# The
# Da Vinci
# Deception

BOOKS BY THOMAS SWAN

*The Da Vinci Deception*
*The Cézanne Chase*

# The Da Vinci Deception

## THOMAS SWAN

NEWMARKET PRESS
NEW YORK

First Hardcover Edition

10   9   8   7   6   5   4   3   2   1

*Library of Congress Cataloging-in-Publication Data*
Swan, Thomas.
The Da Vinci deception / Thomas Swan.
p. cm.
ISBN 1-55704-352-3 (hc)
1. Leonardo, da Vinci, 1452-1519—Fiction.   I. Title.
PR6069.W344D3  1998
823'.914—dc21                                        98-4913
CIP

QUANTITY PURCHASES
Companies, professional groups, clubs, and other organizations may qualify
for special terms when ordering quantities of this title. For information,
write Special Sales Department, Newmarket Press, 18 East 48th Street,
New York, NY 10017, call (212) 832-3575, or fax (212) 832-3629.

Book design by Joe Gannon
Manufactured in the United States of America

*To my wife Barbara and to my children Sally and Greg.*
*And to the cherished memory of my son Steve,*
*who would approve and be proud.*

# Part One

The bee may be likened to deceit, for it has honey in its mouth and poison behind.

—Leonardo da Vinci

# Chapter 1

He pulled a thin blanket over his head to blot out the noises. He wanted to sleep. To get past the last of more than fourteen hundred nights in the state prison at Rahway. He tossed away the blanket and sat cross-legged on the narrow bed; hugging a pillow against his chest, he began rocking and humming. Then, abruptly, he rolled over onto his feet and switched on a fluorescent light that hovered over an artist's table. Taped to it was a letter he had read so many times he could recite it from memory. He stared at the words and they all rushed into his head at once:

Dear Curtis,

In ten days you will leave prison. I can only imagine your joyous anticipation. Though we have not met, I feel we have been friends for many years.

You possess an incredible talent, which you badly abused. You have paid a great price for that indiscretion, and have a clean slate on which to write new successes.

You have immense skill with the pen, a unique gift that if put to proper use shall bring rewards greater than any you have ever imagined.

I believe we are striving toward common objectives, and for that reason invite you to meet with me in order to discuss these matters of mutual interest.

Arrangements have been made at the Intercontinental Hotel in New York on the evening of your release. Upon arrival at the hotel you will receive another communication which will advise you of a meeting place and time.

Enclosed you will find five hundred dollars for expenses.

Stiehl's fingers explored the worn folds of the letter. He looked at his watch. It was 4:35. The incessant snoring of the other inmates had grown obscene. He fell back into bed and recalled his visit to the warden's office three days earlier.

Warden Connolly had pointed to a thin box wrapped in blue paper on his desk. "For you, Curtis. It was delivered this morning by messenger."

Stiehl picked up the box. "It hasn't been opened." He looked quizzically at the warden. "Isn't someone going to check it out first?"

"We'll do that together," he smiled. "I have a strong suspicion there aren't any hacksaw blades in that little box."

Stiehl noted the box carried a mid-Manhattan postmark and had been dated January 3, 1994. He opened it and found a letter and an envelope that was sealed with a daub of red wax. He began reading the letter aloud, then to himself. After reading it he folded the letter and slipped it into his shirt pocket.

Connolly had watched this closely. "Good news?" he asked.

"I'm not sure. Someone thinks we've got mutual interests to talk over."

Stiehl examined the envelope. The paper was heavy, expensive, and in the wax had been impressed the initials "JK" in intaglio. Each letter was voluptuously formed with serifs appended to serifs. He carefully separated the upper flap of the envelope. Inside were five one-hundred-dollar bills. He held them out and fanned the money as if he were holding a winning poker hand.

"You have something in your hand worth talking about."

Stiehl did not reply. He picked out two of the bills and rubbed a thumb and forefinger over each. Then he took hold of the corner of one and carefully tore it. In the light from the large windows behind him he could see the tiny fibers. A very slight smile crossed his lips. Then he replaced the money in the envelope.

"Maybe we will have a talk." He closed the envelope. "Maybe we will."

Connolly held out a hand. "We'll keep the money until you leave. It will be safe."

"I'm sure," Stiehl answered, and turned to the door.

"Stay and we'll have a chat, Curtis. You'll be leaving in a few days and I make it a practice to talk with each man before he moves on. Though I usually end up having a monologue."

In front of the windows two chairs faced a low table on which was a tray and a pot of coffee. "Let's be comfortable." The coffee was hot and Stiehl noted it actually smelled like coffee.

"It's just a few more days. Got any plans?"

Stiehl held the cup with both hands and gently blew on the rising wisp of steam. His prison garb was faded nearly white by the strong detergent used in the prison laundry. Yet it fit him perfectly. His hair had grayed slightly, enough to contrast with skin tanned even now at winter's end. He had a good face with a small cleft in his chin and blue eyes that had an inquiring brightness. He was nearly six feet tall but his hands belonged to an even larger man. His fingers were long and slender.

Stiehl searched for an answer that would not invite further questions. "No sir. I've some ideas but no plan."

"When I talk to the men before they leave, each one wants to dump their anger, but they don't know how. So I do the talking. Is that going to happen with you?"

Stiehl avoided eye contact, "I didn't ask for a meeting, Warden. Sure I'm angry. Damned good and angry, but I'll handle that." He stood and walked to the window. "Four years in a place like this and you don't know who to believe or who to trust."

"You can trust me. They say you're a hell of an artist. Is that so?"

"I can't claim to be an artist, Warden. That file on your lap probably says something about my ability to copy things."

Connolly patted the file that Stiehl correctly guessed contained his dossier. "The file tells us many things, but not everything. You are an artist, and a good one. Why not admit to that?"

Stiehl shrugged. "All right, I'm an artist. A good one, some people say. But there are a ton of very good artists to compete against and I haven't decided if that's what I want to do."

The warden leafed through the papers in Stiehl's file. "I can't find anything about the schools you attended. Do you mind sharing that information?"

Stiehl resisted the invitation to talk about himself.

"There wasn't much. The usual schools." He rummaged through his pockets for a pack of cigarettes. "Okay to smoke?"

Connolly nodded. "Did you study art or sketching?"

Stiehl lit a cigarette, then grabbed an ashtray from the warden's desk. "I took some courses."

"I understand your reluctance to talk about yourself"—he motioned toward the window—"but that's a real world out there and people are going to ask questions that you'll have to answer. And consider the handicap you'll have. A prison record is not easily put aside no matter what special talent you can offer."

Stiehl drew heavily on the cigarette then slowly exhaled the smoke. He looked out to the long stretch of wall and the exercise yard where he had spent so many boring hours. But all of prison life is boring. And all too often, very frightening. Just to be in the warden's office was a reminder of the early days. He had been here once before. It was on his thirty-fourth day in prison. There had been an attempted break. A guard and an inmate were killed. He was questioned from one in the morning until after sunrise and was accused of being an organizer. He had known of the escape attempt but played no part in it. But it had gone on his record and destroyed any chance for early parole.

"When did you first show an interest in becoming an artist?"

Stiehl's back was to the warden now. He stared down to a patch of ground where he and another inmate had raised a few anemic-looking flowers and tomatoes that would never ripen on the vine. In prison you trust no one, he thought. He wanted someone to believe in him. He turned and faced Warden Connolly.

"My dad died when I was nine and I was raised by my mother and her sister. My aunt was crippled with polio. She never married and never seemed to resent that she wasn't. She would read all the time and read to me when I asked. My mother . . ." His voice trailed off to barely a whisper. "She was sick a lot, too. She was a teacher. She taught art at the high school, and turned the dining room into her studio. By a window she had a big easel and she would sit there for hours on the weekends trying to paint something she had seen or wanted to see. There was always paint and paper.

"She taught me how to make a brush from a handful of bristles. I began to paint, but all I was able to do was copy her paintings. I remember how she would encourage me, always saying I could be a great artist someday."

Stiehl stopped. Dormant memories were stirring.

"Then what? School? Art lessons?" Connolly asked.

"Mother died from some damned thing. We never learned what it really was. She came home from school on a Wednesday and went to bed. On Friday they took her to the hospital and on Sunday"—his voice trailed off—"she died."

"How old were you?"

"Thirteen. I remember wishing I was a Jew. I had Jewish friends who had bar mitzvahs and I wished I could, too. Then I'd have money for my aunt. Lutherans don't have bar mitzvahs, so I got a job after school and on weekends. My aunt kept coming up with money from somewhere and with what I made we managed. She encouraged me to take lessons."

"Did you?"

"I tried. In high school first. Then a year at Pratt Institute in Brooklyn. Then my aunt went into a nursing home and I was alone. I didn't know what to do, so I enlisted in the army. I got into the Signal Corps, where I learned I could copy maps that looked better than the originals." He said it as if he had wished he had gone on to another subject.

"From then on it was a course in sketching or learning about watercolor, then oils. I guess I taught myself, too. I liked going to the museums with a pad and pens. I'd go where the art students didn't go. I liked the Dutch and the Italian painters, and I liked paintings with intricate detail. Strands of hair, stitching in the clothes. It was a challenge and I copied them exactly."

He turned and faced the warden. "The rest you must know about."

"Pretty much," Connolly acknowledged. "I'm aware that while you've been in prison you have worked very conscientiously on your painting skills."

"It passes the time."

"And when you are free to take up a new career, you'll steer clear of municipal securities. The financial community doesn't need any more of your near-perfect copies."

"No more securities," Stiehl echoed.

"Or hundred-dollar bills?"

"No comment."

"Too many men go back out to the same thing that brought them here in the first place. I don't suggest you try that." The warden joined Stiehl by the window. "The treasury boys have long memories."

"I'll be careful."

Connolly extended his hand. "Good luck, Curtis. I don't want to see you in this place ever again." He smiled.

They shook hands and Stiehl returned to his cell.

"C'mon, move it! Get your ass in gear!"

Barking the command was Bull Harvey. None of the guards could win a popularity contest but Harvey, at least, possessed a semblance of humanity.

"Hold your water!" Stiehl yelled back. "I'm writing farewell notes to the cockroaches."

Stiehl emerged from his cell holding a thick package of papers and sketches in one hand and a cardboard suitcase in the other. In it he had packed brushes, pens, and a few personal items.

Harvey led the way, muttering a stream of obscenities.

In the administration office Stiehl signed a half-dozen papers including a receipt for $387.37. Among his personal belongings was the wallet his wife Jean had given him for his thirty-eighth birthday. In it he found an expired driver's license, an out-of-date calendar, scraps of paper with long-forgotten notes, and a photo of Jean and his daughter Stephanie, who was ten when he began passing counterfeit municipal securities. He might be with Jean and Stephanie now if the original certificates he'd copied hadn't contained an error and been recalled. Unfortunately, he made precise duplicates—error and all. Jean divorced him two years after he was sentenced. She was now remarried, living somewhere near Princeton. At the right time he would locate Stephanie.

Also in his folder was the envelope with the wax seal. He withdrew the five hundred-dollar bills and carefully placed them in the wallet.

"Okay, Harvey. This is it!"

They were a seedy duo. Bull Harvey's rumpled uniform was pulled tightly over his fat front and his short trousers revealed socks rolled down to the tops of scuffed, thick-soled shoes. Stiehl had been issued a striped, cotton shirt, chinos, and a well-worn raincoat.

They were waved through the east gate. Harvey extended a limp hand, his eyes unable to meet Stiehl's. "No hard feelin's for all the bullshit I threw at you. All the swearin' and pushin'. It's my job. I try to do it decentlike."

"No hard feelings. Thanks for bringing me out."

Harvey flashed a broad smile. "Look, Stiehl, the weirdos are behind you and all the nuts are right on down that driveway. Walk to the end, turn left, and go about a mile to the first traffic light. That's Route 1. Most of the buses are marked Port Authority."

Stiehl picked up his miserable belongings and strode briskly away from the high walls surrounding the prison that had been his home and private hell for so long. He glanced back and saw the bright sun reflected off the golden dome atop the rotunda of the prison. A strange sight, he mused. A gold dome belonged over a merry-go-round in Atlantic City.

The sun had curved up to the highest point it would reach on a cloudless, cold March day. He stepped up his pace as he approached the noisy traffic on Route 1. Within minutes a New Jersey Transit bus pulled to the curb. He stepped aboard, took a seat, and rejoined the world.

On arrival at the Intercontinental Hotel he was handed the letter he had been told would be waiting for him. He did not read it until he was lying on the king-size bed in the pale-blue-and-rose-papered suite reserved in his name.

The letter was in an envelope with the same bold red wax with the initials "JK" in large, flowing script. He propped himself on the huge pillows and opened the envelope.

Dear Curtis,

This has been your first day of freedom in four years. An exciting time!

Tomorrow you shall begin a new life, with new challenges and opportunities and foreign lands to visit.

This evening you will be treated to fine food and wine in the dining room, where a special table is reserved in your name.

And then rest for our meeting in the morning.

Come to the address shown above. I shall look for you at nine.

I am most cordially,
Jonas Kalem

# Chapter 2

The elevator doors opened like a theater curtain, slowly revealing Curtis Stiehl's eagerly anticipated new world. Directly ahead was a bronze plaque: JONAS R. KALEM & COMPANY, and beneath: NEW YORK LONDON PARIS. He turned left off the elevator and walked into a paneled gallery displaying an exquisite collection of paintings. A voice emanating from concealed speakers welcomed him. Mr. Kalem, the voice said assuringly, would soon join him. He walked anxiously about the gallery, noting the paintings, in styles ranging from Romantic to Postmodern. He stopped, facing a wall on which were a small primitive portrait, a George Stubbs horse, a Manet, and a Childe Hassam. His attention was on the Manet when an opening suddenly appeared in the wall and a man of enormous proportions emerged from the dark void.

Jonas Kalem stood six feet four inches tall and weighed not an ounce under three hundred pounds. He wore a dark blue vested suit accented with a fine gray stripe and punctuated with a maroon tie. He was smiling, all but his eyes, which peered through thick, trifocal glasses. His hair was too black for his sixty years. His voice was deep and resonant.

"Welcome, Curtis. My congratulations upon your release from that great unpleasantness." He entered the gallery, his hand extended in greeting. "I am delighted you accepted my invitation to discuss our mutual interests."

Stiehl, still showing his surprise, shook hands gamely.

Jonas led the way through the opened panels to a conventional office with rows of desks and files all surrounded by clicking printers and phones with their blinking lights and electronic chimes. Fax machines spewed out incoming messages and drawings from clients. They paused at a room jammed with video recorders, closed-circuit television screens, and elaborate audio transcribers and players. Five screens displayed each wall of the gallery and the elevator; several smaller screens showed workers in other departments, none apparently concerned that the cameras were trained on them.

"Our security and communications center," Jonas said. "Damned expensive but it's paying off. The insurance people like it and collectors don't mind loaning us their precious paintings."

They moved through a narrow corridor, the spirited music of Offenbach filling the air. They approached three massive double doors spaced thirty feet apart. Jonas opened the first set of doors and they entered a cavernous room. The room was forty feet wide and nearly seventy-five feet long. Leaded windows reached from the floor to a twenty-two-foot ceiling created by breaking through to the floor directly above. The room was divided into three parts: the first, where they stood, was a library; the second was designed as a conference space and contained a variety of tables and chairs; and the third was an office setting with high-backed chairs and leather sofas surrounding a desk Stiehl estimated at eight feet in length.

The library held more than five thousand volumes, many first editions. Aside from standard reference works and encyclopedias, the entire library was devoted to art and art history.

A balcony ran along the interior walls ten feet over the floor. More paintings filled spaces where there were no bookshelves or windows. Some belonged to Jonas, some were on loan, still others were the works of artists Jonas represented and for whom he secured commissions. Suspended from the ceiling over the conference area was a brass and porcelain chandelier with a spread of over twenty feet.

"I apologize for this ostentation, but I spend too much time here to feel confined. I'm a big person and need space." Jonas guided his guest to a chair near his desk. He offered a box of Monte Cruz. Stiehl declined, his eyes continuing to inventory the grand room Jonas called his office.

"If I speak bluntly, forgive me," Jonas said quietly. "I obviously know something about you, including, of course, the reason you spent nearly four years in prison. I feel badly we did not meet before you decided to compete with the American Bank Note Company."

Stiehl shifted uneasily in his chair. He felt intimidated. "How would that have changed matters?"

"In many ways, I am sure. First you should know what we're all about." Jonas lit his cigar.

"We provide a complete range of art services to the communications industry, including the advertising agencies here in the east as well as throughout Europe. But I grew weary of the tasteless art directors that crowd those businesses and looked for new opportunities. Art has been my love since I was a child, and because I have an eye for fine art, I decided to put my knowledge to more profitable use. I added a number of promising artists to our staff and found them commissions for serious work. Their murals and paintings are displayed throughout this country and abroad. I'll show you the scope of our work."

Jonas touched the controls of an electronic switcher and a television screen rose from a nearby credenza. Images appeared and Jonas described the client, the assignment, the art, and the artist.

"Very impressive, every one," Stiehl said. "I wish I had half the talent of any of your artists."

"Your abilities surpass all that you have seen."

"I've never painted an original painting that was worth a damn, or a dime."

"What you can do so exquisitely is worth infinitely more. But you require direction." He paused and twirled the cigar between two fingers then took several puffs and blew the smoke toward the ceiling. Then he added, "My direction."

Jonas touched another button and on the screen appeared the photograph of a municipal bond certificate issued by the city of Paterson, New Jersey. "Recognize that, Curtis?"

"Of course, but what in hell does that have to do with your direction?" Stiehl's irritation clearly showed.

"And what of these, Curtis?" In clear focus was a fifty-dollar bill. Then a hundred-dollar bill flashed onto the screen. Two of the hundred-dollar bills Stiehl had received in the envelope sealed with red wax were identical to the one on the screen.

"Very clever, Mr. Kalem. Where did you find those notes?"

"I can't divulge all my secrets. Suffice to say I have gone to considerable lengths to learn all I can about you. And most especially about your true potential."

Stiehl was confused. Jonas was slapping one cheek with an old indictment and caressing the other with his praise.

"There is more." Now there was a photograph of a modest white frame house on the screen. "You will recognize your home. The one where you were living at the time of your arrest. I understand a small army of treasury agents tore up the house searching for a set of printing plates they suspected you made to counterfeit the fifty- and hundred-dollar notes we saw on the previous slides."

"They found nothing."

"Quite true. Your wife remarried and the property was finally sold a little more than a year ago. I bought it."

"You bought my house? Why?"

"Let's say it was speculation. The real-estate market had been quite bullish and I decided to remodel the home and put it back on the market. But I had another reason. I had a hunch I might find something the agents had overlooked."

Again the picture changed. On the screen was a photograph showing two sets of engraving plates. "Setting them beneath the metal insulation strip in the front door was brilliant. A metal detector would be confused by the strip and it was otherwise a much too obvious hiding place for those precious plates. The agents were anxious to search inside the house and, not finding them, literally tore the gardens and garage apart."

With another touch of the controls the screen disappeared.

"My little show is over and you have learned what I know of you. I have come to know that your skill with the pen is at the genius level and so I want you to work under my direct supervision.

"Doing what? U.S. Savings Bonds?"

"No need for a sharp tongue. I have a very challenging assignment for you." The huge body struggled free of the chair and walked toward a table directly under the wide-spreading chandelier. "Come with me, Curtis."

From leather folders Jonas extracted a dozen sheets. Ceremoniously he placed each on the table.

"These lithographs are from the collection of Leonardo da Vinci's anatomical drawings preserved in the Royal Library at Windsor Castle. There is great beauty here and I believe these drawings prove the Master's incredible genius. Consider that he had little formal education, yet his curiosity was so intense that he would spend hours with a putrid corpse, dissecting it by the light of a lantern, then create these minutely detailed drawings." Jonas peered intently through his thick glasses at Stiehl. "Leonardo knew that to paint the human form he had to know what lay beneath the skin. Study these drawings carefully, Curtis. Note his technique, his mastery of shading and shape."

Stiehl picked up one then another of the drawings. He had a vague familiarity with Leonardo's anatomical works but could not grasp the point Jonas was making. He was at an even greater loss to understand what bearing it had on him.

Jonas continued. "Leonardo was left-handed. His stroke was from right to left."

"And he wrote in reverse," Stiehl added. "I've seen examples."

"It is most convenient that you are left-handed, Curtis."

"You knew that?"

Jonas nodded. He then took one of the drawings and placed it in front of Stiehl. The sheet contained two human skulls, one drawn above the other. "Can you duplicate what you see on this page?"

"Why would I want to?"

"The question is not why. Can you? And exactly as you see them?"

Stiehl studied the skulls. "Yes, I could do that. It would take time before I'd be sure of myself. It's pen and ink, and all line. But the handwriting. That's far more difficult."

"I had no illusions it would be simple." Squinting eyes stared out from behind thick glasses. "It is critically important that you tell me you can, after sufficient practice, create an exact duplicate of what you see on that sheet of paper."

"That would be impossible. Only a camera could make an exact duplication."

"But suppose Leonardo had never put these skulls on paper. Could you draw them so they would appear as if they had been drawn by Leonardo?"

"I can't be sure that I could. Perhaps."

"You are unsure. Yes or no," Jonas shot back, his good humor fading.

"Damn it, I *can't* be sure. Not until I try. Copying is one thing, creating is another. And it's not my strong suit."

"You underrate your own talents. You'll have hundreds of his sketches and drawings to guide you. And there are a thousand more skulls in the medical books."

"Suppose I could draw the skulls. The handwriting would be difficult. It requires an entirely different technique."

"You will have expert assistance. There are countless studies and references dealing with his handwriting. Just as you will have writing instruments and inks that are authentic to the period. The paper will be hundreds of years old, also dated to the time of Leonardo. You will not make a copy of this lithograph. You will have the genuine Leonardo drawing to guide you."

"You have a card to the Royal Library?" Stiehl smiled.

"They're not in the habit of lending their Leonardos," Jonas replied. "But come, let me explain why I must know if you can produce a duplicate of the skull drawing." He returned to his desk.

"The most valuable collection of Leonardo's manuscripts is at Windsor. Nearly two-thirds of Leonardo's surviving drawings are in the Royal Library. Note I said drawings. There are many volumes and notebooks in other libraries and museums; however, those contain Leonardo's theories and observations on a wide variety of subjects. Scattered through those manuscripts are the remaining drawings.

"It is known that when he died, Leonardo left other notebooks and drawings. Perhaps a thousand pages have never been discovered. No one knows how many fine drawings are on those lost sheets. Some have probably been destroyed. But what of all the others? What drawings have been lost? And more importantly, if they were found, what would they be worth?"

"Can you guess how many drawings there might be?" Stiehl asked.

"Several hundred, perhaps more. Leonardo's Leicester Codex was recently auctioned for nearly six million dollars. It consisted of thirty-eight pages and contained but a few unimportant sketches. One sheet holding an early study of the *Mona Lisa* could bring ten million alone. When a Van Gogh goes for more than eighty million a da Vinci will bring an untold amount.

"No one knows what the missing manuscripts contain, the experts can only speculate. Any that are found will be subjected to intense scrutiny and a battery of highly sophisticated tests. The first criterion is that they must be perceived as authentic.

"And that, my new friend, is where you enter the picture. I plan for you to create a generous supply of the missing Leonardo manuscripts."

Stiehl's reaction was immediate. "That's insane! No one can do that. It's craziness!"

"It is none of that," Jonas shouted, and slammed his fist to the desk.

"You were serious about taking a Leonardo from Windsor," Stiehl responded, his voice raised to match Jonas's. "I thought that was a pretty bad joke. I was in prison for four years and I have no intention of going back."

"And I won't let that happen. You will have privacy and total security. You'll have every protection."

"Sort of the honor system," Stiehl said with more than a little irony. "We protect each other."

"You can become wealthy, Curtis. Beginning immediately you will have a substantial income and a studio with every amenity. Consider also that it is I who must present the manuscripts to the community of art historians. Should they discredit them, then I would merely say I had discovered worthless copies. There is no crime in being misinformed."

"Why must I duplicate the skulls so precisely if you plan to create Leonardos that have never been seen before?"

"If you can duplicate a known Leonardo drawing with flawless accuracy, it is very likely that you can create a new work that will go unchallenged."

"Who else is involved in your little game?"

"There will be three of you involved directly in the development of the Leonardo drawings. I will direct the project, and be aided by my assistant."

"Who would I work with? When would I meet them?"

"You will proceed alone for at least six months, and then you will work in close association with a former professor of Renaissance studies at the University of Milan. Giorgio Burri is an acknowledged Leonardo scholar."

"Six months is a long time."

Jonas smiled indulgently. "Exercise the patience you so painfully learned, Curtis. It has taken more than three years to put this plan together. In the beginning you will receive written instructions from Giorgio and will communicate with him through me or my assistant. When the two of you meet, it will be as if you have known each other a long time. No one is more essential to our success than the one who puts pen to paper. Before you attempt to make a precise copy of the Windsor drawing, you will need all of six months to master Leonardo's style and technique, and ultimately you must write as he did. No small accomplishment."

"What if I fail?"

"You won't. I have complete confidence that you'll carry it off."

"Who is the third member of the team? What part does he play?"

"*She* is a highly qualified chemist with advanced degrees from the University of Chicago and MIT. Her name is Eleanor Shepard; when I met her, she was most unhappy in her assignment with the FDA in Washington. I persuaded her to undertake a special research project in Italy."

"What kind of research?"

"First she will locate the paper, then find or make the inks and pens you will use. Secondly, she will develop techniques for aging documents. And finally, Eleanor will study the modern methods for detecting the age and authenticity of art and manuscripts. All the more reason we must have the genuine Leonardo from the Windsor Library."

"Then she knows what you are up to?"

"Not at all." Jonas blew a thick cloud of smoke. "I have commissioned Eleanor to gather the information and the samples, then prepare a complete documentation of her findings, which I have told her will then be published.

"Will I meet her?"

"You would like that, she is a very attractive woman. But she must never know how the Leonardo manuscripts come into being."

"At some point the whole world will know you discovered them."

"And she, too, must believe that I have rescued them from some obscure hiding place. She must not suspect you and Giorgio have created them."

Stiehl now realized how brilliantly Jonas had put his plan together. One of his conspirators would supply the raw materials for the missing Leonardo manuscripts, and then be the same person to test their genuineness.

"Where is she doing all this research?"

"In Florence. She must be where Leonardo lived most of his years. And where she will find paper of the kind available five hundred years ago."

"I can't believe paper that old can be found. And if any is located, could it be handled and worked on?"

Jonas swiveled around to the credenza and took from it a leather-bound book. "This is a rare Elzevir manuscript, printed in 1611. The end leaves have never been touched; the paper has merely yellowed a bit. The paper was made in Holland, possibly Belgium. Feel how supple it is after nearly four hundred years."

Stiehl was no stranger to paper. He rubbed the sheet between his thumb and forefinger. "You expect the Shepard woman will find five-hundred-year-old paper?"

"She will. You can depend on it."

"You have an assistant. Another woman?"

Jonas smiled broadly. "My assistant's name is Anthony Waters, or Tony as we prefer to call him. Tony fills a special niche and will have a variety of assignments. The first, which will occupy him between now and September, is to borrow Leonardo's drawing of the skulls from the Royal Library."

"You said it isn't a lending library."

"Tony is particularly adept at what I like to call 'role-playing.'" Jonas added confidently, "Come September we will have folio number 19057 in hand."

Jonas unwrapped a package of cashews and poured the contents into a bowl. "Any more questions, Curtis?"

"Not a question, just a statement. I haven't said that I'm coming in with you."

Jonas calmly popped a few of the nuts into his mouth. "You have an abundance of talent, Curtis, but a very undisciplined memory. Perhaps we should review those photographs."

"Goddamn it! I'm the one that's just out of jail and I'm not talking about Monopoly, where all you do is wait for the next roll of the dice. Forty-seven months...thirty days shy of four years shot to hell. If this scheme blows, I'm back for five, maybe ten years. You haven't been there, and be damned well assured I'm not going back."

"You won't, Curtis. You have my word."

"Your word? I never laid eyes on you until an hour ago. What goddamn good is your word when the jury says guilty? It seems I'm pretty important to your plans and that convinces me that I hold some high cards."

"Not high enough. I would desperately hate to lose you, but having brought you into my confidence, I can ill afford to take any risks. The statutes haven't expired on your counterfeiting escapade and a conviction would return you to that repugnant hell."

Jonas leaned forward and continued in a low, husky voice. "It would seem that your choice is very simple: risk a return to prison or join us in creating Leonardo manuscripts that will bring make you financially independent."

"You were talking about honor, about trust. And now you talk about blackmail."

Jonas's voice became little more than a whisper.

"I detest the word 'blackmail.' But I like the thought of a very painful and fatal accident even less."

# Chapter 3

"Here's to Ellie Shepard. May she enjoy fame, fortune, and happiness." Steve Goldensen downed the champagne in a single swallow. He refilled the tall tulip-shaped glass and raised it as if to make another toast.

"No...right words...wrong order. Here's to fortune, happiness, and fame. Or should happiness come first? And health, Steve. Shouldn't health be in there someplace?" Ellie asked, a cigarette in one hand, the other holding her champagne.

She giggled as she sipped. Her laughing stopped and she set the glass on the table and stared at it. Even with a frown spreading over her face, Eleanor Shepard was a stunningly beautiful woman. Long auburn hair contrasted with her pale, clear skin and her hazel eyes were flecked with strong green accents. Her lips were full and sensuous. "Oh God, Steve, that sounds horribly selfish. Why can't I say the right words? I came to Washington with such dreams. I'm the gal who was going to be the first female director of the FDA and after three years I've managed to become an expert on analgesics and skin ointments."

He took her hand to his lips. "Ellie, my sweet, you haven't lost that impetuous drive. You came with a thousand stars in that pretty head and expected Washington bureaucracy to bend to your will. It didn't and it won't...not for you or anyone. It's all part of the fabric around here."

Steve was right. Steve was always right, Ellie thought. She looked at his dark, handsome face.

"But it has to change. This city will cave in from its own flab. If I don't run into sheer incompetency, I crash into idiotic mediocrity and there's mile after mile of both."

"So you're going to run away from it."

"No, I'm not running. That's not the way I do things. I was told that if I wanted to make a contribution, I should become involved. To get on the inside. Well, I've done that. But I've become what's happening on the inside. I've become one of *them*, and I don't like it. All I've learned is how a single piece of this government works—slowly, stupidly, expensively. The waste, Steve. The mountains of paper, the meetings, the endless hearings, the pompous asses."

"Hey, hold on. If you got rid of all that, you'd put us lawyers out of business."

"Then they would have to hustle to earn an honest living. Is that so bad?"

"Poor choice of words."

"I'm sorry if I offended you. I didn't mean you were being dishonest."

"Of course you didn't. But you're getting all hung up on feeling you must make a contribution. That things have to change. Ellie, it's a lousy system but it's the best there is."

Ellie snuffed out her cigarette. "Look at me. Three years with the Food and Drug Administration and I'm still smoking."

"You're changing the subject."

"I think we should. We're not being very happy right now."

"I have a happy subject. Let's get married." He raised his glass. "Now."

"Steve, I hoped you wouldn't bring that up tonight. I know you love me—"

"Very much."

"Yes, you love me very much. And I...I love you, too. But it's not the same kind of very much. Not so I can say yes."

"How far from saying yes are you?"

"In centimeters? Or how my heart feels? Or the way I think I ought to tingle? You're a fine person, Steve. You're very good-looking, you're bright, we'd make beautiful children, you have a future, but . . ."

"But what?"

"Please don't be offended." Ellie looked intently at him. "I don't want to be a Jewish Princess and I believe you would want me to be one."

He slumped back in his chair, his eyes closed. She reached for his hand. "Oh, Steve, you sweet thing. I did it again. Believe me, it isn't a religious thing. I don't care that you're Jewish or Moslem or nothing at all. I know you too well. You'd give so much, I'd be stifled. At sixty I might like it, but not at thirty. Right now I need a lot of independence, the freedom to move and do as I please. Does that mean I'm selfish?"

Steve smiled weakly. "I'll take you home. We still haven't finished that toast." They left the hotel and walked in the chilled February air to Steve's car.

Ellie was subleasing a choice apartment in Georgetown, one owned by an undersecretary in the State Department and an old family friend. The Frederick Youngs were completing a year's assignment in Vienna and delighted to have Ellie look after their apartment and the valuable paintings and antiques they had accumulated during thirty years of government service.

Ellie turned the keys in two locks on a thick door, then switched off an intricate alarm system. Steve knew the collection and took a fast inventory, including a Matisse that hung directly over a Queen Anne desk in a small study. "All safe and cozy, the Young Collection has survived another day."

"It's no joke, Steve. I feel a terrible responsibility and I just know I'm going to forget to do something and come home to find the place in shambles and the paintings gone."

He caught her by the hand and engulfed her in his arms. He kissed her forehead and cheeks then pressed his lips to hers. His eyes were moist, his voice slightly choked. "I can't help loving you like I do. It's not fair to lose someone because I want to give so much."

Ellie returned a warm kiss. "There's a split of Mumms in the refrigerator. Let's have a damned good toast and get you and me straightened out."

"Okay, you're on. I'll meet you in there." He nodded toward the hall and beyond to Ellie's bedroom.

She looked up and was silent. She ran a finger down his nose and over his lips and chin. "You need a shave," she whispered. Then her fingers ran across each eyebrow. "I've never made a champagne toast in bed." She kissed him sweetly, her tongue reached for his. Then she pulled away and started for the bedroom. "Glasses are in the cupboard over the cutting board."

Steve found a large, white napkin, which he neatly folded over his arm, and set the still uncorked bottle and two glasses on a small, silver tray. He entered the bedroom to find Ellie sitting at the head of the bed, a sheet drawn around her shoulders. Her auburn hair fell against the white bedclothes, a single light on the vanity spread a warm light through the room. He placed the tray on the bed, then sat beside her. She unknotted his tie and slipped it away from his shirt. Then each fumbled to unbutton the shirt and giggled as four hands tried to loosen a single button. The sheet fell away from her shoulders and he tenderly rubbed her swelling nipples. He leaned forward and kissed her on the mouth and then across her neck. Then, slowly, his tongue caressed the tips of her breasts. He straightened and kissed her firmly on the lips.

"Shall we have that toast before the champagne is as warm as you?" Ellie said brightly.

"Not while I'm fully dressed. I'm still wearing my socks."

She reached down and pulled off his socks, ran her hands up his legs, across the thighs, then with both hands cupped his penis and gently rubbed it. She pulled away, pointing to the champagne. "First things first."

Steve fussed with the cork and forced it free. A loud pop was followed by a gushing of the champagne, which sprayed over them. They looked at each other and laughed, their eyes glistening. "It's only a little bottle, darling, we can't waste it." She nestled closer and licked his chest.

Ellie took her glass and held it in both hands, staring at the bubbles rising to the surface. Her smile disappeared. "Oh, cripes, Steve, the toast. I still don't know what to say."

"Why not keep it simple? No great pronouncements...no promises. How about the simplest of all: 'Here's to us...if it's to be...let it be.'"

"Would that make you happy?"

"Right now I want you happy. I'll just take a big dose of patience and wait it out."

"That's sweet, and thank you." She made her glass touch his. "Here's to us. If it's to be...let it be."

With their eyes fixed on each others, they drank. For an hour they were lost in their love, each giving to the other unselfishly. Their passion was intense, their lovemaking bold and beautifully sincere. He could make her tingle, and she was carried to an ecstasy of pleasure when his tongue flicked across her taut stomach then slowly moved down to her rhythmically pulsating groin and stopped to dwell on the tiny, hidden erection of flesh. His tongue caressed it, sending shudders of total pleasure throughout her body. She felt it everywhere but would not let it enter her heart. She feared that and didn't want to undo a commitment made in the euphoria of their lovemaking.

At the end they lay close together, their hands clasped tightly, their lips silent.

Ellie interrupted the stillness, turning first to kiss Steve, then rolling off the bed onto her feet. She wrapped herself in a pink-and-white dressing gown and, sitting at the vanity, brushed her hair until it glistened.

"Steve, do you have any friends in Italy?"

"What an incredible coincidence...how did you know I was lying here thinking of all my Italian friends?"

"I'm perfectly serious, silly monkey. Do you?"

"I know a few guys from State stationed in Rome. Stuart Larson went over on a special assignment for Agriculture. Old Stu's been studying the Italian wine industry. Call that tough duty?"

"Where's he located?"

"I don't know. Probably travels all over the country. Why the sudden interest in Italy?"

"It's not so sudden. I haven't mentioned this before because it didn't matter then. Now it does. If I make some coffee, will you let me tell you what it's all about?"

"Now who's the silly monkey. Of course."

Ellie entered the kitchen, set a kettle on the range, and spooned coffee into an old drip coffeemaker.

They sat at a small table, and after taking several sips of the hot coffee, Ellie's expression turned somber, and without looking up she said, "I haven't told you anything about this because when it happened, it seemed so strange I didn't think it was real. Well, it's real, all right. Very real.

"The Youngs are great art collectors, and they've taken me to the galleries and introduced me to their friends who are really into collecting and that sort of thing. Just before they left for Vienna we went to the National Gallery for a patrons' reception. There were two lecturers and one of them fascinated me. His subject was the Renaissance masters; painters like Raphael and Leonardo and Michelangelo."

"I recognize the names," Steve said smugly. "Did you learn anything?"

"Some. The little-known things about the great painters and the times they lived in. But the man who spoke was...well, he was fabulous."

"Should I be jealous?"

"Let me describe him. He's enormous; over six feet and must weigh three hundred pounds. He has squinty eyes, thick glasses—probably terribly nearsighted—and a funny mouth. When he smiles, it goes like this." Ellie's mouth formed a little "O." "His name is Jonas Kalem, and if this Jonas had met the whale, I'm not sure who would have swallowed whom.

"I was introduced after the talk and he started grilling me about my background and my education—"

"Ah, now I become jealous."

"He was perfectly charming," Ellie teased. "When he discovered I had a masters in chemistry and wasn't overjoyed with the FDA, he invited me to have a drink."

"The plot thickens. Did you fall in love right away?"

"You have a one-track mind. When we left the gallery, I found we were a threesome. I figured the newcomer was an assistant of some kind. His name is Tony Waters. Now, Tony you could be a little jealous over. He's English and good looking in a menacing way. He'll attract a lot of women but he's definitely not my type. So the three of us went to the bar in the Hay-Adams and Jonas asked three thousand more questions about me and my background and what I want to do and how much money I want to earn. Then he said he might have a position for me, but it would be in Italy and I would have to live there for as long as a year.

"He asked me to think it over and invited me to New York a week later. I had some shopping I wanted to do up there and decided to have one more talk."

"So you went to New York and fell in love with Tony Waters."

"I told you he was not my type. Jonas has the most incredibly strange and beautiful office I've ever seen. He's an art dealer and runs a commercial art studio and has branches in London and Paris. He told me about the assignment . . . he needs someone who can analyze ancient paper and ink and trace their origins."

"Origins to what?"

"He didn't really get into that. I guess that in his work he needs to know about these things. It's like a research assignment and you know that I'm good at sticking my nose into strange places. And he did say that it's all very hush-hush. I'm not supposed to be telling you about it."

"Why the mystery? He wants you to leave a perfectly sound position in Washington and go off looking for old pieces of paper without knowing why or what it's all about?"

"For God's sake, Steve, I am not leaving a sound position—it's a stupid one, and I hate it. If this man wants me to find old pieces of paper and study how inks were made hundreds of years ago, then I believe there is a real purpose in doing it. The idea of living in Italy is exciting, and I think I will be doing something more important than trying to prove that six million aspirin tablets will give a poor little mouse thrombosis of the colon."

"So you accepted his offer?"

"With a proviso. I agreed to give him my decision tomorrow."

"What's it going to be?"

"What do you think it should be?"

Steve got up and poured a cup of coffee. Then he leaned against the counter and for several moments said nothing. Ellie looked up at him, aware that his legal mind was wrestling with facts and conjectures. She remembered that she said they would make beautiful children and now she imagined what their son might look like: Steve's long nose and his squarish chin, a gangly runner's body. But mostly a warm and sincerely friendly face.

"Where would you be living?" he asked quietly.

"Florence."

"That's better than Rome or Milan. I've been in Florence but just briefly. Hot as hell in the summer but a great city. You'll go crazy in Gucci."

"Are you saying I should go?"

"No, but I don't think it matters what I say. This is your decision. It's a god-awful long time. A year..."

"Maybe less."

"Sweetheart, you're fed up with Washington. I'll survive if you go, but don't be surprised if I turn up on your doorstep."

Ellie took a deep breath as if she had just passed beyond the dangerous rapids in a fast-moving stream. Steve had a thin smile that suddenly grew broader. Now the tears came to Ellie's eyes and she said softly.

"Only a year, my love. Maybe less."

# Chapter 4

The day Curtis Stiehl became a member of the Art Department was March 17. It was St. Patrick's Day and a Thursday. Tony Waters remembered it well. He had watched and listened via the closed-circuit television hookup, and he had been angry to learn that Jonas had given him the assignment to relieve the Royal Library of a valuable Leonardo drawing, and furious to learn of it while watching Jonas and Stiehl on a television screen.

Each time a new member of the Art Department was recruited, Tony felt his importance diminish and his relationship with Jonas grow less secure. Tony had been witness to the way Stiehl had dug in his heels, then surrendered to the ominous scenario laid out by Jonas. Tony had been in Cernobbio on Lake Como when the flamboyant Giorgio Burri came to an uncertain agreement after a long and contentious session accompanied by too much wine. And he had been in Washington when Jonas enticed Eleanor Shepard to accept a year's assignment in Florence.

He had striven to be essential to Jonas, and indeed, Jonas had frequently consulted with him as the master plan slowly took form. But when Tony's small empire began to show cracks, he resolved to prove his importance. To reestablish himself he worked with increasing intensity and from mid-March until mid-July he was certain that no member of Jonas's Art Department, or Jonas himself, had worked as hard or made as many sacrifices as he had.

His resolve began immediately. He searched through every conceivable reference source in New York for information about the Royal Library—its location in Windsor Castle, its size, its staff—and he hoped he would come across a description of the security placed around both the royal residence and the rooms he must enter without creating suspicion. It was after two weeks, surrounded by books, brochures, and microfilms of years' old newspaper accounts of attempted robberies in the Castle that Tony realized he had absorbed a mass of information but precious few hard facts that would enable him to make an assault on the library. Of one thing he was certain: no successful plan could be developed in New York City. He reported his conclusions to Jonas.

"I'd rather you go over in the summer, but it's too important to leave to chance," Jonas had concluded. "It's April. You have five months to bring out the drawing." Jonas was not keen on giving Tony complete freedom. He knew his strengths but was equally aware that with Tony's volatile temper it was tantamount to setting loose a heavy cannon.

On the day he flew to London he spent six hours with Jonas, who lectured him on security and the absolute requirement that he not take unnecessary risks. But Tony knew the entire venture was a risk, that his return to London posed serious risks. And that excited him. He left New York on Saturday, April 9, traveling under the name of Gregory Hewlitt and carrying business cards that introduced him as a department manager in the firm of Wade & Reisen. He was a master at assuming a new identity. Safely on the plane, he could relax. It didn't matter that for several months he would be Gregory Hewlitt or some other person. What mattered most to Tony Waters was the fact that for a while, at least, he could put himself aside and become another person.

Tony Waters began his career under the tutelage of a certain Timothy Sean Saunders, once an actor, then in succession bank teller, solicitor's secretary, and finally procurer. They met when Saunders was handling an expensive stable of beautiful women. Tony was asked in to be a strong arm, at the ready to thwart the sometimes violent activity of Saunders's rivals. Tony fit in with the beautiful people. He had a toughness and an athlete's lithe and incredibly strong body. His features taken individually were not particularly good ones, yet women found him very attractive. His skin was swarthy, his deep brown eyes hard and unafraid.

Toward the end of a year's association, Tony took on two thugs that broke into Saunders's sprawling flat off Hyde Park. The scuffle erupted into a bloody fight. The back of Tony's right hand was severely cut, yet in spite of the wound, he overcame the intruders and sent their unconscious bodies down the elevator to the lobby, where they were discovered by a dowager who let out an earsplitting scream, then fainted.

Tony left Saunders and moved on to be his own man. Initially he operated as an estate agent, collecting advance payments on land speculations in Bermuda and Florida. His unsuspecting clientele never saw their money or titles to the land they thought they had bought. He developed other cons but shrewdly changed his identity after several successful hits and moved to another section of London to start afresh.

He preyed on Americans who attended the auction galleries and who were disappointed to lose out on bids they made on silver or antique furniture. Tony promised delivery on similar items that he claimed were in the inventory of other dealers in London. He sweetened the proposition by asking for a mere half payment with the order, the balance, including his fee and shipping, to be paid upon delivery. For several months his clients were delighted with their good fortune. Only when time passed and their valuables never appeared did they finally realize they had been duped.

Tony's final ploy at the auction galleries was not so successful. An American bidder failed to pull down two Samuel Palmer etchings. Unknown to Tony, there had been a rash of Palmer forgeries, and when Tony met him on the following day to receive half payment, he was asked to produce either the etchings or unqualified proof of their authenticity. The mark he had chosen was a colossal American with squinting eyes, a man of discerning taste and deep knowledge of the major eighteenth-century English painters. Tony had met Jonas Kalem.

Jonas knew a dealer's agent when he saw one, and Tony was clearly masquerading. Yet he saw in his rugged handsomeness and the bold attack of his sophisticated cons a man who might fit the plans he was slowly piecing together.

And now Tony was making judgments. He found fault in the choices Jonas made for his Art Department. Though each was eminently qualified, none merited Tony's endorsement. He concluded that Giorgio Burri had been too bold, and his Italian temperament too disrespectful of the offer Jonas had made. Curtis Stiehl was simply an enigma and Tony was distrustful of people he didn't understand. But he marshaled his most intense opposition to the selection of Eleanor Shepard. She was a woman. That was a mistake. She was a beautiful woman and a beautiful woman may not be easily influenced.

He arrived in England and settled in a small flat in West Kensington. From there he had easy access to central London and was but a short drive from Windsor. He began to grow a beard and after two weeks grew accustomed to it and the role he played as a free-lance journalist. He wrote to Sir Robin Mackworth-Young, the Royal Librarian, requesting an interview and the opportunity to research a feature article on the library. In reply the librarian agreed to the interview but said that unfortunately it could not take place until after proposed major alterations to the library were completed. Tony learned that the library would officially close on April 26, then reopen October 1.

The news of the library's closing came as a disastrous blow to Tony's plans. He drove to Windsor still another time, hoping he had overlooked a way into the library. The library was located off the royal apartments on the second level of the ancient gray-stone building. Access to the library, other than from the Royal Chambers, was through the tradesmen's entrance, always heavily guarded, and never open to the public. The library's windows looked over the North Terrace, where Tony walked among the crowds of tourists, continuing his search for a chink in the impregnable walls.

The transformation to Gregory Hewlitt was complete, except for a nagging problem; his full beard was shot through with gray, which to some might be a sign of maturity but to Tony was a weakness. And so he dyed his hair and the beard a coffee brown color. In his pocket he kept a pair of glasses, which he occasionally wore, adding another minor blur to his true identity.

He continued to frequent familiar pubs, hoping a friendly face would appear and he could enlist their aid in solving his apparently insuperable problem. Yet he did not want an accomplice; that would be complicating. And time would soon be an important factor. Then on the first Friday in May his daily reading of the London *Times* paid off.

In the arts section he learned why the Royal Library was to close. Sir Robin Mackworth-Young formally announced that funds had been allocated to install a new air-conditioning system and the equally important humidity controls which were designed to *"... maintain the critically necessary levels required to prevent further deterioration to our vast collection of old documents and rare first editions. We will also install new windows with double-thick glass."* The article concluded, *"There is an imperative need to protect our growing collection of irreplaceable papers, works of art, manuscripts, and royal diaries."*

Tony's spirits soared. He was quick to realize that new faces would swarm over the library: carpenters, electricians, sheet-metal workers, plumbers, painters. He would be among them. While in his teens he had worked at the Hull shipyards in Liverpool, where he apprenticed as an electrician and had later been assigned to a crew that replaced the complicated ventilation systems on large freighters.

His attempts to learn the identity of the contracting firm were unsuccessful; no one in the library was inclined to divulge that information. Nor could the writer of the *Times* article locate the name in his notes for the story. But on Sunday, with a dozen newspapers strewn about his flat, Tony came across an advertisement on the "Appointments Vacant" page of the *Guardian*. Heldwicke Air-Control Systems, Ltd. was the contractor and they were looking for a field engineer.

On his first interview he manipulated the conversation in order to determine the precise qualifications required for the position. Armed with the information, he phoned Jonas and listed the items Curtis must create: references, letters of recommendation, a diploma indicating successful completion of an engineering course in air-conditioning design and installation, and evidence that he served as shop steward in a local union in Connecticut.

He returned the next day for a brief meeting on the pretext that he would like more information on the Heldwicke company. He was following a plan: show great interest in the company, the importance of the installation, and the dedication he would give to the assignment.

He spent a day in the National Gallery, where he sought out a young technician in the museum's Operations Department. He learned that the most important function of an air-control system is to eliminate fluctuations in either temperature or humidity, that the ideal relative humidity was between forty and fifty percent, and that the temperature should remain between sixteen and eighteen degrees Celsius.

Three days later Jonas phoned to advise Tony that the package had been put aboard British Airways Flight 176, due to arrive Heathrow at 9:00 A.M. the following morning. Tony phoned Heldwicke for an appointment in the afternoon.

He sat in front of Barbara Randall for the third time and noted that the young woman spoke very directly as she had in their previous meetings, but she was less severely dressed, her lips were a shade redder, and her hair had obviously been fussed over. "I want to thank you for the opportunity to present my qualifications for the position, Miss Randall. It would be a great honor to be a member of the construction team." He set a thick folder in front of her.

She read through the material, pausing to ask a question then listen to the bearded applicant give an articulate response. After more than an hour together, Miss Randall said, "Perhaps if you have a few more minutes, I would like to confer with one of my colleagues."

"Yes, that would be fine. I'm free until an appointment I've got later this evening," he lied.

He sat alone in the room for nine, perhaps ten minutes. Though he had frequently masqueraded, there were times of uneasiness; always the possibility someone might break through his disguise. Playing the role of Gregory Hewlitt, he had won over Barbara Randall. He always won women to his side when it suited him. All but the damned Shepard woman. He stroked his new beard and, as he did so, made a mental note to use his left hand for making the thoughtful gesture, not the right hand with the long scar. He felt anxiety building. It was a familiar feeling, which, instead of depressing him, sharpened his senses. It was a touch of the old thrill, the game he enjoyed playing. He breathed deeply then slowly exhaled. The door opened and Barbara Randall returned. She smiled and extended her hand.

"Congratulations, Mr. Hewlitt. I'm happy to tell you that we have found your experience suitable and appropriate for an assignment as assistant crew supervisor reporting to Chief of Installation Charles McKean."

He accepted her outstretched hand. Firmly and slowly he allowed his fingers to wrap around hers.

Tony's enthusiasm began to tarnish at about the time he reported for work on the eighth of May, and for the very good reason that Jonas Kalem was going about the business of speaking at every opportunity on the subject of the lost Leonardo manuscripts. His itinerary included Boston, San Francisco, and Chicago in the States, and there were plans to participate in three symposiums of the Leonardo da Vinci Association in Madrid, Amsterdam, and Paris. Normally, Tony would accompany Jonas on these excursions, acting as aide and associate and at all times enjoying the grand and occasionally sumptuous style that distinguished the big man.

Instead of the luxury of first-class travel, Tony was working harder than ever. He received regular praise from Charlie McKean for his performance on the job, but reacted to the accolades with disdain. He remained in frequent contact with Jonas and was able to stay abreast of the progress both Stiehl and Eleanor Shepard were making. Stiehl's major problem was in duplicating Leonardo's handwriting. Jonas was growing

concerned and was looking for a way to put Giorgio Burri and Stiehl together before September as planned. The Shepard woman was on schedule with her assignments.

Then in mid-July Jonas flew to Bern, where he had been invited to
participate in a festival of the Renaissance arts. Again, he charmed his audience and made a daring prediction that immensely valuable Leonardos
would surface within the year and that he expected to participate in their
discovery. With each speech his credibility grew. The rumor mills began
speculating on which of the missing Leonardos would surface. Jonas was
becoming a celebrity and he loved the attention and the applause.

He was not applauded by all for the same reason. A small man wearing large spectacles made notes in a small notepad. Outwardly he
cheered Jonas on, clicking snapshots, asking for an autograph, and otherwise acting as if he were about to form a new chapter of the Jonas
Kalem Fan Club.

At the conclusion of the meeting the little man wrote a detailed report and sent it off to the Metropolitan Police in London.

Attached was a brief note:

Branch C13
For Superintendent and Central File
Cross reference requested:
    Strange doings with this Kalem chap. Is he in file and if so, pull
all details. Switzerland awfully damned hot in July.

                                                            Oxby

# Part Two

I find my head swimming...the body
disfigured in death, seeming to be
buried in its own belly.
                    —Leonardo da Vinci

# Chapter 5

Motor traffic chattered along Datchet Road headed to or away from the borough of Windsor. From an elderly Morris estate wagon crossing the bridge over the Thames, Tony Waters in his guise as Greg Hewlitt peered directly ahead to the looming Round Tower and the great encircling walls of the Castle.

He had passed the small village of Datchet minutes earlier and was traveling the mile and a half to Windsor for what seemed to be the five-hundredth time. He turned onto a narrow, curving road that led to a restricted entrance to the royal residence. A guard waved him through a security station. He parked alongside a trailer marked with the corporate logo of the Heldwicke company. From the rear of the wagon he pulled several large rolls of engineering drawings and a thick, scuffed briefcase. He followed a familiar route to the tradesmen's entrance in the Upper Ward. Close by stood the fourteenth-century Norman Gate, its portcullis poised menacingly as if ready to crash in front of the terrible enemy. He exchanged greetings with a cheerful older man wearing a stained, wrinkled uniform.

"Good morning, Mr. Hewlitt. Not a bad one it'll be . . . once the sun gets workin' on the fog." His smile revealed yellow, slanting teeth. The old gent pointed to the briefcase, "What's for today? Egg and sausage sandwich?"

"Not even close. Today I lunch with the queen."

"In a pig's eye." The old man, whom Tony knew only as Gumpers, winked.

Over the weeks Tony had developed a good rapport with the security staff, yet had been careful not to become too familiar. He turned and followed a series of passageways leading to a flight of deeply worn stone steps that coursed up to the Royal Library. But on this morning he turned to another corridor leading to the North Terrace, where in an hour, hordes of tourists would gather to take photographs or pause between tours of the Royal Palace galleries and chambers.

The air was stirring and a thick roily fog began to clear. Bits of it, like torn rags, drifted off the meadow and swept over him. Its refreshing, wet coolness touched his face. He paused in the stillness to reflect on the last four months and anticipate the culmination of his patient work. On this day he would relieve the Royal Library of a drawing of two skulls by Leonardo da Vinci, identified as folio number 19057.

He recalled those first weeks when he realized how much he needed to know and how quickly he had learned. Just when he feared his charade would collapse, he had been able to get on top of the job. His crew was a good one, and Charlie McKean proved to be a bright, energetic, and very patient Scot. Whenever Tony was baffled, McKean blamed it on his American experience. "Look, my friend, we're putting a system into this old building that was standing thirty years before the American Civil War."

Then, in early August, McKean was handed a second assignment, which meant his time was divided between the Royal Library and a hotel in Maidenhead some ten miles west of Windsor. "You'll be able to handle things, Greg, we're past the gritty part of this installation."

The added responsibility was more than Tony bargained for, yet there were compensations. He could move freely through all the rooms and justifiably remain in the library after the crew and staff were gone.

He discovered the Windsor Library was a repository of state documents and other treasures accumulated by English sovereigns over the centuries. During these hundreds of years the quantity of official papers, diaries, correspondence, and decrees had grown to uncountable numbers, all bequeathed by forty English kings and queens from the time of William I. Twenty-six monarchs had reigned since Leonardo's birth in 1452.

Leonardo's anatomical drawings were representative of the treasures owned by the Royal Families. The collection had come into the possession of the Earl of Arundel early in the seventeenth century, then disappeared and was rediscovered by Robert Dalton, Royal Librarian to George III. But the drawings created little excitement until 1876, when Jean Paul Richter published *The Literary Works of Leonardo da Vinci*.

Fascinating as all the tens of thousands of items in the library might prove, Tony concentrated on the Documents Room, where the Leonardo manuscripts were filed: each page slipped between two sheets of clear acrylic. The manuscripts were indexed: *Sheets from Leoni's, originally from one bound volume, six hundred drawings, including the Anatomical Manuscripts A. B. and C.*

Number 19057—the single sheet he would take—was a designation made under the Royal Library system of cataloging. The cabinets were not locked, but the Documents Room was, and Tony had long since made duplicate keys to it and other rooms in the library.

On September 4, during his weekly phone conversation with Jonas, he received his final instructions. Make a clean swipe of the drawing on Friday, September 9, avoid detection at all cost, deliver the drawing to Curtis Stiehl in the Dukes Hotel in London, and arrange for the safe return of the drawing to the library on Monday morning.

The fateful day had arrived.

During the installation of the air-control system the library staff remained at full strength. It was vital that the routine of the library remain unchanged and the habits of each employee hold to predictable patterns. Robin Mackworth-Young was again in France and his senior assistants (who were masters at stretching out their own weekends) were certain to leave in midafternoon. The others tended to adhere to normal hours, leaving at five o'clock. One or two might linger, then be gone shortly before 5:30. All, that is, save Reginald Streeter, senior researcher, who punctually left at 5:40, and a new assistant named Sarah Evans, who on previous Fridays had remained in the library until after six o'clock.

Tony had failed to determine Sarah's duties, observing that she had short, brown hair, was reasonably attractive, and possessed a very prominent bust. She was pleasant enough, usually flashing a bright, toothy smile. He judged her to be in her early thirties.

He excused the crew early, then spread a week's accumulation of notes over a table and began the task of preparing his weekly report. He was aware of who had left and who remained. At 5:40, Streeter silently exited, and as before, only Sarah Evans remained. She flitted from her desk to a file cabinet to one of the numerous book stacks. She seemed in constant motion, accomplishing little but annoying Tony, who hoped she would wish him a jolly weekend then disappear.

"Miss Evans, will you be staying long? I'll be stuck for a while with this foolish report."

"I have all sorts of end-of-the-week loose strings to gather up. Am I disturbing you?"

He grimaced. "Not at all. Will you be staying in Windsor for the weekend?"

She stood near the table, her arms hugging several books to her ample bosom. "Oh, no, Mr. Hewlitt. I live in London." She was breathing heavily, inhaling in short, nervous gasps. Her perfume had a sweet, floral scent. "You were in the States for a while, I understand."

"Yes. How did you know?"

"Library people talk. It's not all silence."

"Not much silence with my gang around."

"The noise hasn't bothered me. I could carry on if they shot off cannons down below."

"What sort of assignment have they given you?" He chafed at not knowing how to urge her to leave.

"Mostly clerical, nothing terribly important." She paused. "But then there is something else I have been doing here. I—" She stopped abruptly and stepped away.

"Yes, what is that?" He eyed her curiously. "What is that?" he repeated.

"Some other time. I'll tell you then. You're busy now."

"Miss Evans, I can lock up. I'm sure the traffic has thinned by now."

"I'm really in no hurry. It's raining, and I have nothing to rush off to."

He wanted her out of the library, yet now she spoke as if she were about to proposition him. If so, it was an offer he would not refuse. "I have an idea. You have a boring weekend ahead, and so do I. Suppose we start it off in a right proper way. Would you join me in the Garden Room at the Old House in thirty minutes? We can have a nip and commiserate with each other over our poor weekend planning." He flashed a warm smile for good measure.

"Why yes, Mr. Hewlitt. That's a splendid idea. I would enjoy that very much."

She slammed the books on her desk, gathered up papers and files, and shoved them into a drawer. "There! All the loose strings tied up neat and tidy."

In another minute she was gone.

Hurriedly Tony scratched out his report and slipped the papers into his briefcase. He stepped out to the reception room, where he bolted the great double doors. Then in the Documents Room he went directly to the cabinet containing Leonardo's anatomical drawings. Each folio was separated by a stiff divider and sequentially numbered. He knew exactly where to find the 19000 series. 19057 was in the top drawer of a cabinet in the middle of the room. He held Leonardo's drawing of the skulls. He placed it in a metal container then slid it neatly into the false bottom of his briefcase.

He returned to the reception room and lifted a phone to call the night security guard who routinely inspected then locked the library. As he raised the phone he looked directly at the huge carved door he had bolted minutes before. His eyes widened and the hand holding the telephone froze. The bolt had been drawn back. The door was unlocked.

The only sounds were the low whirring of the new air compressors and the buzzing in the telephone receiver. He set the phone down and walked toward the door. Then he smelled the distinctively sweet perfume Sarah Evans had been wearing.

The Old House was aptly named. Christopher Wren had designed it, then lived there in a suite overlooking the Thames. Behind the lobby was the Garden Room, incongruously decorated with a wallpaper resembling jungle vines and garish tropical plants. Tony elbowed past the crowds of weekenders after spotting Sarah at a small table near the windows.

"Sorry to keep you waiting. Those bloody reports are positively a damned nuisance."

Sarah seemed not to be smiling. "Yes, they are a bother. The more so when no one reads them. That's my luck."

Tony ordered two whiskeys. He held up his glass. "To an unexciting weekend."

"We sound awfully dull."

"I agree. Perhaps you can suggest a toast to more stimulating exploits."

Sarah looked at the bearded face then lowered her eyes. For a brief moment she was silent. "I suspect we're each involved in something unusual at this very moment. Something neither you nor I wants to tell the other."

"I'm not sure I understand," Tony said.

"When we were in the library, I wanted to ask you some questions, but we were alone, and then you suggested we come here. I realized there would be others around us and I—"

"You have me totally confused," Tony interrupted.

She breathed deeply. "I must tell you right off that I am not a permanent member of the library staff." She tried to lock her eyes on his and at the same time drive the tightness from her voice. Instead she fell silent, her eyes fixed on her hands clenched firmly around the glass.

"How do you mean 'not permanent'?"

"Precisely that," she replied. "I'm on a temporary assignment."

"Up from London, then? Filling in while we split open the library and put in all those blasted tubes and odd-looking pieces of machinery?"

"In a way, that's true. But there's more." Her eyes turned from his and Tony could feel her uneasiness. She took a deep swallow of the whiskey.

"You're a bit on edge," Tony said. Something gone wrong?

He spoke kindly, then added, "Are you on loan from the Victoria and Albert?"

"No, from the Arts and Antiques Squad, Branch C13 of the London Metropolitan Police."

Tony's face tightened and immediately he forced a weak laugh. "Well now, that's a bit more exciting than being a librarian." They were empty words meant only to fill time while he thought.

"If you know anything about police work, you know that much of it is routine."

"Yes, I'm sure that's so," he replied mechanically. His brain was racing.

"My responsibility is to augment security in the library while the new air-control system is being installed. The royal librarian insisted on an officer from our squad, and because Windsor Borough is beyond the Yard's jurisdiction, it took a bit of doing for him to pull the right strings."

"You must be pleased." He checked the time, then said absently, "There is no price that could be placed on the collection, so it seems the assignment is an honor."

When Sarah did not respond, he asked, "But why are you telling me this?"

"Because I learned yesterday that you are not Gregory Hewlitt," Sarah answered quickly and with little thought to any fear that she had felt minutes before.

"I'm sure there is a mistake."

"It was necessary for me to obtain fingerprints of everyone in the library, including, of course, you and your crew. As all of the regular staff are civil employees, we have a complete record on each. It was not difficult to secure fingerprints. Your men constantly handle pieces of metal or glass."

"If what you say is true, what will you do with the information?"

"Just as you must file weekly reports, so must I."

"And your report will state that I have been employed under an assumed name?"

"I think there is more than that. I haven't read the files, but apparently there are a number of open charges on Anthony Waters. The fact that you are using an assumed name was the extent of my report on you. Up to an hour ago, that would have been all. Women are vain creatures and I went to the lavatory before coming here to the hotel. The main door was bolted and I looked about for you. I saw that you were in the Documents Room and you were looking for something and found it in one of the cabinets. Whatever it was, it's now in your briefcase."

Sarah talked slowly, measuring her words. Tony noticed that she had not completely overcome her anxiety and guessed that this was her first solo assignment. Running off was not an option. That would preclude any hope of returning the drawing on Monday. More ominous was the threat of facing up to old charges. That could mean years in prison.

"I do have something in my briefcase, but you must not consider it stolen. It is simply something I have borrowed." He spoke with contrition. "I've taken advantage of these weeks in the library to study some of the old masters and occasionally I take one or two drawings with me on the weekend. It seems harmless enough."

"But why take them from the library? You can study hundreds of them if you wish."

"Perhaps, but with someone peering over my shoulder and another holding a stopwatch. They're terribly protective. You must know that."

"You're a puzzle, Mr. Waters. You impress me as being very competent, but you are not who you claim to be and now you have taken a very valuable piece of art."

"Yes, it's a poor show." Tony was well aware Sarah was showing a touch of assertiveness and had quickly assumed the dimensions of a major obstacle. He desperately wanted to outmaneuver her, to find the words to defuse the accusations she might put in her report. His thoughts narrowed on another solution: get her out of the way... *remove her.*

A loud chorus of happy voices swept through the crowded room. To Sarah the sounds were a sanctuary, to Tony a distraction.

"The report. When will you file it?"

"Tomorrow. I have a review each Saturday."

"And if the drawing is returned to the file tonight, would you strike that from the report?"

"That would be difficult."

"Please?" He crammed all his emotion into the single word.

"I could withhold that information, but I can't promise."

Tony asked himself who in bloody hell she thought she was. Anger replaced fear but he kept it in check.

"Thank you, Miss Evans." He raised his glass again. "To you, and to the weekend."

Sarah was obviously relieved that the conversation had ended. She hesitated, then downed her drink. "Shall we go?"

A steady rain greeted them as they exited a side door to the parking area. "We'll use your car," Tony said. "I'll get my briefcase."

Before Sarah could reply, he darted away. He returned with the briefcase in one hand, an umbrella in the other. Tony suggested they drive to the service entrance off Datchet Road. "William is on security tonight. He'll unlock the library."

Sarah steered her dark green Rover out of the narrow drive, turned right onto Thames Street, and several hundred yards later turned onto Datchet Road. The service entrance would be on their right, a half-mile away. Thick clouds blotted out the remaining daylight, and the intensifying rain was aggravated by a swirling wind. It set Sarah's full attention to the wet road and the bright headlights of an occasional oncoming car. Tony turned in the seat and placed his right hand behind Sarah's head and his left hand next to her right shoulder.

"I'll signal before we approach the turnoff," he said reassuringly. She was about to acknowledge when suddenly one strong hand pushed her head forward and the other struck down hard on her neck below the ear. She slumped, immobilized. He pushed her hands off the steering wheel, and took control of the car. His right foot found the brake pedal and several seconds later he brought the car to a stop just off the road.

Sarah was not completely unconscious but Tony would now take care of that. He reached both hands to her neck, feeling for the pulse from the carotid arteries. He was gentle; should he press too hard, he risked leaving marks on the skin. He found her pulse, first the left then the right side. Slowly his powerful fingers pressed the arteries against the bone behind, shutting down the blood flowing to her brain. He counted the seconds until he reached fifty. Sarah would remain unconscious for approximately five minutes.

He pulled her onto the passenger's seat then reentered the driver's side and drove off. In Datchet he stopped under a street lamp and carefully sorted through Sarah's briefcase. He was relieved to find her report written in longhand. He was sure there were no copies. He slipped the report in his pocket. Her handbag was deep with zippered compartments, and contained a fat wallet bulging with cards, a comb, pencils, pieces of paper clipped together, and a packet of snapshots. He leafed through all the papers and was satisfied all the notes were personal: a shopping list, a reminder for a hairdresser's appointment, check stubs, a doctor's name. Some notes were scribbled in shorthand. He searched the glove compartment and the trunk. He copied her address. Her wallet held more than fifty pounds and he was careful to leave it intact. He carefully wiped clean everything he had touched.

The ignition key was attached to an oval-shaped ring that contained no fewer than a dozen more keys. His first inclination was to leave them, but he chose instead to take them and separated the ignition key from the ring.

The road running east from Datchet to the M4 twists through farmland and Tony knew every intersection and curve. Since he would have to walk to Windsor to retrieve his car, he did not wish to create a longer distance than necessary. But if Sarah Evans was to be killed because she lost control of her car on the slippery road, he must select the most likely spot for such an accident to occur.

He chose a straight, sloping section of road with a sharp bend several hundred yards from the crest. He stopped the car in the middle of the road. Then he eased her back to the driver's seat and brought her arms through the spokes in the steering wheel so she was leaning forward. He wedged her foot down onto the accelerator pedal. The motor raced, a high whining sound. Finally he lowered the window to allow his arm to reach in so his hand could touch the gear lever.

In one continuous motion he opened the door, released the brake, closed the door, and pushed down on the gearshift. The wheels turned wildly, spinning on the slickened surface. Then they gripped the asphalt.

The car lurched forward and sped down the road. At the turn it shot straight ahead, crashed through a low stone fence, then flew into the air and slammed on its side, rolling over before crashing into a high wall of rocks.

Tony ran toward the wreck, hiding once as a car passed, its head-lights searching the wet road. He ran again and was careful to step on grass and rocks so as not to leave a telltale footprint. He reached the wreckage and saw Sarah's body.

Glass had cut through her head and neck. In the final light of the darkening evening he could see that her blood was everywhere.

He backed away from the wreck and the blood and the smell of gaso-line. Then a powerful rush of exhilaration swept over him and he thrust both arms over his head as a sign of victory. "You're dead, damn you. You had no business meddling." A car rounded the curve and he sank quickly to his knees. Headlights briefly shone over the wreckage like a flash from a photographer's strobe. In that instant he saw the ugliness of Sarah's bloody body slumped back on the seat, her head tilted up to the black, wet sky.

After another car passed he began his trek back to Windsor. He knew it was two miles to Datchet and another mile and a half to Wind-sor. Even at a fast pace—though allowing for the need to avoid being seen by passing cars—it would take fifty minutes to reach his car. The rain had become a steady drizzle, and though tempted to throw away the umbrella, he held on to it as he began to half run, half walk.

It took fifty-five minutes. He was chilled and damp and without re-morse. Cheerful laughter came from the barroom but he was concerned only with the deserted streets and the parking area, which he happily found was empty of people. Not until he was back on the Datchet road did he switch on the headlights. At the fatal turn in the road the lights shone on the field where Sarah's dead body lay, and as he pulled through the curve he was able to catch a brief glimpse of the shattered car. In the murky darkness it was unlikely the accident would be discovered be-fore morning.

# Chapter 6

Curtis Stiehl had waited six months to have Leonardo's drawing of the skulls in his hands. He had learned patience under terrible conditions, but there was a different urgency attached to the assignment Jonas had given him. He had drawn the skulls dozens of times, and had tried other subjects as well. Now he was ready for the actual drawings.

Tony was due at 6:30 and Stiehl's impatience began showing several hours earlier. He fussed over his cameras and took unnecessary inventories of film and chemicals. At seven Jonas phoned to say he would be detained. Stiehl continued his lonely wait.

*Alone. He hated being alone. It brought back bitter memories.*

He went to the window where the view was down to the driveway and the entrance to the Dukes Hotel. Jonas had chosen to headquarter in one of London's small jewels. An in-crowd of Americans liked its quiet intimacy, tucked away on a narrow, cobbled street yet accessible to the shops and services.

The morning Stiehl arrived he immediately began the task of converting a hotel bedroom into a highly sophisticated art and photographic studio. Everything he had asked Jonas to provide was in cartons piled atop each other in the small salon that separated two bedrooms in the Gloucester suite. A large drafting board was set up near one window. The bed was pushed against the wall, and two large tables occupied the middle of the room. Each was equipped with a pair of high-intensity photolamps. A Hasselblad camera was mounted to a copy stand. Under the camera were close-up rings and an assortment of lenses. Two ultraviolet lamps in their reflectors, boxes of assorted films, and filters completed the photographic fixturing. Next to the drafting table was a three-drawer cabinet filled with jars of ink, boxes of chalk, and an array of pens, pencils, and assorted writing implements.

The bathroom had become a darkroom, complete with enlarger, safety lights, developing trays, rinser, and dryer.

Throughout a hot summer Stiehl learned how Leonardo took a quill across paper and created the countless images he had drawn in his manuscripts. He had spent hours in the museums and libraries, and had devoted many more to reading books by Lord Clark, Pedretti, Vasari, and others.

*Goddamn it! The drawing was supposed to be in my hands an hour ago.*

Darkness had come with the rain. He sat by the window, staring down at two drawings he had rendered a few days before leaving New York. They were copies of Leonardo's drawings of the skulls. One drawing was on a sheet measuring slightly more than seven inches by five inches, the other on a sheet four times as large. The smaller drawing was identical in size to the page from the Royal collection. He would compare it to the genuine Leonardo. The one numbered 19057.

*Hurry, you son of a bitch . . . there's not much time!*

He was anxious to see how well he had written in Leonardo's oddly personal style. He was mostly concerned with his ability to write in the bastardized Italian that Leonardo created and wrote in reverse. Like many left-handed persons, Stiehl performed numerous functions with his right hand. He was naturally ambidextrous and had mastered the trick of writing with both hands simultaneously. Leonardo entertained his students by drawing with each hand as if the hands were controlled by a divided brain.

He had not been able to sleep and the brief naps he managed came with the help of Nembutal or Librium. Jonas was off to a meeting he said was of great importance. Stiehl was both angry and frustrated that Tony was late. To this he added the fear that something had happened, that he couldn't get the drawing.

Then came loud knocks on the door to the suite. He unbolted the door and in walked Tony. His raincoat was soaked through, his beard matted with dampness.

"Where have you been, for Christ's sake? Why didn't you call?" The angry words exploded from his mouth.

"From where? Some goddamned ditch? Where's Jonas?"

"He's been delayed. He called an hour ago expecting you'd be here. He was ticked that you weren't."

"Does anybody care about *my* fucking problems?" Tony tossed off the wet coat and rubbed his beard with a towel.

"I care about the drawing. Do you have it?"

"Of course," Tony snapped. "Did you have any doubt I could pinch it?"

"Not until you didn't show on time. It's possible something could happen. Even to you."

"A tire blew out. On the M4. No one came by, I had to fix it myself."

"After you fixed it you should have called."

"Go to hell, Stiehl. I've spent a miserable summer preparing for today. Too bad if you don't like the way I handled my assignment. Let's see you do as well."

"What about your car? You've got to get the drawing back on Monday."

"It's an old clunk, but it'll do. I know the doorman from the old days. He works with the garage operators and knows who's open on the weekend."

"He recognized you?"

"Patrick's in my pocket. He'll put a note in the car telling me where to have the tire fixed. I'll pay him for that and for any other help he can give us."

"Will you tell Jonas the doorman knows who you are?"

"I tell Mr. Kalem what he needs to know. Nothing more."

They stared at each other, neither blinking or speaking. Stiehl could see past the beard and saw a face that was either tired or frightened. Tony's skin was white, his eyes were unfocused and twitched nervously. He went to the window and looked down to the hotel entrance. Then he pulled the draperies closed.

"The drawing," Stiehl said.

Tony took a thin metal box from his briefcase and from that he withdrew the drawing and set it on the table. Stiehl pulled on a pair of white gloves, removed the drawing from its plastic sleeve, and placed it on a piece of clear vinyl. He positioned a magnifying glass attached to a stand over the drawing, and then put his copy next to the Leonardo. He smiled. The similarity was incredible. Tony made his own appraisal.

"My God, Stiehl, you made your drawing from reproductions?"

"Did you have any doubt?" he said, aping the same confidence Tony showed a moment earlier. "That's what I did with my summer. But don't be fooled. They're very similar and yet they're very much different. Now that I have the original I can find what those differences are.

"Aside from the inks and the paper and the instruments Leonardo used, there are a dozen more—call them fingerprints—that separate the genuine from the copy." Curtis lifted the priceless little drawing of the skulls. "The front side of the sheet is the recto, the back is the verso. When the pages are bound, like in a book, the recto side becomes a right-hand page, the verso a left-hand page. When the pages are removed, one edge tends to have small tears where it's been torn from the binding. You see it along this edge." He pointed to the left edge of the recto side.

Though Tony was showing interest, he occasionally returned to the window and looked out to the cars entering or leaving the grounds. Curtis placed a large sheet of paper beside the drawings. The sheet was divided into one-inch squares and the page was exactly three times the dimension of the original drawing. He had lightly drawn an outline of the manuscript's content on the large sheet.

Over the Leonardo and his copy he placed a clear sheet of acetate film; it, too, had ruled lines forming half-inch squares. As he compared his copy with the original and spotted an error or change he wished to make, he made a mark on the overlay grid and at a corresponding position on the larger sheet. Stiehl had devised his own code and the marks he made on the large sheet were also recorded in a notebook that was divided into sections marked: *drawing, shading, writing, paper, ink, age and distress,* and *miscellaneous.*

Twenty minutes passed and Stiehl had not scanned the first row of half-inch squares.

"My God, Stiehl, it will take a fucking bloody millennium at the rate you're going."

"Patience, Tony. Remember the long summer we spent. And besides it will go faster after I've evaluated the top row. I made an accurate copy of the reproduction, but that doesn't mean I've made an accurate copy of the real thing. With the original I'm able to see how Leonardo drew in the deep, shaded sections around the eye socket and in the mastoidal passages."

Tony stared down at four detailed drawings of human skulls, two by Leonardo, two by Stiehl. He couldn't turn away and he began muttering. Then he covered his eyes with shaking hands. He moaned. A low, muffled cry.

Stiehl turned to him. "Hey! You all right?"

Tony dropped his hands. "Yes. Of course. Get on with what you're doing."

"Have you had anything to eat?" Curtis asked.

"I'll wait for Kalem. The dining room's open until eleven."

Stiehl continued to analyze the first row of squares. His notations included the condition of the ink and the deterioration to the paper. From a heavily inked area he scraped off a minuscule amount of ink and carefully put it in a sterilized vial. He repeated the process on the verso side. Next he sliced away a small piece of the paper, careful to take a sample large enough to contain the original fibers, yet not too large as to be detected.

He then placed the Leonardo in a glass frame and set it on a copy stand in front of two flood lamps. He positioned the camera and took a half-dozen exposures of each side of the folio. Then he moved the ultraviolet lights into position. "Now for a critical test," he announced softly to Tony. "This will tell us if there is any faded ink or traces of silverpoint on the drawing." He switched on the lights and carefully examined each side. "See? A few faded lines show up under ultraviolet. We can handle those."

He noted the location of the faded lines on the control sheet, inserted ultraviolet film into the camera, and took several exposures.

Throughout, Stiehl had moved with speed and confidence. Tony retreated to the bed and sat on the edge, watching every move with grudging respect. Stiehl knew he was being watched closely, and he had also sensed Tony's growing uneasiness. He completed his camera work and turned off the hot lights. "I'll develop the film and make sure I've got everything."

Tony returned to the window and parted the draperies again. He watched Patrick open a taxi door. A huge man stepped out and entered the hotel.

Jonas Kalem was a punctual man. To be nearly three hours late could only be justified by a matter of overwhelming importance. His lips pursed into a small "O" signifying that the time had been well spent. He called the Duke of Gloucester suite and, content that the Leonardo was safely in hand and Stiehl was progressing with his work, instructed Tony to meet him in the dining room.

Jonas approached the evening meal with a ritualistic fervor, and this evening it was to the complete consternation of both the dining room and kitchen staff. Two of the six tables in the small room were occupied as they entered. Maître Servio's plastic smile turned more genuine after a quantity of pound notes fell into his hand. He snapped a waiter to attention and alerted the chef to keep a flame under the poacher. The pink salmon was served perfunctorily but Jonas ate with his usual enthusiasm. After the meal Jonas ordered a snifter of Remy Martin VSOP. He inhaled the rich fumes and without turning his eyes spoke very softly.

"Something is dreadfully wrong. I feel it."

"Stiehl has the drawing. I was late getting it to him but he has it."

"That's obvious. There's something else."

"There was a hitch."

"What kind of hitch, for God's sake?"

Tony began. He talked slowly, never raising his voice above a quiet monotone. "I had no reason to suspect one of the assistant librarians had been planted by the Metropolitan Police. In fact she didn't begin until the middle of August, long after I'd screened the other staff members. Most have been there since Charlemagne, to see them creak.

"She came in with her big tits in front of her and a smile frozen to her face. On the last two Fridays she stayed after the others had gone home. She did the same this afternoon. It was a nuisance but she might have stayed for the entire bloody evening. I suggested we have a drink together, then I'd have her out of the library. I thought she had gone on ahead but she stopped at the loo. Then as she was leaving she saw me at the files."

"She saw you take the drawing?" Jonas's fat jowls sagged.

"She saw me 'take something' was the way she put it. When we met for our drinks, she told me she had run fingerprints on me and said I was Anthony Waters. That's when I learned she was on special assignment from Scotland Yard. She's in C13 and I've run into that bunch before."

Jonas spilled his brandy. "Who knows besides this policewoman?"

"She planned to file her report this weekend. Tomorrow. I'm guessing no one else knows."

"She cannot file a report." Jonas slammed his hand on the table. "You hear me? There must not be a report."

"There won't be a report. Sarah Evans is dead."

Jonas's eyes for a rare, split instant were changed, as if an involuntary muscle spasm popped them wide open. "Dead? What in God's name did you do?"

"It rained tonight, the roads were slippery. Her car is in a field beyond a sharp curve." Tony took the brandy down in a single swallow. "She lost control and crashed."

"Explain. How did she lose control?"

The big man listened incredulously as Tony accounted for every action from the time he and Sarah left the Old House until he returned for his car and drove to London. His description of Sarah's car crashing over the wall and the gruesome condition in which he found her were related in vivid detail.

"No more...I don't want to hear it!" Sweat glistened on Jonas's face and he dabbed at it with his napkin. "We're hardly started and you've put everything in jeopardy. You realize they won't stop until they've found who did it."

"It will look like an accident. I'll wager that's their conclusion."

"And you'll make a bad bet."

Tony knew an investigation was automatic, but he was trying to keep Jonas's anger in check.

"You took the report she was going to submit this weekend. Obviously there are other papers. Her files on the crew, and the fingerprint report that gave you away. Where are all those pieces of paper?"

"She told me she received the report on me yesterday. I'm certain she hasn't passed that information on."

Jonas fell silent. He leaned forward as if to speak, then slumped back. All the while he tried to rub away the wetness that soaked his shirt collar. Finally he spoke, his round mouth quivering. "You were a damned fool! An impetuous, unthinking, stupid fool. I have spent too much time and too much money to have this project go wrong." His fat body shook in angry frustration. "I warned you to curb your impulsiveness, and I don't know what alternatives you had, but this way there are none. After they discover the body the police will swarm over the library, all of Windsor, and half of London. They do that when one of theirs is killed. Accident or not. Everyone will be questioned. You were seen with her in the hotel."

"The place was crowded with weekenders. We didn't leave the library together; in fact the guard saw Sarah leave before I called for him to lock up."

"Small points but in our favor. Tomorrow you will do two things. First you will go to where the Evans woman lived and search for other papers. And second, you will return the Leonardo to the library."

"I'm not a bloody lackey and I'm not a magician who can slip in and out of a strange house because you snap your damned fingers and say so."

Jonas reacted instantly. He thrust a hand at Tony's face and snapped his fingers twice, then once again. "You'll do as I tell you. Suppose a team of investigators goes through her papers, and suppose there is a complete file on you, and then suppose they get suspicious and find the slimmest piece of evidence you were in her car."

Tony gave an acknowledging nod. "But the drawing. You said Stiehl needed it for two days. And the police. They'll come prowling."

"I'll deal with Curtis, and as to the police, it seems that if you had anything to do with the woman's death, the library would be a most unlikely spot for you to be."

"But there's a risk."

"You sent someone off on a death ride and didn't think that was taking a risk? Are you completely stupid?"

Jonas shook with anger. "You had four months to bring the drawing out, and when you did, you bungled. There's still a chance you can cover yourself but you must find if she had a file on you. You have until the morning to find a way to clean up the bloody trail you've left."

Another snifter of brandy arrived and Jonas waited until the waiter was out of sight. "Where is her home?"

"In Battersea," Tony answered. "I've got the address."

"Did she have a family?"

"I don't know. There was a photo of a small girl in her purse."

"I want you to meet me in St. James Square after you've gone through her papers. Be there no later than 9:30."

Tony looked at his watch. "That's less than twelve hours from now. That's bloody goddamned impossible."

Jonas stood. "Which will it be? Run from a murder charge until they catch you or deal with the impossible?"

Jonas did not swirl the heady liquid onto the sides of the snifter, then patiently inhale the rich fumes. Instead he drank it in a single swallow, then strode quickly from the room.

# Chapter 7

The rain had ended but the air remained heavy. The early-morning sun could not penetrate the thick, low clouds. Detective Superintendent Walter Deats's car turned off Datchet Road and stopped near a low, stone fence. A police sergeant came to the car and touched the peak of his cap in an informal salute.

"Sorry to bring you out but we might have a puzzle here and I thought you ought to see everything before we remove the body."

"Just my luck, Randy. It's my first free Saturday in a month."

The superintendent climbed from the car and the two set off for the torn Rover that still lay on its side. Deats was a man of medium build, in his mid-forties, and nattily dressed. His full mustache curled up at the ends and he wore dark-rimmed glasses that were more often held like an actor's prop than worn to aid his vision. They covered half the distance when Deats stopped. He looked back to the stone fence and then to the wrecked car.

"Have you measured this? It's an incredible distance for the car to travel considering that it hit then went over that fence."

"It's over a hundred feet. A hundred and six to be exact."

"No wonder he's dead," Deats mused aloud.

"It was a woman," the officer said.

"I got a message that someone from the Yard was killed."

"It's a woman, all right. Detective Constable Sarah Evans. She was attached to the Arts and Antiques Squad. We checked early this morning. On special duty with the Royal Library."

"At Windsor?" Deats asked.

"Been there since August first."

"Good Christ. One of my oldest friends heads up that operation and he didn't have the courtesy to tell me they'd spotted someone right under our noses. That's their bad luck."

"The girl took an awful beating. It's a wonder she wasn't thrown clear of the mess."

Walter Deats had seen the results of knife killings and motorcycle accidents and knew how difficult it was to accept the sight of a maimed and bloodied victim without feeling an awful sickness deep inside. When he reached the car, they shined a bright light on Sarah's face. He instructed the officer holding the flashlight to put a sheet over the body. "Set the car upright," he said quietly. "No point having it look like a circus tragedy."

Sergeant Randy Pelkinton handed him a clipboard. "Here's what we've come up with so far, Walter. On the surface it looks like she was speeding and lost control at the turn. A few things don't jibe, but nothing much to put your teeth into. Like we don't find skid marks, but the road was wet and there's been traffic over that same stretch. Maybe she dozed off and didn't have a chance to brake."

Deats began his own investigation. Notes on a clipboard would be early observations, nothing more. One of the men was searching for fingerprints inside the car. Deats ordered him to look for prints on the outside when the car was dry. He spoke into a miniature tape recorder, capturing his typically terse judgments and the questions still requiring answers. The coroner had not appeared; it always bothered Deats that the medical people were the last to show. It would serve no purpose to have the poor woman declared dead again; that fact was clearly established at 5:30 in the morning when the accident was discovered by a motorcyclist who chose to relieve himself at the very spot the car crashed over the stone fence. Deats wanted an autopsy and knew there would be a minor skirmish over having it performed immediately. It was Saturday. A comment entered into the tape recorder had to do with the fact that Sarah Evans had not been thrown clear of the car in spite of the obvious crashing the car received in the hundred and six feet it traveled. "Seat belt?" was the question to be considered. He noted also that her right foot was actually bent against the accelerator pedal. He would request that the medical people examine the foot. After the pocketbook and contents had been checked for fingerprints, he took it to his car and examined every item, making audio notes as he went along. When he completed the chore, he recorded two final thoughts. First he would phone Elliot Heston, a senior officer in CIP, Scotland Yard. They were old friends and the tragedy was a cheerless excuse to get together. Policy dictated that accidental deaths must be fully investigated and he would assist in whatever way his old friend might request.

His other note was a reminder to choose two men to break the news to Sarah Evans's family even though Scotland Yard would send their own emissaries. But the accident occurred within the jurisdiction of the Windsor police, and he would send one officer in uniform, the other in his Sunday best. It was an unpleasant assignment that Deats wanted carried out as early in the morning as was practical.

During the drive from the Dukes Hotel to his West Kensington flat, Tony had an opportunity to put the day's events into some kind of coherent perspective. The very simple task of taking the Leonardo drawing had escalated into the nightmare of killing. Now he faced the challenge of getting into Sarah Evans's home to purloin potentially incriminating files, then return the drawing to the library. He was cold and tired and angry. But somehow he began formulating a plan for the morning and by the time he fell into a restless sleep a strategy was taking shape.

In the morning before the sun had risen, he sat in front of a mirror, a box of stage makeup before him. Experienced fingers molded pliable putty into a nose somewhat larger than his own, and with a slight bend to it. Over his face and neck he applied a pale cream, blending it carefully into the tiny lines between the putty and his skin. Next he fashioned a pair of bushy eyebrows and glued them in place. With a black liner pencil he drew crow's-feet about his eyes and furrows across his forehead.

To his beard, hair, and new eyebrows he patted on a white powder and combed some of the whiteness away so as to change the brown to gray. From another box he selected a pair of metal-rimmed spectacles.

Next he assembled an ordinary costume: a plain shirt and tie, gray pants, a mud brown sweater, and over all of it a soiled raincoat. He put on a battered hat with a broad brim, which he pulled to the top of his new, bushy eyebrows. He practiced walking with a stoop and added a limp to his gait. Under his arm he held a flat briefcase. During his transformation he talked to himself, practicing an indistinguishable London City accent bordering on cockney.

From his collection of business cards he chose one that read "Jerome Black, Sales Representative." Beneath the name: "Usher & Leeds—Computer Professionals."

At 6:30 it was still nearly dark on the streets. He drove to Heathrow Airport. With his limping, slanting walk he made his way into the terminal and the Godfrey Davis car-rental agent. He handed the attendant a deposit, located the English Ford, then drove across Chelsea Bridge to Battersea. Beyond the huge park with its racetrack and band shell the streets narrowed and came at each other in odd angles. Sarah's apartment was on Ursala Street off Shuttleworth Road. He parked at the end of the street. The time was 8:20.

He walked slowly, inspecting the cars that passed and those parked along the street. An ambulance, its siren screaming, roared past. He glanced back to his car, wishing he had parked closer. He hoped there would be no cause to leave hurriedly yet realized that when Sarah's body was identified, all hell would break loose. Even now he might be too late, might encounter a team from Scotland Yard consoling the family. He set his mind on the character he was about to play. He knew the game of masquerade, and he was incredibly good at it. He continued on to the apartment building. He pulled on thin leather gloves as he approached the entrance. He pressed hard on the button under Sarah Evans's name. Sarah's flat was on the first floor in the front if he figured correctly. He rang again. He would try a third time, then ring the superintendent. His finger was poised to press one more time when a thin voice came from a recessed speaker.

"Yes, who is it?"

"It's Jerry Black—Usher and Leeds. Is Miss Evans at home?" He pitched his voice higher and tried to sing the words, dropping *h*'s and trilling his *r*'s.

The female voice answered. "No, she's not home. I hoped you was her saying she lost her keys."

"She was in our shop a short time ago and asked that we come to look things over before she put in an order. Seemed very important to her. May I come in?"

The little voice did not respond immediately. Then: "She said it was important?"

"I'd say very definitely, ma'am."

There was another pause. "Come in, then: 100A."

A buzzer sounded and the door opening into the lobby was unlocked. He climbed a flight of stairs and found 100A. It was at the front overlooking the street, as he had hoped. He tapped on the door and it was opened by a small girl, perhaps five or six, with blond hair falling below her shoulders onto a pink bathrobe. She was holding a small white-and-tan dog of indiscernible lineage, which promptly jumped from her arms and scurried to a corner, where it sat growling.

A short, stout woman appeared behind the little girl. Her face was pleasant and she managed a weak smile. "I'm Mrs. Evans's mother, and this is Cynthia, my granddaughter."

Tony greeted Sarah's mother and daughter as if he were milling among the congregation at a church tea. His cordiality lacked eye contact. He flashed his business card and just as quickly slipped it back into his pocket. "Your daughter, ma'am, she was looking to buy a computer for her records and correspondence. She asked that we look over the place where she wants to have it installed."

"I wish she was here. Oh, heavens, you have no idea how I wish she was here. She didn't come home last night. And she didn't call and that's not like her. She's in a special kind of work, you see, and I worry about her. Cynthia here, poor child, she's been cryin' most of the night."

"I won't be takin' much time, ma'am. If you could show me the room where she does any work when she's home, that's probably where she'd want to put it."

"I wish she had said something to me about all this. She gets so closemouthed at times."

"Mr. Evans, her husband, would he know?"

"Oh, there isn't no Mr. Evans anymore. That's the problem around here. She doesn't have her man to help."

"Well, we can sort it out. Is there a desk where she'd be doing some of that work she was tellin' us about?"

"Yes, there, in her bedroom."

Tony had surveyed the sitting room and determined it was Cynthia's playroom. In the bedroom was a desk on which was piled a stack of files, and next to it a typewriter table with an old Olivetti on top of it. "I'm sure this is where she wants to have us put the computer."

He pulled out a metal tape and began measuring distances from the desk to the windows and to the electrical outlets. He scribbled numbers on a pad. Sarah's mother and daughter stood in the doorway watching in silent curiosity. He patiently continued, waiting for them to leave. *Didn't they know to leave? Didn't they know he needed to be alone?* Time was passing and he expected the phone to ring or the bell to go off signifying that representatives from Scotland Yard had arrived in the lobby. He turned to Sarah's mother as he made a pretense of sniffing the air through his putty nose. He asked if he smelled coffee burning on the stove.

Sarah's mother said the woman next door always burned coffee, but that she did not. "I can brew you a cup if you would like."

He seized the opportunity. "That would be nice, ma'am." It would take several minutes to bring water to a boil. Important minutes.

Sarah's mother started for the kitchen, Cynthia tagging after. "Come with me, Clover," she said, but the dog took a position inside the door and watched Tony search through the desk.

One drawer was locked. He tried the small keys on the ring he found in Sarah's pocketbook. The second one fit. He took out a half-dozen manila folders and hurriedly sorted through each. One was marked "Staff," and in it were brief write-ups on each employee. Another was labeled "Heldwicke." The name on the first file was Charlie McKean. Quickly he jammed the folder into his zippered briefcase. As he did, he knocked a pen to the floor and it rolled toward Clover. As he reached for it, the dog leaped at his hand. Sharp little teeth punctured the glove and sank into his flesh. "Damn it!" he shouted, and flung the dog against the door. The startled spaniel raced from the room squealing and yapping. He closed the drawer and locked it just as Cynthia ran from the kitchen and chased her pet under the sofa. She sat on the floor and began to cry.

"My God in heaven, what's the calamity?" The grandmother ran from the kitchen to see Cynthia trying to placate the dog while all the time tears streamed down her reddened face.

"I dropped my pen, and when I went to pick it up, I frightened your dog. It bit my hand, ma'am." Tony peeled the glove back, revealing two punctures in the skin, one on each side of his scar. Before he could pull his hand back Sarah's mother saw spots of blood oozing from the teeth marks.

"It'll be fine," Tony said, attempting a cheerful tone. "Is your dog all right? I didn't mean hurting it." The question was aimed at Cynthia but he was not interested in an answer. He had moved to the window and could see that a black sedan had pulled to a stop directly across the street and two men were about to enter the apartment building.

"Thanks for the coffee but I'd best be gettin' back to work out the details for Mrs. Evans. Please tell her to call when she's of a mind to have us go ahead." He stood at the door and looked back at the woman and the little girl, sadness and unhappiness in their faces. In minutes they would learn of the crushing tragedy, but he could not let that be of any consequence. A little smile froze on his face and he said indifferently, "I'll be going now, and thank you for helping me."

Through the closed door he could hear the intercom bell ring as the police announced their presence. He ran down the steps and hid in the shadows of the hall until the two men were admitted and began climbing to the first floor. Then he exited to the street and walked toward his car as fast as the crooked limp would permit.

From Battersea Park to St. James Square is a distance of about two miles. Tony covered it in eleven minutes, including a momentary delay caused by a crowd of tourists in front of Buckingham Palace. He was to meet Jonas by the statue of William III. He was early and saw that Jonas was also ahead of schedule. "It's me, all right," Tony announced as he shuffled forward. "I got the papers, no problem about that. The police showed just as I was leaving."

Tony took a copy of the morning *Times* from Jonas and felt for the thin box in the folds of the paper. He slipped it into a pocket of his raincoat.

"Curtis was a very angry man when I told him to spend the night with the drawing," Jonas said in a solemn tone. "He'll presume something's gone off the track very quickly, so its best you stay away."

"I've got no reason to mix with him. Besides, I've got enough to worry about. I've thought it through and there will be no Greg Hewlitt after today."

"If Hewlitt disappears, they'll know for certain the woman was killed."

"They may still find it out. Where will that leave me?"

"You made it look like an accident. Now you've got all her papers. If you should suddenly evaporate, someone is bound to be curious. Tell your supervisor you have a family matter to settle, that you must be away for several days."

Tony returned to his rental car and proceeded to Heathrow, claimed his own car, and drove to Windsor. After exiting from the M4 he pulled off the road where he removed his makeup, brushed the powder from his hair, and changed clothes. He proceeded on his usual route to Windsor, aware he would pass the accident scene. As he neared the fatal bend his hands tightened on the steering wheel, causing him to feel a twinge where Cynthia's dog had bitten him. Flashing red lights atop a wrecker's truck marked the spot. A dozen or more cars were parked off the road and photographers were using their flashes in the still-murky light. His pulse beat more rapidly as he drove through the curve.

Approaching the service road leading to the castle, he slowed then, with an abrupt change of mind, stepped heavily on the accelerator. He continued into Windsor Borough and to Kings Road, leading south out of the town. In minutes he was in rolling farmland. He turned onto a narrow, unpaved road and stopped.

He gathered the disguise he had worn earlier, remnants of makeup, and the briefcase containing Sarah's papers and wrapped it all in the old raincoat. He hid the bundle under a pile of leaves behind a row of shrubs. He removed the right rear tire and replaced it with the spare. He then punctured a hole at the base of the valve stem on the tire he had removed. His last act was to cut the skin on the back of his hand where he had been bitten. The cuts were only deep enough to obscure the marks of the dog's teeth. He then drove back to Windsor.

The library was empty, save for Reginald Streeter, the punctilious history scholar. He was a gentle man with a puckish face and balding pate. Streeter read voraciously and in midproject would lay out a dozen references, reading from one source, then another, then finally concentrate on the extensive notes he was compiling in several thick notebooks. His life was wrapped up in the lives of English royalty and his expertise on the subject was widely acknowledged.

Tony spread his engineering drawings on a desk near the new system's control panel and busied himself rewriting the report he had prepared the previous afternoon. All ducts, compressors, blowers, and controls were installed and the system was receiving its final fine tuning. The room was silent except for the low whir of the compressors.

Tony was surprised by the soft voice of Streeter, who had quietly come to his side: "The weekend is a good time to hear how quietly the new machinery performs."

"Yes, thank you. We're pleased about that."

"Are you just as pleased that the humidity levels are correct and constant? That's been our big problem, you know."

"We have good control for the most part, but we're getting too wide a fluctuation in the rooms with large windows. Some of the new windows weren't as tightly sealed as specified and that's something I'm looking into today." Tony pointed at two windows in the adjacent room. "I'm afraid those are the culprits."

"My, that's an angry cut on the back of your hand, Mr. Hewlitt."

Tony retracted his hand quickly. "It's nothing. Looks bloody nasty but I only scratched it changing a tire."

"Wash it clean," Streeter said amiably. "You don't want an infection."

He stepped away, then turned back to Tony. "You have a quite nice accent, Mr. Hewlitt. Accents are a hobby of mine and I place you near Liverpool. Are you a Liverpudlian?"

Tony reacted quickly. "No, I was brought up in Leeds."

"Surely you spent time in Liverpool when you were young. Perhaps in Manchester?"

"No, Mr. Streeter. Neither city."

"Then these old ears are playing tricks on me. People are constantly moving about these days, perhaps that's the problem." The older man sighed. "Well, I must get back to my unhappy Queen Anne. Such a poor dear she was."

Again he started away, then turned back. "There is one thing more I must not forget to say. You and your men are owed our thanks for the splendid work that's been done. The great treasures in this library will be enjoyed by many more generations. You have indeed made a valuable contribution to our country's great heritage."

"Thank you, Mr. Streeter," Tony said earnestly. He was happy to see the old scholar finally return to his work and ask no further questions about cut hands and telltale accents. The apprehension he felt when he entered the library at five minutes past noon had not lessened, and while he was not looking forward to a confrontation with the police, he preferred they begin their investigation while he was diligently working and involved in the rhythm of his job and the engineer's role he had learned to play so well. Shortly after 1:00 P.M. his hopes were realized.

Streeter answered a rap on the door and admitted a police sergeant and a well-dressed man who walked through the reception room and on to the First Gallery. Neither man spoke until they had made a complete sweep of all the rooms and found that Streeter and the bearded man were the only occupants. The well-dressed man spoke to Streeter.

"I am Superintendent Deats of the Windsor police and this is Sergeant Pelkinton. We're making inquiries into an accident that involved a member of the library staff. Perhaps you might first tell us your name."

Deats spoke slowly and quietly. Tony continued with his report, not looking up but able to hear the conversation across the room.

"My heavens. Nothing too bad, I hope. Who has had an accident, Superintendent?"

"Miss Evans."

"Oh, dear Sarah. Sarah the smiler, I call her. Is it serious?"

"She was in the library yesterday?"

"Indeed. I believe she was here when I left last evening."

"When was that?"

"My usual time. Five-forty. I meet friends at Boar's Tavern and I try to be there promptly at six o'clock."

"Were there others here when you left?"

"Yes. I believe one or two. Mr. Hewlitt, to whom we owe our gratitude for the splendid new air-control system, was still hard at work. He's the gentleman over there."

"And after leaving the library, did you see Miss Evans again during the evening?"

"Not at Boar's Tavern," Streeter said with a smile. "We don't encourage the ladies to come there in the evening. It's all but a men's club nowadays."

"Thank you, Mr. Streeter. If we have further questions, we'll contact you."

"But you haven't told me what happened. What kind of an accident did Sarah have?"

"Automobile."

"Was she hurt badly?"

Deats did not reply. Tony was aware that the detective was walking toward him. He sized up Deats as a professional who knew how to ask questions and knew when to answer questions fired at him.

"Mr. Hewlitt, my name is Deats, Windsor police. May I ask a few questions?"

Tony looked up as if he had only at that moment become aware that Deats and his sergeant were in the library. He stood, his right hand in his pocket. "Of course. How can I help?"

"One of the employees of the library, a Sarah Evans, was involved in an automobile accident last night. Mr. Streeter has stated that you and Miss Evans were in the library when he left at 5:40. Were there any others here at that time?"

"I don't recall that there were."

"You are sure of that?"

"Sarah went on before I did, then I phoned the security guard after completing my work. He checked all the rooms before locking."

"What time was that?" Deats took his tape recorder from his pocket and turned it on.

"Sometime after six, I believe."

"And did you see Sarah Evans after you left the library?"

Deats had asked the big question, the one Tony hoped might end further police questions and speculation.

"Superintendent, I'm not on staff in the library. I'm employed by Heldwicke Air-Control Systems and the installation is near completion." He forced a weak laugh. "It's no jolly fun winding up one of these things, weekend work and all that rot." Then with a very concerned expression, he asked, "What has happened to Miss Evans?"

"She was killed."

"How horrible. How very, very horrible." Tony slumped into the chair and stared at the papers in front of him. "I knew her only slightly but she seemed such a pleasant person."

"Please answer my question. Did you see Miss Evans after you left the library?"

Tony looked up, his face expressionless. Slowly he shook his head and answered softly, "No. No, I last saw her when she said good night and left the library."

"Quite so. Well, thank you for your help, Mr. Hewlitt. We may contact you for further questioning."

Tony remained motionless until Deats and the sergeant were out of the library. Streeter had edged closer and heard the inspector's final comments.

"What a dreadful thing, Mr. Hewlitt."

"Yes. I suddenly feel bloody awful, not much like working."

Streeter did not reply. He returned to his table and stood silently over his work for several minutes. Then he gathered and stacked his books and notes, disappeared briefly, then returned with a coat and hat and called out, "Good afternoon, Mr. Hewlitt."

"Good afternoon to you, Mr. Streeter."

The wide doors closed and Tony waited an endless minute before locking it. This time he explored every room and corner, taking no chance that he was not alone. In the Documents Room before the Leonardo cabinet he paused again, then swiftly returned the original drawing.

It was nearly three o'clock when he returned to his desk. Fifteen more minutes, he thought, then call security. Rereading his report, he was pleased to discover it was complete and businesslike. Heldwicke had no cause to suspect his duplicity; he had performed well.

A guard Tony did not recognize answered his request to inspect and lock the library. Anxious to complete his one remaining chore, he hurried to his car and drove onto the service road. Familiar faces at the security station waved him to a halt, then asked that he leave his car.

"Hey, Mr. Hewlitt. You've heard of the terrible accident. Seems that pretty girl was on police assignment and we've got instructions to check all the vehicles leaving the grounds. Of course it's just procedural. Only take a minute."

They made a cursory search of the old station wagon. Any of the items Tony had hidden on the other side of Windsor would have prompted questions.

"You're okay, Mr. Hewlitt. Sorry for the delay but orders is orders."

Tony slipped behind the wheel and with a friendly wave drove off. "Ruddy damned good luck!" he exclaimed to himself. He headed the car into Windsor and continued south on Kings Road to the turnoff where he retrieved the bundle containing Sarah's papers. Instead of returning through Windsor, he chose a different route to the city, through Old Windsor and Staines. It would add fifteen minutes to the drive but it avoided Datchet Road with its deadly sharp turn.

# Chapter 8

The three hours after Tony placed Leonardo's drawing of the skulls in his hands, Stiehl completed his initial assessment of the drawing he created during the summer. The list of his big and little mistakes was a long one, and he discovered that even in a simple drawing, Leonardo left dozens of "fingerprints." But the distinguishing marks were not necessarily bold strokes of the pen or flourishes of shaded lines, but his avoidance of elaboration. As he studied Leonardo's drawing his attention was on the direction of the lines. His text was Bernard Berenson's *The Drawings of the Florentine Painters:* "Leonardo's stroke was invariably from left to right, with the rare exception of shaded areas where he used a counterstroke." And so Stiehl used every test the brilliant art historian applied to his appraisal of drawings ascribed to Leonardo. Stiehl was confident of his technical skills, but as Berenson had decreed, it was the spirit and quality of the drawing that determined authenticity.

His own spirit had been crushed when Jonas returned from dinner and announced that the Leonardo must be returned to the library the following morning. Stiehl's anger was white-hot. He argued that a single night with the drawing was too little time, that he was no longer responsible for delivering a perfect copy.

They argued. Stiehl demanded to know why the drawing must be returned so quickly. "For six months I've prepared for the two days I would have Leonardo's drawing, now you give me twelve hours. What started as impractical is now impossible."

"Anything but," Jonas replied, then continued in an unctuous manner. "You have not disappointed me. Your skills are greater than I imagined. Obviously I must deal with an unexpected problem and we cannot take the risk that they may discover one of their Leonardos is missing."

"They chose this weekend to run an inventory on drawings of skulls?" Stiehl said sarcastically. "There's more to it."

"I'll decide what's a risk and what isn't," Jonas replied in a stern voice. "You'll have the drawing until nine tomorrow morning."

Stiehl knew to argue would be fruitless. He returned to the board and continued his microscopic examination of Leonardo's two dissected skulls. Because he must surrender the drawings in a matter of hours, he made certain his photographs accurately duplicated the original. Then he recreated the tiny folds and tears, and the minute stains or stray blobs of ink that had fallen from Leonardo's quill. All were painstaking efforts. And his efforts would be repeated exactly when he had the proper ink and pens and centuries-old paper. He continued through the night, pausing only for coffee. After four hours of intensive work he stopped for a tension-relieving shower.

At nine o'clock Jonas took the precious drawing and slipped it into the thin metal case. He leaned down to examine the progress Stiehl made during the night. The familiar "O" formed on his lips. "Excellent, Curtis. Excellent indeed."

Stiehl's anger gave way to an intense desire to prove he could recreate Leonardo's masterful style using his photographs and the twelve hours he had had with the genuine drawing. He ordered a breakfast but barely touched the food. Then he turned his attention to Leonardo's difficult handwriting and the task of copying nine lines of commentary. Jonas urged him to stop but he stubbornly pressed on.

By late Saturday night he could no longer focus sore eyes, and a throbbing headache intensified. Numbed by nearly twenty-four hours of continuous bending over the board, he struggled to bed, where he instantly fell into a deep sleep, as if shot through with a powerful drug.

Early Sunday morning the great bells from Westminster Abbey pealed out to join others from nearby churches. He dressed and walked along Pall Mall, then Marlborough Road to St. James Park. Beyond the park he could make out the Houses of Parliament and he began walking toward them, now suddenly aware that he had left the hotel grounds for the first time in several days. It was as if he were walking away from the penitentiary again, but now he was in a London park, the grass greener than any he could remember. He stopped to take in the broad vista. In another direction was Buckingham Palace at the west end of the park beyond the Victoria Memorial.

For a half hour he walked along the paths in the park until the thought of food turned his direction back to the hotel. He stopped for a copy of the *Sunday Times* on his way to the dining room. As he sliced away the last bit of meat from a chop, and before settling comfortably to sip fresh coffee, he felt the presence of Jonas Kalem behind him.

"Good morning, Curtis." The big man leaned his hands on Stiehl's shoulders. He meant it as a friendly gesture but Stiehl pulled away. Jonas waved a waiter to the table and ordered a mountain of food. Stiehl's edginess returned and he was in no mood for conversation or the sight of Jonas wolfing down a breakfast banquet.

"Have you recovered from your pique, Curtis? You mustn't let a minor change of plan be so upsetting."

"Minor? We move heaven and hell to equip a world-class art studio complete with a state-of-the-art photo lab so that after I've knocked myself out for six months preparing for the big bang, I'll have the original Leonardo for enough time to duplicate it in every detail. But we had, as you put it, a minor change of plan and I had twelve nighttime hours to perform my magic. I'm good for a little magic, but no miracles. It's all bullshit. Pure unadulterated bullshit."

Jonas did not reply, choosing to wait for Stiehl's steaming anger to dissipate. A bowl of fruit disappeared seconds after it was set in front of him.

Stiehl continued, "Tony brought us the drawing without a hitch and then, without reason, I must give it up. It makes no sense that one drawing in a collection of thousands had to go back into the obscurity of a vault that only a few scholars and Prince Charlie are allowed to visit. I'm sure they are at this very moment anxiously anticipating the chance to marvel over the beauty of those two goddamned skulls."

"While that might seem unlikely, it is possible. We must not take any risks."

"Come off it, Tony's not putting the drawing back to please the prince or a few itinerant art scholars. I don't know why he's returning it but I have a strong hunch it's not for a very good reason." Though Jonas had attacked the meal with his usual gusto, it was obvious to Stiehl that the big man's morning was not going smoothly.

"There have been unexpected developments and for now that will end all discussion about the drawing. We must learn to adjust to change. You had the Leonardo for twelve hours, and had that been the original plan, you would be totally satisfied."

"But that was not the original plan," Stiehl retorted. "Maybe I can adjust to a change of plans. But I want to know why the change." He was staring directly at the squinting eyes behind the thick glasses. "Tell me why that damned drawing had to go back. Tell me about the unexpected."

Jonas turned to face Stiehl squarely, and as he did the great size of the man seemed to magnify and grow ominous. "You will be told what I choose to tell you." There was anger in his voice. "You will make no demands."

Stiehl knew there was little reason to pursue the argument and remained silent as Jonas continued to eat a glutton's breakfast. When the last of the dishes had been removed and fresh coffee was brought to the table, Jonas began conversing in his familiar rich, deep voice. He spoke softly, mindful that they were not alone in the dining room.

"You have taken samples of the ink and the paper. That fact, more than any other, has been the most critical reason for having the original drawing in our possession."

"But without the original I can't make an accurate copy."

"There's no need for a copy. You've proved beyond question that given the time, you could pull it off. But now we can duplicate the inks and the paper. Your training is at an end and now you can begin the most important task of creating the missing Leonardos."

"Just like that!" Stiehl snapped his fingers.

"Yes, just like that. Perhaps you remember our conversation on the first day you visited my office. I touched only briefly on the lost Leonardos. It's a fascinating story."

Stiehl was in no mood for one of Jonas's art lectures, but he was a captive audience and was soon swept away by the charm and majesty of the twisted tale of Leonardo's thousands of manuscript pages, of their passing from hand to hand, of how some were mysteriously lost then rediscovered, of how others simply disappeared. Jonas told the story masterfully and Stiehl became an attentive listener.

"The trail began in 1519 when Leonardo died while in the service of Francis I. The French monarch had provided the aging artist with a comfortable villa and servants in Amboise on the Loire River. All of the manuscript pages were willed to Leonardo's legally adopted heir, Francesco Melzi. Melzi's son Orazio inherited the pages from his father, and it has been assumed that Orazio sold the manuscripts, gave them as gifts, bartered some, or accidentally destroyed others. Kings, dukes, lawyers, artists, and thieves all played a part in the unrecorded dispersal of the priceless pages. Had Orazio known of their potential value, it is possible there would be a different story to tell.

"If Orazio Melzi sold or gave everything away, then the missing pages could be anywhere. But perhaps not all of the manuscript pages passed out of Melzi's hands. I took the advice of no less than Leonardo himself, who wrote, 'Everything loses strength the more it separates itself from its origin.' Where is the origin of the Leonardo manuscripts? First it was in Amboise where he died. Where next?" Jonas paused and looked inquisitively at Stiehl.

Stiehl was surprised that he answered the question immediately. "With Melzi."

"Exactly. Not Orazio the son, but Francesco, who had become the devoted friend and assistant to Leonardo and who very likely sought to preserve the master's works."

For the moment Stiehl was content to put aside his angry frustration and allow Jonas to unravel his story.

"And after nearly five centuries, Giorgio Burri enters the scene. Giorgio, the retired professor of art history at the University of Milan, perfectly suited to research the Melzi family records. Giorgio, who has also been an outspoken critic of the Venetian experts and who has openly pooh-poohed their outdated theories of the lost manuscripts. His retirement from the university was nudged up because of his contentious statements. But to his credit he has equally strong support from the younger scholars. You must realize, Stiehl, how sanctimoniously art historians have acted over the years. They're a clubby lot and detest challenge. They react by digging in their heels deeper."

Stiehl made a mental note to remember that the old guard were clubby and stubborn. "When will I meet Giorgio?"

"Soon. It is vital that you and Giorgio work closely together but that time is not now." Jonas found a sweet roll and finished it off.

"When Giorgio lost the backing of the university, I offered mine. For a year he poked about the Melzi family homes near Vaprio d'Adda and Cascio. He learned how the old Melzi estate had been picked clean but he also discovered that the family owned a smaller estate near Bellagio. It was there that Giorgio discovered a wardrobe chest. Beneath the old clothes and hidden in a compartment at the bottom of the crate he found an amazing collection of Francesco Melzi's personal records and other notebooks.

"Most of the papers consist of personal correspondence, bank records, and property deeds. But the remaining papers are pure gold. Melzi had made an inventory of the volumes he inherited, an astounding collection of information by itself. Further, he had begun to copy Leonardo's manuscripts and either stopped in frustration because of the immensity of the project or, as is most likely, he died."

"He had started to make duplicates of Leonardo's work?"

Jonas laughed and patted Stiehl's arm. "No, he didn't possess your talent. Though remember, Melzi was an artist of fair ability, trained by none other than Leonardo.

"He copied three hundred and six pages, perhaps more, but Giorgio discovered that number. Two hundred and fifty pages are Melzi's copies of Leonardo's sheets that are now in various libraries—principally the Ambrosiana and the Institut de France in Paris."

Jonas leaned forward and whispered, "But hear this, my young friend. Fourteen folios contain what Giorgio is convinced are Melzi's copies of Leonardo's drawings and commentaries." Jonas was whispering, "Can you imagine the value if they were original Leonardos?"

"How valuable?" Stiehl whispered back.

"If they were authentic and each half folio had at least one large drawing to a side, each half folio would go at auction for not a penny under five million dollars. So much depends on the drawing—its size, whether or not it can be recognized as a preliminary study for one of his paintings.

"As there are fourteen folios, or twenty-eight sheets, the value reaches to as much as a hundred and forty million dollars." His lips curled to form the familiar "O," his pleasure duly recorded.

"Why haven't you told me this before?" Stiehl asked.

"You were fresh out of prison, remember? I had no idea how you would react to such numbers. More importantly, I wanted you to prove you were as good as I hoped. You've worked hard and your only motivation has been to prove you could draw a picture equal to the great Leonardo da Vinci." Jonas slipped the cellophane wrapping from a cigar. "Giorgio will be in London on Wednesday and will turn over his research on the Melzi papers."

"I'll see them? And meet Giorgio?"

"No." Jonas put a match to his cigar. "Giorgio is temperamental and I can't always judge his mood. You'll get on with him but there's no rush."

"But I need his help now," Stiehl protested. "I'm getting more comfortable with Leonardo's handwriting but I need help with the language. His notes contain a shorthand I can't decipher and none of the references are any help."

"That will all come in time. We've just taken the paper and ink samples and Eleanor needs them to continue her work. She's located paper near Florence but her tests for age and fiber content aren't complete. In a few days I'll know when we'll be able to move the Art Department to Italy and then you'll have Giorgio at your side more than you might wish."

"Then what's my next step?"

"Return to New York. I have you booked on Continental's evening flight tomorrow. I'm remaining in London for my meeting with Giorgio, then will fly to Italy to spend several days with Eleanor. Tony will deliver Giorgio's material to you on Friday."

"You had it all planned before we left New York, didn't you?"

The big man's mood shifted suddenly. "Not everything," he said solemnly. Then he sat silently for nearly a minute. "Until I compared your copy to the original I couldn't be absolutely certain you were the right man." He got to his feet and placed a hand on Stiehl's shoulder. "You are the right man, Curtis." He leaned down so their heads were almost touching and said, "You will preserve absolute secrecy at any cost. That's an ironclad condition that cannot be breached."

Stiehl looked up to see a determined, almost threatening face peering down at him. Without words the two exchanged an understanding that had not existed until that moment. Jonas patted Stiehl's cheek as a father might show affection for a son. Then he turned and walked from the room.

Stiehl did not move. His eyes were riveted to Jonas until he disappeared. He replayed the conversation in his mind, and when he recalled the number one hundred forty million dollars, he could not control the smile that brightened his face and made thoughts of giving up the drawing of the two skulls seem of no consequence.

He looked again at the *Sunday Times,* scanned the front page, and spotted a headline over a story that dealt with the death of a Scotland Yard policewoman who had been assigned to the Royal Library at Windsor. She had died in an automobile accident a few miles from the royal castle.

He tore the news article from the page, folded it, and put it in his pocket. He would ask Tony if he knew Detective Constable Sarah L. Evans.

As Jonas passed through the lobby he gathered up a copy of all the newspapers at the concierge's counter. He knew the press would give the policewoman's death front-page coverage, speculating on foul play or murder if they could create a plausible motive. He waited until he was in his room before reading the headlines. His face reddened and he began breathing in short, heavy gasps.

He threw the newspapers on the floor, then took the telephone and called Tony Waters.

# Chapter 9

$S$uperintendent Walter Deats turned into the express lane and sped toward London to keep his appointment with Elliot Heston, a deputy assistant commissioner in the Criminal Investigation Department of the Metropolitan Police. Heston commanded Branch C13, under which was the Arts and Antiques Squad. The two met while at the Metropolitan Police Training School at Peel Centre, Hendon. They attained Detective Sergeant status several years later and received permanent appointments to the CID. Heston's first assignment was to C11, Criminal Intelligence. Deats served on the Illegal Immigration Squad. Heston transferred into C13 and began a successful rise through the ranks. Deats transferred out of the Yard, joining the Windsor police. They maintained their friendship over the years and vacationed in Scotland every year, joined in their mutual enthusiasm for salmon fishing.

Deats reviewed the few facts that were known about Sarah Evans's death. For an instant the sight of her cruelly cut and bloodied face flashed in front of him. He winced and shook the image from his mind.

A compulsory investigation was immediately ordered after Sarah's identity had been confirmed. Deats had spent hours going over her correspondence and reports, but the effort did not produce information of even the most remote relevance to the accident. He phoned a Dr. Goldring, whose name was on one of many slips of paper, discovering he was a pediatrician caring for Sarah's daughter. Another number was to a bank branch on Albert Bridge Road where Sarah had applied for a small loan.

And there were two slips of paper containing notations in a gibberish resembling shorthand. But no secretary in the Windsor Police Department could make out the scribbling. Deats had faxed copies to Elliot Heston with a request that the notes be deciphered. He realized that while the accident occurred in the jurisdiction of the Windsor police, Scotland Yard would press its own investigation and issues of jurisdiction would be swept aside. Yet he hoped that his meeting with Heston might minimize the interference and confusion two groups of investigators inevitably created. Besides, Deats preferred working alone, a principal reason for transferring to a smaller force.

The memory of the pretty dead face was further motivation to pursue the case.

As he drove he recorded his thoughts:

*"Monday, September 12, 10:45 A. M. . . . En route Windsor to Yard for Heston meeting . . . Interviewed library staff from 9:00 to 10:30 . . . Drew blanks . . . Evans popular and diligent worker . . . No one seemed to have socialized with her . . . or knew much about her . . . didn't know her personal ways . . . Only royal librarian knew she had been posted to keep an eye on things . . . and he's still miffed it took so long to put someone on duty."*

He switched off the recorder and searched his memory for the occasions when he had been involved in the death of a fellow police officer. He thought of a young detective constable who had been under his command and who attempted to defuse a pipe bomb discovered in the rail station at Slough, a transfer point for tourists traveling from London to Windsor. A needless tragedy. But then he thought that all such misadventures were unnecessary. He remembered Paul Durgin. The promising Durgin had trailed two brothers suspected of armed robbery to their mobile home, where apparently he intended to make a routine arrest. Instead he was shot in the throat and left to bleed to death.

There were others and it was fixed in Walter Deats's mind that police officers don't die from natural causes, that not one instance of death had been purely accidental. He applied that logic to the death of Sarah Evans, and unless an intensive investigation proved that indeed it had been an accident, he would assume she had been murdered.

Whether or not it had been an accident, Deats had four pieces of information to work on: it had rained steadily for several hours, the window on the driver's side was open nearly seven inches, her foot was lodged against the accelerator pedal, there were no skid marks. Each fact might bear directly upon what actually happened, but even the accuracy of some were open to challenge. For example, the extent to which the window was open was determined by the shards of glass remaining in the door, then by estimating the position of the window crank. Deats wondered why in all the rain it would have been open at all.

He repeated these thoughts into his recorder. When he replayed the tape and listened to his own voice intone the fragile clues, he blurted out: "That's bully, Sherlock, and so much crap in the bargain. What does your brilliant mind say to the question of motive? Think about that now. She was assigned to the library to protect the Queen's Collection and no one's walked off with a paper clip."

Yet he could not shrug off the fact that the accident had been so violent. A report from the garage people indicated the brakes had been in working condition, yet the car had obviously shot straight through the curve. Had she blacked out? Fallen asleep? Had she been medicating? Perhaps the autopsy would shed light on those questions.

Then the rain. There had been a long dry spell before the rains fell Friday afternoon. That usually set up a slippery road condition as the water tended to sit atop the fine buildup of oil on the tarred Datchet road. It's part of police training to respect road and weather conditions. Had she been careless and the car simply hydroplaned on the slick skin of water and her foot gone from accelerator to brake, then back, as would be the case with a frightened and inexperienced driver? And thus no skid marks?

Not much to go on, he thought. Besides, the poor girl is dead, and I'm not sure I want to learn that she was murdered. He was now in Victoria Street, a short distance from Scotland Yard.

London's Metropolitan Police initially occupied space at 4 Whitehall Place when the Bow Street Horse Patrol, the Marine Police, and four other law enforcement agencies were consolidated in the police headquarters building in 1829.

Elliot Heston greeted his friend with a firm handshake. He was tall and angular, his hair fell uncombed over a high forehead. and his eyes brightened at greeting his old comrade and fishing partner. He wore a yellow sweater, his tie pulled away from an unbuttoned collar. His gold-rimmed glasses perched on a long thin nose

"Well, Wally, we finally get to work on something together. Too bad it's a sorry mess."

"My sentiments, too." They bantered briefly, enjoying the sort of exchange two old friends might have. Then Deats went to the crux. "What's your book on Sarah? We have no background on her or her family."

"Here's her file. Pretty straightforward. Her husband was second officer on a merchant ship. Poor chap had a burst appendix, developed uremic poisoning, and died at sea. Sarah joined the force before her marriage and had a daughter. She lived with her widowed mother. She was a terribly hard worker. We tabbed her for undercover work and this was her first assignment. Her supervisor felt it would be good training. Low exposure and, God knows, no danger."

Deats fanned through the brief file. "What was her assignment?"

"You know what kind of treasures you've got up there in the library, and you certainly know that security at the Castle is imperfect. The royal librarian didn't want to take chances with all the tearing up and new people prowling around, so he sent a personal request up to the commissioner asking for a surveillance officer from my squad. There wasn't any good reason he shouldn't ask you chaps at Windsor but I guess Sir Mackworth-Young would rather do business with Sir Albert Waye."

Deats nodded. "I'm afraid I knew that. I was hoping for more." It was a perfect opening to ask Heston why he had not told him previously about assigning Sarah to the library. But he pressed on. "Did she file any reports? Anything to indicate she might be onto something?"

"There were a few reports, but all the routine sort of thing. She indicates that she was compiling a dossier on each employee and, well— here, let me read from a report filed two weeks ago." Heston fingered through the folder and extracted a page. *"I am assembling a personal file on each member of the library staff, all that is except Sir Mackworth-Young, whom I assume we can safely exclude. I have also contacted the personnel people at Heldwicke Air-Control Systems for a report on all members of the construction crew assigned to the library. Most of these files are in hand, with several yet to complete. I shall include these papers in a future report, possibly the first or second week in September.'"* Heston looked up. "None of the dossiers has been filed."

Deats stuffed tobacco into his pipe and lit it. "Interesting. Interesting indeed." He smiled. "Damn it all, it *is* interesting and just could be something. If you don't have any of those dossiers and none were found in her briefcase, where the hell are they?"

Heston rubbed the point of his nose. "She hasn't used her desk here at the Yard. I plan to send a deputy to her home to relay official condolences. We'll get all of her paperwork at that time."

"Two of my men visited the mother on Saturday. I don't think she needs further commiseration. Was Sarah under orders to prepare the dossiers?"

"It was part of her training. Her first responsibility was surveillance."

The phone rang and Heston answered. He handed the phone to Deats. "I think it's your autopsy report."

Deats took the phone and spoke with his assistant. He gave Heston a summary: "Fractured skull and her chest was badly crushed. Never a chance. The only good news is she didn't suffer. It's what you'd expect, except for one wrinkle. She had a point-oh-three blood alcohol count. No obvious evidence of drug use, but those tests aren't complete. Apparently she stopped for a drink before driving home."

"With a friend, do you suppose?"

"I haven't learned anything about her personal life. She was a friendly sort, I'm told, but didn't mix with the others. I'm sure she had friends. She was much too pretty."

"There was alcohol. That's something."

"A low count. Sounds like a single whiskey or a glass of wine. I'm not interested in how much she drank but who she drank it with."

Heston moved to the window where his view was down Claxton Street toward Westminster Chapel. "What do you want me to do about the investigation?"

"Let me handle this on my own. I promise to yell if I get onto something and need help. God knows you have facilities we only dream about. I'll send reports directly to you, and if I get any strange hunches, I hope you'll let me talk to you about them."

"I know you would, Wally, but I can't avoid department policy. I have to put someone on the case."

Deats relit his pipe, then fixed his eyes on his friend. "Put yourself on it."

"The accident occurred in your jurisdiction, but the victim was one of ours. You have a duty to investigate and I'll see that you get our full cooperation." Heston returned to his desk. "I've got the perfect man for the assignment, except for one thing."

"What's that?"

"You hate his guts."

"I'm a tolerant man, Elliot, but around here that can only be Jack Oxby. I thought you were transferring him out of C13."

"No one will have him." Heston laughed. "No, that's not true. I didn't want to lose him. In spite of all his character defects, the little son of a bitch gets the job done."

"Character defects? You make him sound like the bad boy in a church choir. The bastard's deceitful, immoral, a liar, and you know that someday he'll go a step too far and you'll be the one to suffer. He'll survive. That kind always does."

Heston's eyes were closed and his head was nodding ever so slightly. "I've thought of that. Oxby also knows more about art and art thieves than all of Scotland Yard and Interpol combined."

"Are you saying there's no one else? It's Oxby or nothing?" Deats tapped his pipe on a heavy glass ashtray with a series of loud bangs. "Put yourself on it. It'll be like old times with you and me."

"I can't do that, Wally. For all practical purposes I am on the case and you'll report directly to me."

Slowly a smile began to cross Walter Deats's face. "If I were in your position, I'd probably put Oxby on the case, too. In some perverse way I admire him."

"You too, Wally? I didn't think a conservative old fart like you could find any redeeming qualities in Oxby. Besides, I might find it difficult to dislodge Jack at this time. He's genuinely interested in the art owned by the Crown, so he has a personal attachment to the whole matter. He's worked up a backgrounder on Sarah Evans which I'll send you."

Deats acknowledged that that would be helpful. "Better yet, I'd like to meet with Oxby while I'm here."

"That's not Jack's style." Heston pointed at the city beyond his window. "He's out there someplace, gumshoeing in his own strange way, as the Americans might say."

"He still assigns himself to the cases he likes and works up his own agenda. And you let him."

Heston nodded. "Yes, and for a quite simple reason. Those are the ones he always solves."

In the apartment-building lobby Deats took a deep breath then pushed the button next to Sarah Evans's name. A male voice sounded on the intercom, and after Deats announced he was from the Windsor police, a buzzer sounded. He walked the flight of stairs and was met at the top by a short, heavyset man.

"Officer, I'm pleased to meet you. I'm Teddy O'Mara, brother to Sarah's mother, who's tendin' to matters at the funeral home." His face was pink and sad and his heavy Dublin-accented voice was pitched high and nearly squeaked as he spoke.

Deats extended his hand. "I'm terribly sorry we're meeting under these circumstances. Please accept my condolences. I'm hopeful you might let me look around the room where Sarah worked on her police matters. I'm looking in particular for some reports."

"You come right in, lad. She was a hardworking girl and would want you to have whatever belongs to the department." O'Mara led Deats to Sarah's bedroom.

He surveyed the room then quite methodically began a search of the closet and bureau. The papers he came across were of a personal nature. Then he sat at the desk and sorted through a dozen or so files that lay next to a framed photograph of Sarah and her husband. He pulled at the single drawer and found it was locked. He tried to force it open. He stopped pulling at the drawer and stared at the keyhole. "Keys!" he said aloud. "We didn't find any keys."

O'Mara had been standing in the doorway. "You're sayin' no keys was found at Sarah's accident? She carried a pound of keys, she did. I joked she looked like a night watchman with all them keys."

"I could be wrong, Mr. O'Mara. I don't recall seeing them."

Cynthia was now standing in the doorway, the spaniel sitting beside her.

"Is it the key to her desk you're lookin' for, Superintendent?" O'Mara asked.

"Yes, do you know where one might be?"

"No, I wouldn't be knowin' where Sarah kept it. Here now, that's Cynthia over there. Maybe she knows."

Deats sat at Sarah's desk. He spoke quietly to the little girl. "Cynthia, my name is Superintendent Deats. I'm very sorry about your mommy."

Cynthia didn't stir, nor did she cry. Her tears had been exhausted when she came to the realization her mother would never return. Now she was in the numbing twilight that shock brings on.

"Cynthia, did your mommy carry a lot of keys in her pocketbook?" When the child did not respond, he tried again, a warm smile across his face. "Did mommy have keys like this?" He showed her his own set of keys.

She looked at his hand and nodded.

"Mommy carried lots and lots of keys?"

Again Cynthia nodded. Deats pointed to the desk drawer. "Do you know where to find the key to this lock?"

She stepped closer and shook her head negatively. "My mom has the keys and she won't be home anymore." Her voice was a whisper but she spoke clearly and looked directly into Deats's eyes when finally she broke her silence.

Deats tugged at the drawer, then concluded he would have to force it open or wait for help. "May I use the telephone, Mr. O'Mara?"

"Certainly, Superintendent. It's in the other room next to the television."

Deats reached his office and confirmed that no keys had been found. He ordered another search of the car and grounds surrounding the accident site. "Check the desk she used at the library again. Notify security at the Castle that we're looking for them and advise all foot and patrol constables to be on the alert."

As Deats returned to Sarah's room the dog suddenly began barking. Cynthia picked him up and stroked his long ears.

"You must forgive the little animal," Mr. O'Mara said. "He'll be skittish with strangers since he got tossed about last Saturday."

"Oh? What was that about?" Deats asked almost absently.

"Some gent was here lookin' to install a computer here in Sarah's room. Clover got scared and snapped at his hand and got throwed against the door."

"Who was the man? Did he give identification? A card?"

"Can't say that I know. I can't say that anybody here knows. My sister said she thinks his name was, oh dear, what was that name...Mr...."

"Black." Cynthia spoke up.

"Black. That's right, Cynthia. Good for you."

"He hurt Clover. See?" Cynthia held out the dog's paw to Deats. She had wrapped a piece of gauze over a small wound. "Clover bit his hand," she said triumphantly.

"What did he look like, Cynthia?"

"I dunno," she replied, shaking her shoulders. "He had whiskers all over and a funny hat."

Deats realized he couldn't rely on Cynthia's description of Black but perhaps the grandmother could furnish more details. "Mr. O'Mara, here's my card. When your sister returns, and if she's up to it, ask her to phone a description of this Black fellow. Ask if she remembers anything else about him—the way he was dressed, the name of his company— that sort of thing."

"I will, Superintendent, but don't be expectin' a fast call. Wendy's pretty upset right now. I should be with her but, well, Cynthia here."

"I quite understand. There's one last favor I'm going to ask. It's important for me to see inside the desk, and if you have a long, flat knife in the kitchen, I might be able to open it."

O'Mara inspected the desk drawer and took a penknife from his pocket. He deftly slid the blade between the drawer and wood strip above it, jiggled it a couple of times, and the drawer opened. "I was a cabinet maker a ways back, learned a few tricks that come in handy now and then."

"That's an excellent trick, Mr. O'Mara. Thank you."

Deats sifted through the folders and papers and letters still in their envelopes. After sorting through all the papers he concentrated on the folder marked "Library Dossiers." Sarah had designed a two-page form, much like one might complete when applying for a position. On the form she was able to record a brief biographical sketch of each employee, and had somehow managed to secure a fingerprint on an index card or piece of stationery that was stapled to the report. A few prints were clean, others smudged. All part of her training, Deats concluded. He counted eleven completed forms, all library employees. Beneath the completed record were additional blank forms. He thumbed through the sheets and discovered that the bottom page contained a mass of scribbles and red lines.

It was a single sheet of lined notebook paper and on it were two columns of names. One was headed "Library Staff" and the other "Heldwicke Workers." Sarah had recorded tiny notations and dates in pencil and ink on what was apparently a summary or worksheet. Deats glanced again at the completed forms, noting that all the names matched those under the "Library Staff" heading.

A red line was drawn through each name except for one in the Heldwicke column. Next to Gregory L. Hewlitt's name was a penciled comment that Deats had difficulty reading. After several attempts he made it out: "Awaiting report from C4 and fingerprint confirmation."

# Chapter 10

At precisely 9:00 A.M. Monday morning, Jonas entered 6 Grosvenor Street and took the elevator to the top floor and the London offices of Jonas R. Kalem & Company, Ltd.

His mood was dark, and he immediately went to a corner office reserved for his occasional visits. The room was spartan compared to the sprawling opulence in New York. He grunted a "good morning" to Claire Haydon, the very competent general director of the London operation. Claire was of substantial British stock—good breeding, fine education, considered a first-rate manager, and destined never to arouse the sexual appetite in the men with whom she associated. Claire was effective. She had tapped into the phenomenal growth of London-based advertising agencies with their appetite for expansion throughout Europe and the States. Accounts in the London office had reached a new high in the year ended, and Jonas knew the reason why. But this morning he chose to be alone and instructed Claire to take all messages and turn visitors away.

He threw the morning *Times* on his desk and stared at the paper folded to reveal the short article that had soured his humor. The headline leaped off the page: INVESTIGATION INTO POLICEWOMAN'S DEATH CONTINUES. He crashed his fist onto the newspaper. "Goddamned stupid luck!"

He stared out the window. Below was Mayfair. A few blocks distant was Regent Street, where tourists and tarrying office workers brought the street of shops alive at this morning hour. His glance fell to two photographs on top of the credenza, obligatory decorations that somehow lent respectability to a shattered personal life. One recent photo was of his son David and daughter Ceil, both caught with a hint of happiness on otherwise dull, expressionless faces. The other picture was of Jonas with his estranged wife Margaret, who had been captured in one of those self-conscious poses that magnified her plain looks. He felt as he often did that he was totally removed from these people who were his family. Why did he regard them simply as people he knew, not as his flesh, not attached to him in any way? Why not even a trace of the sweet love he once felt for the children? He knew it was because they could not meet the standards he set for himself. He had set the hurdles too high for his family to leap over and so they remained on the other side.

The world would look differently on Jonas Kalem once it was announced that he had discovered the missing Leonardo manuscripts.

But his careful plans were threatened by Tony's impulsive solution to the meddling policewoman. Tony, the enforcer and valuable asset, had turned himself into a dangerous liability. He took the phone and dialed the library at Windsor Castle. Fearing a tap may have been put on the lines into the library, he spoke in what best could be described as South London Yiddish. He asked for Mr. Hewlitt.

"Mr. Hewlitt, this is Mr. Braymore. You inquired about some mercury switches last week. I think we can help you."

Tony's response came slowly. Jonas had not forewarned him he might use the Braymore name as a cover.

"Ah . . . yes, Mr. Braymore. That's good news."

"You didn't give me all the information and said you'd call. You've got my phone number; perhaps if you still need them, you'll ring back with the specifications."

"Indeed. I'll check on the matter."

Jonas was satisfied that Tony had gotten his message and would find a public phone. Fifteen minutes later Jonas answered a ring on his private line.

"Yes?"

"Did you figure they spiked the lines so quickly?"

"No more risks, no matter how slight. I've decided you should retire from the air-conditioning business. Immediately. Do as we discussed. Take leave to visit your family."

"The police were waiting for us this morning. One from Windsor, another said he was from Scotland Yard. We all had to fill out a damned bloody form asking for personal information. Where we live and the cars we drive. That sort of thing."

"I told you to clean house, now be damned sure you do. Be careful how you leave matters at the library. Make it appear you'll be returning."

"My flat's clean. All that's left are some clothes and a toilet kit."

"Listen closely." Jonas breathed heavily into the phone. "Shave off the beard, buy a new suit, then meet me at the Tate Gallery cafeteria at 2:30. No hitches and don't leave any trails."

He put the phone down and stared at the instrument. The intercom light flashed and a buzzer sounded.

"I'm sorry to disturb you, Mr. Kalem, but there's someone on the line who insists on talking with you. He's called before and claims it is extremely important." Clair Haydon's voice was low-pitched and had a certain Margaret Thatcher-like authority.

"Who is it?" Jonas asked.

"He won't identify himself. I told him you were busy, that you would call him back. He has an Oriental accent, if that helps."

"I'll take it, Claire." Jonas waited a full minute before answering. When he spoke, he was all business.

"This is Jonas Kalem. What may I do for you?"

"Thank you for coming to the phone, Mr. Kalem. I know you are very busy." The voice was strange sounding, as if it were in falsetto, and the accent decidedly Oriental. "I will be brief. For reasons of great confidence I cannot reveal my identity at this time. I represent someone who shares your interest in art—particularly the work of the great masters. Leonardo da Vinci specifically."

"There are many thousands who are similarly inclined," Jonas intoned.

"But none who have the intense interest you have shown in recent months."

"We have nothing in our inventory. For that matter there are no Leonardos available. Not even a sketch."

"But in your speeches you have been saying that there will be new discoveries."

"That's true," Jonas replied. "We have every hope that will happen."

"As do we. And for that reason I should like to talk with you in person. Perhaps Thursday evening?"

"I don't know what we can discuss."

"Large sums of money and the continued safety of your associates. Those seem worthy topics for discussion."

This was preposterous talk, yet Jonas maintained his composure. "Large sums of money in the art world are commonplace. As for my associates, I believe none are in any peril."

"I disagree, Mr. Kalem. Valuable works of art and millions of dollars are often a formula for danger."

"You must identify yourself. I will not agree to a meeting until I know who you are and who you represent."

"You seem to forget, Mr. Kalem, that you have appeared in public to make predictions concerning new Leonardo discoveries. We interpret these presentations as an invitation for serious collectors to contact you. Often the collectors must be anonymous."

"I understand. But I am not now prepared to hold discussions. If you will give me your name, I shall contact you when the time is right."

"Your speech to the DaVinci Association in Paris was most compelling. I wish to hear in person the progress you and your associates have been making."

The presentations Jonas had given had attracted more than a hundred responses, but this was the first invitation to meet. The reference to his associates was particularly disquieting. Did they know about Curtis and Eleanor?

"It's out of the question that I meet with you until I know who you represent and who will be present."

"You must not make so much of identification. It will be very much in your interest to follow the instructions I will give you. Please make note of them."

Jonas cupped the phone to his ear and jotted down the procedure he was to follow on Thursday evening.

"When we meet, you must be alone. Do not come accompanied." There was a click and the phone went dead.

The Tate Gallery on Millbank along the Thames is Britain's home to its own great artists. The permanent collection includes Turner, Blake, Constable, Reynolds, Gainsborough, and the works of more recent painters not yet listed among the famous. Jonas reached the gallery at two o'clock and mingled with the crowd viewing a special exhibition of Whistler who, while American, had been adopted by the British.

A few minutes past 2:30, Jonas descended to the lower-level cafeteria. A clean-shaven Tony was seated at a corner table. Jonas moved slowly through the line then carried his tray to Tony's table. They met as strangers, talking idly about the Whistler exhibition and other gallery offerings. Satisfied that they blended into the noise and crowd, Jonas became all business.

"Is your flat cleaned out?"

"Like a bloody whistle. Tidied up my work at the library, then contacted the field manager. Told him I had a family emergency and that
I'd be away for several days. The work's nearly done, only a carpenter
and the painters will be there until the end of the week."

"Excellent. There's a good chance you won't be missed for a week,
about as long as it will take them to discover that Gregory Hewlitt is a
fiction." Jonas studied the face across from him. It was lightly flushed
where the beard had protected his skin and contrasted with the ruddi-
ness of his forehead and upper cheeks. Jonas detected a lift to Tony's
eyes and a mouth set as if to speak some piece of brash arrogance.

"This insane thing you've done is all over the papers. We have no
choice but to adjust our plans and move ahead. I want you to assume a
new identity. Shorten your hair, wear glasses, you know the tricks. Remember that Greg Hewlitt was tweeds and a beard, and I want you in
serge with a close-trimmed look. Buy a new wardrobe. Conservative, dark
colors. You'll stay at the Connaught. Giorgio arrives Wednesday afternoon. We'll study the material he will bring with him, then on Friday you
will take it and my instructions to Curtis in New York. I'm flying to
Milan on Sunday, then on to Florence, where I'll meet with Eleanor
Shepard for several days. I'm going to give you an envelope. It contains
five thousand pounds, enough to cover expenses. Any questions?"

"I'll need new papers. Passport, visa, personal cards, that sort of thing."

"Of course you will." Jonas spoke impatiently. "You have your old
sources for those items."

"They're expensive."

"I would expect so. How much?"

"A few years ago a passport was over three hundred pounds. It is a
great deal more today."

Jonas slid several large-denomination notes into the envelope. "That
should cover it. Can you trust the people you're dealing with?"

"They're in a high-risk business," Tony answered. "They don't keep
records and they don't stay put for very long."

Jonas placed the envelope on his tray. "Remember that you can never
be Tony Waters again. If they haven't made the connection, they will
soon. Have you picked a new name?"

Tony rubbed his cheek where it still itched. "Yes. Before the day is
over I'll be Keith Habershon."

Jonas repeated the name several times. "That seems all right. Just handle everything carefully and don't leave a new trail for your new friend at the Windsor police. One last thing. What have you done with your car?"

"It's in the public garage at Victoria Station. Cars are parked there for weeks."

"Clean it out. Now be on your way. I'll see you at the bar in the Connaught at eight on Wednesday."

Tony swept the envelope off the tray and slipped it into his pocket as he rose from the table. Jonas watched him disappear into the crowd.

Tony set off for Victoria Station at a half walk, half trot. He was about to lose all traces of his connection with Gregory Hewlitt, and his attention was fixed on creating a new personality and total change of appearance. At Belgrave Road he hailed a taxi. As he rode, he thought of the new character he was about to become. Experience taught him that when he assumed a new role, the fewer lies he must live, the more truthful his masquerade. But those thoughts did not block out the excitement he felt as he began piecing together all the parts that combined to make a new person. He knew what he would do to his hair and face. Now he thought of the clothes. The change would be quite different this time, he concluded.

At the Victoria Station long-term parking area he walked past cars with many days of accumulated dust. He gave the old Morris a thorough search. Next he took the underground to Oxford Circle, transferred to the Central Line, and rode on to Chancery Lane. When he exited, he was at the northern edge of what once had been London's newspaper district—two blocks east the *Daily Mirror,* nearby the *Evening Standard,* and to the south within short walking distance had been the *Times* and *Evening News.* This concentration of newspaper publishers had spawned numerous ancillary services, including typesetters, electroplaters, commercial photographers, and small printing companies. Near the *Daily Mirror's* old offices, north of Fleet Street, he paused in front of a small shop with the name FLEET TYPESETTING, LTD. painted on a sign that hung aslant on two nails over the door.

In the tiny office he waited for a man known to him as Morris. He didn't know if it was his first or last name, and had never asked. Chances were it was neither.

"This card. You printed it for me when you were on Salisbury Court."

"This here shop's never been on Salisbury. Good you remember that."

"My mistake," Tony replied. "I need more cards." He handed Morris a business card on which was printed the name "Frank Pearson." He had used the name frequently and in fact was using it when he first met Jonas Kalem.

Morris examined the card. "Yes, how many?"

"Fifty. Exactly fifty. But a different name."

"Costs as much for two hundred as fifty," Morris said laconically.

"Fifty is all I need. I doubt I'll use that many."

"Anything else?"

"Yes. One of these."

Morris took the passport and flipped through the pages. As he did, a hand dropped beneath the counter and pressed a button. His expression changed when he found a single identifying clue that proved the passport was his handiwork. A door opened behind Morris and two burly toughs came in. One went to the street and after several minutes returned, gave a hand signal, and disappeared through the door he had entered earlier.

"A necessary precaution, Mr. Pearson."

"Habershon. Keith Habershon. Here's the other information you'll need." Tony handed Morris a sheet of paper. "I'm leaving for New York on Friday."

"Where is your photograph?"

"I'll have it tomorrow. Before noon."

"You'll leave a deposit of a thousand pounds. Another thousand when you pick it up."

"That's a bloody fortune. I paid three-fifty for that old one."

"That's the old price, all right. Inflation hits us all, Mr. Habershon. My competitors charge twenty-five hundred, but I see we have done business before. The balance must be in Swiss francs. Small-denomination notes."

"That may be awkward."

"Perhaps, but not difficult. Most times I require full payment in Swiss francs. Shall we proceed?"

Tony placed a thousand pounds on the counter. "I expect everything to be ready on Thursday."

"It will be if your photograph is here by noon tomorrow. I'll ask you to leave now."

Tony's next stop was at Bermans and Nathans Costumers in the theater district in Soho. He went directly to the makeup department, where he bought a band of hair, a tube of spirit gum, and scissors. Next stop was a barbershop, where he had his hair cut in a conservative style with short sideburns. He then went to the Regent Palace Hotel, where, in a small dressing room in the men's lounge, he fashioned a thin mustache, glued it in place, and neatly trimmed it.

Off Piccadilly Circus he located a sleazy shop advertising triple-X-rated videocassettes, magazines, and passport photographs. He was photographed by an overly lipsticked girl who was surprised he actually wanted a passport photo. "Are you sure you don't want to take Polaroids of me? I'll do some tricks you ain't seen, mister." Her accent was thick and straight from Galway County. "Forty pounds plus film for ten minutes. For sixty you can have me for a half hour in a private room. Just me and you."

He thanked her agreeably and added a generous tip to the bill. "Later, perhaps. Yes, later." He meant it. The tawdry girl excited him. He hadn't slept with a woman for too long, and now suddenly he wanted this one. He lingered momentarily, then turned to the door and was soon absorbed by the commuters.

Bright neon lights contrasted with the heavy gray sky. Long lines waited for buses and homeward-bound office workers clogged the entrances to the underground. Too late to buy a wardrobe, he thought, and so he fell into line and inched his way down to the platform where a train would take him to Bayswater and a short walk to Cordova House, a small tourists' hotel.

He bought an evening tabloid. On the train he unfolded the paper and saw on the third page that Sarah Evans's death was being sensationalized. A headline screamed: WAS POLICEWOMAN RAPED?

He ate at a neighborhood pub where he sat at the counter. He kept to himself and, after the meal, drank another pint of dark ale. All the while he was observing two men who were having an animated conversation. The younger man was Tony's age and had an affected, nearly effeminate manner. He studied the way the young man waved his hands and how occasionally he would turn up his chin and shake his head vigorously. Tony was preparing for the role he would begin playing the next day.

The next day was Tuesday, the day he would find a new suit to match the personality of Keith Habershon. Tony resisted the temptation to shop on Saville Row, but chose Harrods, where he would be unnoticed among the horde of shoppers. He also knew that the difference between a Henry Poole label and one from Harrods was several hundred pounds. The morning was nearly spent when he emerged from the giant store, hailed a taxi, and ordered the driver to the intersection of Fleet Street and Fetter Lane. He wore a dark blue suit and paisley tie and carried a small portmanteau filled with his other purchases. His scarred hand was covered with a black leather glove. In that hand he held his other glove and practiced the movements of a fine dandy. He slapped the glove against his thigh with a sharp thwack. He tilted his head slightly, then touched the peak of his new suede cap. All the while he rehearsed a new accent, conversing with the driver about the endless stream of tourists flowing in from Japan and more recently from Southeast Asia.

He walked the short distance to the Fleet Typesetting shop. He waited several minutes in the cramped office, certain that he was being observed from behind a wall blotched with peeling paint. Then Morris appeared.

"You cut a handsome figure, Mr. Habershon. A successful business-man, are you now?"

Tony answered dryly, "None of your bloody business. My calling cards. Have you printed them?"

"All fifty of 'em right here." Tony accepted the small package and slipped them into a pocket. He placed the new photograph on the counter.

"We'll have the rest of your order completed tomorrow. Two o'clock should do. And I was thinkin' that if you'll be travelin' abroad, you might need a driver's license. That's a simple matter and I can have one along with the passport."

"How much?"

"Eight hundred Swiss francs to our good customers."

"Do it. I'll be here at two."

A walk from Fleet Street to Mayfair and the Connaught Hotel is two and a quarter miles. It is nearly a straight line with a jog at Trafalgar Square, then up Haymarket to Piccadilly, on to Berkeley, then Mount, and finally Carlos Place. Tony elected to take that walk, to practice his new role, and to buy a traditional black umbrella along the way.

And he wanted to think. He knew that Greg Hewlitt would be dis-covered as a nonperson. Very quickly, perhaps even at that moment, the search for Anthony Waters was under way. If he were found, he would be linked to Sarah Evans's fatal accident. But he had left no clues, and besides, why would he want to kill an assistant librarian?

Now his thoughts centered on the full impact of being the object of a countrywide search, that his life would forever be played out in a masquerade, that for all time he would be a hunted man.

At that instant a black police car sped by, its blue light flashing, the distinctive hooting horn blaring. He ducked into a doorway, stunned by an alien fear that swept through him.

The sound of the bleating siren faded and he continued his walk. He breathed deeply and felt a sudden exhilaration course through every part of his body, and he smiled. Every sense was sharpened. He was obsessed by a single thought that he, the hunted, was prepared to play what would soon become an even more deadly game.

# Chapter 11

The maroon Lancia sped through the curving narrow road and without slowing turned ninety degrees onto a graveled driveway, moved ahead two hundred yards, and skidded to an abrupt halt. Eleanor Shepard jumped from the car and ran across a pink-stoned patio toward what looked like a three-story stone house sliced in half. A phone was ringing.

"I'm coming...I'm coming!" She leaned against the thick door, pushed it open, and continued her dash to the phone.

"Steve, I'm here. You're too damned punctual!" she blurted out.

"You're panting," Steve Goldensen chided.

"I'm out of breath...there's a difference."

"You mean if I were there, you'd be panting?"

"I mean if you had to fight the Florence traffic and a zillion tourists, you'd be out of breath. Tell me your news."

"I'm coming over. A problem came up in Paris and I drew the assignment. But I can tack on a long weekend in Florence. How's that for news?"

*"Mille bene!"*

"Say again?"

"That's super news! When?"

"End of next week. I have to meet with the client for a couple of hours. That means I'll fly out of New York, damn it."

"Don't say damn it. That's good. You can pick up some books from the library in Jonas Kalem's office. I can't buy them over here and they're important."

"Okay, but there's a limit. I'm traveling light."

"I'm excited! You know it's been six months? Half of the year I asked for."

"I damned well know. I keep a special calendar."

They talked for many more minutes. Their weekly conversations had become ritual; Steve placed his call every Tuesday at 5:00 A.M. Washington time. While it played havoc with her schedule, Ellie managed to scramble back to her villa to receive them.

"We've talked enough," Ellie said. "Save your money because everything costs a fortune over here." She smiled at the phone as she put it down. She was dressed in white: slacks, shirt, espadrilles, and a bandanna tied over her red-brown hair. She retrieved several packages from the car, then climbed the curving stairs to the top of her half-house... her *mezzo casa,* she called it.

The formulas for the inks were nearly completed and over thirty flasks and bottles lined a table set against a white-plastered wall. She sat on a high stool and set her day's work in front of her. From her perch she was able to gaze out the window to the hills of Florence. The sun probed the haze and brightened the sea of red-tiled roofs.

Memories of the past six months pushed aside all thoughts of proving out a recipe for an ink the Renaissance artists might have used. Half a year had flown by, and now it seemed like a terribly long time. Her hand reached out to touch a thick notebook that had become her diary.

*March 9*

*I never want to forget the thrill of flying over France, then Italy when the air was pure and the early sun's beams seemed to dance off a million little spots of water and made everything below look like I was above a fairyland. But Malpenza airport was more like a zoo with armed guards. I slept, but not well, and was dead tired when we landed. It took forever to get through customs, find my car, and get out to the highway.*

*The main roads are incredible, and everyone passed me as if I were poking through an Alexandria school zone. By the time I reached Florence (I'll learn to say Firenze) I was going a hundred and forty but that's in kilometers. Try that on the Baltimore–Washington Pike!*

*I know I'll love Florence if I don't have to drive around it. The motorbikes come at you from all directions and sound like three-hundred-pound wasps. Cecilia Grosso from the real-estate office was delightful and I hope we'll be friends. She showed me some shortcuts from the city to my precious villa, and on the way pointed out I Tatti. I'm happy I knew about it and I plan to spend as much time there as I can. I fantasized that Bernard Berenson was still alive and had invited me to be his guest and browse among the eighty thousand books in his library.*

*My villa is on a hill behind a home occupied by the Gambarellis. I met Jean Gambarelli, who is English. She's tall and thin with white hair pulled back in a black ribbon. She must be sixty, but acts younger. She's terribly friendly and had stocked the kitchen so I wouldn't have to run out for food the first few days. Jean promised to help get a phone installed.*

*I'm falling asleep as I write. More about my new home later.*

*April 14*

*Today it rained. The first rain in nearly two weeks.*

*I thought I had fixed up everything the way I wanted it but spent the entire day doing all the things I kept saying I would do "tomorrow." I learned that I'm living in a building that is over three hundred and fifty years old. It was built as a barn and stable with living quarters above, and was once twice the present size. It was built into a hill, and somehow it got sliced down the middle and that's why there's just one room on each floor. Except the first, where there's a living room and a kitchen with awfully high ceilings. The second is my bedroom, which was the hayloft, and the third level is my studio and opens out onto the hill behind. Thank God they put in plumbing somewhere along the way. The water pump has a mind of its own and the hot water is either the temperature of lava or cold enough for iced tea.*

*I'm brave now and drive into the city and park a few blocks from the Duomo. From there I can walk to the University of Florence, the Uffizi Gallery, and the library.*

*May 2*

*My English friend, Amy Howecroft, invited me to spend the day in the restoration rooms in the Uffizi Galleries. I met Amy in the checkout line in the new supermarket near the Piazza Nobili. She's on academic leave and working on her doctorate. Amy's been great! She helped me find the ancient paper Jonas asked me to locate. I found it in art and book dealers in small towns, in out-of-the-way galleries, and the archives of cartieres, and small producers of handmade paper. A few of the small family-owned companies traced their origin to the Middle Ages and I saw paper being made in tiny factories along the Pescia River not far west of Florence. I saw a vat big enough for Jonas to take a bath in. It was four hundred and eighty-nine years old. I bought a centuries-old family ledger. I paid a hundred thousand lire (about sixty dollars) for it. The end papers are the perfect size and look new!*

*June 17*

   *The saga of the telephone continues! To review: it took four weeks to get one installed, four more weeks to have it put where I wanted it in the first place (bedroom), but when I got home that afternoon, three men came to make the change but left and took the phone with them! Today it is back in the living room.*

*August 6*

   *Steve warned me it could get hot in Florence and he was right! This afternoon I got home and changed into a two-piece bathing suit. Jean Gambarelli hovered over me like a sailor back from six months on the water. I rarely see her husband. Giuseppe is older and I wonder if everything is okay between them.*

*August 18*

   *It's frustrating to get phone calls from Jonas. They're always so in-conclusive and vague. I get the feeling that what I'm doing isn't too im-portant. But he keeps sending money and I continue collecting old paper and reformulating inks. It's great I found Patzi at the University. She's good company and I can send her on errands when I get tied up.*

*September 5*

   *I never thought I'd go this long without seeing someone from home. I do miss Steve but I'm no closer to saying I'll marry him than when I came over. Amy's in Scotland for three weeks. I see a few new friends I met through Cecilia and I like the woman at I Tatti. Her name is Miriam Klein and she's from Milwaukee. She's employed by Harvard University. I'm homesick and the way I feel tonight I may tell Jonas I want to go to Washington for a while.*

   She slammed the notebook shut on the last entry, recalling how she had grown lonely and self-pitying. "Dumb broad," she said aloud. "You made this decision all by yourself. Steve will be here soon. Jonas is com-ing and you can have it all out with him." She smiled at what she heard herself say.

   Then she turned to face the clutter accumulated over the spring and summer months: the bookshelves overflowed, a cabinet beside it was crammed full with bottles containing ink samples, carbon black, and gallnuts. More bottles contained chemicals, a box was filled with centuries-old bits of iron, and others held chalks and pigments. An array of mortars and pestles suggested an apothecary's shop. On the floor were tall flasks of distilled water, two propane cylinders, straightwalled ceramic jars, and a light stand to which was clamped an ultraviolet lamp.

On top of another table was Ellie's collection of ancient paper. She had cataloged each sheet by its age, original use, where she bought it, price paid, fiber content, watermark identification, and *cartiere* in the case of twenty-seven sheets that were her prize discovery. She knew that at least two sheets had been made by the same craftsmen that produced paper used by Perino Del Vaga and Leonardo da Vinci.

A long table positioned directly under the skylight was Ellie's command center. Near the door leading to the patio was a smaller table for Patrizia Tozi, her assistant. "Patzi" was an art history student at the university, ideally qualified to investigate the pens, quills, and other drawing tools used by Leonardo. Disarray of a different sort surrounded her work area.

The phone rang. Its distinctive, metallic sound reached every corner of the stone house. She slipped down the steep steps, damning the bureaucratically bogged-down telephone company. It was Jonas.

He spoke quickly, dispensing with the amenities in a sentence, then went on: "I shall be leaving for Milan on Saturday. I will take the train to Florence and arrive late afternoon. You needn't meet me. I'll stay at the Excelsior and will call you at six."

Ellie was puzzled by his abruptness, by his slow, almost stammering speech. She began to worry that somehow she had displeased him.

# Chapter 12

The quiet dignity permeating the lobby of the Connaught Hotel was shattered when Giorgio Burri stepped through the door, spewing forth a seamless stream of Italian, French, and English, climaxed by a thunderously emphatic *"Mio Dio!"* He was surrounded by the doorman, a taxi driver pleading for his fare, an assistant concierge, and a greatly agitated receptionist, who had dashed from behind his desk to discover what wild storm had blown in off Carlos Place.

"This man"—Giorgio was pointing at the driver—"deliberately drove to the wrong hotel so his fare might be increased."

"I've been tryin' to tell you I made an honest mistake and I ain't chargin' you for it." The driver, cap in hand, set himself in front of the highly charged Italian. "Twenty-four pounds and it's all square."

The receptionist spoke up. "That's quite fair, Signore Burri. You are Signore Burri?"

"Of course. You are expecting me."

"The fare from Heathrow is often more."

"I have not been deceived? Then I must apologize." A broad smile replaced the scowl. *"Sono molto dispiacente.* I am sorry. Here are your twenty-four and three more." He handed over the notes.

"I'm obliged, sir. Thank you." The driver spun and returned to his taxi.

"No more misunderstanding. *Va bene!"* Giorgio yanked at the collar of the raincoat he wore as a cape. Long, graying hair covered his ears, framing a lean, expressive face dominated by an aquiline nose that was doubtless a distinguishing Burri family feature. He was tall and trim for a man of sixty-two. He was not the conventional image of an art scholar, not with the toughness he exuded and the ruddy, deeply lined skin that showed weather-beaten evidence of his love for skiing and hiking.

"If you will come with me, Signore Burri, we can arrange for your accommodations." Giorgio followed the greatly relieved receptionist to the desk.

As he registered, his eyes never strayed from the porter standing by his luggage. He was handed a message. It was from Jonas, requesting he phone upon arrival. When the porter suggested he take the bags and meet him in his room, Giorgio said with finality, "*Bene,* but the black one stays with me."

From his room he phoned Jonas. Giorgio treated phones as necessary evils, somehow never relying on the instrument to carry a sound from one place to another. And so, he shouted.

"Jonas, my friend, it is Giorgio. What may I do for you?"

There was silence for a moment and Giorgio looked skeptically at the telephone as if to confirm his suspicions. Then he heard a familiar voice.

"Welcome to London, Giorgio. I have planned dinner for tonight."

"What a pleasure. I am anxious to see you and place my files in your hands."

"We'll meet at the bar. Eight o'clock."

"*Sì, exccellente. Addio.*"

At eight Giorgio was in the Connaught Bar, ensconced at a table opposite the wide door leading from the lobby into the wood-paneled room. A tall glass filled with ice, a section of orange, and a bottle of Pellegrino water had been set in front of him. Resting against his leg was the black bag he had not let out of his sight since leaving his villa in Cernobbio earlier in the day. He wore a heavy tweed jacket with a printed silk scarf tied loosely around his neck beneath an open shirt. A gaily striped *mouchoir* drooped from his breast pocket. The colors and fabrics might normally clash, yet they came together remarkably well.

His eyes swept the room, pausing to enjoy a dark-haired young lady with an absolutely perfect profile. She sat to the right of the great door. Then he saw Jonas make his entrance. He stood and greeted him effusively, confused at seeing Jonas accompanied by a man he did not know.

"You remember Tony," Jonas said as he fitted himself into a chair next to Giorgio.

"*Sì.* But he is very much changed. Perhaps it is the mustache. You did not tell me we would have the honor of Signore Waters's presence."

There was a sharp edge to the way he said the name and a clear indication his business was with Jonas.

Jonas signaled to a waiter and ordered a double Dewars. Tony pointed to the Pellegrino water and asked for the same.

"We are approaching that time when too much is happening in too many places. Tony will help me keep an eye on things, particularly the work that can now commence in earnest."

"I mean no disrespect to Mr. Waters, but you have emphasized most eloquently that we maintain the greatest—how do you say?—discretion."

"All the more reason Tony joins us. I rely on him to keep meddlers away. We must have absolute secrecy." Jonas held his glass to Giorgio. "Agreed?"

"*Sono d'accordo.*" Giorgio returned the gesture. "I drink to our success."

They finished their drinks and moved into the grill, where Jonas played host. Thin slices of smoked salmon were prepared at a small buffet nearby, followed by an entrée of Scottish beef served from a huge silver-domed cart wheeled to their table. Giorgio relished the outpouring of food but could not resist announcing his preference for the simple Chianti wines and sturdy Barbera d'Asti. If the wines Jonas selected had not excited him, the offer of a stout Havana did. A cup of espresso and the cigar added to Giorgio's contentment. He rambled from subject to subject, then praised Jonas for his ambitious undertaking. "There will be many in the academies and universities who will applaud your incredible discovery. You will be famous, my friend. And deservedly so." Jonas accepted the flattery by puckering his lips to form the familiar "O."

"Only this"—Jonas held out his arms as if to embrace the entire dining room—"would delay me from seeing what you have brought to us." Then his mood changed abruptly, and he said very solemnly, "But it is time we go to your room, Giorgio. We have much to discuss."

In fact, Giorgio had a suite: a bedroom and a handsomely furnished sitting room. It had pleased Giorgio; now Jonas added his approval. He shed his jacket. The grill room had become intolerably warm and perspiration showed across his broad back.

"I shall be very happy to show you what is in my black bag. I have not let it out of my sight, even to go there." Giorgio nodded toward the bathroom. "It is true, every day another pair of eyes would visit me, and I grew tired of hiding the papers. I have shielded them even from Ivonne, and it is the first time in thirty-six years that I have kept a secret from my wife. I told her that what I was doing was a surprise and that someday soon I would take her to the United States." Again he laughed and a sprinkling of gold crowns sparkled from amid straight, white teeth. "Ivonne wishes to visit New York and San Francisco as if they were a hundred kilometers apart."

He unlocked the briefcase and withdrew a leather-covered box. Jonas edged closer and Tony pulled a chair up to the table around which they were gathered.

"In this box are fifty-six sheets of paper representing twenty-eight leaves. That means there are fourteen folios. I have classified them in two groups. Eight leaves contain Leonardo's architectural studies, which we must claim are missing from similar manuscripts now at the Institut de France. Twenty leaves contain drawings and sketches Leonardo prepared in anticipation of one or another painting he later completed, and are similar to the folios at the Uffizi and on which Leonardo drew his early thoughts for *The Adoration of the Magi*. But these which I have prepared represent his early studies for the *Mona Lisa*, *The Last Supper*, and the *Leda*.

"The size of each sheet differs slightly from the others, yet most are of the dimensions Leonardo preferred: approximately twenty-one-by-twenty-eight centimeters. The folios containing sketches for his paintings were once part of a bound book. Leonardo's sketchbook, one might say. I think, Jonas, you must suggest that someone at some time took the book apart and changed the size of the sheets to fit into another volume.

"I am pleased with my imitation of Leonardo, but my skills as an artist have long since departed me. Even so, I have been more faithful to Leonardo's style than was Melzi. As I told you, I have taken Melzi's copies and eliminated what were obviously his additions or interpretations. Strange how even in those days a student considered himself more skilled than his teacher. As well as I believe I have remained true to the Master's style, your artist must do even better. He must render every tiny line with absolute precision and with an unhesitating flow of the pen—a task I do not envy.

"My drawings will be his guide, but he must place each drawing on the sheet in the precise position I have indicated. I have, in another box, copies of enlarged sections and details of Leonardo's finished paintings or drawings, and it is these the artist must duplicate with the change in perspective and angle I have indicated. You must show each page to me as he completes them, and of course we shall eventually work side by side as the drawings are completed. This shall be of great importance when Leonardo's commentary is written. The handwriting will be most difficult to reproduce, and so I have used only the barest amount. And here also are complete instructions for the execution of the Master's handwriting. They must be followed without exception."

As Giorgio spoke, his attention was squarely on Jonas. Tony might well have been simply another piece of furniture. Now with the preamble concluded, Giorgio opened the brown box, took out a packet of papers, and handed them to Jonas, who placed it on his broad lap. He examined the top sheet, which contained sketches of a swan, its curving neck held by graceful hands.

"You are looking at the drawing Melzi was certain to have referred to when he painted the standing Leda. *Il Cigno.*"

Jonas motioned for Tony to come to his side. Both men stared at the drawing for several minutes, then Jonas set it on the table. No sooner had he put it down than he picked it up again and brought it within inches of his myopic eyes. He waved the sheet at Giorgio.

"This is a copy!"

"Are you surprised we have Xerox machines in Como? They are everywhere and produce an excellent copy. In fact, the copy may serve the artist better than the original."

"That's not our agreement. You are to turn over everything. You keep nothing."

"We have no such agreement. True, that is what you asked, but I did not agree to those terms. When we struck our bargain, I agreed to create a number of Leonardo's lost folios—fourteen, in fact. Then, when they were transformed to appear as the genuine work of Leonardo, I would provide evidence they had been discovered in the hands of a descendant of Francesco Melzi. I further agreed to vouch for their authenticity and encourage others who share my views of Leonardo to do the same. For all this you have paid me the sum of fifty thousand dollars."

"Precisely so. You were paid the money well in advance. I have gambled, not you. We agreed that you would turn over all the drawings. Not some worthless copies." Jonas tossed the sheet to the floor.

Giorgio picked up the sheet and very calmly placed it on top of the other pages still on Jonas's lap. "You have gambled with money, I with my reputation. Remember, there was more to the arrangement we made. You offered to pay a fixed amount each time you succeeded in selling a half folio at auction or to a private buyer. I did not agree to that arrangement. But we did touch our glasses on my proposal, which provides that I receive ten percent of the price you receive for each manuscript page you sell.

The agitation showed clearly in Jonas's reddened face. The heavy meal and too many glasses of wine and now the obstinacy of the art-historian-turned-capitalist caused the perspiration to flow freely.

"There is no quarrel with our financial arrangement. The terms are generous. But our agreement was very specific regarding the disposition of the drawings. You are to give each one to me. If you violate the agreement, then I am no longer obligated to pay any additional money after the manuscripts are sold."

"But you will pay," Giorgio said slowly and without his usual smile. "You are taking an unreasonable position, Jonas. You will need my cooperation when it is time to work closely with your artist. The manuscripts must never be discovered as forgeries."

It was the first time the word had been used and Jonas was struck by the realization that Giorgio was fully tuned in to its ominous significance. He loosened his tie and rubbed a handkerchief across his neck.

"The matter is simply resolved. Give me all the drawings and—"

"I will not do that. They are my assurance that the risks I am taking will be rewarded. And they are quite safe. I have hidden them behind two feet of stone in an ancient villa overlooking Lake Como."

"This—this is . . ." Jonas was spluttering anger and frustration showed in his eyes. "This is extortion."

Giorgio permitted his smile to return. "No, it is what we call good business in my country. It will be easier for us to trust each other if the original sheets are in my possession. As each manuscript page is sold, I shall present you with the original."

Giorgio watched the huge man twist nervously in the chair that was too small for him. He saw him look to Tony for support, but the impeccably dressed aide appeared to be completely uninvolved in the argument. Finally Jonas broke the long silence.

"My congratulations, Giorgio. Your precautions are unnecessary, but I commend you for taking them."

"It is true I have taken precautions, but there is something more to all of this. We are honorable men plotting a dishonorable deed. Such action can twist a man's mind, and I only wish to be protected against consequences I cannot control. I have worked long hours to produce these papers and I have learned something quite profound. No one has ever put his mind to the task of creating a page from the missing

Leonardo manuscripts; no researcher has ever dared put his speculations on paper to suggest what those sheets might contain, and yet I have given you fourteen complete folios.

"I have come to know Leonardo as if he were my brother. And I know the other minds and artists of his time. Hear me, Jonas, just as his contemporaries, he copied what he liked. It was a way of learning. We would say they were plagiarists and be wrong. The times required it. And they were honorable men. If Leonardo knew what I have done, he would ask only that it be honest. Every drawing on every page is one I know was set down by that great man. But his sheets are lost. Now, the world will see them again. If I receive a reward for this work, I shall consider that I have earned my compensation honestly."

Giorgio's ramblings ceased and he took a chair across from Jonas. Both men remained silent for many minutes until Jonas returned to the manuscript pages and began the slow process of studying every drawing on every page.

Wednesday became Thursday and finally at 2:00 A.M. Jonas confessed that he could no longer focus his eyes or his attention. They agreed to reassemble in the morning.

Tony became a full participant when they met again at ten o'clock. Each of Giorgio's sheets contained at least one drawing and Leonardo's commentaries. Two of the sheets formed a page or leaf, and two leaves made a folio. Tony in effect assembled a catalog of all fifty-six sheets and assigned a number to each. His notes were intended to help Curtis schedule the work he would soon commence.

They agreed to assign a three-digit number to each folio and began with the architectural drawings. These four folios were designated 201, 202, 203, and 204. The folios containing drawings that related to Leonardo's paintings, and which would have far greater value, were numbered 401 through 410.

The pages that formed the 200 series were devoted to studies and ideas Leonardo found most challenging. Some of the drawings had military overtones, others touched on details of a basilica that very likely might have been a commission from Lodovico Sforza. Four were exquisite renderings of Leonardo's own ideas for a cathedral in Florence. Giorgio had not lost his ability to draw architectural subjects, nor would the drawings in the 200 Series prove difficult for Curtis Stiehl. Offsetting this advantage was the requirement to place more of Leonardo's handwriting on each page, a complicated task.

After much discussion, the forty sheets comprising the 400 series were paired and paginated. The first through the tenth pages were Leonardo's preliminary studies for the *Mona Lisa*. Pages eleven through sixteen contained drawings of a maiden and a swan thought to be important in the lost *Leda*. Giorgio showed these pages with particular pride. "I am sure that what I have done here will add further controversy to the mystery of the *Leda*. It is said that the finished painting has not survived, but I feel that gives us license to suggest that Leonardo treated Leda and the swan with greater sexual feelings. As you see, Zeus is shown as a small figure in the background."

Ten pages were devoted to head and hand studies of the disciples in *The Last Supper*. Leonardo's notes revealed how difficult it was for him to secure models for Judas and for Thomas. Eight pages contained Leonardo's famous warrior horses, intended as preliminary to *The Battle of Anghiari*, the mural he painted in the Council Hall in Florence. The last six pages were densely packed with sketches of the Virgin and Christ child. One drawing showed the babe clutching a lamb and another with His hands reaching out for the animal. Either drawing would be hailed as preliminary to the lost *Madonna of the Children at Play*.

Giorgio lifted four sheets. "These comprise folio 400-1M as I wish it to be identified, and contain sketches for the *Mona Lisa*." He took two more sheets. "And these become the first page in folio 400-2C. Judas and Thomas. Your Curtis can concentrate his efforts on these pages. I am providing him with many references, all works of the Master to guide him." With a smile he added, "They will create much excitement at the auction, Jonas. The studies for the *Mona Lisa* will be the first ever to be discovered."

The little "O" on Jonas's lips disappeared quickly. "Perhaps we shouldn't be so bold. We should establish credibility first. Let's begin with an architectural study, it will be less controversial."

"I disagree, Jonas. As I have said, while the architectural drawings are more easily drawn, the writing on a typical sheet is extensive and can be very difficult. The value of these pages will be far greater once the others have been sold. But there is something else to consider. I come from the world of art and I know how they think. There will always be the nay-sayers, but there are as many, even more who will cheer at the suggestion that new works of Leonardo have surfaced. There will be many, many art experts who will want these new drawings of Leonardo to be—as we would say—*autentico*. They will argue most loudly in your support for the full accreditation."

"Your point is well taken; however, I believe we should have a choice when it is time to present the first manuscript page."

"*Bene.* I suggest these drawings of fountains for a new palace that Leonardo planned for Lorenzo di Piero, who was the nephew of Pope Julius. The fountains are beautiful and should not present a problem for Curtis. What Leonardo had to say about them will be more difficult."

Luncheon was served from a cart wheeled into the room. They ate sparingly, even Jonas picked at the generous array of meats and cheeses. The day had been overcast and not until the gray sky turned black did they complete their close study of Giorgio's many pages. During a brief break in the afternoon, Jonas broached the subject of the original drawings Giorgio claimed were safely hidden. He argued once more that all of the drawings were rightfully his property.

"*Basta! Basta!* There is no more to say about it."

Giorgio let loose with a sample of his fiery temper. He had no intention of backing down. After the brief outburst, he returned to his gentle, patient manner. He shared his immense knowledge of Leonardo's life and precious heritage. At times he spoke with awe and reverence, then regaled Jonas and Tony with ribald stories of the great artist's private life.

But now Giorgio was tired. The long hours without fresh air or diversion had taken effect. "Forgive me, I do not wish to be rude, but I am very tired. I did not rest well last night and I feel now I could sleep forever. Ah, and to make matters more unhappy, I must be up early to visit several shops for Ivonne and be at the airport in the early afternoon."

Jonas poured a tumbler half full of scotch. The time for the meeting he reluctantly agreed to attend was not far off and he felt a nervousness somewhere in his very generous stomach. "I am flying to Milan this weekend," he blurted out.

"Then you can visit with us. The lake is beautiful at this time of year."

"Lake Como is beautiful at all times of the year. You showed me that. Soon I will ask you to be my guest."

"*Sì?* You have bought the property you told me about?"

"Another one. It is on the eastern side of the lake. Below Torno."

"The Villa Grigio?" Giorgio's face showed his excitement. "That is the Vescova estate and has been vacant for many years."

"That is the one," Jonas replied. "It is larger than I had planned, but I couldn't pass it by."

"Ah . . . that explains the busy activity. Many workers and boats anchored by the docks." He shot a knowing glance at Jonas. "It is very costly to bring such an old building to life again."

"It's an investment, Giorgio. Perhaps I shall sell after it has served its purpose."

"I took my boat to the dock and tried to land so I might learn what was being done to that great villa. But I was waved off by a guard aiming his rifle at my heart."

"I'm sorry if you were frightened," Jonas said. He swallowed the last of the scotch, then added, "The security I demanded is apparently in effect. But to your discomfort, I am afraid. Soon you'll be free to tie up your boat and visit *Il Diodario.*"

"That is what you call it? *Il Diodario?*"

"You know that name?"

"It is most unusual. I have heard the word but cannot remember its meaning."

"I'll refresh your memory. Leonardo used the name in one of the myths he was so fond of writing. It's obscure—one I like very much."

"Ah, I think now I recall something. *Il Diodario* has to do with money, or with the treasury. Is that not so?"

"That's the interpretation I chose," Jonas replied.

Tony clutched Giorgio's black bag and trailed Jonas to the elevator. In the lobby Jonas snapped instructions for Tony's return to New York and handed him a sealed envelope marked for delivery to Curtis Stiehl.

"See that Curtis reads this letter before he unpacks Giorgio's drawings. He's not expecting Xerox copies any more than we did."

Tony pocketed the envelope. "He hasn't forgotten how little time he had with the Windsor drawing; now he gets a pack of copies. He'll be sore as a bloody boil."

"There's a check in there to ease his discomfort," Jonas said without conviction. Before going out to his waiting taxi, he added, "That Italian bastard thinks he put one over on us. He can become a first-class pain doling out the drawings one by one. You might have to find a way to get behind his two feet of stone."

A small smile trickled across Tony's face and Jonas knew that he had struck home. "Just say the word, Mr. Kalem."

"Keep a close eye on Curtis and handle him gently. For now, the focus of our project is on him."

Tony followed Jonas to his taxi and waved him off. He returned through the lobby of the Connaught and paused to look at the *Mirror*, the only newspaper that continued to put the story of Sarah Evans's accident on the front page. He didn't read past the headline: SEARCH FOR MISSING ENGINEER IN POLICEWOMAN'S MYSTERY DEATH.

# Chapter 13

Walter Deats stood at the bar of the Black Knights Tavern and ordered an ale, which he would ignore save for a sip and then only if the dryness in his mouth persisted. The pub was a mecca for Windsor tourists and their numbers were growing.

He showed his identification to the woman serving him. "I'm Superintendent Deats," he said quietly. "I have pictures of a man and a woman. Tell me if you recognize either of them."

"Superintendent, I'll tell you right off I see a hundred faces a day—"

"I know you do, but just on the chance they were here and you saw them, I'd appreciate your help." He set a photograph of Sarah Evans on the bar.

"Is this to do with the poor girl that was in that awful crash? She's a pretty thing, but I don't recall seeing her."

"She's the one," Deats acknowledged. Then he placed a drawing of Greg Hewlitt next to Sarah's picture. Hewlitt's likeness had been developed by the forensic lab, following interrogation of library employees then piecing together Hewlitt's features by the Penry Facial Identification Technique. Deats vouched for the accuracy of the drawing.

"No, I haven't seen that one either. Wouldn't mind if I did." The woman smiled.

"He has a scar...here." Deats pointed to his own hand.

"I've not seen him. Scar or no scar."

Deats smiled at the woman and returned the two pictures to his pocket. "Thank you." He turned to leave, then moved back to the bar. "Were you tending bar last Friday evening?"

"Superintendent," she answered wearily, "I'm behind this bar every hour it's open."

"Was someone helping you?"

"My husband's always here. But in the kitchen most of the time."

She nodded in the direction of a door beyond a noisy group flinging darts at a well-riddled circle of cork.

Several thirsty patrons had grown impatient and tapped their empty glasses on the bar top.

"Sorry I'm no help, Superintendent."

"I may be back," he called to her.

Deats made a note to return when the Black Knights Tavern was less crowded. He checked the number of pubs and hotel bars he had visited. Seven. Then he looked at the next name on the list. The Old House Hotel.

Jonas was inclined to disobey instructions and have Tony follow him. Involving Tony might be a risk worth taking, at least until he knew who was behind the Oriental voice. But his decision was made. He would go alone. "The Berkeley," he called to the driver.

The hotel's lounge was in warm browns and accents of gold and burnished brass. It was a quarter to nine, time enough for a strong drink to fortify him before the meeting. The theater crowds had long since gone to their entertainment, yet the lobby and bars were teeming with men and women of every nationality chatting or drinking and otherwise preparing to launch themselves on an evening's spree. Somewhere in the crowd a pair of eyes was watching him, and he could sense it. But his full attention was not focused on what lay ahead; rather he brooded over the obstacle Giorgio had placed in his way. "Damned Guinea," he muttered. He finished the drink and went to the newsstand.

His instructions were to pick up a copy of the *Financial Times* and begin to read it. Immediately a voice came from behind him.

"Good evening, Mr. Kalem. Thank you for accepting our invitation."

Jonas turned to find the smiling face of a man he judged to be about twenty-five. He was immaculately dressed in an expensive suit of Italian tailoring. Jonas was intrigued with the young man's features: only the shape of the eyes betrayed his Oriental blood. They were a startling gray blue. The wide smile revealed straight, white teeth. "Please come with me."

In the elevator the young man said, "That business with the newspaper was pretty corny. Someone saw it in a movie." They continued to the sixth floor and Jonas was led to the end of the corridor. A door was unlocked and he was ushered into a suite of rooms. He had formed a vague picture of the man who phoned three days before and was totally unprepared for the sight before him. Standing in the center of the room was a woman dressed in a shining, richly brocaded red dress. A gold necklace framed a very striking face. High cheekbones and arched eyebrows were delicately accented by makeup. She was barely five feet tall, yet there was a majesty to the way she stood, head held up and her arms gracefully crossed in front of her. She greeted her guest with just the suggestion of a bow.

"Thank you for coming, Mr. Kalem. We were not certain that you would accept our invitation." Her slightly accented English was precise.

"Nor was I until this evening."

"Please join me." She motioned toward a high-backed chair. "We have presumed you may wish a taste of your favorite whiskey."

Jonas eased into the chair, and as he did so, the young man offered a small silver tray on which was a glass filled with ice and an amber fluid that Jonas took without hesitation. He took a long sip then said, "We have not met."

"For the present, I ask that you know me as Madame Sun. You have met James?"

The young man stepped forward and bowed. "It is a very poor joke, but I am the son of Sun."

"I am happy to meet both of you," Jonas said, "but who phoned me on Monday?"

"You were contacted by Mr. Dong Shim," Madame Sun replied. "He will not join us today. Perhaps another time."

There were two doors leading to other rooms in the suite. Jonas was sure that Mr. Shim was behind one of them. He watched Madame Sun take a chair close to him. Her skin was clear and white and contrasted with the bright red dress. He studied her face and decided that only one word properly described her. She was truly exotic. A foreign and tiny expression of mystery that was simply unfamiliar. At forty-five or six, as he judged her, she had not lost a trace of her sexuality.

"Then we can begin," he said. "I'm anxious to learn why you wish to meet with me."

"I am prepared to tell you what has brought us together, but I cannot divulge everything at this time. You may have surmised that my son and I are Korean. My husband is an American who fought in the war, returned to the States to complete his education, then decided to make his career in Korea. He has consulted with the men who built our trading companies. You know the names of Hyundai and Samsung?"

Jonas nodded. He had heard the names, but had no familiarity with the men who acquired power and wealth as leaders of Korea's giant trading corporations.

"My husband is a lawyer who prefers the world of art to the tedium of business and international law. Over the years he has helped two of these wealthy men accumulate private art collections. One has an insatiable appetite for very expensive paintings and it seems he is more impressed by how much they cost than their value as works of art."

"You represent this collector?" Jonas asked.

"That is possible," Madame Sun replied. "It is also possible that my husband will make purchases in his own name."

"He is a collector?"

"There have been many opportunities," was her terse reply. "I have asked you here so that we may discuss the provocative statements you have made about the Leonardo manuscripts. It is obvious that you will soon announce the discovery of Leonardo's drawings. Is that not so?"

Jonas poked at the ice in his glass, then took a long sip. "Just as you have said, it is possible."

"You can be more definite, Mr. Kalem."

"With all respect, Madame Sun, if the time comes when I have the great fortune to make such an announcement, I will choose the forum most carefully."

"You have made announcements in four countries and your predictions have been widely reported in the press. You have chosen your forums with great skill. I am merely asking when you will tell the world what you have discovered."

"In less than a year. Six months, if all goes without complications. The matter of authentication is extremely critical."

"Who will authenticate the drawings?"

"Harold Pimm heads up the Old Masters Department at Collyer's and could assemble an outstanding panel. They would be my first choice."

"We will be disappointed if you choose Collyer's. If a gallery is chosen it should be Sotheby's. A board of independent scholars is our first choice."

"Collyer's reputation is superb, particularly for their knowledge of the Italian Renaissance Masters," Jonas replied. He put his glass down as if the conversation had ended and he was about to leave.

Madame Sun raised a hand and waved him back into his chair. "I will speak candidly. If the purpose of your speeches is to arouse interest among potential buyers of the Leonardos, you have achieved your goal. But I have gone beyond mere interest. I have studied your astrological chart and confirmed that you will be at the center of an event of international importance." She nodded to James, who handed his mother a leather notecase. "This news is good, yet I find distressing complications. Clearly you shall tell the world of your good fortune, but it is also apparent that there is blood over some portion of your life. I see in this picture the hand of death."

Jonas ranked astrologers with fortune-tellers, lumping both into his own agnosticism. But he could be gulled by a superstition, and this woman had tied together his inevitable announcement of the Leonardos with death. He emptied his glass. James took it from him and refilled it.

The two were seated with but a small table separating them. The contrast was remarkable: Madame Sun so very small compared to Jonas's hulking eminence.

"Your speeches about the lost Leonardos have been widely reported and you have shown no reluctance to provide the journalists with personal information. From this I learned your date of birth and New York hospital records revealed the time you were born. I follow the ancient form of astrology known as *Ming Shu,* which requires that I know the correct date and time of your birth. And so, Mr. Kalem, I have recorded that you were born on June fourteenth in the year 1938."

"I suppose that makes me a Gemini," he said amiably. He felt the alcohol's warmth and allowed himself to ease into the discourse.

"In Chinese astrology we do not have the signs of the zodiac because we are more concerned with the year of birth. The years are named after animals, and like the months, there are twelve. Before we continue, I must tell you that I am most fortunate to have the ability to accurately read the signs that are different with each of us. There are a great number of persons who will listen only to Madame Sun. You may have little regard for the messages the heavens send, but I know that for many years I have seen the truth and have received much respect for my skills."

"I've no reason to doubt you are a very gifted astrologer," Jonas replied, "but I know nothing of it and cannot take it seriously."

"Many feel as you, until they hear what I have found in their chart. Keep an open mind, Mr. Kalem. Listen to my words."

Jonas shifted his weight back into the chair. He sensed a strange power flowing from the small woman. She was confident; he saw that in her eyes looking intently into his. Madame Sun opened the ornately tooled leather cover and removed several sheets, which she carefully placed on the table. Her hands moved gracefully and with practiced assurance. Her lips moved as if in prayer, and she hummed. Then she spoke in a soft voice, speaking in a rhythmic cadence that had a hypnotic effect.

"The time, day, month, and year are your four Pillars of Fate. Your animal sign is the Horse. This means you have strong masculine traits and are more comfortable with men. The Horse may fear members of the opposite sex, ignore them, or worship them, but rarely can the Horse relate to them. The Horse personality requires that you achieve success and be recognized by your peers. I find this particularly true in your case. You find social contact important, and in fact you are very happy to be with other people, and are particularly pleased when you are asked to speak to a group.

"We are in the year of the Dragon when the time is ripe for extravagant schemes and flamboyant gestures. It often is a time of increased activities in the arts. It can be a profitable time for the Horse because there will be exciting challenges and opportunities. But it may also be a year when the Horse may exceed his abilities and become involved in unplanned difficulties.

"All of what I have said merely puts very broad brush strokes on your astrological canvas. It is a very large canvas with many events occurring at a time when I feel great caution is required on your part."

Madame Sun unfolded a large parchmentlike sheet and turned it so Jonas could see the Chinese characters and the colorful symbols that filled the page. The images did not focus clearly. The drinks were taking effect.

"*Ming Shu* provides you with five elements that are determined by your four Pillars of Fate." She handed Jonas a bright orange card on which were printed Chinese characters and under each the words "Wood, Water, Fire, Metal, Earth."

"Each element represents a personality trait. There are twelve element positions and the frequency each element appears in your birth chart determines personality strengths or in some cases severe weaknesses. I find the dominant element in your chart is Metal. Metal is the sign of harvest and business conflicts. In plainest terms, Metal means money and your Metal rating of four is quite high."

Jonas nodded. So long as Madame Sun spoke of positive matters, he would listen.

"But Metal indicates the sharpness of a knife, particularly when Fire has a high rating. I find a Fire rating of three, which signals danger. It is real danger, the danger of death. It is not clear if it will be someone close to you. But you will know."

The comfort he was feeling vanished. He drained his glass and no sooner did he put it down than James picked it up. Jonas waved as if to signal that he did not want the glass refilled, then just as quickly indicated he would take another. Madame Sun waited until Jonas was holding a fresh drink.

"Throughout your chart I find the contradictions of good fortune and troubling periods when you shall incur serious losses. Your Fortune Stems chart reveals nothing of particular concern, but your Branch Stems fall on the chart to indicate disharmony and conflict."

Jonas swallowed nearly half of his drink before realizing it tasted different. It was bitter. A trickle of the liquid fell down his chin and he wiped it away with the back of his hand. He smelled the glass and couldn't detect anything unusual. Then, for nearly a full minute, he stared at his chart filled with Chinese writing, circles, and odd-shaped boxes. What was the message? he wondered.

"All that you have said might be true for anyone. I cannot run a business without conflict. And people die. I'm happy to know I am a Horse, that's better than a Rat. And I'm most pleased to learn I rank high in Metal and Metal means money." He looked at his glass and decided that paranoia had attacked him briefly and he was drinking straight Dewars with a dash of water. He downed the rest of his drink but held on to the glass.

"You've obviously gone to great lengths to find I am a Horse dominated by Metal and fear women, which is an outright absurdity. Yet you haven't told me what you want from me."

"It should be clear, Mr. Kalem. My husband and I are interested in your discovery of the Leonardos, and if the manuscripts are authentic, we are prepared to offer you a very significant price. My knowledge of *Ming Shu* has allowed me to know what is happening in your life and be forewarned of any reasons why we should not begin a relationship with you."

Jonas hesitated for an instant, then asked, "And you have found none?"

"To the contrary, there are many troubling signs. Death hovers over your chart. Who dies, or why, I cannot say. In the Dragon year there may be many conflicts." She pointed to a group of Chinese characters. "I see that more than once you have extended yourself into schemes of bad judgment."

"Now you are making judgments . . . wrong ones at that." Jonas stood, but found he was unsteady. He knew he had been given strong drinks and suspected there had been more than his favorite scotch in the glass. "You asked me here to talk about the Leonardo manuscripts, read my horoscope, and ply me with drinks made with some sort of Korean sorcery." He took one step and was overcome by an awful dizziness. James saw the huge body begin to sway and he quickly was by Jonas's side and caught the nearly three hundred pounds before it sagged to the floor. James showed he had the strength of several powerful men. He eased Jonas back to his chair. "Why are you doing this to me?" Jonas said in an almost disconnected way.

"The sorcery you allude to, Mr. Kalem, was merely an amount of alprazolam, which you Americans consume in alarming quantities. No harm will come to you, but it was important that you learn of our interest in the Leonardos, and also that you hear the wisdom of *Ming Shu*. We have listened to your speeches and followed you and your associates from New York to London. We will continue to observe your progress." She rose up and moved to Jonas's side.

"We shall do what is necessary to add a Leonardo to our collection."

Without another word, Madame Sun and James walked from the room, leaving Jonas alone with his astrological chart on the table before him.

# Chapter 14

On the seventh day of the investigation, Walter Deats concluded that Sarah Evans had been murdered. The evidence was circumstantial, but abundant. A strong feeling in his gut had a lot to do with it.

The media had grown impatient with the noncommittal communiqués issued by the Windsor police, and Deats was anxious to make some sort of announcement to stop the bizarre speculation cropping up in the newspapers. Before releasing a statement announcing his murder theory, Deats knew he must positively identify Gregory Hewlitt. Not until four days after the accident was Deats certain that Hewlitt's disappearance went beyond coincidence.

A waitress in the Old House remembered seeing Sarah and Hewlitt, and Sarah's mother recognized the police artist's drawing, adding that the beard and hair were grayer and that her granddaughter's dog bit his hand. Reginald Streeter reluctantly noted seeing the bleeding hand of the man who had worked with such dedication "to preserve the valuable heritage of the Royal Library."

Deats interviewed Barbara Randall at Heldwicke Air-Control Systems but neither the dismayed personnel manager nor Hewlitt's file shed light on the impostor's true identity. The papers Hewlitt submitted to Heldwicke were sent to C3 at the Yard for fingerprint evaluation. Deats supplied other samples of Hewlitt's prints found in the library.

Deats concluded that Hewlitt had driven, or at the least had been in, Sarah's car the night of the accident. He was so positive that when a fingerprint examination of the car turned up only a few of Sarah's smudged prints, he became even more convinced that Hewlitt had wiped the car clean before sending it on its death run. The fact that the car was so clean of prints prompted Deats to demand that it be reinspected for "even the slightest trace of the bastard's marks . . . and if it's not admissible in court, it will be good enough for me."

At two in the afternoon on Friday, Deats learned he was no longer searching for Gregory Hewlitt. Elliot Heston phoned.

"I just got a complete file on your man from CRO and confirmed by C3. You're looking for Anthony Waters alias Douglas Laurie alias Brian Purcell alias a dozen other characters who ran some of the best con operations the Fraud Squad ever tried to close down. Freddie Conklin heads that up and he'll give a month's free beer to the man who puts a claim on Waters."

Heston had cut through the Yard's departmental maze; C3 in the Criminal Investigation Department is closely linked with the Criminal Record Office known as C4 or CRO. Tony Waters's records were released from CRO after fingerprint identification linked Hewlitt to Waters and his well-documented con exploits. The Fraud Squad, C6 in the alphanumeric identifying system, kept their books open on Waters, but the old-timers gave long odds on his capture. With some admiration they had given him the code name "Chameleon." Duplicate files were delivered to Heston's office and after a quick perusal he called Deats with the news.

"Anthony Waters." Deats repeated the name softly. "Any arrests?"

"None by the Yard, but according to the file, City of London Police picked up his trail off a report from the emergency ward at St. George's Hospital. That's when they added a scarred right hand to his ID. They were zeroing in on him when he vanished. That was two years ago."

Two-year-old reports were of little use, Deats thought. "What are you going to do about all this?"

"Issue an all-branches notice and release everything we've got on him. Standard stuff but a necessary first step. We'll cover all exit points immediately."

"You know nothing will come of it," Deats said emphatically. "By now he's become a Hasidic rabbi."

"Have a better idea?"

"You're stuck with the rule book, but can you forget your ruddy damned policy for two days?"

"Two days I can handle, but what sort of miracle are you planning to pull off in forty-eight hours?"

"I don't honestly know, but as soon as Waters learns we're onto him he's going to put more distance between us. I'm coming over to see those files."

When Deats arrived at Heston's office, he learned there had been an important development since the two talked less than ninety minutes earlier.

"Good news, Walter. We found his car at the Semly Place Car Park near Victoria Station. A crew's gone to check it out."

"I want to check it, too. I don't know why, but for some reason I think it's important."

Deats was driven to the garage by one of Heston's men and waited while a crew from the forensic lab examined the old Morris wagon. There was little that could be done beyond search for prints, extract soil samples from the tire treads and carpet, and determine when the car had been abandoned. Deats sat behind the wheel making audio notes of all the seemingly inconsequential details, which when all lumped together might suggest something in Tony Waters's personality that he could take action on. Why was the car parked near Victoria Station? Did it matter? The garage was as close to several international airlines terminals and bus stations as it was to the rail station and the underground. Perhaps he would be back for it? These were the fragments of information that Deats recorded. He was disappointed; he had hoped for more. He tapped the tape recorder against the palm of his hand, then turned it on again.

*"Waters's car is clean and doesn't tell us much. I'll request that it be impounded in the event there's something we should be looking for and as yet haven't put our finger on."*

Deats flicked off the recorder and sat silently. He stared straight ahead, his eyes focusing on the rearview mirror. From the mirror he shifted his glance to the sun visor and, with an idle wave of his hand, flipped the visor and discovered a piece of paper wedged between the welting and the ceiling fabric. He grabbed at the paper, unfolded it, and saw that it was imprinted "Dukes Hotel—St. James Place." Penciled below was the name and address of a tire shop.

He put in a call to Heston. "I just found something, Elliot. Maybe nothing but worth the check. I'm going to look into it before coming back to the Yard."

Deats ordered the driver to the Dukes Hotel. His luck was holding a little better now. The young concierge did not recognize the note, but the doorman did. Deats introduced himself, eliciting the talkative Irishman's name and working schedule.

"I ain't talked to a Windsor policeman in nearly four years. Not since me and the missus was up to see the Castle and some bloke was tryin' to hold up the passengers on the bus we was on." Patrick was in an expansive mood.

Deats smiled. "I remember. He almost got away with it, too. He was more frightened than the passengers." He waited patiently while the doorman recounted his experience. Then he held out the police artist's drawing of Tony Waters. "Recognize this face?"

"I certainly do," Patrick said without hesitation. "That's Mr. Waters. He was here about a week ago. Is he in some kind of trouble?"

"You recognize him with the beard?"

"Oh, sure. I knew it was Mr. Waters when he showed because there's a way about him that I know. Maybe the eyes or how he walks. It's my job to remember people. I know Mr. Anthony Waters, all right."

"We'd like to talk with Mr. Waters, but he's disappeared. Do you know where he might have gone?"

"No, I can't help, Superintendent. Fact is, I never did know where he lived. I do recall him once sayin' he was goin' to the States. That's right, but I wouldn't know where."

Deats held out the paper he found over the sun visor. "Know anything about this?"

"'Course I do. I wrote that name down for Mr. Waters the night he was here. Nasty weather that night. He had a flat. That's right, a flat on the M4 and he wanted to know where to get a new tire. I told him I'd put it all down on a note. I figured he'd know where to look for it."

"Did he stay at Dukes often?"

"Well now, he didn't stay here this last time. He was with an American gentleman, the same one he'd been with on other visits. But I know Mr. Waters from before. Always very generous, he was." Patrick winked and rubbed a thumb and forefinger together.

"How do you mean 'from before'?" Deats asked.

"It goes back some years. Mr. Waters had a business in London. Successful was my guess. At least he would come here and spend the night with some expensive ladies. All very proper to talk to, all dressed fit for the queen's ball. But whores, they was."

"The American. Tell me about him."

"He's a big man with a deep voice. Wears glasses, thick ones." Patrick frowned. "They stayed in the Duke of Gloucester suite."

"They? He wasn't alone?"

"There was one other. I didn't see much of him. He stayed cooped up in the rooms most of the time."

"That's strange, or didn't you think so?"

"Not so strange as all the special packages and boxes that was delivered up there."

"What kind of boxes? What was in them?"

"None of the hotel staff could touch them. The people that brought them in took every one up to the suite, then the same blighters took 'em out."

"Any visitors?"

"Not on your life. They was particular about who went through the doors and they blocked off one of the bedrooms and no one was allowed there the entire while they was 'ere. You can ask Mrs. Palmer about that, all right. She's in charge of housekeeping on that floor."

"When did the big American leave?"

"Only this morning. Too bad I wasn't on duty. He was generous, too." Patrick looked sad.

"And the other American?"

"He left on my day off. Bad luck all around for me. That was the day they took all the cartons out of the suite."

Patrick had been cooperative and had made no bones about trading his information for coin of the realm. Deats handed him several pounds.

"Not a word of our conversation to anyone," Deats said gravely, fully aware that Patrick would break his silence a dozen times before nightfall. "Here's my card. Phone immediately if any of the men who were in those rooms comes back."

Before returning to Scotland Yard, Deats met with the manager, a Mr. Proquitte, and the senior concierge. They added little to Patrick's testimony. The dour concierge, who had more the air of an important guest than one who wore crossed keys, described the cartons that were delivered by a crew from Kalem's London office. Mr. Proquitte reluctantly divulged Jonas Kalem's business address in New York.

"Waters didn't stay at the Dukes and I don't have the foggiest notion where he's been staying. I doubt it would help if we did know." Deats summed up his findings for Elliot Heston with a final conundrum. "The big man named Kalem obviously has something to do with whatever Waters is up to and the gang of them were using the hotel for some hush-hush purpose. Last anyone knows, he was off to Heathrow."

"We can put a trace on him but don't count on fast results," Heston said. "We'll do better picking up on him in New York."

"I'm not sure he went to New York. No one at the hotel handled his tickets. I have a hunch he went to Paris. He has an office there, too."

"We can check both offices. We can do it by phone."

"Anonymously, I hope."

"By all means."

"There's a third man. Curtis Stiehl returned to New York on the twelfth. Monday. The hotel confirmed his reservation."

"If Kalem and Stiehl have left the country, what does that suggest our friend Waters may have done?"

"I say he's in New York," Deats replied.

"Under what name?" Heston tossed a thick file onto the desk. "There's a dozen aliases in that file and you know damned well he isn't traveling under any one of them."

"I wonder if he'd have the balls to use his real name in New York."

"Not likely. You said he's become a rabbi, and God knows he might have."

"What do you suppose his relationship is to Kalem? He's not under hire to put in air conditioners."

Heston nodded but did not respond. He lifted his phone and asked for a connection to the chief of detectives' office in the New York City Police Department. A line cleared in less than a minute and he heard the phone ring on the other side of the Atlantic. He glanced at his watch: it was 3:30—10:30 in the morning in New York.

"Chief Tobias, please. This is Elliot Heston, Metropolitan Police in London. If he's not there, please tell me how I can reach—Tobey, it's Elliot Heston, you old scoundrel....I understand you were in London last month and I never heard a peep from you....I'll excuse you this time...when will you join us fishing up north?...Just keep me posted.... Tobey, I need your help. I just lost a young special agent—we think a homicide....We've got a suspect, only we don't know what name he's using and I can't give you an accurate ID on him but we've some things to go on....He may have used the name Anthony Waters when he was in New York....We think he was employed by a Jonas Kalem....I'll fax over everything we've got on him and the Kalem chap....There's a third person—name of Curtis Stiehl....Don't bother about the spelling now....Yes, there's a rush....The press is beginning to put all their bizarre twists on the case....It was a young woman, quite pretty, and she had a

daughter we didn't know about, so the department is getting flak....
Good...you understand...thanks, Tobey...I'll get the information
started. Cheerio."

For the balance of the afternoon the old friends pored over Waters's
files hoping to uncover a clue to the way he handled himself on previous occasions when he changed identities.

"There's no clear pattern to the way he operated," Deats concluded,
twirling the glasses he had not worn while reading the files.

Heston leaned back, his head cradled in his hands. "If Greg Hewlitt
is really Anthony Waters and he sent Sarah to her death, then we're
dealing with someone completely different from what we're reading
about in these reports. Waters was a confidence man, a professional
ripper-offer. When he was threatened, he responded with force, but
there's no record of violence, not yet. I have a feeling he won't surface
in the suburbs selling bogus cemetery plots."

Deats fidgeted with his glasses then folded them and tucked them
into his shirt pocket. "Gregory Hewlitt killed Sarah Evans. But there is
no Gregory Hewlitt. There is an Anthony Waters who is tied up with a
very large man named Jonas Kalem. Add Curtis Stiehl to the stew. They
stayed in the Dukes Hotel, where they moved many big cartons in and
out. Stir it all up and you have everything but a motive. I'm going to
New York."

"You can't do that, Wally. Your department won't send you."

"I didn't think they would. But you can."

"Now you are out of your mind."

"Not at all. A deputy assistant commissioner knows where the strings
are. Pull one of them."

Heston rubbed a hand across the back of his neck. "I'd like to go myself"—he shook his head—"but I can't. I'll see what I can do."

# Chapter 15

Morning came painfully for Jonas. His head throbbed as if it had been pummeled by a hot iron bar, and his eyes were little more than red slits. His memory of the previous evening was all too vivid up to the point when Madame Sun placed a note with the terms of her offer next to the astrological chart she had prepared. Then the glasses of whiskey that contained more than his favorite scotch. After that his memory was blank until he wakened to find himself sprawled on the floor of his bedroom. Even the sight of the huge tray of food in the sitting room could not evoke a memory of what had transpired after leaving the Berkeley Hotel. He bathed in water as hot as he could tolerate, then stood under a cold shower. Slowly he rallied and was able to pack and be at Heathrow in time for his flight to Milan.

He alerted Ellie to his arrival and was gladdened by her cheerfulness. Nothing had dimmed his appetite and on the train to Florence he found the dining car, where he remained for the entire trip.

Jonas had been in Florence on two previous tours, but had stayed briefly each time. He was familiar with that part of the city radiating out from the Piazza Goldoni, site of the Excelsior and the recently revived Grand Hotel. There, too, is the Church of Ognissanti containing the crypt of Botticelli. From the hotel it was a five-minute walk to the American consulate, less than that to the British. Around the corner was the Palazzo Corsini with its rarely seen treasure of early Italian art.

He had made swift visits to the historical heart of the city and the great Duomo, the Cathedral of Santa Maria del Fiore with its baptistry and Giotto's bell tower, gleaming in white, pink, and green marble. Once he walked to the Pitti Palace on a day that had been insufferably hot only to quickly retreat to the relative comfort of the Uffizi Gallery. In spite of the great city's rank among the world's art capitals, Jonas had done very badly. He had actually seen a small portion of the treasures about which he had so avidly read and routinely included in lectures delivered with the fervor of a native Florentine.

If Jonas was a relative stranger to the city, he was not so considered by the manager and chief concierge in the Excelsior. He had phoned personally, asking for the Belvedere suite, a magnificently appointed penthouse complete with a secluded terrace and commanding view of the city. He uncorked a bottle of Freisa d'Asti, a sparkling red wine with the distinctively unique aftertaste of raspberries. He downed a tumblerful.

The late afternoon sun cast its orange aura over the city. Jonas stood on the terrace gazing past the Duomo to the slopes that rose in the east, where, tucked into the hills, was the ancient town of Fiesole. Somewhere in the scope of his vision was Ellie's villa. He returned to the sitting room and his briefcase. He took out the two vials of ink samples Stiehl had extracted from the Windsor drawing. A third contained the sliver of paper sliced from the same sheet. Jonas was impressed with the ordinariness of the treasure; the vials appeared empty and the slender strip of paper would surely be discarded by a zealous charwoman. They told a different story to Jonas—millions of dollars and a slain policewoman.

He planned to spend the weekend, stretching his stay until Tuesday. He would monopolize Ellie's attention to gain her unquestioned loyalty and also observe her progress in finding or making the materials Stiehl would use in the final execution of the manuscripts. To this point, she had no reason to suspect the role she was actually playing. At all cost, Jonas had to keep it that way.

A sound of bells from surrounding churches announced the hour of six. He lifted the phone.

Ellie welcomed the challenge of guiding Jonas through the galleries, the museums, the piazzas and palazzos. She displayed her growing Italian vocabulary and took near-childish delight in taking him to the sanctified Print Room in the Uffizi and stunned him when he was introduced to the complete staff in the rarely visited restoration laboratories in both the Uffizi and the Laurenziana Library. There Jonas held sheets of centuries-old paper and priceless manuscripts. Through the influence of the Gambarellis, doors were opened to private collections and specially conducted tours by *direttores* of the Pitti Palace and Medici Museum. Ellie planned the daily itineraries and, like a conscientious Girl Scout leader, followed a tight timetable that left Jonas in a state of exhaustion at day's end.

On Sunday a hot September sun shot the temperature above ninety, and by midafternoon Jonas complained that his feet had become too pained to walk another step. They stopped for a sweet at the Trattoria Cantinetta in the Palazzo Antinori. He breathed heavily and wiped perspiration from his reddened brow.

"Tomorrow we'll be in the country," Ellie said. "It's cooler there and we are prepared to show you how much progress has been made on the paper and inks." She smiled, anticipating how proudly she would show Jonas her *mezzo villa*.

"We? Have you been working with some others?" Jonas asked, alarm in his voice.

"I have an assistant, a student from the university whom I turned loose on researching the chalks."

"You didn't tell me."

"It didn't seem worth bothering you about."

"This is wrong, Eleanor. Your work is highly confidential."

"But Patzi's just a college girl. In Florence there are many art historians and college people doing research and they all hire young people to run errands or help with the language."

He forced a weak smile to mask his anger. "You may continue using this Patzi person for another week, then you must dismiss her. Under no circumstance may she spend time in your studio. We cannot have her suspicions aroused."

"What's to suspect?"

He leaned forward and said in a near whisper, "There's been a critically important change in the nature of our work. The Royal Library has commissioned us to create precise duplicates of Leonardo's anatomical drawings." Barely a shred of the statement was true, but Jonas uttered it with the sincerity of an angel.

"Why would they want duplicates? They can make reproductions by the thousands."

"They want to match the drawings as authentically as possible. That's why you are searching for old paper...and inks. Several attempts have been made to steal the original drawings when they've been loaned for exhibition. Now the drawings never leave the library."

"Sounds a little crazy. Next the French will display a copy of the *Mona Lisa*."

"It hasn't come to that, but great art has become so valuable that drastic steps are being taken. Now you can see that our work must continue in total secrecy."

Ellie tilted her head and stared through the thick lenses to his squinting eyes. "I'm pretty good at keeping a secret as long as everything is on the up-and-up. I'm not very good on shady deals."

Jonas's lips formed a small "O" and he said with forced humor, "We're making too much of this. Let's enjoy our day and tomorrow I will see all of your accomplishments."

Ellie had been surprised by the news that her papers and inks would be used to make copies of Leonardo's drawings. She could not sleep, worried that her ink formulations would be detected if subjected to any modern technique for testing the age of a painting or the page from a manuscript. Yet she put on her happy face when Jonas arrived, and proudly showed him her *mezzo villa*. The tour ended in her studio and Ellie was in turn amused, then concerned that Jonas was struggling for breath after climbing two flights of stairs.

He sat at the long table and took the vials from his pocket. "We were permitted to take one of the anatomical drawings from the library and that allowed us to scratch ink samples from each side of the page. We also snipped out a sliver of the paper. You can match your inks and paper to these."

Ellie held the tiny bottles up to the light. "There's barely enough in each for a mass spectrometry evaluation and with luck we'll get a chromatography reading as well." She frowned. "I think we can match the inks exactly, but I'm not sure I can put the ink on paper, dry it, and pass it off as original to Leonardo's time."

"Why is that?" Jonas asked.

"When ink dries, it is absorbed into the paper. The chemicals in the ink migrate into the paper . . . into the tiny vegetable fibers that make up the paper. That migration forms a pattern that requires many years to become established."

"I read something about that," Jonas said. "Can we solve the problem?"

Ellie shrugged. "I didn't think it would be a problem. Why would the Royal Library care, as long as the drawings look exactly like the originals?"

"Can you solve the problem?" Jonas repeated.

"I'm not sure. I'll see if we can accelerate the aging process." She sat on her stool and ran her hands through her hair. "Damn, it'll take time. And money."

"You'll have the money," Jonas assured her.

"I'll see what my new friends at the University of Pisa can do."

"You must tell them it is a research project..."

"Shush! I will be very discreet." She placed a finger on Jonas's lips and smiled.

Jonas smiled back. He seemed mollified and clapped his hands and said jovially, "Show me what else you've been up to."

Ellie described her work area. "You can see where I've spent your money, but I promise I haven't been frivolous. I'll have inks tests made at the University of Pisa."

"Be sure to include a test for a paint sample, anything to draw attention from the inks."

"I can do that," she replied. Jonas's concern for security was obsessing him, she thought, but perhaps it was all part of the assignment.

"The test will tell me exactly what ingredients were used in making the inks used on the original manuscript. After formulating matching inks, I'll apply them to the papers, dry them, then scratch off samples just as you did with the original drawing. Then I'll run new mass spectrometry tests and compare the new to the old. I can't predict how the inks will be absorbed by the paper, but I'm aware of the problem and will find a solution."

"Won't that depend on the paper itself? What tests will you run on the paper?"

"There are several to test the fiber content, but I won't have to age-proof it. After all, every sheet is dated to the late fifteenth or early sixteenth century. Some have beautiful watermarks verifiable to a period from about 1460 to 1510. No one knows exactly when the marks were first or last used. Each sheet is a minimum of thirty-by-twenty centimeters...just as you specified."

Jonas leafed through the assorted sheets. "Nothing more than pieces of paper," he said with mild amazement. He brought each close to his squinting eyes. "Yet they are exquisite."

"This was a gift." Ellie held up an old piece of paper. "And I paid four hundred dollars for this one," she said, pointing to another. "That's almost three quarters of a million lire! But look at the watermark." She held it in front of a strong light. Then she held others to the light.

Jonas leaned close to see the distinctive thin lines running in one direction, more widely spaced and thicker lines running in the opposite. Near the center of the sheets was the outline of an animal or flower. The designs were crude, but identifiable, whether of a turtle, a bull's head, or a religious symbol.

"Watermarks on the paper of fifteenth-century drawings in the Uffizi are similar to these," Ellie said in a scholarly tone.

"What luck with the chalks?" Jonas asked.

"Not good news. I have red but no black."

"Strange. Why not black?"

"Black chalk used during the Renaissance was quarried somewhere in Italy, but no one seems to know where. Naturally black chalk hasn't been available for three hundred years. We can't compound it either, not so it couldn't be detected."

"That is bad news. You feel that black chalk could be detected as something made in the last three hundred years?"

"There would be that risk."

Jonas heard the word "risk" and shuddered. Would the skeptics be suspicious if none of the drawings contained black chalk? That would be a problem for Giorgio.

Neither he nor Ellie had seen Patzi enter the studio from the patio. She stood by her desk waiting to be acknowledged by Ellie. She wore jeans and a cotton blouse. She stepped noiselessly in her white Nikes. Her brown hair was cut short, the whites of her eyes contrasted with a deeply tanned and rather pretty face. Ellie looked past Jonas and saw her.

"*Patzi, salve!*"

Jonas turned, surprised they were not alone. He stared at the girl, who had quietly returned Ellie's greeting.

"How long have you been standing there?" he demanded.

"A minute, signore," Patzi responded, intimidated by the huge man's thunderous question.

Ellie stepped between them. "Patzi, this is Mr. Kalem. You've heard me speak of him. He has paid us a visit and wanted to see my studio and the work I've been doing. I thought you would be in classes today."

"I forgot some books, Ellie. I . . . I did not know I would disturb anyone." She gathered the books and dashed for the door. "*Scusi*, I am sorry."

Ellie watched Patzi scurry down the terrace to her car and laughed nervously. "You scared the hell out of her."

"What did she overhear?"

"Nothing she and I haven't discussed before."

"You talked to her about making black chalk and five-hundred-year-old inks?"

Ellie smiled. "In the scheme of things, chalk really isn't very important to Patzi. Her biggest concern these days is a young man named Amedeo."

Jonas returned to the Excelsior. His mood was mixed; Ellie was making excellent progress in spite of the problem with the black chalk. But she had brought an outsider into her confidence. Perhaps he made too much of it but a curious student could talk to friends, and however innocently spoken, her words would be remembered at a later time when news of the newly discovered Leonardos would be on the lips of everyone in Florence. Ellie must tell Patzi she was no longer needed. A week was too long to wait.

It was nearly seven o'clock. Stiehl had had several days to study Giorgio's drawings. Jonas placed a call to New York and was greeted by Stiehl's angry voice demanding to know why he had been "dealt a stack of Xerox copies."

"They're crisp and clean, all right. That's the damned trouble," Stiehl continued. "I have no feel for the original material... there's no depth or character to the shadowed areas.

"Giorgio insisted on retaining the originals. When you execute the final drawings, you'll have both the originals and Giorgio to guide you. Your instructions were clearly spelled out and I'm sure Tony can answer any additional questions you—"

"Screw Tony. I should have been with you when Professor Burri turned over the drawings. The same goes for the paper and inks. And the quills. It will take months to learn how to use them without dropping blobs of ink. If Leonardo were alive today, he wouldn't use a goddamned goose quill."

"You agreed to use authentic instruments."

"And I will. A quill is a crude device to carry ink and draw a line. I have to constantly dip the damned thing into an inkpot. Leonardo devised pens that held ink. I know that's true. Besides, it's the result that counts and I doubt there's a person in the world who could detect whether I used a quill or a pen I made myself. And, incidentally, that's what I'm doing."

"Have you discussed this with Tony?"

"No, and I don't plan to."

"I've authorized Tony to speak for me."

"Then unauthorize him. I'm not taking orders from Tony and that's final."

Jonas paused for a full minute, then interrupted the long transatlantic silence. "Keep an open mind, Curtis. Don't start any arguments. Tony can be very stubborn. *Very* stubborn."

Each said their good-byes. The line Tony used to monitor the conversation was the last to go silent.

# Chapter 16

Tony waited until he heard two clicks and a dead phone line, then he turned off the monitor and rewound the cassette. He listened to the conversation twice before going ahead with the inevitable confrontation. Stiehl's new studio was secluded in the northeast corner, isolated and blessed with abundant natural light.

Quietly Tony entered the studio. He edged to within a few feet of Stiehl before the surprised artist discovered he was not alone.

"You might show the courtesy of knocking."

"Was I being rude? I thought I was quiet as a church mouse," Tony said in a mocking way. "I've come to see how you're getting on and how I might help."

"I'm getting on as well as all this secondhand crap will permit." He waved at the mounds of drawings, reproductions, and photographs spread over his drawing table and the work surfaces surrounding him.

"You've bitched and criticized from the moment I gave you all that 'crap,' as you call it." Tony leafed through a stack of Stiehl's sketches. "Now I find you're taking your complaints directly to Mr. Kalem."

"How would you know?"

"It's my business to know. We're engaged in a bloody damned expensive project and we each have our responsibilities. Part of mine is to see that you live up to yours." He thrust the phone receiver at Stiehl. "You were complaining to Mr. Kalem about Xerox copies, and you don't like the quills you agreed to use."

Stiehl suspected that his call from Jonas had been monitored. Now Tony confirmed it. "I'm not going to argue with you about quills and pens. If I achieve the correct result with a five-hundred-year-old quill or a pen I made yesterday, it won't matter."

"You agreed to use quills. Anything else and you've violated your agreement."

Stiehl pushed a box toward Tony. It contained a dozen pale yellow turkey quills. He selected one, cut it to a length of about eight inches, removed the feathers, tapered the end, then created a writing edge by cutting squarely across the quill and narrowing the shaft to a point. Next he cut a slit three quarters of an inch long and inserted a sliver of steel shaped like an "S," positioning it so that it formed a well for the ink.

"If you'll keep an open mind, you might learn something." He handed Tony the quill. "That pen is the same design that's been used for fifteen hundred years. Whether its a goose or turkey feather or a bamboo reed, the design and the problems it creates are the same."

He spilled the pens onto the table. He chose one from the pile. "Here, this looks like the best of the lot. I'll put ink in it and you write a couple of sentences on that piece of paper." He squeezed a small amount of ink from a medicine dropper into the hollow shaft of the reed, then handed the instrument to Tony. "Write slowly," he cautioned.

Tony aimed the point of the pen to the paper and slowly began writing. He carefully wrote across the page, then lifted the pen and returned to the left side of the paper. A drop of ink fell onto the sheet. "You put too much ink in it," he complained.

"Then you load the ink. Put in too little and you have to reload after every two or three words. That's no good, I can't draw that way. Too slow. It causes an uneven stroke."

"You'll have to practice more. If that's how it was done, you can do it, too," Tony said firmly.

"I'll say it again, and for Christ's sake, listen to me. I don't have to master the quill. It makes no sense. I've researched writing instruments from the Egyptians to the ballpoint. I can make pens identical to those used by Leonardo, and in fact I turned my apartment into a quill factory until I realized it was nonsense to use such an unreliable device." He smiled, amused by the memory of gathering turkey and goose feathers from New Jersey farms. "I threw out the feathers and bought a small metal lathe and reshaped the nibs on these fountain pens. They're specially made for calligraphers. I get an ink impression identical to a quill and without the problems. Here are the pens I've made." He held several in his hand and offered them to Tony for examination.

Tony took the pens, unsure of what to look for. "There must be a damned good reason you've been instructed to use a quill."

"Not a good one. Every writing instrument imparts a distinctive mark to the paper, thick or thin lines depending on how the nib is angled. With a microscope the expert sees the peculiar characteristics of the quill; uneven ink flow, an erratic wear of the nib, imperceptible splotches of ink, and imperceptible scratches in the paper a smooth metal tip wouldn't create."

"You're saying an expert can detect the differences, that he can discover minute differences under a microscope."

"Yes, he can see those things. I can, too. So I make a pen that holds ink, won't drip, and makes marks just like a goose quill. There is only one difference: I can begin to draw immediately instead of training myself for a year before I've mastered a technique I really don't need."

"Are you saying that an expert can't distinguish between your pen and a quill?"

"No more than you can tell me he can."

"Then damn it, there's a risk and you must use the quill." Tony had referred to risk-taking with the same trepidation he recalled hearing Jonas invoke many times.

"You're welcome to an opinion, but I'm using my pens and that's final."

"You conceded there's a risk..."

"That's your conclusion. I said I doubted that a difference could be detected. For that matter, Leonardo probably used a metal pen. After all, his manuscripts aren't covered with ink droppings, and so my drawings and all the difficult handwriting must also be clean. Right-to-left handwriting in an unfamiliar language isn't something I want to tackle using a quill."

Tony showed his impatience, "You're to follow instructions."

"Tony, you've grown tiresome with this bullshit about orders and instructions. I'm responsible for creating the drawings. That's what I'm doing, and the sooner you leave the quicker I'll get on with it." He returned to his high-backed swivel chair, leaned over his work, and gave Tony his back.

Tony's reaction was spontaneous. He gripped Stiehl's right shoulder and spun him half a turn so they squarely faced each other. He thrust the pointed end of a quill to Stiehl's throat, scraping the skin. A smudge of ink mixed with a line of blood that oozed from the scratch. "The quill... the bloody, fucking quill. Your orders are to use it. Now use it! You hear me?" Tony shouted.

Stiehl's right hand reached behind him and pawed at the table until his fingers wrapped around a pair of long-bladed scissors. With his left hand he pushed Tony away, then raised the scissors threateningly. "I asked you to leave so I can get on with my work."

The chromium blades reflected the bright studio lights. Tony retreated. There was no doubt he could overcome his slight disadvantage, but it appeared he would concede a small defeat. It buoyed up Stiehl's confidence. He asked a question that had been on his mind since his meeting with Jonas in the Dukes Hotel.

"Did you know a Constable Sarah Evans while you were at the Royal Library?"

He noticed that Tony tightened the grip on his hand and shifted his eyes to the window.

"Of course I knew her. But as an assistant librarian. It wasn't until after her accident that I learned she was a policewoman."

"What did you think of the way she died?"

"It was bloody awful, but it's none of my business and none of yours. Now I'm saying for the last time that you're expected to use quills, not some homemade pen that could shoot down the whole project. If you refuse, I will tell Mr. Kalem."

"If you don't, I will," Stiehl said.

He lay the scissors on the table and stared in silence at Tony who seemed to be struggling with his parting words. Stiehl had stood up to him. Finally, Tony spoke.

"We've gotten rather worked up over the issue of pens and quills. I apologize for pushing the matter. But it is something you will have to face with Mr. Kalem."

Stiehl picked up the scissors and slapped the closed blades against his palm. "Yes, it's been foolish." He showed no sign of accepting Tony's veiled offer of peace.

Without further comment, Tony turned and walked off.

Tony shut himself into Jonas's cavernous office. The draperies were pulled across each window, shutting out the afternoon's bright sunlight. The dim light from a single lamp did little to penetrate the vast darkness. He sat behind Jonas's oversized desk, his arms crossed, his head bowed. He retraced everything that had happened since he last sat on the other side of the desk. He recalled the rainy night in Windsor when he sat beside Sarah Evans, driving toward Windsor Castle on the Datchet road.

He remembered looking at her, how she had leaned forward to look for the turnoff into the Castle grounds, how only the instrument lights on the dashboard illuminated her. He remembered that she was very pretty. He clenched his fist as he remembered striking the paralyzing blow to her neck... then, the sounds of the car crashing against the wall.

"Mr. Waters? Mr. Waters, are you in here?" Edna Braymore stood inside the door at the far end of the office. She was dressed in a severely tailored charcoal suit, her graying hair combed back. Edna Braymore had been Jonas's executive secretary and office manager for twelve years. She was humorless, diligent, and effective. "The police are on the phone; a Detective Tobias inquiring about you and Mr. Stiehl."

Tony was on his feet. "What have you told them?"

"I've said nothing. He asked for Mr. Kalem, and when I told him he was away, he asked if you were employed here. I said I would find someone to answer his questions and came to find you."

"You did the correct thing. I'll take the call."

"He's on line one."

He waited for her to close the door, then pressed the button for line one. "May I help you?" He spoke without a trace of an accent.

"This is Alex Tobias, New York police. Who am I talking to?"

"Albert Kalem, Jonas Kalem's brother."

"Sorry to intrude, Mr. Kalem, but do you have an employee named Anthony Waters?"

"Waters... Anthony Waters..." Tony repeated the name slowly as if he were scraping at the far edge of his memory. "Oh, that would be Tony Waters. He has never been what we call an employee, but my brother did use his services from time to time."

"Do you know where I can find him?"

"Not here, certainly. He and my brother had some kind of falling-out. Waters moved away from the city, I believe."

"When did this happen?"

"Within the year. I don't recall exactly."

"Do you have an address... a phone number?"

"I don't, Inspector... or is it Detective?" Tony asked innocently.

"I'm chief of detectives, Mr. Kalem."

"If the matter is urgent, I'll check with our personnel people but you'll have to call tomorrow."

"That's all right. We'd like the information if you can help us. Do I understand that your brother is out of the country?"

"I don't keep tabs on his whereabouts," Tony replied sharply.

There was a pause, then Tobias asked, "Mr. Kalem, I'm also interested in a man named Curtis Stiehl. Does that name mean anything..."

"Isn't this a bit irregular, Chief Tobias? Perhaps you should tell me the purpose of your inquiries."

"I understand your concern, and I can only ask for your cooperation. I received an inquiry from London Friday afternoon on Waters and Stiehl. My hopes are that you will tell me if they're employed by your company."

"Of course we'll cooperate, if it's important."

"It is. Do you recognize the name Cutis Stiehl?"

"I don't know the names of all our recently hired people but will look into it."

"I'll call in the morning."

"If I'm not here, ask for Miss Braymore." He set down the phone and signaled for Edna Braymore.

"Chief Tobias was making inquiries for the London police. A most embarrassing affair, Miss Braymore, all over an incident that occurred during the summer. It involved a contract for the purchase of a piece of land south of London, which, when I investigated, proved to be worthless. I considered the arrangement fraudulent but the estate agent thought otherwise and has pursued it in the courts. As I felt obligated to complete my assignment for Mr. Kalem, I have assumed another identity to avoid harassment. It's all so petty. Can we let this be our secret?"

Tony played the scene flawlessly. He forced an ingratiating smile. "This Tobias chap will phone tomorrow and I want you to answer his call. You will say you have no further information on Anthony Waters and you will acknowledge that Curtis Stiehl is an employee and was in London with Mr. Kalem. But do so only if Tobias specifically indicates that he knows Stiehl was with Mr. Kalem. I told Tobias I was Mr. Kalem's brother. Albert was the name I used."

"But Mr. Kalem doesn't have a brother," Miss Braymore interrupted. "What if that's discovered?"

"Unlikely. Please understand that I did not wish to have my personal embarrassment involve Mr. Kalem in any way. Tell Chief Tobias you have no record of my whereabouts... that I have not been seen for several months."

Miss Braymore dutifully recorded her instructions in a shorthand pad. Her usual calm was becoming unstuck; she was plainly confused by

Tony's deception. "I'm afraid Detective Tobias may come to the office to speak with us in person."

"That crossed my mind. Give him as little time as possible, but be courteous. Reveal nothing more than what I have told you."

"But if he should talk to others. They have seen you here in the past few days."

"They've seen me as Keith Habershon. And I've kept apart from the staff since returning."

"It all seems so strange . . . that they would ask the New York police to search for you because of a misunderstanding over the purchase of some property."

"You don't understand the English." Tony smiled. "A contract is a bond not to be broken. It's tradition and it's a bloody bore."

Miss Braymore easily saw past the effete Keith Habershon disguise to Tony Waters's strong, smiling face. "I think we can take care of Detective Tobias, Mr. Waters, but please don't get into any more disagreeable situations."

Tony waited until he was alone, then returned to sit behind the great desk. There was risk in bringing Miss Braymore into his confidence, but the greater risk was in silence. It had taken Walter Deats seven days to uncover his identity; his Keith Habershon cover could crumble in less than two days. Stiehl had become obstinate, his growing independence made supervision of his work nearly impossible, and he had asked about Sarah Evans. Tony was the clear loser in the earlier confrontation over the quills. *He had turned his apartment into a pen factory. What else was he doing without Tony's knowledge or Mr. Kalem's approval?* Stiehl could grow careless and may have shifted more of his work away from the security of his studio.

Tony stayed in the office for the remainder of the day, then minutes before five o'clock asked Miss Braymore for Stiehl's address. He departed through a small door off a narrow balcony suspended halfway up the high library walls.

# Chapter 17

Stiehl was living in the small city of Hoboken, New Jersey, because he knew the territory and would be closer to his daughter Stephanie. A square mile of ethnic neighborhoods, Hoboken was chockful of family-owned grocery shops, taverns, and small churches. The first-ever game of baseball was played on its Elysian Fields, and John Jacob Astor built a summer home along the Hudson River, though no plaque marked the spot. There was the little stuff of history in Hoboken but no greatness. But then, Hoboken had never laid claim to any.

A cab took Tony the short ride through the Lincoln Tunnel. Police barricades were set across the streets leading off the main avenue, and lights had been strung over the streets; bunting and flags fluttered from wires stretched between houses and telephone poles. Stiehl lived in a converted brownstone in a second-floor apartment. A bay window overlooked the intersection of Garden and Eleventh Streets.

"There's a street carnival goin' on," the driver announced.

"Drive as close as you can to Garden Street," Tony directed.

"I've been here three times in my life, mister. All I know is it's down where them people are. You'll have to walk."

Tony walked toward the sounds of a steel band and a blue haze rising from smoking braziers. The humid air captured the odors of broiling sausages and skewered lamb; the sweetly spiced scent of peppers, nuts, and pastries blended with unshucked corn roasting over charcoal. A trio of accordionists dressed in Bavarian costumes marched past. Crowds were gathering—chattering, laughing, some dancing a polka to music that had not yet begun.

On Garden Street the strings of lights were even more profuse, the colored bulbs casting their variegated glow in the growing darkness. Emblazoned across a banner that stretched the width of the street were the words ST. TERESA BLOCK PARTY.

Tony continued on Garden Street to 126. He had picked either a poor night or the best of all nights to break into Stiehl's apartment. The crowds concealed him when he stationed himself across the street, where, unnoticed, he sized up the situation.

He studied the building, his eyes moving from window to window. The curtains in the bay window were pulled aside and Stiehl could be clearly seen looking down to the crowds. A young girl was beside him. His daughter, Tony correctly assumed. The figures disappeared, then the lights in the bay window went out. Minutes later Stiehl and Stephanie walked from the entrance and were quickly absorbed by the crowd.

Tony waited until he was certain that Stiehl was caught in the spirit of the block party. Then he moved out of the shadows and crossed the street. He reached the steps leading to the vestibule when two men ran by him and into the building. Again he waited. Lights went on in the rooms where the men had gone. Tony darted up the steps.

In the dimly lighted vestibule he found six mailboxes with a name and doorbell under each. Stiehl's neatly printed name was under a box that had a crudely stenciled "2A" above it. The door leading to the upper floors was locked. A phonograph played behind the door leading into the first-floor apartment, the music contrasting with the jumble of street sounds. He took a set of steel probes from his pocket and kneeled to pick the lock. The dim light was less a handicap than was the noise from the street. He wanted to hear the pieces of metal in the lock sliding against each other. Then new sounds came from laughing voices and footsteps growing louder as they raced down the stairs. He stepped beside the door just as two children flung it open and continued through the vestibule and out to the party.

Tony caught the door before it closed and quickly ran up to the second floor. The lock to Stiehl's apartment was a Schlage—durable, common, and easily picked. He inserted a thin probe, then with a vibrating motion moved the tumblers into position and turned the chamber. It did not move. He tried again with a stouter probe: this time the handle turned. He entered into what had formerly been a bedroom and now served as a living room with its wide, high bay windows. Glints of red and blue light shone eerily through the curtains. In the middle of the bay he could make out a long table, and on it a metal lathe, assorted power tools, and a small drill press. Before turning on a light he pulled the curtains.

Street noises blotted out the soft creaking sound of the dry floorboards, and just as he switched on the lamp he realized he was not alone. He swung around expecting to find Stiehl glaring at him but he saw only a dark object falling toward his head.

He turned to avoid a direct blow and a thick length of wood glanced over his ear splitting the skin. He was thrown off balance but his instincts remained sharp. From a crouch he reached out to grab his attacker.

The weapon arced through the air again, this time crashing into the lamp. Now only a trickle of light came through the curtains. Tony lunged forward, his powerful hands searching for the legs of his assailant. Then the hunk of wood crashed painfully onto the bone at the top of his shoulder. As he frantically reached out again he was struck a final time. The last blow was devastating and sent him sprawling on the floor.

Immediately the attacker turned Tony onto his back then pressed an ear to his chest. He found a towel in the bathroom, soaked it, and wrapped it around Tony's bleeding head.

He retrieved the lamp, found another bulb, then set it in the center of the table. He next took a camera and took shots of the machines, the boxes of pens and quills, and the half-dozen pages of sketches and notes found beside the lathe. Finally he shone the light on Tony and finished off the roll of film.

The attacker turned Samaritan inspected Tony's ear and the cuts higher up on his scalp. Apparently satisfied that the damage was not serious, he switched off the light and left Tony to the emptiness of the apartment.

Tony remained unconscious for ten minutes, then experienced additional minutes of semiawareness. The pain in his head and shoulder intensified, and when he was fully conscious, he discovered the wet towel and ran it over his face, then pressed it against his bleeding, hot ear. He attempted to push himself into a sitting position but his shoulder felt as if a barbed needle had been twisted deep inside him. He fell to the floor and lay motionless.

He could hear the singing from the crowds outside the window; a brass band playing off-key paraded by. The pain became near paralyzing, then lessened. He gripped the leg of the table and pulled himself to a sitting position. For an hour he sat, painfully awake at times, thankfully asleep at others.

The door to the apartment opened, and the light from the hall spilled over him.

"What in hell..."

"It's me. Tony." He struggled to his feet, reaching for an anchor to steady his unsteady legs.

"You sneaking bastard. You've gone too far." Stiehl flipped on the ceiling lights.

"Stop acting so damned tough and help me." Tony found a chair and fell into it, his head sagging and the towel now soaked in blood. "You might thank me for taking this beating. He'd've given it to you if you'd returned sooner."

"Let me see what he did to you."

Stiehl gently probed the cuts then dabbed the wound with peroxide and applied a bandage. While first aid was administered, Tony explained he had come to fulfill his obligation to Jonas Kalem.

"Precautions are necessary. The fact someone's been in your apartment is proof that without tight security the entire operation could be exposed. Who was it, Stiehl? What was he looking for?"

"I'd guess it was a Treasury guy who knows I'm out and thinks he can hang another bad-paper rap on me. I was told they might come snooping."

"Could it have anything to do with the da Vinci papers?"

"Only four people know what we're doing." Stiehl shook his head. "No. Nothing to do with Leonardo."

"Don't be too sure only four people know about Leonardo. A call came in today from the New York police. They've been asked by Scotland Yard to find you and me and ask questions."

"Questions about what?"

"I don't plan to find out. They won't know to look for Keith Habershon, and I want to keep it that way."

"I asked you earlier about the policewoman. Is that why they're looking for you?"

Tony didn't answer. He went into the bathroom and put cold water on the cuts. Then he sat at the table that held Stiehl's metal-working tools and the pens he had made.

"I came to see your goddamned pen factory and, having nearly lost my life doing that, feel entitled to an explanation of what I'm looking at and what you've been up to." There was the tiniest glint of humor in the way he said it. He may well have been on a fool's errand, but had came close to a tragedy.

"It's all right there," Stiehl said. "A few tools, some strips of thin steel, and a box of pens."

Tony picked up several pages of drawings. "What are these?"

"Designs for the pens I've made. They can't be bought, so I made them."

Tony was hurting and was in no mood to prolong his investigation. "Mr. Kalem won't be happy with our news." He reached the door, a hand to his head. "I predict he'll want both of us out of New York. And soon. My advice to you is stay clear of the other workers."

"Why are the police looking for us? I've done nothing." Stiehl went to Tony's side. "The police have linked me with you and it's you they want. Why?"

Tony didn't answer.

"Why, damn it?" He grabbed Tony by the collar. "Did you kill that policewoman?"

"You're out of your bloody mind." Tony broke loose, opened the door, and rushed down the stairs and out to the laughter and music.

# Chapter 18

September was ending without a cool wind to relieve the humid dreariness. Walter Deats tried to fight off the unaccustomed heat but his wardrobe was suited to the English countryside, not the phenomenon of a hot, breezeless Bermuda high smothering Manhattan.

His plea to Windsor's chief of police for the opportunity to trail Anthony Waters had been agreed to only after Elliot Heston interceded with an informal deputation and a small financial subsidy. But a final decision wasn't made until late on Monday, and Deats scrambled to catch a flight on Tuesday afternoon. His plane was on the ground at 2:48 and the taxi deposited him at his hotel on West Thirty-fourth Street at 4:45. Quickly he registered, sent his bag to his room, and was back in a cab on his way to meet Alexander Tobias at police headquarters.

Chief of Detectives Alexander Tobias stood at the door to his office at the end of a long corridor that linked the chief's command center with central reception. Tobias was in his mid-fifties. He had a broad, friendly face and a full head of salt-and-pepper hair. He advanced down the hallway to greet his guest.

"Welcome, Superintendent. Sorry it's like a sauna in here but our air conditioner's on the fritz."

Deats gripped the detective's hand. "Elliot sends his regards."

They entered the office exchanging the idle banter of two professionals. Tobias closed the door then sat on the edge of his desk. "Let me update you." He opened a manila folder and leafed through the pages.

"On Friday Elliot telephoned and asked that we check on the whereabouts of Anthony Waters and Curtis Stiehl and develop a profile on Jonas Kalem. The best I could do was phone Kalem's office yesterday, but that didn't give me much. Kalem wasn't in and I spoke with his brother, who said that Anthony Waters had been mixed up in their organization but there had been a quarrel and Waters was booted out. The brother claims to have no personal knowledge of Curtis Stiehl... said he'd look into the records and asked that I phone the next day."

Tobias stepped behind his desk. "I decided against another phone call and paid them a visit. Quite a layout they've got. Entrance from one elevator bank, exit from another. Tight security. Considerable art on display, most of it good stuff, but I'm no judge of that. The brother wasn't there so I spoke with an Edna Braymore, Kalem's personal secretary, who's also the office manager. She was tight-lipped and nervous as hell. She claimed Waters hadn't been in the office for six months." He sat on the edge of his desk. "Kalem's in Europe, and I find it unbelievable that she doesn't know where to reach him. She confirmed that Curtis Stiehl was an employee but that he wasn't to be disturbed. And when I asked when the brother would return, she said she didn't know."

Deats played with his glasses. "Anthony Waters hasn't been seen for six months?"

"Yep. That's what they claim."

"Strange. We know he was with Kalem less than two weeks ago. Even so, with the exception of Stiehl, no one is minding the store. A bit extraordinary, wouldn't you say?"

"We accumulated some good information today, however." Tobias flipped open another folder. "Waters is one of your boys, so I put him aside, but I ran the other two names past the FBI's Identification Division. Kalem showed up in the New York files, and Stiehl had quite a write-up in the federal records as well as in New Jersey."

Deats tossed his heavy jacket onto a chair. "Good show, Alex. Please go on."

"Eight years ago Jonas Kalem was indicted on a charge of extortion. He overcharged several of his clients who saw to it that the charges were paid, then were paid off for their cooperation. It was a sophisticated kick-back scheme that involved several million dollars. An audit tripped him up and eventually he was caught in the conspiracy. When he was brought to trial, he agreed to make full restitution. A number of prominent companies were involved and they dropped the charges rather than face the bad publicity."

"And Stiehl? What's his background?"

Alexander Tobias did not reply but walked to his office door and gave a signal. Into the room walked a man who appeared more distressed by the heat than Walter Deats. He carried his seersucker jacket like it was an old gunnysack and his tie dangled over a soiled, damp shirt. From his unshined shoes to his scraggly hair he was a tonsorial disaster. But he wore a grin and his face was touched with mischievousness.

He held out a hand and said in a nasal voice touched with an unmistakable Bronx accent, "Hi, Superintendent. I'm Len Bascom, U.S. Treasury. Alex here told me you'd be here today and could I come meet you."

They shook hands. Deats was slightly amused by this most unlikely representative from the august United States Treasury Department. But he was also confused and looked to Tobias for an explanation.

"Leonard goes back a long way with Curtis Stiehl. His story might interest you."

"Stiehl's a convicted counterfeiter," Bascom began, "served a four-year stretch." Bascom described the fraudulent New Jersey municipal securities scheme, Stiehl's apprehension and trial. "I was involved in counterfeiting at that time. Stiehl operated alone, never on a large scale. But he's a pro. Best we've ever seen." He took a hundred-dollar bill from his wallet. "I've carried this for four years. I'm not turning it in until Stiehl goes with it."

Deats ran his fingers over the note. His impression was that it was excellently produced. "What do you need to make a charge?"

"The usual. Passing his homemade bills, locate his presses, or get hold of the goddamned plates that I know were in his house when he was arrested."

"Tell Superintendent Deats why you're so sure," Tobias urged.

"During Stiehl's trial we went through his home with everything but a bulldozer and came up with nothing. Three years later his wife gets a divorce and sells the house. I don't learn about the sale for another couple of months, then I go back to see if it's occupied. The house is empty and I see everything's changed—doors moved, new windows, fresh paint. I check the local real-estate people and find it's up for sale again. I'm thinkin' we shook that house down—Christ, we didn't scratch the surface. They tore the bricks out of the fireplace, then built a new one. Somebody knew about the plates and wanted them more than we did." A drop of perspiration formed on the end of his nose. "Jesus, it's hotter'n a whore's snatch in here.

"There have been two owners since Stiehl's wife sold it. The first was a man named Frank Pearson. He paid with a certified check. No mortgage. Two weeks later he sells it. Again, for cash. The deeds are filed all nice and tidy. Pearson sells to a pension trust account being administered by the Barclay Bank in New York. The deed gets filed under the name J.R.K., Ltd., London, with the bank as agent."

Deats looked up from his notebook. "A London company bought the property?"

"Damn right. The money came out of London but control was here in New York." Bascom turned to Tobias. "Does he know?"

The chief shook his head.

"When the inquiry from Scotland Yard hit the computer, I got alerted that activity's being churned up on Stiehl. I traced it to Alex here. Then I learned you fellows were also interested in Jonas Kalem. Stiehl works for Kalem ... has since he was released from prison."

"We assumed that. They were together in London," Deats said.

"Kalem has a branch operation in London, goes under the name Jonas R. Kalem, Ltd. There's the J.R.K., Ltd. connection."

Deats continued writing in his notebook. "Kalem and Stiehl are a pair, that's confirmed. Who's Pearson?"

"That lead's dead. Probably a nobody to muddy the trail."

"How does Anthony Waters fit in? He was with them in London."

"I don't know this Waters guy," Bascom answered. "Give me an identification on him."

Deats replied, describing Waters as he had seen him in the library in the role of Gregory Hewlitt. He showed the police artist's drawing.

"I've had surveillance teams on Stiehl's apartment all summer. We went in once but didn't find anything more than some drawings and scribbling that one of my men says looks like Latin. I can't get a search warrant or tap his phone, so I'm taking a chance on breaking in. Then we see he's bringing home some heavy packages and what we think are metal-working tools and I say we got to get in there again. Fuck the warrant. I want to do it at night but he never goes out. Last night he does. A big street festival's going on and he has a young girl with him. I take my best lockpicker and we're in his apartment in forty seconds. But somebody has the same idea. I know it isn't Stiehl coming back and I don't think introductions are in order. I coldcock him before he has a chance to run. I photograph the machines and the guy. Here are the shots."

Deats asked for a magnifying glass. Tobias obliged and Deats examined the photographs more closely. "He's not counterfeiting with this kind of machinery. Not money at any rate. But these photos, the ones of the guy you put to sleep. I'll wager it's Anthony Waters. Look here ... across the back of his hand. Can you have this enlarged?"

"'Sure thing. Have it tomorrow."

Then silence, each waiting for the other to speak. Alex Tobias was the first: "Quite an interesting trio we're dealing with. An extortionist, a counterfeiter, and—"

"A murderer." Deats completed the sentence.

Twenty-six blocks north a lone figure stood at a window in an upper floor of the Fifth Avenue Hotel. Tony had not heard Jonas's voice since he monitored the call to Stiehl on Friday. His calls to the Excelsior went unanswered, then on Sunday he was told to expect a call from Jonas on Tuesday. The day was drawing to a close when finally the call came through. An angry voice gave instructions. Tony read them back and was relieved when the conversation finally ended.

He looked down from his window to the famous avenue and the landmark arch at Washington Square in Greenwich Village. He had ventured onto the streets to a drugstore, then a liquor store for a fifth of gin. He was surprised the bottle was nearly empty. Tony Waters knew loneliness. It somehow suited him.

The phone rang and he jumped to answer it before it could ring a second time. It would be Edna Braymore. Only she knew where to reach him.

"Tony? It's Curtis. Are you alive?"

"Of course," he snapped. "How did you know where to reach me?"

"I told Edna Braymore to give me the number. You're not the Prince of Wales, for Christ's sake."

"She's under instructions not to give this number to—"

"Bug off, big shot. Have you heard from Jonas?"

"He wants both of us in Como. I'm going on Friday. Kalem will call with your instructions as soon as he's made the arrangements. You're not to see or talk with anyone. Is that clear?"

There was silence. "Is that clear?" Tony repeated.

"Yeah. It's clear."

Stiehl hung up the phone.

# Chapter 19

Alex Tobias assigned Detective Larry Culp to the stakeout at Fifty-fourth and Lexington Avenue. The black, unmarked police car became an oven: only wisps of air kicked up by passing traffic trickled through the open windows. Deats was persistent: "If Waters is still in the city, our only chance is finding him going in or coming out of that building."

"If you recognize him," Culp said skeptically.

"I will. Somehow I will."

Culp was a new breed of police officer. He was perhaps thirty, a state university graduate, and dedicated to law enforcement. He had earned his lieutenant's bar in June. Tobias had been watching his progress for several years and had the angular, blue-eyed officer assigned to his staff within a week of graduation. Occasionally they closed the windows and turned on the air-conditioning. Then the engine overheated. The relief was momentary.

Deats wrote in his notebook: *Wednesday, 24 September. New York blazing hot and no time to be on the trail. Alex Tobias cooperating. Tell Elliot. Good chance Waters here. Officer assigned to me has arrest warrant. Identification is the key. Assume Waters has changed appearance. Will visit Kalem's offices but expect no better luck than Tobias met with.*

A rear door opened and Len Bascom slid onto the backseat and handed a large envelope to Deats. "Here're the blowups. You won't need a goddamned magnifying glass."

A single, medium-sized suitcase was on the bed. It was tan with stout leather flaps, two polished brass locks, and a long, thick handle. It was double-stitched throughout, and with the unmistakable scent of newly tanned leather. He had seen it at Loewes & Kroll, Ltd., one of two indulgences he felt he deserved as he had shifted to the role of Keith Habershon. The second was in the bottom drawer of Jonas Kalem's desk. He finished packing, then phoned Edna Braymore.

"Are the flights confirmed?"

"Yes. I picked up the tickets this morning."

"You paid in cash?"

"As you instructed."

"Put them by the phone on Mr. Kalem's desk. I'll pick them up in forty-five minutes. I'll need money. Three thousand in tens and twenties."

"It will be in the same envelope."

"Any calls?"

"Not this morning."

"If there are, the message is the same. I haven't been seen for six months."

"I understand." Edna Braymore paused, then asked solicitously, "Are you in any danger?" The voice was soft, the coldly efficient tone gone.

"Not at all, Miss Braymore. They'll tire of chasing and it will all smooth over. Remember, it's our secret and I'm relying on your help."

On the street he hailed a taxi and instructed the driver to take him to the intersection of Fifty-fourth and Third Avenue. He paid the fare and handed the driver an extra hundred dollars.

"Circle the block and pull up in front of 284. If I'm not back in fifteen minutes, you made an easy hundred. If I am, you've been tipped for a fast ride to LaGuardia."

The surprised driver folded the bills and slipped them into a shirt pocket. "You're on, mister. Remember my number: 5603."

Tony crossed to the north side of Fifty-fourth Street and mingled with the sweating office workers hurrying to or from an air-conditioned haven. His attention was focused on the parked cars lining both curbs, his eyes searching inside the cars for a stake-out crew. He saw the black sedan just as a man opened a back door and got inside. He did not quicken his pace, but fell in with all the others who were returning from lunch. He waited his turn, then pushed through the revolving doors and into the lobby.

Deats opened the envelope and drew out two photographs. The enlargements were heavily grained but sufficiently detailed to reveal a scar running across the back of the right hand. The second enlargement was less clear; a shadow obscured half the face. "Do you remember the face?" Deats asked.

"Not too well," Bascom replied. "I was in a hell of a hurry."

"I think I see a mustache."

"Yeah, I think so," Bascom acknowledged.

Deats turned his gaze from the photographs to the building entrance. The sidewalks were crowded. A man carrying a tan suitcase turned into the building and disappeared through the revolving door. Deats stared at the spinning panels of glass and steel.

Tony walked to the bank of elevators marked "39–55." He pressed 39. The thirty-ninth floor was immediately above the two-story-high office Jonas had created for himself. He turned into a hallway off which were the floor's utility rooms. At the end was a single steel door marked NO ADMITTANCE. He took a key from his wallet, unlocked the door, and stepped into the blackness.

He felt along the wall for a light switch and flipped it on. He was in a narrow corridor. Twenty feet along the wall he pushed open a small door and stepped onto the balcony by which he had left the office several days earlier. He descended the library ladder and stepped quickly to the desk. The envelope was by the phone. He checked the contents and slipped it into his pocket. He opened the bottom drawer to the desk and withdrew a Walther PPKS revolver; his second indulgence. Then he went to the center area of the room and pulled open a drawer in the oversized table. He picked out a folder. Twelve of Giorgio Burri's drawings were as he had left them. He opened his suitcase and slipped the folder under several layers of shirts. He returned up the ladder, through the corridor, and back to the thirty-ninth floor.

Deats got out onto the sidewalk and peered over the top of the police car toward the entrance and the twirling door. Then he leaped back into the car. "The suitcase! The one carrying it is Waters."

"Describe him," Bascom asked.

"Look for a tan suitcase with a wide handle and brass fittings. Whoever's carrying it has a mustache. Bet on it."

"Lieutenant, you stay here and get your radio working." Deats started for the entrance, then returned. "Is there another entrance to that building?"

"Through the shops and the bank. I've got the Seventeenth Precinct on the phone. They're three blocks south on Fifty-first."

"Tell them what you know and ask for help."

Tony reached the lobby and paused. His taxi was double-parked in front of the entrance. The black sedan was beyond on the other side of the street. One of the men got out of the car and started to cross the street. Tony edged toward the revolving doors, then damned himself for not planning to leave through the bank offices and out to Lexington Avenue. His taxi was no use to him now; he would have to find one on Lexington Avenue and travel south before turning uptown toward LaGuardia. *Don't take any risks.*

He went into the bank.

Deats walked toward the building, through the revolving doors, and into the lobby just as a man carrying a tan suitcase went into the bank. Deats could see into the bank through smoked gray windows that caused the lights inside to give off a muted iridescence. He was sure it was Waters. He ran into the bank and saw the man and the suitcase exiting onto Lexington Avenue.

Tony pushed through the crowds and waved to a taxi that had pulled to the corner across the street to discharge a passenger. He turned to see Deats running from the bank. Tony shouted at the driver but was ignored; everyone shouts at New York cabbies. Tony yanked open the door and fell onto the seat. "LaGuardia. And fast!"

"Look, buddy, my off-duty sign is on. I ain't about to go to LaGuardia in the middle of the day and sit on my dump in this heat."

"A hundred bloody dollars says you can go someplace and get cool."

The driver pushed down the flag.

Tony saw Deats running toward the cab. "Go, damn it!" he yelled.

Deats reached for the door handle, his eyes glaring, his screams unheard in the traffic's roar. His fingers gripped the door handle as the taxi moved forward. The door was locked and he reached with his other hand to pull up on the lock. Tony had pulled out the Walther and smashed the butt end of the gun on Deats's hand. The intense pain forced Deats to fall against the door, and as the cab gained speed he ricocheted to the street in front of a trailing delivery van. The driver veered left, braking simultaneously. Deats's head had crashed against the street and he lay limp in the heat-softened asphalt.

"Did you hear that idiot?" the driver yelled over his shoulder. "He near kills himself trying to get a ride. You see all kinds."

"Keep going, he's all right. Might teach him a lesson." Tony turned to see a crowd gather around the fallen superintendent. "How quickly can you get to LaGuardia?"

"This time of day...no traffic...thirty minutes if we don't boil over."

Deats had seen him clearly. Tony checked the time. It was 1:10. The next shuttle to Boston was at two. Deats would identify him, he was certain of that. New York and federal police would be alerted. They would cover Kennedy or Newark Airport where overseas flights departed. But he was leaving from Boston. How did Jonas Kalem know to arrange that? *Minimize risks.* His Boston-to-Paris ticket was TWA Flight 810 leaving at 6:40. The shuttle would put him in Logan International at 2:45, and he could be in a room at the airport motel by three. Four hours to kill. He would change clothes. He looked at the expensive Loewe valise and knew he must get a less conspicuous piece of luggage. He stroked his mustache and put the thought out of his head.

"Thirty minutes? See if you can do it in twenty-eight."

"I saw him run right into the car. He was screaming like a lunatic." A bystander who had seen Deats dash toward the taxi was trying to get the attention of anyone who would listen. Lieutenant Culp saw the commotion and was the first to kneel over the fallen superintendent. A patrol officer arrived, then another. Culp showed his badge to the first. "Radio for an ambulance. This is a police officer."

The officer responded. "Four-twelve to headquarters. Need ambulance at five-four and Lex. Repeat, ambulance to five-four and Lex. Police officer injured."

Deats's head lay in a pool of blood; three fingers on his right hand were ripped and bleeding. His eyes twitched open, then closed.

"Get these people away," the lieutenant ordered. The police, now joined by others called from the Seventeenth Precinct, pushed back the throng. The incessant sound of a siren could be heard; then another. A white-coated medic cut through the ring of onlookers as Deats was regaining consciousness. The superintendent tried to rise up but a firm hand urged him back. "Stay put," the medic said sternly, "let's see what we've got here."

Deats lay stretched on his back. His body was going into shock, acting as a massive dose of novocaine to dull the pain that would soon grow in his head and broken hand. Deft fingers felt for further damage. A stretcher was set beside him, then almost magically he was levitated onto it. He was carried to the ambulance and, despite the heat, covered with a blanket. He lay still, his eyes searching the eyes of strangers peering down at him. "Lieutenant Culp, is Lieutenant Culp here?"

The medic applied a thick gauze pad to the bleeding scalp. Another hand touched his shoulder.

"I'm here," the voice answered reassuringly.

"That was Waters," Deats said hesitantly. "He was in that taxi, I let him slip—"

"No, you tried."

"He'll get away—airport... London..."

The officer tapped Deats's shoulder reassuringly, then returned to the sedan and raised Alexander Tobias on the phone.

"A hundred damned bucks and the toll's on me," the driver laughed and pulled in front of the Air Shuttle Terminal at LaGuardia. "Thirty-four minutes was the best I could do."

Tony was out of the door before the taxi came to a stop and placed five twenty-dollar bills in an outstretched hand. "Get yourself a cold beer and stay off these bloody hot streets."

There were no police in sight, only two shirt-sleeved skycaps. He stopped inside the terminal and surveyed the ticket counters and the gangways leading to the departure gates. The two o'clock would depart from

Gate 3. The line of passengers moved slowly past an agent. He started for the line as a red-faced police guard entered the terminal from a door marked NO EXIT. He was speaking into a portable phone. Tony spun, slipped the gun into the suitcase, returned to the front of the terminal, and handed it to one of the sky caps. "That goes on the two o'clock to Boston."

"You can take that right on with you, sir."

"I'd prefer checking it," Tony replied, plucking several bills from his wallet. He waited until the suitcase was on the conveyor belt and traveled out of sight.

Back in the terminal he looked for the red-faced guard. He was standing behind the agent at Gate 2, the phone against his ear. A newsstand was between Tony and the gate. He stopped and bought a magazine and immediately opened it. Then, head lowered, he began reading it as if fully engrossed. A digital clock over the door read 1:54. Tony edged toward the agent.

"Goddamn it, I don't care when the first flight leaves for London. Put a net over every airline that flies there. We can't get him coming into the airports but surer than hell we can stop him from flying out of it!" Alexander Tobias paced behind his desk. "No, we don't have the cab's number! Superintendent Deats nearly lost a hand trying to stop it." He gave a description based on the little he picked up from Deats and Bascom. Culp thought Waters had been wearing a dark suit and added what he knew about the expensive suitcase with the brass fittings. The detective punched a button on the telephone console. "Get Elliot Heston at Scotland Yard."

"It's seven o'clock over there, Chief," a female voice replied. "He's probably left for—"

"Get him at home if you have to." Tobias slammed down the phone. He stared at the squares of plastic, waiting for a light to flash signifying his line was active. He thought of Kennedy Airport, the huge sprawl, the number of airlines connecting New York with Heathrow and Gatwick: Continental, British Air, Virgin, United...even Air India. Newark wasn't as big, but from there a dozen lines flew to Europe.

"Did an alert go to LaGuardia? Why for Christ's sake not? Do it!" He slipped the phone onto its cradle, his exasperation heightened by the trickles of perspiration sliding down his back.

Tony showed his ticket and walked past the redfaced guard holding the phone tight to his ear.

The whirring of the jet engines crescendoed and the DC-9 rolled away from the terminal onto the taxi strip leading to Runway 1331. At 2:07 clearance for takeoff was radioed.

"Elliot, sorry to get to you so late but we've got an alert on Anthony Waters at our airports. Deats nearly had him but he slipped off." Tobias swiveled his chair and rose. "He's pretty banged up. He grabbed hold of the door to the taxi Waters was in and got his right hand badly smashed. His head got a good whack, but X-rays are negative."

"Thank God he's alive," Heston said. "Should I come over?"

"It's not critical, Elliot. Let's wait for tomorrow's report."

"You believe Waters is returning to London?"

"We all think so."

"You don't know what we've turned up. Jonas Kalem was traced to Milan last Friday."

"Are you suggesting that Waters may be headed—"

"I'm not suggesting anything straightaway, but it's just as likely he's headed for Milan as London."

The Boston shuttle taxied to a stop and the passengers began filing off the plane. Tony reached the ramp, where he stood to the side and scanned the corridor leading into the terminal. There were no uniforms in sight and he proceeded into the terminal and to the baggage-claim area. He stood to the side until the bags began appearing on the carousel. Eventually his Loewe bag tumbled off the conveyor. In it were the drawings and the revolver. He concluded that there was little chance he could tell if the area was under surveillance or not. He gambled and went to his bag, showed his claim check, then went quickly to the airport motel.

"Superintendent? Mr. Deats? It's Larry." The lieutenant stood at the side of the bed. "I've got good news. You're a hundred percent except for a couple of fingers and they'll be okay. How about that?"

Walter Deats had no sensation in his right hand; a local anesthetic had deadened the nerves. But there was an ache in his back and his head throbbed. His eyes opened but all was a blur. He turned toward the voice.

"Lieutenant, the American version of one hundred percent differs vastly from the British. I'm in exquisite pain and I can barely see you."

"You're just coming around. They gave you a double jigger of Seconal."

"Where's Waters? Did you get him?"

"Not yet. There's no way he can slip through security at the airports."

Deats's vision cleared slightly and the lieutenant came into focus. "Does Tobias know—"

"The chief is on top of the whole operation. He phoned London. Your friends know what happened and that you're all right. I've been told to tell you that Jonas Kalem was traced to Milan on an Alitalia flight last Friday. The chief wants to know if that information suggests where Waters may be headed."

Deats blinked and turned his head but was quickly jolted by a piercing pain at the back of his head. "Kalem in Milan? No, he won't be there. He's . . . damn, I don't know. I can't think." He looked plaintively at Culp. "Understand?"

"Sure. It's okay."

In the airport motel Tony changed from the dark suit into a pair of brown slacks and a yellow sport shirt. He unpacked the suitcase and carried it to the floor above and jammed it into a refuse container next to the soda dispenser. He wanted to keep the expensive Loewe bag but it was becoming a trademark and it was essential that he blend in with his fellow travelers.

The time was now 3:25. He returned to the terminal and the TWA counter, where he checked on his flight to Paris. Then he took a limousine to the Sheraton Plaza in Boston. A telephone directory led him to a luggage shop, where he chose a conventional dark blue two-suiter. He returned to the hotel and took the limo back to the airport motel.

At 4:15 he was in the TWA lobby. He presented his ticket, passport, and blue suitcase. The agent was solicitous. "I'm sorry there's a delay, Mr. Habershon. We have an equipment problem."

"How long a delay?" Tony asked.

"We're posting an estimated 7:30 departure."

Without a word, he picked up the suitcase and went to the men's room. In a stall he opened his bag and took out the revolver. Something wasn't right. *Don't take risks.* He wiped the revolver then wrapped it in toilet tissue. He opened the door and dropped the package into the towel receptacle. He returned to the ticket agent and checked his bags.

Tony clutched his boarding pass and walked to the passengers' lounge. The sun was falling toward the horizon, creating long, sharp shadows beneath the fuselage and wings of a 747 sitting just beyond the windows. There had been no police in the waiting room before, but now there were two. One was talking with the senior agent, the other stood by the departure door to the aircraft. Then each was joined by a man in streetclothes.

Tony stood at the window, staring out at the planes on the tarmac. Maintenance men swarmed over the plane, but no special crew of mechanics was evident. But there was a special group that was offloading all the suitcases and packages that were being put aboard the plane in Boston. They set them in rows under the left wing of the plane. Two men walked among the rows of suitcases, examining each. They neared a dark blue suitcase, then continued past. Tony sighed perceptibly.

Examination of the luggage was finally completed and at 7:41 the last piece of baggage disappeared into the stomach of the huge plane.

*"Attention all passengers on TWA Flight 810. We apologize for the delay. We will now commence boarding the aircraft."*

It was the last hurdle. But some irony was attached to the delay and the apprehension it caused. The search of the luggage had been a test, occasioned by the recent bomb threats from the South American drug lords.

When the plane left the runway, Tony was deeply relieved; he was reminded of a cloudless day many years before when his crude kite finally took to the wind. He had run faster than all his friends, but the sticks and cloth he called a kite skittered over the ground. His father was away once more. They never shared those monumentally important successes like the one that day when his kite flew above the others.

# Chapter 20

Terminal Building One in the Charles de Gaulle Airport was bedlam. Tourists and businessmen clogged the escalators and aisles; a long line had formed in front of the men's room. Tony inched ahead and, when inside, waited again. He locked himself into one of the cubicles, shaved, and changed to a shirt and tie.

He bought a ticket on Swissair to Zurich. The noon flight would arrive at 1:10. At the Godfrey Davis counter he reserved a BMW.

Alex Tobias sat across from Edna Braymore in her richly decorated office. He dabbed at his neck with a handkerchief. "New York is like a furnace," he said offhandedly.

"It is extremely hot, Mr. Tobias, we're all too familiar with that distressing fact." She showed her agitation; her hands gripped the arms to her chair as if she were being catapulted through a violent storm in a crippled airplane.

"Miss Braymore, there was a near-fatal accident just outside this building yesterday. It happened during the noon hour. Were you aware of it?" He asked the question in the same measured tone as he had remarked on the weather.

"I heard talk among the office workers. I didn't go to lunch yesterday. It was more pleasant to stay at my desk."

Tobias waited for her to continue but she remained silent. He studied her face, then the way she moved her shoulders and legs. Tobias had written the book on body language.

"A man ran from this building and hailed a cab on Lexington Avenue. He was followed by another man, who, as it turns out, was a police officer from England. The officer tried to stop the cab, but instead was thrown to the street. It's a miracle he wasn't run over. His right hand, Miss Braymore, was seriously injured by the man in the cab." He put his hand in front of her. "These fingers were crushed. We don't know if he'll ever be able to use them again." His exaggeration scored the point.

"That would be a terrible thing. But you did say he might have been killed but wasn't. That's something of a blessing." She smiled weakly.

"Don't you think it's interesting that he was an English police officer?"

She did not reply immediately, then said, "Yes, I suppose that is unusual."

"Miss Braymore, two days ago I sat in this chair and heard you state that Anthony Waters had not been seen in these offices for six months. Is that a true statement?"

"I have nothing to add to that conversation, Mr. Tobias." Her nervousness turned to irritation. "I answered your questions and now I must ask you to excuse me." She rose stiffly and walked to the door.

Tobias did not move. "You are perfectly within your rights. You can refuse to answer my questions today, but in due course you will have to respond. I strongly urge that you listen to what I have to say."

She remained by the door. "Then say what it is."

"If it is determined that Anthony Waters was in these offices during the time you say he was not here . . . and if it is proven that you were in any way involved in his escape, then, Miss Braymore, there would be sufficient cause to suspect you of complicity and the harboring of a suspected criminal. That may bring great unhappiness into your life."

She returned to her desk and faced the detective. "For what horrible crime is he accused?" A touch of sarcasm tinged her words.

"For killing an agent of Scotland Yard. A young woman, perhaps of an age to be your daughter. She was merely carrying out a routine assignment but not so unimportant to stop Anthony Waters from brutally murdering her." He lowered his voice. "I'm told she was pretty, but that night she became a distorted, mangled mess. Her face was torn and cut, her chest crushed by the steering wheel of an automobile that Waters converted into her death weapon. Her scalp—about here—along the hair line of what had been soft, blonde hair, was cut clean to the bone, and—"

"Stop! You can't force me to hear more."

"Miss Braymore, when did you last see Anthony Waters?"

She sat staring blankly at an abstract oil that hung on the wall directly behind Tobias. She answered in a soft voice. "Monday. Monday afternoon. But you must understand...he said there had been a problem over a piece of land he planned to buy...that he had gone to see the land and that it had been misrepresented." She shook her head slowly. "He said there was a contract and there might be inquiries. He said it was all very 'petty' and that it would be our secret. Mr. Tobias, he is not a murderer."

"You saw him on Monday? Not since?"

"No."

"When he got into that taxi, where was he going?"

"I can't answer that."

"You know you can. It's best if you tell me."

"He instructed me to get a ticket on the air shuttle to Boston, then on to Paris."

"After Paris—where?"

"I don't know. I really don't know."

"Money. Did he ask for money?"

"He asked for three thousand dollars."

Tobias shrugged. Not a fortune, he thought, but enough to get him anywhere in the world. "Have you heard from Mr. Kalem?"

Again she looked past Tobias to the abstract painting.

"I'll repeat my question. Has Jonas Kalem telephoned?"

"I last heard from him a week ago."

"Where is he now?"

"I don't know, Mr. Tobias, and that is the truth. When Mr. Kalem is in Europe, he frequently travels without an itinerary. We send all urgent messages through the London office."

"Why not Paris? You have an office there."

"The Paris office is really a small apartment. It's more of a convenience."

"The address. May I have it?"

"There's no one there."

"Are you sure? Waters flew to Paris last night?"

Her eyes strayed back to the painting. "I suppose it's easy enough to locate in the directory. Here, the address is in our brochure." She handed Tobias a copy.

He put it in his pocket, then rose. "I trust you understand that we must cooperate with the London police on matters like this."

Edna Braymore finally shifted her gaze away from the painting. "What will happen if you—they—find him?"

"He'll be tried for murder. The English are good at that, you know."

"I hope it's all a dreadful mistake. I can't understand how anyone could take another person's life."

Tobias was at the door. "If that was the way things went, Miss Braymore, I'd be a basketball coach."

The airbus banked gracefully over Lake Zurich, then began its final approach into the airport at Kloten, seven miles north of the city. The temperature on the runway was fifty-eight, a welcome relief from the steaminess of New York.

Tony was in a forward row, and was the fourth passenger off the plane. A trio of arguing Frenchmen preceded him and he fell in so close behind they appeared as a quartet. He showed his passport to an agent who was anxious to wave the line into the terminal without delay. He was relieved that a BMW was available and waiting. The sturdy car could take the twisting Swiss roads and accelerate on the expressways.

His route south would take him through Zug, Altdorf, Bellizona, Lugano, and the border city of Chiasso. In all, a distance of nearly a hundred and fifty miles. He stopped at the central piazza in Lugano for an espresso; from there he could look out over the lake to the distant Italian hills. Except for the brief stopover in Paris he had been in constant motion for thirty hours; now he was at rest, and he reacted to the sensation by letting his memory reverse the chronology of the past three days. Zurich—Paris—Boston—the red-faced security guard—Deats's wild eyes—spiced meats on charcoal grills—the blows to his head. The images came in a rush; he bolted upright, his muscles tightened. He ran to his car.

At Chiasso, Italian police were inspecting every automobile. Passengers stood by as agents rooted through baggage and each car's interior.

A young officer in a tight-fitting uniform asked, *"Passaporto?"*

Tony held it out. "Is there a problem?"

"Have you anything to declare?" The English was nearly flawless.

"No. I've come directly from Zurich," Tony replied.

"Open the trunk, please."

Tony obeyed.

"And the suitcase. Will you open that also?"

Tony obeyed again.

The officer rummaged through the contents. "You may close it." He inspected the interior of the car. Perfunctorily, he smiled at Tony and returned the passport.

"We have had a great problem with drugs coming from the north. Please proceed and enjoy your visit."

Tony followed the traffic into Chiasso, then, led by the signs, drove the final six miles to the city of Como. In the maze of one-way streets he finally discovered the Piazza Volta and the Hotel San Gottardo.

At the reception desk he was handed a message from Jonas. He was to phone upon arrival. He called from his room only to be told by an operator speaking in poor English that Mr. Kalem was not responding to her rings.

"Page him," Tony demanded. The page was not answered.

"Tell him Mr. Habershon is in Como and to return my call as soon as possible."

It was 6:30; the late-summer sun still shone over the old city. He resisted sleeping and paced the confining, small room. His patience grew thin after two hours of waiting. "Where is the fat, bloody bastard?" He stared at the telephone. "Call me, you blubbery son of a bitch! When Stiehl leaves New York tomorrow, they'll be all over his ass. Don't you understand? Stiehl's going to lead them here!" He screamed at the dead instrument.

Not far north on the lake was another phone that had been ringing but was now silent. Jonas Kalem stood on the large balcony outside his room watching a pair of fishermen a hundred yards off the Villa d'Este's pier. Their small skiff rocked in the waves kicked up by a passing speedboat. He glanced south to Como, his lips set in a small "O."

"Patience, Tony. I'll answer your call when I'm ready and you've exhausted your impetuous anger." He was satisfied that Tony had reached Como, Giorgio was a short distance away, and Ellie would join him in another week. He put his attention toward Stiehl and the challenge of managing his safe escape from New York. He put in a call to New York, then waited an obligatory six minutes for the connection.

"Good afternoon, Curtis. The arrangements for your trip tomorrow have been finalized. I suggest you write them down." Jonas proceeded to issue the instructions, then asked Stiehl to read them back.

"Why all the cloak-and-dagger? I can shake a tail on my lunch hour."

"You may think so, but I prefer putting the odds on our side. We wouldn't want someone to stumble onto those printing plates, would we?"

Stiehl was infuriated to feel the cord tighten around his neck. He was about to loose a fusillade of invectives, but cooled instead. "I'll phone you on Saturday."

# Chapter 21

"How is your hand, head, and back...in that order?" Alex Tobias stood inside the door to Walter Deats's room in Bellevue Hospital. "You made the first section of the *Times,* though they managed to misspell your name." He tossed the newspaper on the bed.

Deats looked up from a notebook. "In reverse order, the back aches, the head never was much good, and these"—he held out a bandaged hand—"these fingers hurt like hell, I don't mind saying. If only a misspelled name were my only problem." He glanced at the brief article. "You're good to look in on me."

"Elliot's called three times. I'm beginning to think you're important."

Deats laughed. "He's worried I won't be able to bait his line the next time we go for salmon. The man's got ten thumbs."

Tobias sat at the foot of the bed. "I don't like admitting we blew it when we put out the net for Waters. We covered Kennedy but he went to LaGuardia, then Boston. I've confirmed him to Paris, but after that—"

"After that he went to Italy. Where, I'm not sure, but I've got some ideas. It's certain I won't discover the answer in this antiseptic environment." Deats threw off the sheets and slid his feet to the floor. He sat for a moment, not sure what might happen when he tried to stand. "Are you sure they said my head was in one piece?"

"They'd have you strapped in if they didn't think so. You seem positive Waters went to Italy. Any thoughts on where he might be?"

"None I'd wager on. Let's hope it's not Milan, or worse, Rome. It would take an eternity to search those cities." He stood to test his balance. "There, that's not so bad." He began dressing.

"Look what we've got here," Deats continued. "A man who trades in art and whose ethics are demonstrably questionable, has brought to his association two others with known criminal backgrounds. The first is the elusive Mr. Waters, who I am convinced murdered Sarah Evans, but I'm equally quick to admit I don't know for what motive. It seems most interesting that she had been placed in the Royal Library for the purpose of playing watchdog over an extremely valuable art collection. Obviously Waters was masquerading in his engineer's role and was in the library for reasons other than keeping the queen's humidity under control." He reached for his notebook but threw it back on the bed, realizing he could not write. "Remind me to tell Elliot to have the officials at the library conduct a complete inventory. I can't imagine they haven't already seen to that. Finally, we have Curtis Stiehl—an immensely skilled counterfeiter. The obvious conclusion, at least to me, is they're up to some sort of forgery scheme."

"Interesting speculation," Tobias said. "Any thoughts on what kind of forgery?"

"My instincts tell me there will be superbly crafted pieces of fake art floating about, but, Alex, that is like knowing that somewhere a single grain of sand holds all the solutions to the universe and we must search the beaches and deserts of the world to find it. Rather an insuperable job, eh?"

Deats attempted to button his shirt and Tobias did it for him. "I'm not sure you've got permission to be out of bed, let alone getting dressed as if you're going to leave."

Deats moved in front of a mirror. "Ah, but I am. First I'll have this tired face shaved, then have one of your fine American breakfasts. After that I shall pay an overdue visit to the offices of Jonas Kalem."

"I hope your luck's better than mine."

"You said the reception area is a small art gallery. A man's character is often reflected in his taste for art. In any event, it's my last effort in New York. My allowance is all but spent and destitution is forcing me back to Windsor on Sunday."

Walter Deats pushed on the revolving door with his good hand and stepped into the marbled lobby, then turned to watch the turning door he had seen spin countless times.

He entered the brown-and-gold reception room, aware he was surrounded by music and a mildly sweet and pungent odor. The overhead lights dimmed, and as they did, the spots aimed at each painting intensified and gave off their programmed, subtle changes of color. Then he saw he was not alone.

Seated in the center of the room was a man in a dark charcoal suit who looked up to acknowledge Deats's presence. "Hello," the man said genially.

"Good morning," Deats replied. His eyes went past the man and took in the paintings hanging on the length of each wall.

"Interesting exhibit," the man offered.

"Most unusual lighting," Deats said.

"Are you a collector?"

"Not for my own account. But I represent those who are. Are you?"

"Too rich for my blood," the man answered pleasantly.

The music was interrupted by a pleasant female voice. "Mr. Goldensen, we're trying to locate the books Miss Shepard asked for. Can you spare a few more minutes?"

"Yes, but I hope it won't be too long."

"Give us another minute or two," the voice answered. "The other gentleman... may we help you?"

"Perhaps. Do you have a catalog? One that includes prices?"

"You'll find the literature on the table next to Mr. Goldensen. May I have your name, please?"

"Of course. Geoffrey Beal. I'm a London agent representing several clients."

"Thank you, Mr. Beal. Please feel welcome and if there is any way we can help you, press a gold button on the panel by the chairs." The music returned.

"Have you met the man who owns all this?" Deats asked without turning from the row of paintings.

"No, but my friend tells me he's quite accomplished."

"I've tried to meet up with him but he's deucedly difficult to track down. My clients rather like some of the young artists he's brought along. Is your friend the one whose books you're trying to locate?"

"Yes." Steve chuckled, "Eleanor met Kalem in Washington, and he's put her on an assignment."

As he moved about the room, Deats spoke softly into his recorder: *"There's no particular theme to the paintings displayed... rather eclectic... two photographs stand out... beautiful lake scenes that are somehow familiar... but I can't locate them."*

"Did you say something?" Goldensen asked.

"I slashed these fingers in my workshop before coming over and I can't take notes as I usually do. I find this little recorder quite useful."

"Did I hear London?"

"A suburb." Deats stationed himself in front of the photographs. "Will you be returning to Washington? I'm most anxious to go see the East Wing at your National Gallery."

"I'm leaving for Paris on Monday. Then spend the following weekend in Italy. But if these people don't find the books I've been asked to take over, I may skip Italy. My friend would not be happy with me if I arrived empty-handed."

"I envy you. Paris and Italy at this time of year. Going to Rome, are you?"

"No. Florence."

"Hope you have good luck with the weather. Even now it can be hot."

"My friend is in the country for that reason."

"Is she in Impruneta by chance?"

"Near Fiesole."

Again the music stopped. "Success, Mr. Goldensen. We located Miss Shepard's books."

"That's good news!" Goldensen exclaimed. "You'd think those damned books were printed in gold."

An attractive girl appeared, package in hand. "Mr. Goldensen? Please follow me, I'll show you to the elevators."

"Good talking with you," Goldensen said to Walter Deats, and disappeared behind the sliding door.

"Indeed yes," Deats called after him. "Enjoy your holiday."

Deats spoke again into his recorder. He knew he must capture the names and places: Goldensen, Eleanor Shepard, Fiesole. And the dates: *"Goldensen will be in Italy next weekend. He will leave Paris on Friday, perhaps Thursday afternoon."*

He returned his attention to the photographs and the voice came again.

"Mr. Beal, have you found anything to your liking?"

"As a matter of fact, I have. But I'm embarrassed to say they are the photographs. Can you tell me about them?"

There was no immediate reply. Music flowed again from the speakers. Then the voice returned. "A painting was sold and the photographs are filling that space temporarily. We have no information on them."

"Are they for sale?" Deats asked.

Another pause. "No, they're from Mr. Kalem's collection."

Once more he studied them until the images were fused in his memory. Then he spoke into his recorder: *"Two photographs of an incredibly beautiful lake with mountains rising behind. I don't understand my fascination for them but have a hunch it has not a thing to do with fishing."*

He took a brochure with the prices, then pressed the gold button.

Stiehl made a final inspection of his apartment then wrestled two large suitcases down the narrow stairs to the vestibule, where he was met by a fast-talking young man who gave his name, country of origin, educational status, and list of entrepreneurial pursuits before the luggage was in the trunks and Stiehl was ensconced in the backseat of a car redolent of the too-sweet scent of a cheap aftershave lotion.

Hoboken grew up before the automobile, making garages scarce, and parking spots along the streets even more rare. But as the Gold Coast Taxi pulled away, an inconspicuous Ford Escort followed from its location near the intersection and lagged a respectable distance behind. Neighborhood cars became as familiar as their owners after a time and a new car was greeted with curiosity. Stiehl had seen the Escort on several occasions, but had not caught a glimpse of the owner. He grew more interested in the car and driver after Tony and the unknown intruder broke into his apartment earlier in the week. Everything indicated he was being watched by a Treasury Department detail, perhaps the warden's prophecy being fulfilled.

"Be nice if I knew where we was goin'," the president of Gold Coast Taxi said, "Newark? LaGuardia? Kennedy?"

"Teterboro," Stiehl replied, "and see if you can lose that blue Escort behind us."

"Yeah, I see him. Not real easy around here. Too many lights. Is that guy bad news?"

"He might be. He might also be a guy going to work."

"If he's still tailin' us when we get to the turnpike, he's already at work. Hey, call me Enrico. Okay?"

"Sure," Stiehl replied, his attention on the car behind maintaining a consistent two-hundred-yard separation. For another two miles through the heavy traffic the cars traveled in tandem. He took it as an inconvenience and, for a moment, suspected that Jonas had intentionally planned to have him followed to assure his uninterrupted departure.

They reached the turnpike and Enrico pushed his speed to seventy. The Escort widened the gap to three hundred yards. When Enrico slowed to fifty, the distance closed to a couple hundred yards again. "Yeah. He's workin' all right," Enrico said.

"Screw him. Get me to Airlinx Charters at Atlantic Aviation."

"You got it!" Enrico turned on the speed and in less than fifteen minutes they were at the Atlantic Terminal building.

Enrico helped with the heavy bags and, as he was being paid, asked Stiehl in a hushed tone, "Do you want me to do something with that guy that tailed us over?"

"It's all right. He won't be following me anymore."

A girl wearing pigtails and a tight-fitting pink blouse showed Stiehl the way through a door behind the Airlinx counter. "Hop in." She gestured toward a jeep painted in pale blue and pink and liberally trimmed with chrome.

She drove a short distance to a waiting Cessna 310, its propellers turning. "There it is," she said, pointing to the plane. There were seats for four, but he was the only passenger. He shoved his bags ahead of him, then sat in the first row. He was greeted by another pigtailed, pink-bloused girl, taller and older and prettier than the first. "Good morning, Mr. Stiehl. I'm Linda. Welcome to Charter Flight 3 to Kennedy International Airport."

"I'm not going to Kennedy," Stiehl protested.

"I didn't say you were going to Kennedy, just the plane. Sit tight while I taxi over to the end of the runway. Your flight to Philadelphia is waiting."

Linda taxied to the top of the runway. "I'll swing around beside the plane up ahead."

Stiehl gathered his suitcases and hopped off the instant the plane stopped. He boarded an identical Cessna 310, also marked with the Airlinx logo and painted in the distinctive pale blue and pink. A pilot's face showed from the cockpit. Stiehl thought he looked too young to be a pilot. "Climb in, we're cleared to go."

Stiehl watched Linda's plane move to the edge of the runway, begin its roll, then leave the ground, bank, and turn north. His plane followed. It rose off the runway and quickly banked around to a southerly heading. Stiehl could look directly down to the airport below. He saw a man standing beside a blue Escort. He was holding binoculars and alternately moved from the Cessna heading north to Stiehl's Cessna heading south.

They were on the ground at Philadelphia International in fifty min-utes. At 4:35, Lufthansa Flight 421 met its scheduled departure time. Seven and a half hours later, Curtis Stiehl walked into the terminal building in Frankfurt, Germany.

# Part Three

*...Al Diodario di Sirla Locotentete del Sacro Soltano di Babilonia.*
[... to the Diodario of Syria, Lieutenant of the Sacred Sultan of Babylon.]
—from a letter by Leonardo da Vinci

The chief town of each Turkish province was the residence of a Diodario, who presided over the financial affairs of the province. Hence *Il Diodario*— the Treasury.
—Jean Paul Richter

# Chapter 22

Lake Como is of modest dimensions: thirty-one miles north to south by two and a half miles across the widest point at the area known as the *Centro Lario.* But of Italian lakes, or perhaps in all the world, none is as lovely or so incomparably serene as this blue-watered jewel. The lake is shaped like an upside-down "Y." At the bottom to the west is the city of Como, and across a range of mountains in the southeasterly arm lies the industrial town of Lecco. At the crotch of the lake is Bellagio—old, charming, and overrun with tourists. The northern shore touches Switzerland, the Alps visible in the distance.

South of Bellagio is the ancient village of Torno. Into and away from it twists a road cut through thick layers of stone where years earlier crude tunnels were fashioned. The gray stone blasted from the mountain had been thrown down the steep hill to the water's edge. In the mid–nineteenth century a resourceful and wealthy Milanese banker, Giancarlo Vescovo, purchased land at waterside and set his architect and stone masons to the task of creating one of the most unusually graceful mansions along all of the lake's shoreline. The heaps of gray stone became the building blocks for a great house.

Because the mountain angles sharply down to the lake, the building was designed to sit on a narrow plot. It was forty feet from front to back, and over two hundred and fifty feet from a solarium on the north to a row of stone boathouses on the south. A low portico extended another thirty feet over the water with wide steps leading down into the water.

The villa rose three stories, each with high ceilings and great tall windows with leaded panes. From a boat close in on the water one realized its immensity, yet from across the lake, the building appeared but a large gray dot at the base of the mountain rising behind.

The Vescovos occupied the mansion from the time of its completion in 1885 until Giancarlo died in 1927. It was unoccupied until 1936 when the Italian army commandeered it for use by senior officers and as a weekend retreat for Benito Mussolini. Then Il Duce was captured in 1945 in the village of Dongo, north and west along the lake, and returned the night of his capture to Moltrassio, a town directly across from Torno. Following the war the house fell to the fate of many old lakeside homes. It was simply ignored.

Access to the Vescovo home was extremely difficult, as no automobile could be driven closer than several hundred feet on a road directly above. A rock-strewn path zigzagging up a steep slope had once been used by surefooted mules. One reached the house by boat or, on rare occasions, by a seaplane. A high stone wall stretched along the road, ending where deep ravines prevented even the most daring from making the dangerous descent. At the center of the wall was a heavy iron gate anchored in thick mortar. The gate was welded shut, never intended to be opened, standing only as an ornament.

Over the old welding was a new plaque. It read: IL DIODARIO.

Jonas chose the solarium for the focal point of his retreat. Glass replaced solid walls and the room assumed the appearance of a greenhouse, including tubs filled with leafy plantings and a fountain that spewed columns of water. The furniture was plushly upholstered. An oversized chair was placed strategically at a corner of the room overlooking the lake. Next to it was a console containing dials and buttons for Jonas to control the lights and electronic gadgetry that amused him and gave him a sense of power.

Late-season travelers were still very much in evidence on the lake, particularly on this last Sunday in September. On Saturday, Jonas had accepted delivery of a Riva powerboat at the docks of the Villa d'Este. It looked as if it were in motion even while it was moored. White with blue trim, it was guaranteed to outdistance any boat on the lake.

Stiehl had made his way from Frankfurt to Como. Jonas suggested he spend a day adjusting to the time change, then arranged for a meeting at the hotel. Tony had moved to *Il Diodario* and the last of his frustration melted when he was handed the keys to the boat. Tony gathered up Stiehl and his bags, then sped over the water to the massive gray house. Alone in the solarium, Jonas made a phone call.

Two hundred miles to the south a phone rang. Ellie Shepard lay on a chaise in the patio outside her bedroom. She was naked, a towel draped across her waist. In the breezeless afternoon sun she was hot; perspiration glistening on her tanned skin. She swung her legs to the patio, knocking over a glass, sending it skittering into the garden. She swore at her clumsiness and at the phone company as she raced down the steps.

"Is that you, Steve?"

"Eleanor, hello. It's Jonas."

"Sorry, I thought it was—"

"A friend? I am."

"Of course you are. Don't be offended."

The towel had dropped away during her dash to the phone and she stood naked in the center of the room.

"I want you to drive to Como tomorrow. We've come to the time when we can all be together."

"I think I solved the charcoal problem," she said proudly.

"Excellent. Bring your samples."

She was disappointed by his lack of enthusiasm. "New lab tests on the reformulated inks are being run, but I won't have results for another day or two."

"You can have the results sent here," Jonas insisted.

"How long are you going to keep me?" she teased. A breeze through the open door gave her a chill. "I really have to be here on Wednesday."

"I won't keep you. You'll be free to leave on Tuesday. What's so important?"

"An old friend is visiting. He's bringing the books that I left in New York."

"Your friend...I didn't hear you tell me his name."

"An old friend from Washington. Steve Goldensen. He'll be in Paris on business and I promised to show him Florence. I'm a hell of a guide, remember?"

He laughed. "I certainly do. Plan on a four-hour drive to the Villa d'Este Hotel. Arrangements have been made with the concierge. The last leg of your trip will be by boat."

"Are you on an island?'

"No, but I don't recommend you try coming any other way."

When the weather is agreeable, the population of Windsor swells by such numbers as to please every shopkeeper and restaurateur in the old city. Walter Deats faced less promising problems caused by Sunday crowds—complaints over pickpockets, stolen cars, and lost children with runny noses. The sutures in his fingers made the skin itch and he wanted to break open the cast so he could plunge his hand in ice. On his return flight he promised himself he would spend the long hours studying his notes and listening to the tapes. He had accomplished neither, but fell into periods of needed sleep.

Today, except for the annoying itching, he was putting his attention to finding Tony Waters. Waters was in Italy, he was sure of that. His immediate task was to come up with the resources to go on the hunt once more. He shut himself in his office to pore over his notes. He played the tapes. Over and over. He studied the forensic reports with their horrible description of Sarah's death. He scoured the files prepared by Scotland Yard on the previous exploits of Tony Waters. The Yard had also deciphered the two shorthand notes found in Sarah's pocketbook.

HELDWICKE SLOW IN REPLYING...PHONE MONDAY AND SPEED THEM ALONG. NEED FOR FINAL IDENTIFICATION REPORT ON G.H.

Deats had no doubt that "G.H." was Gregory Hewlitt.

FRIDAY. G.H. BOLTED DOOR THEN TO DOCUMENTS ROOM. TAKE (?) FROM 19M SERIES. WILL INTERROGATE.

Deats read the translations a few times hoping for some kind of insightful revelation to pop up. None did. He turned on his tape recorder:

*"Sarah Evans wrote two notes in shorthand on the day she was killed... she had strong suspicions Hewlitt was using an alias... and possibly knew he was Anthony Waters.... The most significant information is that Waters went into the Documents Room with his briefcase and took something... took what? She will interrogate him... at the Old House... we know they were seen there. As to the Documents Room and the 19M files... a visit to the library should clear that up."*

Early Monday morning Deats was in the Royal Library. It was still closed to the public but he was passed through to the royal librarian's office and a fastidious young assistant with a much-too-perfect BBC accent.

He seemed cooperative and Deats declined the suggestion that he wait for Sir Robin Mackworth-Young to return from his weekend in Bath.

"I'm sure you can answer my questions," Deats said. "Where in the library are what might be called the Documents Rooms?"

"We have more than a few of those, Superintendent. Some contain personal effects of the royal family, others hold works of art, by category to be sure, and they are all now part of the collection."

"How are they cataloged? By number . . . name?"

"Numeric, as a rule. It depends what we're dealing with. Then there are the exceptions that make us all go quite insane." He smiled.

"Does the designation 19M mean anything?"

"I don't see any particular significance to the number nineteen or the letter 'M.' Nineteen is two digits and we have no such classification. Books and manuscripts are classified in a manner similar to the Dewey Decimal system. Statues and pottery and other three-dimensional objects are cataloged by period and type. Art and manuscripts are filed in series, generally numeric, with three, but usually four or five digits."

"You used the word 'series,'" Deats said. "I neglected to include that word. My information comes from very cryptic shorthand notes, possibly very much abbreviated. The specific notation reads: 'one-nine-M series.'"

The librarian wrote the number, the letter "M," and the word "series." "It's so different when one writes it out. The letter M indicates one thousand, perhaps. The reference then might be to the nineteen thousand series. If so, the works would be included among the old masters as we so reverently . . ." he smiled, "refer to them."

"And they would be in one of your Documents Rooms?"

"We use that term, though it's not an official designation."

"The notes were written by Sarah Evans, the young policewoman who—"

"Who died so tragically. She was such a willing worker. I couldn't believe she had been placed here by Scotland Yard." He said the words with deep reverence. "Only Sir Robin knew. But she had learned our particular jargon and probably knew what was kept where."

"Can you show me the nineteen thousand series?"

"Certainly. It's this way."

Deats was led to a room immediately off the reception hall. The room was lined with fireproof cabinets, and two rows of the cabinets were placed back-to-back in the middle of the room.

"You picked a good one. The nineteen thousand series includes the anatomical drawings of Leonardo da Vinci."

Deats scanned the rows of cabinets and looked over the top of the files to the reception area and the door leading out of the library. He recalled Sarah's note. She had seen Waters take something from the files.

"May I see one of the drawings?"

"We can manage that." A drawer was opened and a folder taken out at random. "What have we here? It's numbered 19127 and titled simply *The Brain.*"

Deats was handed a folder and found it held a drawing of a dissected brain. To his unpracticed eye, the paper was good as new, the inks only slightly faded. The drawing was sheathed in clear acrylic.

"Are there any other 'old masters' in the nineteen thousand series?"

"Most doubtful. There may be works by Leonardo's students. This series belongs to Leonardo."

"And this"—Deats returned the drawing—"is it valuable?"

"Of course it would never be sold from the Queen's Collection," the librarian said imperiously, "but it would fetch four, possibly five million pounds."

"That much?"

"It's a Leonardo. And there's only one like it."

The librarian told Deats he had watched Gregory Hewlitt go about his job in a quiet, efficient manner. "Damned surprising he's disappeared."

Deats was unable to learn more from further questioning, so he thanked his host, spoke briefly into his recorder, then returned to his office. He put in a call to Elliot Heston. The familiar voice came on the line.

"Where in hell have you been?" Heston chided. "I've been trying to get you all morning."

"What's so important?"

"Your hand is important. How is it?"

"You've been calling all morning for that? It's coming along, but if I don't get the damned cast off soon, I may lop it off at the wrist. Elliot, I'm coming on to something and I want you to arrange for a special assignment to Branch C13."

"Wally, I can't do that, and you know it."

"I know nothing of the kind. You helped with the New York expedition but that was money from petty cash. Put in a request to assign me to your squad for two weeks. You're a deputy assistant commissioner, you can do it."

There was a long silence. Deats pressed the phone to his ear for sounds to assure him the connection had not been broken.

"Let's talk it over."

"Stay put," Deats responded instantly. "I'm on my way."

Ellie pushed the Lancia to its limits, rushing toward *Il Diodario*. She bypassed Milan and swung onto the A9. The road began to rise, the mountains surrounding Lake Como appearing dimly through the haze.

At Cernobbio she found her way to the grounds of the Grand Hotel Villa d'Este. Carlo Mietto greeted her with his austere, courtly manner. He wore the crossed keys proudly, the tails of his long gray coat signifying his seniority. "Welcome to the Villa d'Este," he intoned with a delightfully accented voice. "Signore Kalem has asked that I call him as soon as you arrive. You will be comfortable on the patio until the boat arrives."

Carlo led her through the hotel and out to a sunlit stretch of white-and-green tile that extended from the hotel to a row of docks. He snapped a young waiter to attention and sent him off for a glass of Campari and soda. Ellie was restless, she had driven hard and was content to stand and take in all the loveliness offered by Lario de Como.

She heard the roar of the boat's engines before she saw it circle around from south of the docks. The man behind the wheel was waving. She recognized Tony Waters and for a brief instant thought of running for her car and speeding away from all the beautiful madness. Instead she returned his greeting, a little giddy and excited that a new episode in her adventure was about to begin. Minutes later the boat skimmed over the deep blue water, a white frothy wake trailing behind. Ellie watched the Villa d'Este recede and the gray spot she marked as *Il Diodario* looming larger.

Eager hands helped her climb the wet steps leading to the portico. She entered a high-vaulted loggia lined with intricate mosaic patterns, the floor of patterned marble, and at its center a round green slab with inlays of pink, white, and black fleur-de-lis. Life-size statues of children stood in granite basins, water cascading over them and spilling in gentle falls to pools sunk into the floor. Broad-leafed plants set in terracotta tubs lined the walls opposite the fountains. Scattered among them were white gardenia plants exuding their powerful perfume.

She walked through the gates into the atrium. It was a square room with a crystal and porcelain chandelier suspended from a beamed ceiling. Into the wall opposite the iron gates was set a fireplace ten feet wide; alabaster figures and brass candleholders were set across the mantel.

"Welcome."

She turned to greet Jonas, who approached her, his arms extended.

"What do you think of my *Il Diodario*?"

"I'm not sure. I don't know if I'm in Disneyland or the Middle Ages."

He took her hand and guided her through another hall to an ornately furnished dining room. The table was prepared for a formal dinner; on it were candles set in crystal and silver holders flanking a centerpiece of white roses and giant dahlias. The table was set for five; two on each side, the fifth at the end in front of the fireplace. Beyond the dining room in a small hallway, Jonas stopped. He pushed a button and a door opened to a small elevator.

"This luxury was installed as a courtesy of the Italian army," he explained.

The elevator rose slowly to the next level. Jonas had not let loose of Ellie's hand and he guided her once more to a wide door. "This is your room." He ushered her into an exquisitely furnished bedroom suite that included a balcony overlooking the lake.

"Do you like it?" he asked almost apologetically.

Her words came slowly. "I'm sorry if I sound unappreciative, but I didn't expect this."

"We shall have cocktails in the solarium at eight. Dinner at nine. We'll be waiting for you."

Stiehl was in the solarium at a quarter to eight. He had exhausted his eyes during a full afternoon devoted to the intricacies of Leonardo's complex handwriting and further attempts to memorize the peculiar shorthand language the artist had invented. He welcomed the break but was anxious, too, for the chance to meet Giorgio Burri and begin the final process of putting finished drawings on paper. And tonight he would meet Eleanor, the "Maiden from Florence," as he had dubbed her. The Art Department would be together for the first time and he knew that was significant.

It was not yet eight when Tony appeared and the two acknowledged each other with a nod. Tony was deeply tanned from hours spent speeding over the lake. Then a loud voice boomed out. Giorgio Burri had arrived, his spirits obviously at high pitch.

"*Buona sera.* It is good to see you again." He pounded Waters on the shoulder as he greeted him.

"*Buona sera*, Signore Burri," Tony replied. "You have heard of Curtis Stiehl, and now you meet him."

"A pleasure, Curtis," Giorgio said with a wide grin. "We can now begin a long friendship."

The two shook hands and Stiehl immediately felt the man's warmth. "I've a hundred questions to ask you."

"And I have a hundred answers. But none of that now. Tonight is special. I have lived on the lake for many years but never have set foot in the great old Vescovo home. It has a richness that only Jonas Kalem could magnify with his... how should I say... *voluttà.*"

Ellie came to the doorway. She wore a plain white dress with a scooped neckline that just showed the swell of her breasts. Around her neck was a gold necklace from which hung an emerald surrounded by small diamonds. She touched it somewhat self-consciously. It had been placed on her dressing table along with a note from Jonas.

The men ceased their chattering as Ellie proceeded toward them. At that moment Jonas appeared and went to her side. "Gentlemen, may I present Miss Eleanor Shepard." The huge man loomed over her, then, with unusual grace, took her hand and kissed it.

Giorgio placed himself in front of Ellie and bowed correctly. "Signorina Shepard, it is my great honor." He gazed at her like a doting father. "You are most beautiful."

Ellie extended her hand. "I've looked forward to meeting you. Mr. Kalem has told me about you." She turned. "You must be Curtis Stiehl."

"Until now you have been the mystery woman in Florence who finds old paper and ink." He accepted her outstretched hand.

"Do I look mysterious?" Ellie smiled.

For that moment Stiehl wanted only to continue holding her hand and not worry about finding the right words for a reply. "Not mysterious," he answered, then added quietly, "but very pretty."

"Thank you," Ellie said. "That was kind of you."

Their eyes stayed on each other's until Tony stepped forward and took Ellie's arm.

"Good evening, Miss Shepard," he said with deference. "The emerald catches the beauty of your eyes."

Ellie accepted the compliment and could think only to comment on Tony's hours in the sun. "You look well with your new tan. I'm afraid I would be burned scarlet." She was polite but her smile had disappeared.

The minutes that followed went quickly for Stiehl, who stepped to the side and observed Giorgio's outspoken, frequently outrageous humor and the effortless way Jonas orchestrated the evening's events. But he could not avoid focusing on Eleanor.

At nine dinner was announced and Jonas tucked Ellie's arm under his and led the group into the dining room. He had chosen a menu highlighting foods and wines of the region. A hot antipasto followed by a pasta in a creamy sauce. Then fish: filets of lake fish—*lavarello* and *salmonrino,* both native to Lake Como. Giorgio seized the commentary from his host rapturing over the *salmonrino.* "There is no delicacy to compare with its flavor, the heartiness of salmon blended with the sweetness of trout." He turned to Ellie. "It is ambrosia, an aphrodisiac should you be unwary."

"That's not fair. I'm outnumbered four to one."

"I shall protect you, Eleanor. But you should know that I am one of the most successful *salmonrino* fishermen on the lake," he proclaimed.

"A commendable accomplishment," Jonas said.

"They are very scarce and difficult to trap," Giorgio continued. "I have developed my own special techniques."

"Will you teach me your secrets?" Tony asked.

"They have required many years to learn and I would be unwise to give them away."

"Your secrets would be safe," Tony replied.

"A secret shared is no longer a secret."

Stiehl was amused by Tony's interest in lake fishing and also took note that Giorgio was not easily bullied.

After the last dish was served, Jonas rose to his feet.

"We have made greater progress than I thought possible and each of you has made immensely important contributions." He lifted his glass and turned to Ellie. "To Eleanor. You have brought the paper and the inks, yes, the chalk and dyes, too. A toast to your hard work and diligence." Glasses were lifted all around.

"And to Giorgio," Jonas went on. "We are indebted to your mastery of Leonardo's life and his works. Your scholarship is the backbone of our collective effort."

"There is no strongest or weakest link in our chain, but if the skilled hand of Curtis Stiehl were not present, there would be no opportunity to succeed." Again the glasses were raised.

"Now, finally, I salute Tony, who is my 'adhering agent.' He adds sharp eyes and a strong body to deal with the endless details which are part of this complex enterprise."

It was Giorgio's turn. "To Jonas. A man who has created a new *Il Diodario*. Because of you, these old gray stones are alive once more."

Stiehl had rarely taken his eyes off Eleanor, and as Jonas toasted each of his guests, he wondered how completely she understood all the ramifications of the "complex enterprise" in which she had become such an important yet innocent participant.

# Chapter 23

From his studio Stiehl could look south to the city of Como, across to Cernobbio, and north beyond the Villa Carlotta to the pre-Alps. Immediately below his windows was the wide stone dock. Not content with the light that flooded through the high windows, Jonas had added panels of lights in the ceiling. Other lamps hung from stanchions spotted strategically around the work area. Bookshelves lined a long wall, and tucked into one were the components of a sound system. Concealed among all the lights and electronic paraphernalia were microphones and a miniature television camera. Buried amid Jonas's opulence was the means to satisfy his unquenchable curiosity and monitor the loyalty of the artist on whom so much depended.

Earlier, Stiehl had joined Eleanor at breakfast. They shared their memories of the previous evening, laughing at Giorgio's flamboyant storytelling. When he said good-bye, he added that he hoped she would return soon. He remembered how she smiled.

He looked below to the water and the sleek, white speedboat. Tony was fine-tuning and adjusting, coaxing every bit of speed the powerful engine could generate. Eleanor appeared carrying a small suitcase. Tony would drop her at the Villa d'Este and return with Giorgio as his passenger. Stiehl returned his attention to his drawings and found that Jonas stood inside the doorway.

"Am I interrupting?"

"I'm still adjusting to this studio, and the sights out those windows."

"Better too many amenities than not enough." Jonas lowered himself into a chair beside the giant drawing board. "Eleanor is confident she's hit on the right formula for the red chalk and the ink, but she needs more samples with both ink and chalk worked into the paper."

"We had a chance to talk about that last night. I told her I would work up a half-dozen short pages."

"What else did you talk about?" Jonas asked with a touch of anxiety.

"Old paper and ink made with iron and gallstones are not my idea of hot topics for such a pretty head."

"Perhaps a hot topic would have been better. I was afraid that if she stayed in Florence without meeting you and Giorgio, she might begin asking questions."

"She asked a few, but harmless, I thought."

"What kind of questions?"

"How did I meet you, for example."

"And how did we meet?"

"I answered an ad for a layout artist."

Jonas smiled. "What else has aroused her curiosity?"

"Giorgio. She wonders why he's so important to what we're doing. I told her he was one of your old friends and besides, he's your neighbor across the lake."

Jonas asked if Eleanor was curious about the Windsor Library assignment.

"Not about the project. She seemed a little homesick and wondered where I lived. That sort of thing."

"Eleanor believes that we have an assignment from the Royal Library. And she knows I have been in pursuit of the missing Leonardos for many years. That's all she needs to know and all she must ever know. She will come back to *Il Diodario* one more time, then return to her friends in Washington. This studio is off limits to her. But of course you know all this, we discussed it in my office many months ago."

Stiehl remembered that first visit when Eleanor Shepard was only a name. Now he could put a face to the name and wasn't sure he wanted her back in Washington.

"I'll be happy to begin work with Giorgio."

Jonas glanced at his watch. "He'll be here in less than an hour. And with his original drawings," he added with emphasis.

"All of them? All forty of them?"

Jonas was suddenly on his feet. "You said forty sheets? But there are fifty-six."

"I only have forty." Stiehl pointed to the forty Xerox copies neatly stacked on the board.

Jonas leafed through the pages. "Forty? Tony was given fifty-six."

"That's what he gave me," Stiehl said flatly.

Jonas picked up the phone and jabbed at the buttons. "*Pronto! Pronto!* Signore Waters, tell him to come to the studio immediately."

"He's about ready to take Ellie across the lake," Stiehl said.

Jonas went to the window. "He'll get the word. Are you sure there are only forty?"

"Of course. I logged and cataloged each one."

The cheeks on the big man were scarlet. "Does he think this is some silly game we're playing?"

The low roar from the engine had stopped. Jonas turned and stared at the door, his hands clamped tightly behind his back, his feet set wide apart. He stood motionless until the door opened and Tony strode confidently into the room.

"I've been informed by Curtis that he has forty sheets, yet you received fifty-six. Perhaps you can account for the missing sixteen?"

"No problem. I have them."

"Why do you have them?"

"For safekeeping. That was my judgment."

"Stupid thinking. Did you think the man was going to sell Xerox copies in Times Square?"

The rebuke was unexpected and Tony showed anger at being dressed down in front of Stiehl.

"Bring them to me immediately," Jonas commanded.

"It was a reasonable precaution," Tony protested. "He can't work on all the bloody sheets at the same time."

Jonas pointed a shaking finger toward the door, his voice low and threatening. "I don't give a damn for your twisted judgments. I make judgments, you follow orders. The other sheets. I want them now."

Tony backed away, glowering. He raised his chin and his lips moved but he said nothing. He turned and walked from the room.

"Forget this incident, Curtis. Tony overreacts at times, and if I treat his mistakes gently, he'll repeat them." He returned to the chair. "How long in hours or days—will it take to complete the first drawings?"

Stiehl shrugged. It wasn't an easily answered question. "I've been concentrating on technique for over six months and I'm confident I can duplicate with a pen—my pen—nearly anything Leonardo ever drew. I'll never master his brush technique or the subtlety of his chiaroscuro, and no one will match his ability to choose and blend pigments. He spent years on a painting, but only minutes on a drawing. To duplicate the fluid line I must draw as fast." Stiehl pushed a small drawing of the infant Christ in front of Jonas.

"If I can't draw that face in minutes, then I won't be able to duplicate the smooth lines he put on paper. To be successful, my drawings have to look like Leonardo drew them. It isn't copying, it's a different technique."

Stiehl stepped back from the table. "When I feel I'm ready to put a drawing on paper, I'll be able to complete it in two or three hours. The trick will be in feeling ready."

"Do you feel you are?"

"Giorgio will help me make that decision."

"It will be favorable, I know."

Tony returned. He handed Jonas a package and was gone as quickly as he had arrived.

Jonas gave the package to Stiehl. "He'll be angrier than hell until he's out on the water." Jonas patted Stiehl's shoulder and walked from the studio.

Stiehl filled his pen and began to draw. His hand moved confidently, the last traces of hesitation gone. At his side were easels holding enlarged reproductions of Leonardo's *Lady with an Ermine,* the *Mona Lisa,* and numerous studies of young women. He had drawn all or parts of them, it seemed, a thousand times. He was familiar with every feature and nuance—with the angle of a head turned and tilted, with the ways Leonardo had broken from tradition, expressing his philosophy of light and shadow. To Stiehl's immense capacity to mimic others he added his understanding of how Leonardo used ink and chalks. From the beginning of his association with Jonas he had sought this inner understanding so that whatever his mind told his hand to draw, the result would automatically appear in the precise style of the Master.

Writing in reverse continued to present a larger problem. He pushed aside the drawings and began again the laborious task of disciplining his hand to move quickly while setting down the unfamiliar words. It required intense concentration to memorize Leonardo's spelling of two or three words, practice writing them with a ballpoint pen on ruled paper, then plain paper, then with pen and ink, and finally write the few words on what would become the finished manuscript with one of the crude pens he had made.

The now-familiar sounds from the speedboat grew louder. He went to the window to watch the boat pull alongside the dock and Giorgio hop out.

"First we must talk." Giorgio said after an inspection of the studio. "I must know you better—how you think, what you know of Leonardo, how you express yourself. Do not be offended by my questions, at heart I am a teacher. I am told you were in prison. Why?"

"I counterfeited municipal securities," Stiehl answered matter-of-factly.

"That is *what* you did. I asked *why*. Why did you counterfeit them?"

"I knew how, and I needed money."

"Could you not use your skills for another purpose? To be an artist?"

"I didn't think so then. I was impatient."

"Who is Tony Waters?"

The shift in the questioning surprised Stiehl. "I haven't figured him out. I know very little about him."

"Do you like him?"

"Not particularly."

"Are you married?"

"No longer. Divorced."

"Do you have children?"

Stiehl smiled. "A daughter."

"Your smile told me it was a daughter." Giorgio touched the tip of his nose, returned the smile, and continued, "When was Leonardo born?"

"1452."

"Where?"

"Near Florence. In Vinci."

Giorgio continued firing questions about Leonardo, and while not prepared for the long quiz, Stiehl was surprised he knew so much. Then Giorgio turned a hundred and eighty degrees and fired more questions about Tony, Jonas, Eleanor, the Renaissance, and finally Giorgio Burri.

"I've never met anyone who has spent a lifetime studying and teaching art. I never thought that is something I could do, and now I think it's the most important thing I could ever do. You could be my father, and somewhere inside I wish you were. But I've known you for too short a time to talk like that."

"Go on. Not to make my ego blow up. You may tear it down. What is it you like about Giorgio?"

"You speak different languages. You like to fish and hike. You have a good life. You smile and make other people happy."

"Those are kind words, and I thank you." Giorgio's tone became serious. "Would you risk going to jail again?"

It was a question Stiehl couldn't give a simple answer to. The quick answer was no. Even in the apparent safety of a studio overlooking Lake Como, he was at risk. He did not give an answer, and Giorgio did not push for one.

The session lasted two hours, and when it was over, both men knew each other as well as if they had experienced many months of a close relationship. As Giorgio asked his questions he roved around the studio. He now stood near a tall bookshelf, and as Stiehl looked toward him, a glint of light caught his eye. He studied the reflection coming off a round piece of glass. Stiehl remembered that first day in Jonas's office, the hidden television cameras and the room with the TV monitors. Jonas was watching and listening. Then came a gentle rapping and a young couple entered carrying trays of food and wine.

They talked as they ate, and after Giorgio drained his glass he began a serious study of the drawings Stiehl put in front of him. His reaction was spontaneous

"*Splendido! Bello!* It is difficult to believe what I am seeing. Your line is fluid and graceful. They are magnificent."

"I worry about the handwriting," Stiehl said apologetically, yet happy with the warm praise.

"*Sì*, there are problems, but you underestimate yourself."

As the afternoon wore on, Stiehl returned to his apprehension over the handwriting. With Giorgio's encouragement, his confidence increased.

It had been a sunless day. The ubiquitous bells announced seven o'clock, and as Stiehl turned on the ceiling lights he was joined by Jonas.

"I couldn't wait any longer," Jonas said. "What is your assessment, Giorgio?"

"It may be a miracle, but in this young man the genius of Leonardo still lives."

Strong praise, thought Jonas, more than he expected, and far more than enough to brighten his round face. "That is the best news of all." He wrapped his arms around Stiehl in a smothering hug. "You are ready, Curtis. When will you begin?"

"Tomorrow, with luck. Maybe I'll have to psych myself up, but if Giorgio thinks it's time, then I'm ready."

"Exquisite." Jonas turned to Giorgio. "You will approve the drawings?"

"That is our agreement."

"Your original drawings," Stiehl said. "Can I see them?"

"Of course." Giorgio opened a small leather folder and took out his original drawings of Folios 4 and 9.

Stiehl examined Folio 4. His first impression was that the Xerox had been an accurate guide. But as he looked more closely, he saw that the writing on Giorgio's original was different from the copies. He compared copy to original and confirmed that a significant change had been made when the copies were run off.

"The writing is different. Why is that?"

Giorgio smiled self-consciously. "Leonardo's words are just as important as his drawings. It is easy enough to decide what sketches he might have made for each of his paintings, but to be inside the Master's mind ... to know his thoughts ... well, that is truly the contribution I have made."

"Are you saying that every damned Xerox has different notations from what Leonardo would have written?" Jonas demanded.

"They are both a fiction, Jonas. However, my originals carry the ideas I am confident Leonardo would have set down. The copies contain what I might describe as idle chatter."

"I've been memorizing idle chatter?" Stiehl asked.

"But not in vain. I gave you Leonardo's vocabulary, and the shorthand he invented. You have not wasted a minute's time."

Stiehl knew that his struggle with the handwriting was not in its content, but in forming the words. He also was aware that Giorgio's news did not sit well with Jonas.

"I see there's more unfinished business between us," Jonas said as he walked quickly to the door. "I am going to the solarium and expect you will join me immediately."

Giorgio sighed heavily. "How unfortunate that trust becomes something to give and never receive. Ah, well, my very talented friend, I must leave you to humor Jonas into a better mood. Begin with the drawings and put Leonardo's writing out of your mind for the present." He placed his hand on Stiehl's. "I will help you. In a few days you will be *una scriba esperto.*"

"You made him out to be Leonardo reincarnated," Jonas said with a measure of approbation. "Or were you building his confidence?"

"If I made him more confident, then I am happy. But you must know that he possesses a rare talent. I have seen many artists at work and I am a failed painter myself, but there is a magic to the way he moves the pen over the paper . . . as if he wills the ink to flow in a way his mind sees clearly."

"All that's to the good. But you deceived me again. First with copies. And now I find there is the genuine manuscript copy and what you call idle chatter."

"I made it clear that I will hold the drawings until each sheet is sold. I have made a concession even so. Two of my originals are with Curtis. It is a fair arrangement."

"You call it fair because you hold the drawings. They must be here in *Il Diodario* where they will be safe. In your hands there's a risk they'll be discovered."

"There's little chance of that. My home is filled with drawings and sketches and old books I have spent a lifetime gathering. A few more drawings would scarcely cause attention."

"But if anything should happen to you . . ."

"Nothing shall happen, Jonas. But neither you nor I are truly safe. Only so long as Eleanor believes what you have told her. If she learns of our plan and how you have used her, then all of us are very vulnerable. I have thought about this and it troubles me."

Jonas slouched into his favorite chair. "I have thought about it, too. How did you come to *Il Diodario* today?"

Giorgio looked at him quizzically. "By that monstrous boat your man runs all over the lake."

"Can you come another way?"

"The road to Bellagio runs behind the villa. There is a gate."

"It has never been used. Welded closed. New chain fences make access from the road nearly impossible. You come by water, and if you leave, you return by water."

"What has that to do with Eleanor?"

"I gave you my answer. You come to *Il Diodario* by water, and *if you leave,* you return by water. There is no other way."

# Chapter 24

Few enterprises run as well as European trains, the Italian State Railway System not excepted. The *conduttore* had noted Walter Deats's bandaged hand and had helped him to his compartment for the last leg of his journey to Florence. The rhythmic sounds of the train were relaxing, and staring out to the mountain ranges with their small towns perched high up, Deats remembered his last conversation with Elliot Heston.

"It's more than a case of murder."

"But what? You've got a queasy feeling about some hanky-panky in the Royal Library?" Heston had replied skeptically.

"Come off it, Elliot, you know that Waters spent the entire summer in the library for a purpose other than installing an air conditioner. It's perfectly clear that he took something. What? Why?"

Heston had calmed his old friend, "I believe you, Walter. I'm convinced you're onto something, and I agree Waters must be found and his friends put under surveillance. But the Yard doesn't go out of the country except on extraordinary cases, and then it's handled very specially. Officially, Jack Oxby is on the case."

"Why is he out of the country most of the time?"

"That's where the stolen art goes."

"That's my point. Oxby chases lost art, not killers."

"He gets his share of both."

"Damn it, Elliot! I've gone this far. I want to find Waters and I need your help. I can't work with Oxby. No one can."

"You know he's damned good, Wally. He's coming at Kalem from another direction."

"Fine. Just help me get to Waters."

"I'm getting heat for financing your New York escapade, and if I authorize travel funds so you can run off to Italy and you come up empty, they'll boot my ass back onto the streets with a rank three below constable."

"I won't fail you, and even if I did, you're too old to be on the streets."

"You're stubborn, Wally. I'll stick my neck out one more time, but if you don't come back with Waters..."

"I'll fish alone."

Crowds jammed the platform in Florence, jostling, shoving, bidding tearful welcomes or more tearful farewells. Italians cry a lot, Deats thought. A porter claimed his suitcase, then led him to a line of taxis. His hotel was near the Arno on the west side of the city. Immediately after checking in, he went to the house physician and had the cast opened and the irritating stitches removed. The hand remained bandaged, all but his thumb. He marveled that such an ordinary part of the body could be so essential.

In the morning he began the task of locating Eleanor Shepard. It proved to be more difficult than he bargained for. Even the articulate manager of the hotel could not extract a phone number from the telephone company. "There is no listing for a Shepard."

"She is living in Fiesole," Deats repeated to the manager.

"A small town compared to Firenze, but there is still no record."

He telephoned the Kalem organization in New York, but if they knew Eleanor Shepard's address, they were under instructions not to release it.

His only hope was that wherever she was living, a real-estate agent had been involved. He asked the assistant manager for a list of agents and began calling them in alphabetical order. The American Agency Real Estate Office was third on the list and the voice answering the phone belonged to a young American girl who said that Cecilia Grosso handled the rentals for Americans. Deats made an appointment for that afternoon.

Cecilia was a short, bubbly woman who had learned her English in Boston. Her accent was an interesting combination of Bostonese and Milanese.

"Miss Shepard is the daughter of a dear American friend, and I should very much like to pay her a surprise visit."

"I haven't seen Miss Shepard in several months. She's living in a sweet villa on Via Bosconi." She talked with her hands and aimed a finger past Deats as if giving instructions. "In the country." She wrote out the address.

"Thank you, Miss Grosso. Remember now, this is a surprise."

A caravan of tour buses preceded him into the center of Fiesole. Beyond the piazza the traffic lightened. Cecilia Grosso was correct, Via Bosconi ran along a high ridge and Eleanor Shepard was nearly eight miles outside of Fiesole. He passed the steep drive leading to her villa, noting first the low house in front. He also noted a white-haired woman in a vineyard that ran parallel to the drive.

He made a U-turn and drove slowly to the drive, pulling off the road under the skimpy shade of a silver-leafed olive tree.

Jean Gambarelli saw him leave the car and walk toward her. She waved a greeting. *"Buon giorno."* A wicker basket was slung under her arm.

Deats turned into the rows of vines. "Do you speak English?"

"Quite well, I think," she answered with a laugh.

Her basket contained assorted bottles, and she was holding a tube with markings along its length.

"I'm a bit lost," he said, trying to appear embarrassed.

"We English have a penchant for that—you *are* English?"

"Indeed. London these days."

"I've observed how tourists react when they're lost. The Germans are too stubborn to admit it, the Americans turn it into some kind of new adventure, and the English come right out asking for help."

"I confess I'm not so much lost as I'm trying to find a rental property for next year. Do you know of any?"

"Yes. We've a beauty." She pointed toward the stone villa. "I'd show it to you but it's occupied. I expect it will be free shortly."

"Perhaps I could see it another time. I'll be hereabouts for a while." Deats pointed to her basket. "Are you preparing to harvest?"

"I hope so. The sugar's not up and we're already a week late." She held up the long tube. "It reads barely twenty and we like to be at least twenty-two."

"I wouldn't know what that means." Deats moved so he was looking past the woman to the stone villa.

"We call it 'Brix' and that's a measure of the sugar in the grape. When the juice ferments, half of the sugar converts to alcohol. So, the higher the 'Brix,' the more alcohol, and with this variety of grape, the better the wine."

"Thanks for the lesson." He turned then looked back with a smile. "I really am lost. How best to get to the city?"

"You're headed correctly. Follow the road into Fiesole then look for the signs."

"Do you expect the house will be available in the spring?"

"I believe so. I'm Jean Gambarelli and you know the address. We usually book through an agent, but you can contact me directly if you wish."

In the car he recorded the scant information. He looked up to see a maroon Lancia edge out of the courtyard onto the drive. The driver tooted the horn and waved at the woman testing for sugar in her grapes. At the Via Bosconi, the car swung onto the paved road, the tires screeching in protest. Deats caught a glimpse of the driver's deep red hair. He saw the license plate and recorded the last four digits. The car straightened and sped off. Miss Shepard was a reckless driver or in one hell of a hurry, he thought.

His old Renault was no match for the Lancia. At the first intersection he continued straight toward Fiesole. He didn't know the Lancia had turned left and, taking the back roads, would be in the center of Florence before he could inch his way through Fiesole's traffic-jammed streets.

He lost her because he had rented an ordinary-looking car that, regrettably, gave ordinary performance. Back in Florence he upgraded to a muscular Fiat. He returned to the hotel, satisfied he had found Eleanor Shepard, but aware his hunt for Waters was still on. Eleanor was the key. He put a fresh tape in his recorder.

*"Eleanor Shepard is in Fiesole, but apparently her friends are not....If I'm to find Waters, she must lead me to him...but one misturn and she's lost....Might even accept help from Jack Oxby...if he'd take instructions."*

He played it back, then asked the hotel operator to connect him with the Gambarelli residence.

"I failed to introduce myself this afternoon. The name is Beal... Geoffrey Beal. I've been thinking about your charming villa. Can you tell me more precisely when I might take a look at it?"

"Sooner than I'd expected. My pretty tenant returned with an American guest, and apparently they'll be driving to Milan's Linate Airport on Friday."

"How delightful," Deats replied jauntily. "I shall call you on that very morning. Cheerio." He smiled as he put the phone down. "That's a bit better," he said aloud.

He recorded his findings. He was certain Eleanor's friend was Steve

Goldensen, and that he was returning to Paris or going to another European city. If he were returning to America, he would fly out of Melpenza, the overseas airport. Not Linate. Still, he was worried that Eleanor might drive to Milan, and he'd lose her in that city of roundabouts and one-way streets. He had expected a message from Jack Oxby telling him how the extradition proceeding against Waters was moving along. *"I could use some help from the local police but too many Italian cooks..."* He didn't complete the sentence.

In the evening he left the hotel and walked along the Arno. When he returned, he had conceived a strategy and by midnight he had fleshed it out.

The next day was Thursday. Early in the morning he found an automobile supply store and a watchmaker. Then he visited the Lancia dealer at 61 Via di Novoli.

In the afternoon he drove to the Linate Airport south of Milan.

As he turned onto the A1 Autostrada, he noted the odometer and the time. The needle of the speedometer turned until it hit 120. Except for in the tunnels, he maintained the speed for the next two hundred and seventy-one kilometers.

At the turnoff to the arterial leading to the airport he slowed. He was looking for a wide shoulder where he could pull off and park. Signs with arrows indicating the turn to Linate appeared. At the second sign, about a mile from the turn, two trucks had pulled off to the side. Airport traffic moved to the right lane, proceeding more slowly than the outer lanes. He pulled to a stop in front of the first truck and watched the traffic for nearly half an hour. Satisfied, he swung back to the highway and proceeded into the airport complex.

For an hour he drove over the latticework of roads, familiarizing himself with every one, then with every parking area alongside the terminal building. He parked, then entered the wing serving intra-European flights.

He recorded the flight numbers and departure times for the airlines flying from Milan to Paris. He would have wagered that Goldensen was ticketed on either Alitalia or Air France.

Next he drove to the airport exit, again measuring time and distances. He continued to the Autostrada, retracing his route to Piacenza, a half hour south of the airport. From the hotel he phoned Alitalia, gave his name as S. Goldensen, and apologized for misplacing his tickets and asking if he could be told which flight he was on. He waited for what seemed an interminable time, then was told he was on the 12:30 flight and to come early and be reticketed.

Friday morning he was up early, returned to the Autostrada, and set off for the airport. It began to rain. He estimated that Eleanor and her friend would arrive at the airport entrance between 11:30 and 11:45.

The rain steadied to a light drizzle, the traffic sending up sprays of water to cloud the air. He arrived at his post at ten o'clock and by eleven had trained himself to recognize the grill and headlamp configuration of a Lancia from a quarter of a mile away. He could pick out the color at about five hundred feet, the license number—those small numbers and too many of them—he could not read accurately until the car was nearly abreast of him.

The target time of 11:30 ticked away.

Then 11:35 ... 11:40 ... 11:45 ... Thoughts of taking an alternative action were crowded out by the fear that Eleanor and Steve were not coming to Linate at all, that Goldensen's plans had changed.

Then he spotted a Lancia in the middle lane, its turn signal flashing. His eyes focused on the license plate. He raced the motor and started moving as the car sped past. They had arrived.

He turned onto the road in front of a long transport truck and was blasted by a screaming air horn. The Lancia turned into the airport and slowed. Deats fell back and followed. At a "Y" intersection the car hesitated. A right turn led to the departure level at the terminal, a sign pointed left for parking. They turned left and Deats sighed in relief.

They turned off to the first parking area. Deats drove past them, stopped, and watched as they walked toward the terminal. Then he pulled alongside Eleanor's car.

It was 11:52.

From a paper sack he took a ring of keys. The Lancia mechanic had demanded a hundred and fifty thousand lire, twice the amount Deats eventually had paid him. Another fifty thousand paid for a brief lesson in the electrical system of a Lancia. None of the first half-dozen keys fit the lock ... nor did the next three. He was not counting the seconds, but knew he was losing precious time. The next key slid into the lock and he opened the door. He reached under the dashboard and pulled on the hood release lever.

From the sack he extracted a length of wire. Near one end was a timer fashioned by the watchmaker and next to it was a two-inch-long metal cylinder. He lifted the hood, then attached one end of the wire to the ignition coil, the other end to a bolt in the car's frame. He did it with his left hand, using only the thumb on the other.

When Eleanor started the car, the timer would be activated, and after four and a half minutes, a solenoid switch would open and electricity flowing from the ignition coil to the car's frame would cause the system to short out. Deats calculated the engine would stop approximately sixty seconds after Eleanor left the airport.

He moved his car a dozen spaces away and waited. It was one o'clock when Eleanor returned. She immediately placed a road map against the steering wheel, but to Deats's consternation she continued studying the map after starting the engine. The timer was ticking. Then suddenly she backed out and, with wheels spinning, sped out of the parking area as if she were leaving the pit at the Grand Prix in Turin. Deats followed, his eyes alternating between the Lancia and his watch. At three minutes after the timer kicked on, she was through the pay booth and accelerating. Deats followed. In twenty-six seconds Eleanor's car would be powerless.

He closed the distance between them just as she turned onto the arterial heading west and away from the center of Milan.

Fifteen seconds to go.

She accelerated into the fast-moving traffic and held her position. Deats was a half-dozen cars behind. The allotted four and a half minutes had elapsed and the Lancia's speed approached a hundred and thirty kilometers per hour. Then the left-turn signal began flashing. "Something's wrong," he said aloud. "Something's damn well gone wrong."

But the Lancia was turning right *off* the highway, though the left-turn signal still flashed. Deats followed and pulled to a stop behind her. She bolted from the car, hands on hips, her expression angry and confused.

She ran toward his car. *"Parla Inglese?"*

"Much better than Italian."

"It quit!" She pointed at her car. "No warning, no red lights, no buzzers... damned thing just died."

"I saw you turn off just as I was looking to get my bearings. Can I help?"

She noticed his bandaged hand. "All help gratefully received, but shouldn't I flag down one of the local *polizia*?"

"Let me check the engine. Italian cars are notoriously like the people who make them. Very emotional." His smile reassured her.

"I don't want to delay you."

"Come now, pull on the hood release."

She jumped back into the car and pulled the lever. Deats yanked the wire free from the ignition coil, unclamped the other end, and pocketed the device.

"Are you going into Milan?" he called out.

"No," she shouted over the highway noise.

"Heading south?" he persisted.

"No again. North."

Deats walked back to her and placed his hand on the roof of the car. "Delightful coincidence. So am I. Switzerland?"

She looked up. "Find anything wrong under there?"

"I think so. If you get going again, I can follow along. That might prove a bit of relief."

"It would make me feel better. I'm going to Como. It's not far."

With the mention of Como, Deats recalled the photographs in Jonas's gallery. "Give the engine a try. Let's see if I spotted the trouble."

She turned the key and the engine came alive. "Hey, what did you do?"

"The fuel line was pinched up. I straightened it out." He might have said the manifold had "lobulated." All that mattered to Eleanor was that the engine was running.

It was an hour's drive to Como. At the last toll plaza she pulled to the side and signaled Deats to come alongside. "I'm going to the Villa d'Este, which is in the first town north of Como. It's not far and I want you to follow me. I owe you a drink for all your help."

"That's not necessary," he said without much conviction. "Will you be staying there?"

"Don't I wish! I'm meeting a boat that takes me across the lake."

"To another hotel?"

"No...I'm visiting friends. Please join me for that drink?"

"Thanks, but I'm running behind schedule. I'll follow you to the hotel."

"Okay, but if you change your mind, the offer stands."

The town immediately north of Como was Cernobbio.

At the north end of the town, Eleanor turned into the grounds of the gracious hotel. She gave several blasts on her horn and waved briskly. Deats slowed, but did not go through the gates when the maroon car was out of sight. He parked in front of a shop near the gate and walked toward the hotel. Two boats were tied to the dock, a small fishing skiff and a white speedboat. Deats sat on a low stone wall that ran beside the shoreline.

A porter scurried from the hotel. He put a suitcase and several boxes in the speedboat. He made another trip with more packages and this time Eleanor was behind him. Holding her arm was a man dressed in white ducks and a blue polo shirt. Deats tensed. A hundred yards away was Anthony Waters.

The road he had followed to the hotel gate continued behind the ho-tel, then rose sharply to a point overlooking the lake. Deats raced back to his car and drove up to the bluff. He arrived to see the speedboat pull away from the dock. As it gained speed, the bow lifted and the sounds from the engine reached him several seconds later. The boat made a wide, white wake, throwing a rooster's tail high in the air. It sped across the lake, aimed at a mass of gray stone at the water's edge.

# Chapter 25

Two drawings were on Stiehl's drawing board. The mellowed colors, to the professional eye, showed their age. He had seen Ellie return and wanted badly to show her the results of more than six months' hard work. He was proud of what he had accomplished and wanted to impress her with his skill. Was that being childish? Perhaps tomorrow, on Saturday, he would bring her to the studio. But Jonas might send her off. Eleanor was not to know. No, she must not see the drawings.

He took one of the drawings to the window and studied it in the late-afternoon light. It was intended as a preliminary drawing of the *Mona Lisa*. Leonardo's brief notes described the clothes he wanted the model to wear and humorously rebuked her for failing to bring his favorite cheese. The ink, applied as black, was now the color of a soft brown *bistre*, faded to barely perceptible lines where a delicately fine stroke was laid to define the strands of hair. He was pleased with the way he rendered the veil, where the seeming transparency of lace laid over lace had been captured with great precision.

Giorgio insisted that Folio 4 appear to have been pulled from old bindings and so instructed Stiehl to create tiny notches at intervals where threads had once held the sheets together and were, in turn, sewn to a leather cover. It was a minor authenticating touch but importance would be attached to the fact the sheet was part of a bound volume, suggesting other pages existed. In the same sheet, Stiehl created a minuscule tear. Again, the detail seemed unimportant, yet Stiehl practiced with scraps of paper time after time before making the imperceptible rip in the actual page.

It all took precision, patience, and, not the least, professional hands.

Folio 9 was to have straight edges except for subtle defects at the bottom. Eleanor's notes had mentioned—and Giorgio concurred—that a straight edge was rare, that handmade papers of the period were imprecise, not standard in thickness or size, and were often marred by imperfections.

Giorgio also wanted to show stains, probably those of carelessly spilled drops of wine. A fragment of a fly's wing was impressed onto the verso, and several tiny holes were drilled as evidence a worm happened on the paper at about the time, so Giorgio conjectured, Napoleon was claiming works of art in the name of France. Minute creases and folds were made at the corners.

Distressing the pages was a plodding effort. It was important that the paper be made supple, as that, too, was a manifestation of age. Handmade paper stored under reasonably good conditions might have indefinite life, Eleanor reported. Many sheets she found had never been printed on. These were often the end papers in large books and ledgers. Some of the papers had rarely been touched, much less handled by an artist or writer. Stiehl wore thin cotton gloves when he was drawing or writing, but at times he wanted his skin oils to soften the paper.

The spectrographic analysis of the papers, chalk, and ink compared favorably to the results Eleanor obtained on the samples from the sheet Tony had taken from the Royal Library. Her detailed report ran to sixty pages and described each of nineteen tests, including certified copies of the methodology and results from the laboratory at the University of Pisa. Eleanor included results of a new process that tested for the molecular migration or absorption of ink on paper. In old documents the ink gradually dried and set into the paper. Recently applied ink, and even inks as authentic as Eleanor had produced, would give off a telltale flaking. Eleanor had designed a way to eliminate flaking. The samples Stiehl prepared had been processed and were now under evaluation at the university.

During dinner, from which Giorgio was absent, Jonas reported on their progress. "Curtis has been more productive than I thought possible. I've made arrangements to take the first of the reproductions to Windsor. All of us, and that particularly includes you, Eleanor, can be very proud of our accomplishments."

Eleanor felt uncomfortable and, like Stiehl, did not respond to Jonas's enthusiasm. Missing was the warmth of that first sparkling evening when Jonas had orchestrated a lively dinner party. Now the only sounds were the clicking of knives and forks.

Eleanor finally broke through. "I might still be stranded near the Linate Airport if one of Tony's countrymen hadn't saved me." Her ex-

perience seemed hardly worth retelling but it interrupted Jonas's monologue.

"What was that about?" Tony asked.

She gamely related how her engine had failed and how a gallant
Englishman had come off the road to help. "He found the trouble right
away ... all with a bandaged hand I thought was useless. Then he followed me as far as the Villa d'Este in case I broke down again."

"Describe him," Tony asked warily.

"Oh, I'd say average height ... mustache ... mid-forties perhaps."

"Wore glasses?" Tony asked again.

"Funny, I don't remember."

"Lucky for you he could make repairs with one hand," Jonas chimed
in.

"Apparently something simple," Eleanor replied. "A pinched fuel
line? Does that sound right?"

"Which hand was bandaged?" Jonas was too far away to notice the
concern in Tony's eyes.

"I don't think I looked that carefully." She put both hands up, then
waved one. "This one, I suppose." She continued holding up her right
hand.

"Hardly matters." Jonas reached to pat Eleanor's arm. "You were
saved and you're here ... safe and beautiful as ever." He glanced at the
others. "Let's have coffee and brandy in the solarium."

The informality of the new surroundings proved no more relaxing.
Jonas repeated his pleasure at having reached the point when he could
present the results of their work to the Royal Librarian. Eleanor sipped
her coffee, then abruptly rose and went to the door leading to the patio. "I'm going for some air, then to bed. Please don't think I'm rude, but
I'm very tired."

"I'll join you," Stiehl said. He opened the door and followed her.

Tony watched them leave. When they reached the outer enclosure, he
turned to Jonas. "New trouble. Eleanor's savior was no casual tourist. She
described the damned police superintendent who was snooping about in
the library."

"How could that be possible?" Jonas's voice turned shrill.

"The description fits ... I did in his hand. And isn't it a quaint coincidence that his car was stuck tight on her ass when she pulled off the
highway?"

"That's improbable. How could he know that on this day and at that hour Eleanor Shepard would be on the highway outside of Milan with engine trouble?"

"I can't say *how* he did it but he did. In some way he learned she was in Italy, then in Florence, and then—"

"It's three o'clock in New York." Jonas lifted the phone and commanded the operator to speed a call through to his office. The connection cleared quickly and he asked for Edna Braymore.

"I want you to get the logs for all visitors to the gallery for the past two weeks. Read the names and notes that were taken for each." Jonas drained the sweet Mantonico, then motioned for Tony to refill his glass.

Edna Braymore began reading the list of daily visitors. She reached Thursday, September 28. Two visitors. Neither name prompted a reaction from Jonas.

"Friday, September 29. A busy day with two sales," she reported. "A Houston dealer named Karle bought the Felix Ziem for eighty-six thousand. Then a Mr. Goldensen and Geoffrey—"

"Wait! Goldensen. Why was he in the gallery?"

"He had come to pick up books for Miss Shepard. I assumed you knew him. I remember how we had a terrible time locating the books—"

"Who else on that day?"

"Geoffrey Beal, a London dealer. He was very complimentary about the exhibit, but was interested only in buying the photographs we'd put up to fill the empty space created when the Ziem was sold."

"Pull the videotape and give me a description of Beal."

"That will take time, Mr. Kalem."

"Of course it will. I'll wait, it's very important."

The phone was cordless and Jonas walked a few steps onto the patio. Eleanor and Stiehl were silhouetted against a violet sky. "Put the PM on them and patch into the recorder. I want everything they're saying on tape."

The PM was a parabolic microphone, a disk some thirty inches in diameter with a highly sensitive microphone at its center. Tony powered the unit, then slipped a short-range transmitter over his shoulder and went out to a position approximately a hundred feet from Eleanor and Stiehl. He listened through earphones to capture a clear signal.

"I'm sorry it's taking so long, Mr. Kalem. I'm in the control room and watching that day's tape on the screen. We've run it ahead to when Mr. Beal was in the gallery. Yes, there he is... he's wearing a tweed jacket and he has a mustache. I can't see his face too clearly.... He seems to be holding a small radio—no, it's a tape recorder. His right hand is bandaged. He's by the photographs of the lake scenes.... He's talking into the recorder."

"I want you to pay close attention. Rewind the tape to when Goldensen and Beal were together. Listen to their conversation and tell me if Goldensen refers to Miss Shepard by name and says he's meeting her in Florence." Jonas returned to his console, dialed up the conversation between Eleanor and Stiehl, and heard Eleanor talking about lights on the lake. Edna Braymore was back on the line.

"Yes, Mr. Kalem. He mentioned both Miss Shepard and the fact he would see her in Florence."

"It's beautiful, Curtis. Even now when the lake is going to sleep and all around the lights are going on as if everything else is just waking up."

"I've never thought of a lake going to sleep. That's a notion I haven't considered. But it's very beautiful, the way you describe it. I've watched the lights come on at night, and I've wondered who turns them on and what they have done that day." He turned to her and smiled. "Is that a postman over there? Or did a bank teller turn that light on?"

"I like that, too," Ellie said softly. "Each light has its own little story. Some happy, others sad. At night when you turn on the lights ... are you happy?"

"I don't let myself think about it. I spent too much time chasing happiness away from me, then wondered who I was and why had I done that. Now I take it a day at a time and so far it's okay."

"You were in prison. Why?"

"How did you know?"

"I hope that's not important. Were you?"

"It is important. Who told you?"

"I'm sorry, it's really none of my business. Please forget I asked."

"Look over there! That hillside came to life as if someone hollered, 'Hey, hit the switches!'" He laughed and Eleanor joined in. Then silence. Without turning to face him, she asked about his years in prison. He had worked up the courage to tell her. But she knew. Who told her?

"It was six years ago," he began. "I was trying to be an illustrator and was good at drawing the inside of machines, but those jobs didn't pay much. When I was in art school, I had a part-time job in a brokerage company. I guess that's where I got the crazy notion about making bonds. Bearer bonds that I could sell easily. I taught myself how to make engravings and began selling bonds. Then I got cocky and figured I could make more money faster if I made my own money."

Eleanor laughed. "You make it sound so easy. You were a counterfeiter?"

"I tried to be. I was just beginning when the feds closed in on my bond business."

"That explains why Jonas hired you. I'm sorry about the other... prison, I mean." She looked up at Stiehl. "You know, I've been in Italy six months and until a week ago I felt I was involved in something terribly important. Now it all seems so crazy. This old place, the isolation, Tony and that awful boat. Why the hush-hush over making copies of the Windsor drawings? You can do that in New York."

"Jonas likes to be dramatic," Stiehl replied. He knew she must not know the truth.

"Curtis, I want to see your drawings." She spoke in a firm voice, as if she would not be denied.

"Of skulls and bones and muscles of the lower leg? There's nothing to see."

"I don't care. I want to see the drawings."

"Ellie." He put his fingers under her chin and lifted her face to his. "There's nothing to see." He kissed her forehead. "It's late, and you said you wanted to go to bed."

"I think you just gave me the kiss-off. You're hiding something and I want to know what it is."

"And I said you must be very tired."

"Then I'll ask Giorgio."

"Come on, let's get some sleep."

The speakers went silent. Jonas ran up the volume but all he generated was a loud hum. Tony returned.

"They've gone to their rooms. You heard? Princess Eleanor is asking questions."

"She's a bright woman. I expected it."

"We don't need her curiosity."

"What do you suggest we do about it?"

"Pay her off before she knows too much. Send her back to Washington, or—"

"Put her in a car headed for a steep cliff?"

"You won't lay a finger on her, right? What will she say when you tell the world you found the missing Leonardos? She'll blow her mouth off about you and where she spent the last six bloody months. What she can't figure out she'll pull out of Stiehl."

"Eleanor is my problem, as is Curtis. You'll have enough to handle in taking care of Giorgio."

"I thought you needed him."

"Only so long as he holds on to his original drawings. After we have all of them, then we might say that he is at your disposal."

Tony broke into one of his rare fits of laughter. "Find where he's hidden them in one of a thousand piles of old stone? It's a crazy notion."

"Not so crazy. On Monday we visit Giorgio for a taste of his wife's celebrated cooking. I suspect the drawings are not far from where he sleeps."

"I doubt he would keep them in his home."

Jonas set his empty glass down. "That is precisely the difference between your deep-rooted suspicions and Giorgio's naive innocence. The drawings are where he lives, not buried behind stone ten miles away."

Tony swigged the last drops directly from the bottle. "You always have an answer. Give me one on Deats. He's here. Your precious princess led the way."

"Superintendent Deats shall be taken care of in proper order. After all, he's just arrived and needs time to get oriented."

"Oriented? Perhaps I should send him a map with a circle around *Il Diodario*. The bastard's come after me...and no disguise will stop him."

"Tony, I'll remind you that Leonardo said impatience is the mother of stupidity. What is needed is a rational approach in dealing with the superintendent. If he was led to Lake Como, then we shall find a way to lead him away."

Walter Deats stumbled onto the Albergo Caramazza in Moltrazzio, a hill-hugging village north of Cernobbio. A lane led to the small hotel, dead-ending in a miniature parking area so narrow that to turn a car around it was necessary to drive onto a rotating platform, then push it a hundred and eighty degrees.

He took a room overlooking the town and the lake. His view was north of the bluff from where he had seen the speedboat literally fly over the water. He desperately needed a pair of high-magnification binoculars.

He learned that Eduardo Caramazza, owner of the inn, had served as civilian adjutant in Mussolini's Department of Defense and had carefully chosen his spoils from the war. Prized among his possessions was a Leitz 22X60 Compofortit binoculars.

"They are nearly fifty years old and heavy," Caramazza said proudly, "but when set on the tripod, they perform with great precision. You can count the cars on a ferry crossing over to Bellagio and that is a long distance from here."

Caramazza joined Deats with the familiarity of an old friend. He was slightly built, but there was strength in his face and voice. The hotel and the town and dozens of relatives living on the lake were his life, all intermingling with the business of the day and the social life at night. Caramazza was the town historian, but with interests ranging far beyond Moltrassio. His knowledge of the lake and its people could be invaluable. Deats became an eager listener.

Deats trained the binoculars on the gray villa Caramazza identified as the Vescovo mansion, "now owned by a fat American."

Through the glasses he discovered two men with rifles slung over their shoulders. Each wore fatigues, the colors blending into the dense shrubbery surrounding the villa. One patrolled along the tree line above the boathouse, the other ranged from the solarium to the north, then would disappear into the trees as if headed up the steep hill behind *Il Diodario,* only to reappear on the other side of the mansion, where he met the other guard returning from his patrol. They would confer for several minutes, then repeat their patrol.

He spotted the white speedboat moored in the boathouse nearest the villa. There were pink-and-lime-striped umbrellas over tables in the patio. The man Deats identified as Anthony Waters took the boat out on the lake, patrolling in ever-widening circles. A blimplike body attired in khaki shorts lay on a plastic cushion. A divinely shaped young woman dove into the water, swam away from the gray stones, then returned and sat on the steps until her deep red hair dried.

A man appeared in the window in an upper floor. He waved to the swimmer, then slipped out of view.

Colorful sails dotted the deep blue lake, and the sky had been ordered up by a photographer taking postcard pictures. The same photograph, perhaps, that Deats saw in the gallery in Jonas Kalem's New York gallery. It all looked so normal. So peaceful.

# Chapter 26

Deats steadied the heavy binoculars on the white speedboat, following it until the bow dropped and it moved out of sight behind a spit of land near the Villa d'Este Hotel.

Throughout the weekend Deats observed the speedboat leisurely plying back and forth in front of the gray villa. When another craft entered the same waters, the boat encircled it, sending up white geysers and forcing the smaller boat to bob violently in the heavy turbulence. Deats assumed that Waters was searching for him, and if he was found on the water, he and his boat would be sliced in two. It would be "an unfortunate boating accident."

He left his perch to find Eduardo Caramazza.

"I'm interested in the white boat that comes from the gray mansion you said was owned by the American. I watched it disappear behind a piece of land below the hotel."

"Perhaps going to Cernobbio. The shops there are more convenient than those in Como."

"Do you have a boat?"

"Not one that matches the white terror, but it's reliable." Caramazza smiled. "To live on the lake without a boat is like a meal without wine."

"I'd like to hire it, but I'm still hobbled by this damned hand."

"You are my guest. Let me run you along the shore and find where the witch from *Il Diodario* has been moored. Is that what you want to learn?"

"Indeed yes." Deats smiled appreciatively.

"Signore Deats, you are here for a special reason, and if I have the time to help you, I shall. I'm afraid that with only one good hand, you may have an accident and we shall both be very sorry. I know the boat, and I know the tricks of the lake and where all the coves and rocks in the shallow waters are hidden."

Caramazza's help could be invaluable. Deats turned to his new friend. "I accept your offer. Let's see where they've landed."

Caramazza smiled. *"Andiamo!"*

Giorgio Burri's villa was set well back from the water. Between the dock and the pale yellow house was a green garden with high walls running the length of the property on each side. Above the dock was a white-latticed gazebo; it was here that Giorgio waited for his guests to appear. He climbed down to the dock, calling out instructions to tie up alongside his wide-beamed fishing boat.

Jonas might have been more easily extricated with a crane, but the lumbering giant finally managed the few feet from the boat to the dock. Tony leaped nimbly to his side, a leather briefcase under his arm.

"You will see we live modestly," Giorgio said, leading the way through the long, narrow rooms on the ground floor. "And we are proud of the art we've collected. Many of the drawings I bought for a few lira." His voice rose. "We were so poor when I was a *professore aiutante* that to buy a small da Montelupo or Granacci would set Ivonne to crying. Today, they will bring a hundred or even a thousand times the little I paid for them."

They had entered from lakeside, from the back of the villa, and were now walking to the entrance hall off of which was a flight of stairs leading to the second level. At the top they faced another long hall leading back toward the lake.

"We allowed ourselves one luxury when we created this study that looks over the water and to the east where the sun rises directly over your *Il Diodario*."

It was a generous-sized room with alcoves and wide plank flooring. The walls were crammed with drawings and paintings, there was a collection of statuary, and many shelves were filled with Giorgio's favorite books. It was a cheerful, bright room that belonged to a scholar and an intellectual who lived in a special comfort surrounded by years of careful accumulation.

"I am Ivonne." A woman stepped toward Jonas, her hand extended. If Ivonne Burri had been in the kitchen since sunup, she did not look the worse for the effort. She was of average height and lean, her hair a silvery blond and carefully coiffed. She looked very trim in a yellow-and-white summer dress.

"Welcome, Signore Kalem. I have heard so much about you." Her accent was a blend of French and Italian.

"And Giorgio never fails to speak of you. He praises your touch in the kitchen most of all."

"The way to his heart is through his stomach." She smiled broadly. "Please sit. We put a table in this room where we can look out to the water."

A tureen of hot *minestra* was in the center of the table. It was followed by linguini and pesto sauce and filets of lake whitefish.

"I apologize I cannot serve the *salmonrino,* but in a few days I will make a large catch," Giorgio exclaimed.

Ivonne laughed. "That is what I hear each week, but the promise is greater than the catch."

"Before these witnesses I say that on Friday I shall return with a basketful."

Tony joined in. "We'll pay close attention to how well you do."

Ivonne's menu concluded with a salad sweetened with fruit. "You are a lover of wines, Jonas," Giorgio said. "I see you filled your glass several times with the wine from a vineyard of which I am part owner. It is east of Como, midway to Lake Garda. It is like Santa Maddalena. Do you like it?"

"Wine from *your* vineyard? I like it. Rich but not too heavy."

"A good balance, we say. I have a supply in our wine cellar and I will ask Ivonne to bring you a bottle."

Ivonne nodded, aware that Giorgio and Jonas were about to begin a more serious conversation. "I'll be in the garden if you should need anything." She took away the remaining dishes.

Giorgio directed his attention to Tony. "In the room directly below is a collection of rare books, some quite old and beautiful. And more drawings, mostly by our Baroque artists. You're most welcome to browse there or anywhere in my home." Tony, realizing he'd been dismissed, went off without a word.

"You enjoyed your food, Jonas?"

"As you told me many times, Ivonne has a master's touch. And I'll tell her." He nestled the leather case in his arms. "But now to more important matters. Curtis has completed two folios, and I have them for your approval."

"I've been curious to know why you brought them here. I should go over them with Curtis in the studio."

"But this is your studio, your references are here. If there are problems, then you and Curtis can meet."

Giorgio took the case to the table as if he were handling the Holy Grail. With appropriate reverence he placed two drawings on the table. He looked at each, front and back, for an initial impression. Gone was his usual smile. Now he was somber. He moved a lamp closer and began a closer examination. He spoke quietly in Italian. Jonas moved away and began a careful inspection of Giorgio's study.

"You must be pleased," Giorgio said without looking up. "For these sheets to stand as Leonardo's, we must sense it intuitively, and here, in the young woman's face, is that unmistakable spirit Leonardo was searching for during all the days when he planned his *Mona Lisa.* Berenson taught that it is in the spirit and quality that are found the umpires of authenticity. There will be disbelievers, but that would be so if Leonardo da Vinci were to rise from his tomb and fly to London with you." Giorgio smiled at his joke. "That's a good one, eh, Jonas? Leonardo in a flying machine?"

"He would approve," Jonas answered.

Jonas was at the far end of the studio, carefully eyeing the art on the white stuccoed wall. He was less interested in the pictures than what was behind each one. He moved the paintings aside, looking for a hiding place or a small wall safe. Giorgio had boasted that his drawings were behind two feet of stone. But nowhere could the walls be this thick. At least not above ground. But below? In the cellar? In the wine cellar?

Tony accepted Giorgio's offer and went first to the room where a collection of old books was waiting to be sorted. Shutters were closed on all the windows except one facing the garden. He could see out to the sunlit garden where Ivonne sat writing in her notebook.

From the study he went to a small music room, then to the dining room. Across from the dining room was the kitchen. It was a square room with a massive fireplace, which gave evidence that the house was more than two centuries old. One door opened to the pantry, another to a black void. Only the first few steps of a staircase leading down were visible. Inside the door he found a light switch. He flicked it on, then started down the wooden steps.

At the bottom he found he was in a cavernous room running the full width and length of the house. Lights dangled off wires suspended from the cross beams. Thirty feet away was a brick enclosure. He was certain it was the wine cellar. A thick wood door was secured by a monstrous padlock he could not pick or break apart. He retreated to the top of the stairs, turned off the lights, and then returned to the cellar to wait for Ivonne to come for the bottle of wine.

"They are nearly perfect, Jonas. The study for the *Mona Lisa* is incredibly beautiful."

"Nearly perfect is not good enough," Jonas said sternly.

"There are minor changes to make, but none too difficult. I have made notes for Curtis and we will go over everything together."

"How much time will it take?"

"A day, no more than two."

"I will need a week and perhaps more to force the inks into the paper and prepare them for the other tests."

"I am happy that is not my responsibility. Eleanor could help, but you have kept her unaware. Am I correct?"

"She is asking questions and has become suspicious."

"Would you expect otherwise?"

"I had hoped to bring her into my confidence, but I put it off. I can't force her to become a willing partner, yet if she knows and won't join us . . ." Jonas didn't finish the thought. He put the drawings back into their plastic sleeves and then into the leather case.

"You could explain that these two are part of your discovery and ask that she prove their authenticity."

Jonas nodded. "That's crossed my mind." The big man held the leather case across his generous girth and looked intently at Giorgio. "When Curtis has made the corrections, he will be free to start on the next pages. One of the reasons I've come to your home is to ask for the original drawings."

"You may ask, Jonas, but I will not give them to you."

"I demand it."

"It is useless to argue. They stay with me."

"What assurance do I have you won't make more Xerox copies and expose the entire project?"

"That would be foolish, Jonas. You have my word."

"That isn't good enough. There's too much money at stake. Once these pages are shown to the world, the pressures on all of us will be immense."

"The drawings are safe with me," Giorgio said calmly.

"But are you safe?" Jonas wheeled about and walked off.

Caramazza's boat was as advertised: solid and comfortable. Deats tried to dress as a tourist, but his wardrobe was as inappropriate for a boat ride as the heavy woolens he had taken to a steamy New York.

From Moltrassio, Caramazza ran his boat slowly along the irregular shoreline. Below the Villa d'Este he swung toward the center of the lake, holding to a hundred feet from the sharp spit of land Deats had seen through the binoculars. After rounding the tip, they turned sharply back along the pebbled beach of Cernobbio.

"There is the landing." Caramazza pointed to a marina where fishing boats had been pulled up to rest on the smooth flat rocks and sand.

Deats looked for the white speedboat but the only white craft was a Sunfish that a small boy was striving to float out to friendlier winds.

Then he saw the gazebo and below it the boat. He touched Caramazza's shoulder. "Look there."

Caramazza put the throttle in neutral. The boat stopped, rising and falling in a nearly imperceptible swell. "That dock belongs to Giorgio Burri."

"You know him?"

"Yes. And his wife. Though we are not close friends, we have known each other for many years. They come to the hotel for some of our specialties and I have been with them at the home of mutual friends."

"What is his business?"

"He is retired from the University of Milan. When he was young, he was a painter. Then he became a teacher of art."

"He teaches painting?"

"Perhaps, I do not know. He gives lectures on the Italian painters at the schools in Como."

"Tell me more about him. How long has he been retired from the university?"

"Two, perhaps three years. I said he retired, but that is only partly true. He was asked to resign." Caramazza waved his hand as if hoping to pluck his next words from the air. "There were rumors he published papers on controversial subjects that caused his superiors to demand he make apologies. But he was stubborn."

"What kind of controversial subjects?"

"As I say, these were rumors and I did not pay close attention. He was a professor of the History of Art, so what can the controversy be over such a subject?" He smiled. "There are politics in the University like everywhere. Am I right?"

Deats sighed. "You are right, Mr. Caramazza. I have seen it."

"There is someone in that boat who interests you very much. But not in a friendly way."

"A man I want to take back to England. He faces extremely serious charges."

"You are a policeman—as I suspected. I think I saw that from the beginning."

"Is it that obvious?"

"We Italians, especially those of us with military experience, have a nose for crime." Caramazza ran a finger down his nose. "It's a national hobby with us, but there is a difference, depending on which side of the law you let your nose do the sniffing."

"Will you help me?"

"Tell me more about yourself, and this man who you have come after."

"I am from the Windsor police. One of the men in that boat is suspected of murdering a policewoman. I followed him to New York where this happened"—he held up his hand—"and now to Como. He knows I'm here." Deats related how he had doctored Eleanor's car, then happened along to play the good samaritan.

"Will you arrest him?"

"With help. I don't have the authority."

"Do you have papers?"

"A warrant and evidence we've filed for extradition. I'll need cooperation from the local police."

"The *comandante* in Torno is a very suspicious man. I would not give your papers to him but to someone in higher authority. I have friends in Como." Once more Caramazza put the throttle in neutral and the boat settled in the water. "Do you know why they have come here?"

"No, but if you could arrange a meeting with Professor Burri, I might find an answer."

"*Sì*, I will do that." He moved the gear to forward and accelerated away from the shoreline.

Tony had nearly given up hope that Ivonne would come for the bottle of wine on the off chance she had found one in the kitchen. He was behind an old chest less than ten feet from the heavy door. He brushed away the stones from the hard dirt floor. He did not want to risk kicking the smallest pebble across the floor in a room with the acoustics of an echo chamber. He heard a scratching noise, like a rake being dragged over gravel. A rat the size of a small squirrel ran past him to the wall, then disappeared into a hole. Then came another noise.

Ivonne was descending the steps. She hesitated briefly, then continued down to the locked door. A key turned, the door opened, and a light was turned on. Tony moved silently to the opened door. Hundreds of bottles lay on dozens of shelves. Ivonne was at the far wall holding up bottles until she was satisfied with her choice. On another wall Tony saw a break in the rows of shelves. The stone wall was interrupted by a section of wood several feet square. He felt certain he had found the vault. He retreated behind the chest. Ivonne locked the door and went back to the kitchen. The lights went out.

Tony followed her. He slipped into the kitchen, then back to the hall, where he continued his tour of Giorgio's collection.

Caramazza turned toward *Il Diodario* and set the throttle forward. Had he or Deats looked back, they would have seen two men get into the white speedboat and begin a similar route across the lake.

"I want to see the faces of the guards protecting *Il Diodario*," Caramazza called out to Deats. "When we are running in front of the villa, I will ask that you take over."

Tony pushed the powerful craft to full speed, thrusting Jonas back in his seat. The fat man clutched the leather case and urged Tony to go slower.

"Softly, Tony, we're in no great hurry."

Tony ignored the admonition. His eyes were on a boat approaching the southern edge of the villa.

"There's no cause to hurry," Jonas repeated. "It's damned uncomfortable on the kidneys when this torpedo slaps the water."

"There's a boat prowling past our docks. I want to see who it is. Hold on to that bar in front of you."

Jonas grabbed the chrome bar with one hand and tightened his grip on the case with the other. They spurted ahead, the propeller digging deeper into the water. Jonas felt as if he had sunk six feet under the surface.

Two hundred yards from Caramazza's boat Tony relaxed speed and came up on the stern of the slower-moving craft, now nearly abeam of the solarium. He drew alongside, closing the distance to less than a hundred feet. Deats glanced left to see the other boat closing on him and immediately dropped out of sight, calling to Caramazza to take over the controls. Caramazza maneuvered his boat very deliberately, as if he were searching for a fishing spot. He knew the waters and aimed for the old landing at Torno. His broad-bottomed boat took little draft and could venture into the shallow waters. At the far edge of the villa's property he saw a man dressed in khaki. "There's one of his guards, Mr. Deats. If my eyes see correctly, he is pointing his rifle at us."

They watched Tony pull into the dock. They were a quarter of a mile away and would easily stretch that to a half mile before Tony could come after them.

Jonas, relieved the ordeal was over, stumbled to the stone dock. "Tie up and meet me in the solarium."

"But Deats is in that boat. I swear it!"

Jonas glared down to a defiant face. "My orders are to tie up."

Tony looked out to see the slow-moving boat turn out to the middle of the lake. Reluctantly, he secured the boat and followed.

Jonas placed the precious leather case on the table next to his command chair. A glower was spread over his face and his eyes still squinted from the bright sunlight on the water. "You were ready to chase the boat down and ram it broadside. I could see it."

"I wanted to follow them. I want to know where to find that bloody bastard."

"You're frightened. That's when you become dangerous."

"You sit there like a raja telling me I'm frightened because some zealous detective is trying to yank me back to face a murder charge." He moved in front of an impassive Jonas. "That might frighten a weak man, but I'm not weak."

"Your bravado is very becoming, Tony. Sit down and let me explain how we shall handle the inquisitive superintendent without violence. We can assume that they have commenced extradition proceedings through their embassy in Rome and that Deats has all the proper papers, including a warrant for your arrest. But where will he take those papers? To the provincial police? To Como? Neither. He must go to the local authorities. We are within the jurisdiction of the town of Torno. The chief of police is named Luciano Pavasi, with whom I have made a contract to protect *Il Diodario* from curious outsiders. Luciano is a very understanding man, particularly now that he has an account in the Suisse Banca in Lugano which grows each month by a million lire."

"If Deats doesn't get cooperation from Pavasi, he'll go to someone higher up."

"But Pavasi will smother him with cooperation. When the superintendent visits Pavasi, they will talk about crime and punishment and the low state of morality in their respective countries. Pavasi will dutifully contact the officials in Rome and receive authorization for Deats to serve out his warrant. They will come to *Il Diodario* and place you under arrest. When Deats is assured you are in custody in Torno, he'll return to Windsor, wait for the extradition process to grind away, then return and escort you to England, where you will stand trial for the murder of Sarah Evans." Jonas looked up. "Would you size it up differently?"

Tony had listened to the scenario in total disbelief. "I sit waiting like the fatted calf?"

"You weary me, Tony. You are so bright, yet so dull. You will sit here but not as a fat calf—"

"You've gone mad! If you think I'm going to be your sacrifice—to protect your ass—"

"Enough!" Jonas propelled himself from his chair and crashed his huge belly against Tony, sending him reeling backward. "I'm protecting you! Let them find you. Let them take you to jail. Let the goddamned Englishman go back to his Windsor. He'll rot waiting for you to be extradited."

Tony gained a modicum of composure. "Stop talking in riddles. What are you telling me?"

"If you continue to run, Deats will continue to chase. So we shall arrange a convenient arrest. You will spend several nights in the jail in Torno. When Deats boards his plane for London, you will simply walk away and join me in the car waiting in front of the police station."

"How do I know Pavasi will go along?"

"All Swiss accounts are not secret, specifically one in the name of Luciano Pavasi. It would be a devastating revelation."

"But when it's discovered I'm not in jail?"

"That will take weeks. Luciano will say you have become critically ill, that you cannot be seen. Eventually he will say you have escaped. By then you will be a thousand miles away. Getting rid of Superintendent Deats is a simple matter." His expression turned again to a glower. "It's Giorgio who presents a difficult problem. He has changed. I saw it in London when he brought his damned copies. Then he tells us there is a version with the words Leonardo might actually have written and another for practice." Jonas's skin had turned pink from the sun, now it was flushed red with anger.

"Either he wants out or is going to demand a larger share. Neither is acceptable. He will be surprised to learn I discovered the hiding place of his drawings."

"You found it?" Tony asked incredulously. "I saw into his wine cellar and there is a vault there. I'm positive."

"While Giorgio was absorbed in Curtis's drawings, I surveyed his collection. I was attracted to one in particular. It's a large pen-and-ink of stones and massive fortifications by a long-forgotten artist. But I was intrigued by the thick frame and heavy backing. Too much for a simple drawing on paper." He spread his thumb and index finger apart several inches. "I'm positive that's where they are."

"But the vault I saw in the wine cellar?"

"If I'm wrong, then the drawings will be there."

"Assume you're correct. What then?"

Jonas got up and went to the window, where he stood, hands clasped behind him. He was taking in short, deep breaths. After several minutes he began to talk in a slow, almost inaudible voice.

"I have given a great deal of thought to Giorgio and have concluded that he will demand payment for the drawings Curtis has completed, then want nothing more to do with our project. He doesn't have the stomach to stay with us. He will live the lie for as brief a time as possible and respond to all the questions that will be asked after our discovery is announced. Then he will want to spend time with his Ivonne."

"But we need him," Tony protested.

"Not if we have his drawings."

"What do you propose we do?"

"Giorgio sets his traps for the *salmonrino* every Friday. He's proud that he has learned to catch the fish alone, but he's no longer a young man, and if he should have an accident, there would be no one to help him."

"And you want him to have an accident?" Tony said to the man who had just ordered an execution. "You've never forgiven me for what happened to the policewoman, but now you are asking me to eliminate Giorgio. Just like that!" He slashed at the air as if he were dropping a killing karate chop."

"We're past turning back. I've gambled everything I own and must sell one of the drawings. No one, including Giorgio, can stop that from happening. How you do it is your business, but it must be an accident. I detest taking a risk. But Giorgio alive would be a greater risk."

"While I'm fishing on Friday, where will you be?"

"I will be in London. Possibly in the West Country."

"You'll have a perfect alibi."

"So must you. There's ample time to prepare for your fishing expedition and remove yourself from any suspicion. But remember, Giorgio sets his traps early. Long before sunrise."

# Chapter 27

"Comandante Brassi, permit me to introduce Signore Walter Deats, superintendent from the Windsor police. He carries a special assignment from Scotland Yard." Brassi bowed slightly and Deats thought he heard the click of heels. Brassi was tall, thin, and blond. His fair skin and narrow face were not typical Italian features. Deats felt he had seen him in an old German war film.

"Signore Caramazza telephoned to say you wished to see me on a matter of urgency. How may I help you?" Brassi's English was smooth, with a bare trace of an accent. Deats summed him up as all business, spit and polish.

"I have an arrest warrant for a man we suspect of murdering a Scotland Yard agent while she was on special assignment for the Crown. I also have copies of a request for extradition which has been filed with your government. The suspect, known as Anthony Waters, is residing at the villa *Il Diodario*."

"May I see the papers?" Brassi had the warmth of a north Atlantic winter wind, Deats thought.

"Correspondence relating to the extradition is in this folder. Also you'll find a copy of the extradition protocol between our countries, though I'm certain that was unnecessary." The comment was meant to flatter Brassi, but Deats didn't want any misunderstandings regarding the terms under which Waters would be arrested and confined.

"Here is the citation and arrest warrant." Deats gave the *comandante* another folder.

Brassi read through the papers. "It seems this man has used many names and disguises. Are you certain that he is who you say he is?"

"I have no doubt." Deats related all that he knew about Anthony Waters and his relationship with the new owner of *Il Diodario*.

Brassi concluded, "He's armed?"

"He carried a gun in New York and I'm sure he has more than that at this time."

"We can assume he'll resist if confronted and escape if he thinks it possible. Would you agree?"

"He's not the sort to surrender."

"Caramazza, what do you know of *Il Diodario*?"

"It is the old Vescovo villa, used by the army. I was there many times."

"*Sì*, I know it, too. My grandfather was a friend of the old man. I went there often as a boy after the war, though no one lived in it."

"It is different today," Caramazza added. "It is guarded by Luciano Pavasi's men."

"That is typical of Pavasi"—Brassi shrugged—"but not unusual for local police to find a job as a guard when not on duty."

"At least two are stationed on the grounds at all times," Deats said.

"There's still no easy way to the villa by land, or has that changed?"

"No," Caramazza answered. "The hill is too steep for a road."

"Will you confirm our request to your officials in Rome?" Deats asked.

"That won't be a problem. First you must capture your man before we need the machinery to send him to England. So often the complicated paperwork is completed and there's no person to arrest. But you know where to find him."

"He's on the lake every day, and I've little doubt that he knows I'm here." Deats told how he had followed Eleanor, then continued to relate what he knew of the two Americans.

"They are friendly with Giorgio Burri. You know him?" Caramazza interjected.

"A familiar name, but that is all," Brassi said. "What are they doing in the old villa?"

"Kalem is the key figure. He deals in art, but why he has brought his people to Lake Como is not yet clear to us."

"Waters knows you are here and hasn't run off. In fact he puts himself on view every day. Perhaps Pavasi is supplying more than armed guards."

Caramazza leaned forward. "Pavasi is corrupt. He lives too grandly for the head of a small police department."

"In the long history of our country, has there been such a person who could not be corrupted?" Brassi stood and thrust his hands into his pockets. "I deal in all degrees of dishonesty and find it necessary to know who can be bought off and for how much. A few thousand lire can buy cooperation at any level. I must assume that Luciano Pavasi has a grander scheme and has learned to ask for much larger sums."

"Who will make the arrest?"

It seemed to Deats that Brassi was going to let the question go unanswered. Then he spoke. "Normally that would be Pavasi's responsibility. As he can't be relied on, I shall consult with the regional administrator. You can count on my cooperation."

"*Bene, bene,*" Caramazza called out. "*Grazie,* Bruno."

Brassi stiffened. "There is no friendship here, Caramazza. We are dealing with a very serious matter. I should expect the same consideration if I were in Signore Deats's jurisdiction." He turned his cold eyes on Deats.

"I will honor your arrest warrant and take the necessary precautions to seal off *Il Diodario* so this man Waters cannot disappear before we call on him. Please return on Monday morning. I will tell you then what action we shall take."

# Chapter 28

The last hurdle facing incoming passengers to Heathrow was a legion of oddly uniformed men and women, each waving a card bearing a name or livery service. Standing out from the others was a nattily dressed chauffeur, additionally distinguished because he held no sign. Seumas MacCaffery had met Jonas on many previous occasions and knew it was best for him to locate his myopic client, not the other way around.

"A good day to you, Mr. Kalem." He took the suitcase in one hand and locked the other around Jonas's fat arm. They went off to a vintage Chrysler, Jonas clutching his valuable leather case to his chest.

"So it's Collyer's you be wanting." The accent was as thick as if he were Robert Bruce himself. "We'll be there soon enough if the traffic doesn't give us fits." The traffic was kind, and after some forty minutes, Jonas extricated himself from the old limousine, then climbed the few steps to the famous old building on Bruton Place.

"Mr. Pimm. I have an appointment," he announced to the receptionist.

He was ushered into a cramped office on the second floor, where a balding, bearded man of middle years greeted him enthusiastically. Harold Pimm, head of the Old Masters Department, pushed bifocals onto his forehead, then extended his hand to Jonas.

"I can't tell you how much I've looked forward to this visit." Pimm's voice was high and musical, and when he spoke, his eyes blinked as if his speech and sight were somehow connected.

"I'm impatient to share my news with you," Jonas replied. "When you see what I've brought, you'll understand my reluctance to reveal it except under these circumstances."

"I reviewed our correspondence and had forgotten how long it's been since we began discussing your search for the Leonardos."

"Four years. But the pages have been lost for centuries and a few years more or less hardly matters."

"Quite so." Pimm nodded. "I must remind you that I cannot make any judgments until after the committee finds for or against. I hardly need add that I hope it is favorable."

"I understand," Jonas replied.

"First I must deal with the paperwork. It's a nuisance to both of us, but as your discovery may be worth millions of pounds, that becomes a heavy responsibility." Pimm handed several documents to Jonas. "Please read them, Mr. Kalem. They're meant to protect you, as well as Collyer's."

Jonas drew the documents close and began reading. Pimm continued talking amiably, observing that Jonas had been brave to travel alone with his valuable treasure. "Someone might have taken the leather case and not cared what was inside."

Jonas signed the papers and put his copies in an envelope.

Pimm took the signed papers from him. "Very good. We're a few minutes late and an extremely impatient committee member is waiting."

Pimm led Jonas to a paneled room where three men were seated at a long conference table. Jonas shook hands with Paul Gilsanon, a tweedy type with leather patches at the elbows, short-cropped hair, and a pipe with the largest bowl Jonas had ever seen. Gilsanon was a chemist and third-generation proprietor of Gilsanon & Knowles, Britain's finest art restoration laboratory. The major museums, including the National Gallery and the Tate, relied on Gilsanon's staff to ascertain age, chemical properties, and the authenticity of art and artifacts.

A man at the head of the table turned in his chair to greet Jonas but remained seated as he acknowledged Pimm's introduction. Doan Chamberlin looked away from Jonas and said icily, "It is a pleasure, Mr. Kalem, though I must advise you that my time is most valuable and I see we are well behind schedule." Chamberlin was an art historian, lecturer, teacher, and acknowledged expert on the extensive collection owned by the royal family. He was in his mid-fifties, immaculately dressed in a blue blazer and gray slacks. His face was handsome—arched eyebrows, high cheekbones, and a long straight nose. Jonas thought he was a bit too precise, from his John Lobb shoes to the aftershave lotion that formed an odorous halo around him.

The third member of the committee stepped toward Jonas. He was Edgar Freebury, thirty-four, a brilliant scholar who had made Lord Kenneth Clark his idol and had achieved recognition for his exhaustively comprehensive knowledge of the Italian Renaissance. Pimm had a deep affection for the younger man, offering him fees and honorariums at every opportunity. He was the archetypal intellectual—blessed with curiosity, an extraordinary memory, and woefully inadequate financial acumen.

Jonas knew each man's reputation. In particular he had made a thorough investigation into the personal life of Doan Chamberlin. He turned his squinting eyes back to Chamberlin, noting he wore a ring on each hand, and his fingers were long and delicate, the nails manicured and covered with a clear polish.

"Gentlemen, the end of our suspense is at hand, and Mr. Kalem pledges that he will not disappoint us. I needn't remind you we have made an extraordinary departure from our long-standing regulation regarding the submission of drawings to the full committee instead—"

"Pimm, old man, please don't say you needn't remind us of something then go straight ahead and do it," Chamberlin interrupted with a wave of his hand. "We're aware of the rules and particularly those we choose to disregard. I'm dreadfully short of time, so let's have Mr. Kalem show us what he has." Pimm nodded his assent and Jonas stepped to the head of the table.

"I'm deeply appreciative of the opportunity that has been extended by Mr. Pimm and Collyer's. Of course, I am honored by the presence of each of you. I shall not fail you by placing an unimportant work on the table, but shall present what I consider the most important art discovery of our generation."

Jonas put two thick folders on the table, each tied with brown yarn. He held the first one up. "This contains the reports on a wide range of laboratory tests that have been conducted on the paper, the inks, the chalks, and also the procedures considered appropriate for ascertaining age, proper chemical analyses, ink absorption, etc. We recognize that in the absence of a provenance, these matters are of extreme importance. We are at this moment conducting additional evaluations and will submit them as soon as possible. I believe the content of this folder will be of the greatest interest to Mr. Gilsanon. The other folder contains an immensely rich amount of documentation supporting our claim for an unqualified attribution of the work. This folder is for you, Dr. Chamberlin."

"At this point I should like to review a statement which has been prepared by Professor Giorgio Burri, whom I retained to coordinate the attribution study and create a credible provenance."

Jonas gave each man a copy of a typed report that ran to seventeen

pages. At the mention of Giorgio's name, Pimm and Chamberlin reacted strongly, but in markedly different ways. Pimm smiled broadly
and Chamberlin showed great anxiety. The latter waved his copy of the
report. "I know this Burri person. He's Italian, of course?"

"Yes."

"University of Milan?"

"Yes, again."

"He's a troublemaker, uh ... controversial. A fraud, did I hear?"

"That would be a strong accusation, Dr. Chamberlin. Do you have
any facts to go on?"

"I'm not the one to ferret out those details. It's simply the man's
reputation."

"Like many of us, our reputations are what different people believe
about us. Professor Burri is controversial, but his incredible knowledge
of the Renaissance masters has never been challenged."

Pimm leaned across the table toward Chamberlin. "Doan, you have
an incredible penchant for slowing things down when you're in a terrible hurry. I think we all know of Burri's unique position on a number of
issues, but the man has never been accused of deceit. He's an extremely
bright fellow, and I've found his scholarship always at the highest level."

Pimm's comment seemed to satisfy Chamberlin. Then, with the conversation centered on Giorgio, Jonas had in one of those brief instants
that can't be measured in a millisecond, a vision of the lake and of a man
standing in a boat preparing his fishing lines. The scene disappeared
and Jonas continued. "Gentlemen, please read Professor Burri's report
very objectively."

The report contained three essential parts. The first dealt with Giorgio's
qualifications. Next was a detailed description of the Leonardo drawings. And the third was a disclosure of how the Leonardo drawings had
been discovered and an accounting of where the pages had been during
the past four hundred and seventy years. It was all heady stuff, presented
in Giorgio's scholarly, competent style.

Conversation ceased as each man read at his own speed. Gilsanon
was the first to complete his reading, followed by Pimm, who pushed
his glasses to his forehead, then studied the expressions of the others.
Freebury turned the final page and in a voice filled with awe said quietly, "An incredible find. Absolutely incredible."

Doan Chamberlin, the last to finish, said as if in response to Freebury. "Incredible if true."

"Excellent," Pimm said. "This will require corroboration, of course, but it puts us off to a good start."

"The drawing, Mr. Kalem, I must see it," Edgar Freebury said.

Jonas placed a thin box on the table. Carefully he pulled out a plastic envelope. He slid the sheet from its protective folders and placed the drawing in front of the committee.

"Gentlemen, I present...Leonardo."

Jonas stepped back so the others could crowd over the drawing. Gilsanon pulled a magnifying glass from his pocket and focused on the paper and the lines of ink forming images of the familiar young woman whose enigmatic expression had, in its completed form, become part of the most famous of all paintings.

The four appeared to be in an attitude of supplication. Pimm's hands were placed palms together at his lips as if he were praying; Freebury was bent forward; Chamberlin, hands on the table, bowed his head; and Gilsanon was kneeling. Without comment, Jonas reached a hand to the drawing and gently turned it over. Edgar Freebury stared down at the *Giaconda*. "First impressions are dangerous, but the delicacy of lines, her eyes...there is a sense of knowing it is from Leonardo's pen."

"Don't be a fool, Freebury," Chamberlin chided. "Your role is to challenge. We're advocates of the very devil until every vestige of doubt is removed. Then you'll have time enough to be emotional."

Freebury replied, "I know my role, Dr. Chamberlin. Suffice to say I have been untouched by some of the greatest art of the world yet deeply moved by the simplest drawing of a schoolchild. I react to what I see and feel. I'll make a judgment of authenticity with my head, and confirm it with my heart."

"You prejudice yourself with emotional dithering," Chamberlin said.

"And you are prejudiced by withholding yours," Freebury retorted.

Jonas sensed an argument brewing. "Gentlemen, I have very precise photographic copies for each of you. Mr. Freebury, I have a set of enlarged photographs which should aid in your analysis. You are welcome to compare the copies to the original before Mr. Gilsanon takes it to his laboratories for analysis. How much time will you require for your tests?"

Gilsanon looked up. "I must have the drawing for forty-eight hours. Most of the laboratory work requires two days and several tests may take longer." He bit on his pipe. "We'll speed everything along."

"Including spectrometry?"

"Indeed yes. And we have newer methods that are more accurate. But today's forger has access to the same technology and it's become our task to stay a step ahead. With the stakes so high, they stay right on our heels."

"What are the newest tests?" Jonas asked.

"Lasers. Chemistry. Autoradiography. Even fiber optics has given us new techniques for age-dating and analysis of dyes and pigments." He put a match to his pipe. "We've had spectacular success lately with a new process for testing old inks."

"Something you might use on this Leonardo?"

"It might be worth trying, but most printing papers were sized with animal renderings, and papers used for drawing were not. Artists, and that would include Leonardo, sized and polished paper differently. That's what I've been looking for." He waved his magnifying glass. "I see the paper was polished, probably with a stone. The red-dyed chalk used as a wash will give us an opportunity to try our new gadgets."

Jonas felt suddenly warm. "I would like to see your laboratories."

"I'll see if that can be arranged. We've been protective of our proprietary methods. You understand."

Jonas nodded. He understood that a single test Ellie had been unable to conduct might uncover the forgery. Masking his disappointment, he said, "Proof of genuineness is in your capable hands, gentlemen. I trust you will go to every length to prove they are genuine."

Gilsanon drew on his pipe. "We shall, Mr. Kalem. You can rely on that."

With the meeting adjourned, Jonas went immediately to the side of Doan Chamberlin. "You've been extremely patient. I'm indebted to you."

"This is not a business where debts are incurred, Mr. Kalem; neither of us can be the other's creditor."

"I meant that our meeting lasted longer than I planned, and time is valuable to all of us."

"Quite so." The slightest hint of a smile crossed Chamberlin's usually dour face. "My accountant cautions me to consider that each hour has a precise value. Rather a tidy sum based on the good fortune I had with my last publication."

Jonas was keenly aware of the book. *Royal Art and Sexuality* had been one of those scholarly works that received popular response in spite of its supposed narrow appeal. It had been twice reprinted less than four months after the controversial reviews. "You must be pleased with its popularity."

"The publisher chose the title. I resisted, of course. And so the public's been fooled to think it's about royal infidelity and salacious secrets."

"And pornographic art, according to reviews in the London newspapers."

"Sensational rubbish. Not a literate mind in the lot and each with a tabloid mentality. My purpose was to investigate the immense quantity of art and literature in the royal collections that is exclusively concerned with sexual relations, both normal and abnormal. You have obviously not read the book, and once you have, we can discuss it further."

"Mr. Chamberlin, I know a great deal more about your book than was in the reviews. We could discuss the role David Latcham played, for example."

Chamberlin's expression froze, his air of superiority suddenly gone. "It's preposterous to think we could talk of such a person."

"Perhaps, but not out of the question. I heard you say that you plan to drive to the country this evening. Undoubtedly that means the Cotswold, and Chipping Camden to be precise. Is that correct?"

"I said only that I was driving to the country. How would you know about Chipping Camden?"

"I learned by accident, but I did learn. I've made arrangements to stay at the King's Arms and suggest we meet there Saturday evening. Is nine o'clock agreeable?"

"That will be very inconvenient."

"The bar is pleasant and private."

Chamberlin's eyes darted left and right, as if he were trapped and couldn't find a way out. Then he lowered his head. "Very well, I will be there, but with the understanding that nothing you say will prejudice my decision regarding the Leonardo."

Jonas did not reply, but nodded his head slowly and smiled. He watched Chamberlin leave the room, then made his way to Pimm's side and thanked him for his cooperation. Then he made arrangements with Gilsanon for the safekeeping of the drawing. "It shall be safe, Mr. Kalem. We've considerable experience protecting art treasures. That's really what our business is all about."

"I'm sure it will be safe, but that won't stop me from worrying. Return it to Harold just as soon as you've run all your tests."

"We'll begin immediately, and I shall personally supervise. You realize that a small slice of the paper must be sacrificed, and ink scraped for other tests."

"We took our own samples," Jonas said knowingly. They shook hands and Gilsanon went to find Pimm. Edgar Freebury folded a notebook in which he had been writing. Jonas handed him a slip of paper. "Please call me if you need further information."

"I have one question." Freebury's voice was soft and his words came slowly. "Your discovery may be the most important contribution to Leonardo scholarship in this century. Greater than locating the Madrid Codex. Have you calculated its value?"

"A great amount of money," Jonas said with what seemed genuine sincerity. "I am much more concerned with adding to our knowledge of the great master."

Freebury continued putting papers into his briefcase. "You said that very nicely, Mr. Kalem, and I trust those are your true sentiments. Yet if your discovery proves to be authentic, it may be worth untold millions. Is that important to you?"

"I have made a large investment in time and money to recover the manuscript, and if there's a high reward, then I feel it will be justified."

"Did you invest for the sake of enriching our knowledge of Leonardo? Or simply to be enriched?" Freebury reached the door and turned back. "I must remember that when I first look at a work of art, I have an emotional response that tells me if I am looking at truth or a lie. Its commercial value cannot influence my judgment."

Then Jonas was alone. Chamberlin and Gilsanon had reacted according to form. While neither was in his pocket, both would, in the end, vote affirmatively. Freebury had put his idealism on the table. Yet he showed keen interest in the drawing's value. Perhaps he was showing, like so many, that greed was one of his character defects.

# Chapter 29

Friday began in the early morning darkness when Giorgio turned in his bed and tenderly ran his fingers over Ivonne's cheek and neck. She no longer wakened on his fishing days to brew the strong coffee he craved, but would set a kettle of water on the stove before going to bed, knowing he could make his own, and find the basket of cheese and fruit. He smelled the familiar combination of her cologne and perspiration, scents that aroused him. He kissed her closed eyes, then rolled away and onto his feet.

It was 4:45, an hour away from sunrise. The weather was as predicted: cool with an intermittent light rain that might end by noon. Giorgio would set his lines in darkness. The waters along the eastern shore of the lake would remain sunless for most of the day, even though the sun might shine on it later in the afternoon.

*Salmonrino* are bottom feeders; a prize catch runs to four pounds. Professionals, and Giorgio considered himself one, laid a series of lines on the bottom, a procedure more easily accomplished with two men. The lone angler devised his own methods. Giorgio recorded selected areas where he had had success, choosing a spot only after studying the weather, the time of year, and the strength of the Tivano wind that was frequently a factor in the early morning. A mild wind and he chose positions away from the eastern shore. Strong winds meant he must stay close to the high, sheltering rocks. He judged that the Tivano was blowing at less than five knots. He could anchor away from shore, and that pleased him. The water was deeper, and, though it was more difficult to set the lines, there were more *salmonrino* to catch.

Steam hissed from the kettle. He brewed strong coffee mixed with chicory and filled his thermos. He had packed the boat the previous afternoon, so the morning preparations were brief. Giorgio was proud of his boat. He had contributed to its design, not that that made it better, but it had features and comforts few others could offer. He flew two pennants, one on the bow and another at the top of the squat cabin perched amidships. The colors were bright—red, yellow, and green, matching the striped pole at his dock. It was a happy boat, but unpredictably troublesome. The powerful motor behaved unreliably at times and on too many embarrassing occasions the boat had lain becalmed on sunny afternoons when Giorgio and Ivonne intended to take friends for a tour of the lake.

A few minutes past five he silently paddled away from his dock. The lights along the public landing in Cernobbio could be dimly seen through the mist, and at a hundred yards out, the lights flickered, then were not seen at all. It was as if he had drifted into a black envelope. He turned on the light in the compass housing, then started the engine. He reduced power and slowly moved on a heading that would take him north and toward the medieval town of Torno.

Tony waited until he heard the motor. Then, alternately dipping a double-ended paddle left then right, he followed the gurgling sound that came from the exhaust of Giorgio's boat. He was as black as the air around him, his face rubbed with an ebony cream made from burned cork and oil. He wore a black turtleneck sweater and a rubber wet suit. The tiny kayak moved faster than the boat it was pursuing and several times Tony had to back off. He shifted the coil of rope slung over his shoulder, then again dipped the oar into the water.

Giorgio put the engine on idle. Dead ahead were the lights at the boat taxi landing at Torno, a bright light on the dock and a red light to his left. When the two lights aligned, he reversed the motor and ran the boat for thirty seconds toward the middle of the lake. At that point he dropped anchor and measured the water's depth. Twenty meters. He pulled anchor and moved farther from shore and measured again. The bottom fell away quickly and he was atop twenty-eight meters of clear, icy water. He turned the motor off.

The light in the cabin shone on the clock. It was 5:35. He recorded his position, the time, and the weather conditions in a diary. He went to the stern and began preparing the lines.

Noiselessly the kayak circled, slowly closing in on Giorgio's boat. When he was ten feet away, Tony could see a shadowy figure pulling his nets from a wooden locker. He dipped the paddle deep into the water and with short, silent strokes drew alongside the bow, where he tied a length of nylon rope to the anchor line.

Giorgio separated six lines, setting them out on the port rail. Four short lines, all with hooks and baited, were attached to each. These lengths were fixed at varying lengths from the main line. Giorgio dropped the first line, pulled on it to eliminate slack, secured it, then placed a bright orange buoy the size of a melon to mark the location. *"Buono. Mille buono,"* he said aloud. The gentle, steady current flowing due south turned the craft's bow to the north. Giorgio loosened the anchor line and played out eight meters. The line had a thick wrapping of tape at eight-meter intervals. He lowered his second line. The eight-meter separation was not a guess; Giorgio had learned from long experience.

Tony had not anticipated Giorgio's action and could not unhitch from the anchor line before Giorgio freed his boat to drift the allotted eight meters. Concealed by darkness, he maintained his advantage of surprise, but had lost valuable proximity to his quarry. He reacted immediately and rolled the kayak over, slipped free, then swam underwater to Giorgio's boat.

Giorgio heard the splash. It was no more than a slap on the water. *"Chi è li? Che cos'è?"* His question went unanswered.

What followed was a fury of motions and sounds.

Tony dove below the keel then shot up beside the boat, broke the surface, and, extending his waist above water, lunged for the rail. He grabbed it with his right hand, then as quickly pulled up with his left. He rolled over the railing and onto his feet. Giorgio could see only a shadowy form in the dull light. He reached for a pike, a long pole with a curved steel hook at the end. At the same time he touched the handle of a nine-inch fishing knife in a sheath hitched to his belt.

*"Che cosa fa?"*

"It's all right, Giorgio. It's me, Tony.

"You are crazy. Why are you here?"

"I like to swim in the morning. Sunrise on the lake is beautiful. Don't you agree?"

"There will be no sunrise this morning." Giorgio could barely make out Tony's shape. "You gave me a terrible fright."

"I suggested you let me come fishing with you." He continued toward the older man.

"And we agreed to make plans. *Scusi,*" Giorgio said, waving Tony away. "This is a critical time. The lines must be set out quickly after the first is put down."

"Let me help."

"There's no time to teach you. Watch, and sit in the cabin."

Tony walked past the cabin door. He closed it and continued toward Giorgio. His blackened face made his body appear headless.

Giorgio tightened his grip on the pike. "Please go to the bow, and after I drop the next line, you can let off on the anchor."

"Then I can help. Good, I want to help you."

Giorgio leaned the pike against the railing and tossed another line into the water. He took up the slack and attached a buoy as before. "Now, if you have come to help, let off on the line until you feel the tape. Then fasten."

There was silence, only a gentle slurping of miniature waves against the hull and the sound of a truck's horn on a distant road. "Tony?" Giorgio called into the darkness. "Have you found the line?"

The answer came from behind Giorgio. "We won't be drifting, Giorgio."

"But we must. If I drop here, it will be too close to the last line. And see, it is getting lighter."

"We won't be dropping any more lines." Tony moved closer, the circles of white in his eyes shining like bright silver coins. "It is regrettable that no *salmonrino* will be caught here today. Perhaps others will have better luck."

"That is foolish talk. If you've come to help, then go and let off on the anchor line. We must move quickly."

"You really don't understand, do you?" Tony raised his arms, brushing the taut rope against Giorgio's throat.

Giorgio had understood there was danger from the instant Tony sprang out of the water. Tony was half his age and strong, but Giorgio knew his boat and the lake. He ducked away from the rope and grabbed the pike. He lunged at Tony, slashing the sharp point across his chest and through the wet suit, missing his skin by the thickness of his sweater. Giorgio's agility surprised Tony, and for an instant he thought the hook had cut into him. Giorgio attacked again. Tony fell back against the railing. He was off balance when Giorgio swung the pike a third time. He grabbed at it, deflecting the hook away from him. He fell to his knees, lurched forward, and grabbed Giorgio's legs, then brought him down on the narrow decking between the cabin and the rail.

"*Bastardo!*" Giorgio yelled. "*Aiuto! Aiuto!*"

Tony wrapped his arms around Giorgio and wrestled him to the railing. Then holding him tightly, he fell into the water.

The sky had continued to lighten and now they could see each other. Giorgio's eyes were wild with fright. He clawed at the black face, thrashing at the water with one free arm. He reached for his knife, but too late. Tony wound an arm under Giorgio's head, took a deep breath, then sank into the water, pulling Giorgio down with him. But the lean body had more strength than Tony bargained for. Giorgio squirmed free and swam to the surface. Tony was after him immediately. This time he wrapped his legs around his victim and pulled his head back into the water. Giorgio twisted frantically, exerting every bit of strength to break the hold. Then, abruptly, his body convulsed, then went limp.

Tony swam the few feet to the boat and grabbed hold of a mooring line. He looped the rope under Giorgio's arms and tied it securely. He climbed onto the boat and hoisted Giorgio over the rail and laid him on the deck. He put his ear on his chest and felt for a pulse. There was none. Giorgio was dead.

Water had seeped through the gash in his wet suit. He was cold and unable to move as freely as before. It was raining. Another fisherman had anchored a half mile away and more boats would soon be on the lake. He sat beside his victim and took stock of the situation. He had planned to make it appear that Giorgio had drowned. But he had had a heart attack and now was on the boat in wet clothes.

He carried Giorgio to the bow, where he coiled the anchor line around his left leg. Then he lowered him until his head and shoulders were in the water. He tightened the line. He returned the pike to its holder and put the long knife back in its sheath. He placed the fishing line Giorgio had planned to drop on the deck. Next he checked for signs of a struggle. There was no blood, and he hadn't touched metal. No fingerprints. He went over every detail another time. It had been an accident.

Another fisherman approached. Tony fell to the deck. He was certain Giorgio's boat was well-known and a friend might come alongside and ask if he was having good luck. A horn sounded three short blasts.

If they came closer, they would spot Giorgio. He heard voices, carried over the quiet water by a rising wind. He crept to the bow and rolled off into the water and swam to his kayak. The engine in the other boat accelerated, and slowly the craft disappeared.

He circled Giorgio's boat. He knew that within an hour Giorgio would be discovered, his body cut free, and a frantic effort made to save him. In the confusion, the details of how he was found and how the rope had twisted around his leg would be obscure. Tony was satisfied. Poor Giorgio became entangled in the rope, lost his balance, and fell overboard. He had fought to free himself but failed. Fear of drowning brought on a heart attack.

The lake awakened for another day. Ivonne set off to market. She would buy some cheeses—*pecorino* and a *quartirolo*—to accompany the wine she and Giorgio would share when he returned.

# Chapter 30

News of Giorgio's death spread quickly through the small towns along the lake. By Saturday noon, Caramazza had received a dozen calls, including one from Varenna, well north of Bellagio. Deats arranged a meeting with Brassi in the *comandante*'s office for two in the afternoon.

"Burri died from a massive heart attack, not from drowning." Brassi looked up. "There was very little water in his lungs; the autopsy showed that."

"Any history of a heart problem?" Deats queried.

"The examiner spoke with Burri's personal physician. The answer is no. He was a very healthy man for his age."

"Are you satisfied it was his heart?"

Brassi leaned back. "No. But then I never like simple solutions."

Deats fussed with his glasses. "What are the possibilities?"

"He was found in the water with a rope around his leg. We can assume he became tangled up, grew frightened—remember, it was dark. And then his heart gave out. He obviously didn't get twisted in the rope after the attack. Would a seasoned fisherman panic in that situation? I doubt if Burri would, based on what I know about him."

"A heart attack could strike a man that age any time. He didn't have to be frightened into it," Deats said thoughtfully. "Who discovered him?"

"The lake patrol. My men recognized his boat, and one of them has fished with Burri."

"Anything to suggest someone was with him when he went out this morning?"

"*Niente.* Lines and bait. Food for one person. But I don't think it was an accident."

"Why do you say that?"

"One detail doesn't have an answer. Burri was found with the upper part of his body in the water. For the moment let us assume he did have an attack, lost his balance, and fell over the railing headfirst into the water but the rope stopped him from going deeper in the water than to his shoulders. Now at this time he may still be breathing, but only for a minute or two perhaps. That would explain the small amount of water in his lungs. Now he is dead, and in the water to here." Brassi pointed to his chest. "It is a small point, but when the report was prepared by the examiner, he wrote that all of his clothes were wet."

The men looked silently at each other. Deats spoke first.

"Have you talked with his wife?"

Brassi sighed. "That is one of the reasons I feel as I do. She's a strong woman and is convinced someone killed her husband."

"So am I," Deats said simply.

"*Perchè?* He was very popular. A friend to everyone."

"I've no doubt there is a motive. The details will become clear in time."

"We would say it is a *rompicapo,* a puzzlement. Someone tried to kill him, but he died from a heart attack." Brassi raised outstretched hands.

Deats was flexing his bad hand, clenching then opening it and rubbing the stiff fingers. "Anthony Waters killed a policewoman and tried to make her death appear to have been an accident. I'm convinced beyond any doubt that is true. For a reason I can only speculate on, Giorgio Burri was murdered and his death was also made to appear as an accident." He kept his hands busy, this time polishing his glasses with a handkerchief. "But Giorgio had a heart attack, and Waters hadn't planned on that. The usual form of death in a boating accident is from drowning. I don't know how it happened, but Waters became confused when he discovered Giorgio died before he could drown him. Without thinking it through, he pulled him back onto the boat, tied a rope to his leg, then put the body into the water up to his waist." Deats stood. "That was a mistake."

"But a motive, a *causa,*" Brassi insisted.

"Money! Incredible amounts of money. It's happening in that gray mansion."

Brassi leaned forward, his expression intense, his eyes fixed on Deats's. "I gave orders for our observers to follow Waters and report when he was out on the lake. But he went in the darkness and came back without being seen. Then, this morning in the daylight, he was on the water in the speedboat racing to Como, then north to Bellagio and back to *Il Diodario.*"

"He wanted to be seen. Was the American woman with him?"

"He was alone."

"What of Kalem?"

"We learned from the taxi driver who drove him to the airport Thursday morning. He took an Alitalia flight to London."

"You should have told me. We might have been able to have him followed."

"This is information I learned early this morning. We rely on primitive technology, Superintendent. We are not a branch of Interpol."

"They might find him at the hotel where he stayed a short time ago. It's worth a call. What are your plans to arrest Waters?"

"Luciano Pavasi's men still patrol the grounds and Pavasi has taken a long weekend in San Remo. It seems he has a weakness for the gambling tables in Monte Carlo. When he returns, I will pay a surprise visit. I must have his cooperation and he will not want to give it to me. But in the end, Pavasi will do as he is told."

"I want an end to the killing. Can't we get this over with before Tuesday?"

Brassi nodded. "Without raising suspicions." He got to his feet and smiled confidently. "Everything is being made ready for Tuesday. Then you will have your man."

On Friday, after his meeting at Collyer's, Jonas told Seumas to drive west on the M40 to Oxford, then into Gloucestershire county and the area known as the Cotswolds. Jonas wanted to be alone and away from responsibilities. He had been on the go since sunrise and had put in a long, tiring day. Their destination was Broadway and the terribly old and charming Lygon Arms Hotel. Seumas found a room in a small inn near a pub filled with happy ale swiggers. Jonas sought a comfortable corner of the hotel's dining room. He ordered a double Golden Grouse, then several more. Finally he ordered an immense serving of roast beef and the usual side dishes. The food and drink were like a sedation; medicine to soothe his feelings of inadequacy or guilt. He went to bed. He wakened early on Friday, but knew when he read his watch that Tony had been up earlier and Giorgio was dead. He had not meant for people to die. He felt strangely sick.

The day was spent driving through the rolling Cotswold hills. The villages were out of storybooks, as if they had been designed for a Disney movie. Everywhere was the honey-yellow Cotswold stone. Seumas spoke when spoken to, otherwise silence filled the venerable limousine. Jonas's brain raced on, even as he sat mute and unmoving, gazing out on numberless flocks of sheep and thickly thatched roofs atop rows of quaint cottages. They returned to Broadway and Jonas telephoned *Il Diodario* to receive, officially, the news that Giorgio had been found dead earlier that day. Eleanor got on the phone and he failed to assuage her outraged grief.

Jonas again sought his own privacy and drank and ate as he had the previous evening. Eleanor's impassioned outpouring served to justify a third snifter of brandy following his meal.

He fell on his bed and went immediately to sleep. He slept fitfully and at daybreak fell into a deep sleep. It was nearly eleven when Seumas rapped on his door. They spent Saturday as they had the previous day, but as they drove, Jonas prepared for his meeting with Doan Chamberlin.

Eleanor pecked at the food she had taken from a buffet table laden with a dozen dishes Jonas selected for each Saturday-evening meal. Giorgio's death had depressed her, and she was still in shock.

"It isn't just awful, it's stupid and goddamned wrong! Men like that don't have accidents. He was a good man and a happy man!" She threw her napkin on the table and raced from the room. Stiehl got up as if to follow.

"Let her be," Tony said stonily. "She'll want to cry and be emotional."

"What the hell would you know about emotion?" Stiehl followed after her.

She had walked to the end of the patio and was rubbing her arms as if to ward off the chill coming off the lake. She turned as Stiehl approached her. "I'm cold."

"Summer's over," Stiehl answered. He put his sweater over her shoulders.

"I'm sorry I'm acting this way over Giorgio."

"Don't be sorry," Stiehl replied. "I'm trying to get at my own feelings. I once told Giorgio that I wished he were my father, and now I feel like I've lost my father. I'm angry he's dead, damned angry."

"He was the kind who let people get close to him. He made us feel happy and important. Now he's gone and we're the losers."

"I don't have many friends. It hurts to lose one."

"I'm your friend."

His hand brushed across her cheek. "I'm happy you are. But can you teach me how to write the way Leonardo did? Giorgio was my teacher, now I'm on my own."

"I can't write my mother a letter she can read. Will you show me what Giorgio was teaching you to write?"

He took both of her hands and pulled her close to him. "Things have changed, and I don't like what's going on. I don't think you should stay here."

"I can't leave. Jonas said I should stay until he comes back from London. I couldn't leave if I wanted to." She pulled on his hands. "Please show me what you've been doing. Please?"

"All right," he said quietly. "But Tony must not know. Tell him you're going to your room. Wait for half an hour, then come up."

She squeezed his hand and went back into the villa. Shortly after nine o'clock she rapped on the door to the studio.

"Tony's been drinking. He didn't seem to care what I was doing."

"It's not like him," Stiehl replied. "Something's going on, and I'm not sure if I like it."

The studio was festooned with reproductions from the Windsor collection and Stiehl had arranged it to appear that he was creating copies of Leonardo's anatomical drawings. He had been aware that Jonas had placed television cameras and microphones in the studio and had carefully picked through the lights and fixtures until he was certain he had located every camera. Locating the microphones presented a different problem. Those he found were tiny and he could not be confident he had spotted every one.

"How's it coming?" Eleanor asked.

"I'm bored with skulls, bones, and muscles," he replied. "You know why Leonardo spent so much time on those things? He had to know what people were made from so he could paint better nudes than Michelangelo. God help me, that's true."

Eleanor held a page filled with scribbles. "What's this?"

"Leonardo's ideas on love, sex, and the senses. Giorgio said that as long as I must practice Leonardo's handwriting I should write about something interesting."

"That sounds like Giorgio." She picked through the layers of drawings, pausing occasionally to comment on one. "They're beautiful. Every one. Will you draw something for me? I've never seen you at work."

"I'm a temperamental artist," he joked. "I must be inspired." His face brightened. "I have it. You're my inspiration."

He placed a chair a few feet away and positioned her so the light struck her face unevenly, creating subtle shadows on her cheeks and chin. He stared at her, analytically at first, then, though her expression was quiet, he saw her high spirit and a hint of her good humor. But he saw, too, her absolute beauty, a precision to her features. His hand moved quickly and an image took form as if it had been on the paper all the while and he was merely peeling away a protective covering.

It took but several minutes to complete the drawing. "There! Eleanor Shepard in the school of Leonardo, by the hand of Curtis Stiehl."

She came behind him and saw what he had drawn. She recognized herself and thought the likeness flattering. There was an intensity to the eyes, and the mouth seemed about to open and speak. "Is that how you see me?"

"I did. Then, when you were sitting there."

"I think it's beautiful. Too much so." She turned to him, then slowly lowered her head and kissed him firmly on the mouth. It was a long and passionate kiss. "Thank you," she said gently.

She backed away and sat in a chair close to Stiehl's drawing board. "You went to prison for counterfeiting, but you didn't go into any details and I didn't ask. Now I want to know."

"Because you kissed me?"

"Because I care about you and know so little about you. I don't want to do the wrong thing for the right reason."

"I'm confused."

"So am I, Curtis. I came to Italy to get away from someone who wants to marry me. I thought if I got away, I could sort it all out and decide if I love him that much."

"Do you?"

"No." She shook her head. "Please, tell me what you did?"

He described how he had counterfeited first the bonds, then the money, and how Jonas discovered the printing plates. He told her about prison life and how he had studied to improve as an artist. He told her the fabricated story of Jonas receiving a contract from the Royal Library—because he knew she must not know the truth. And finally he told her about his wife and daughter Stephanie.

"You miss Stephanie?"

"I love her very much."

"Did you spend much of the money?"

He laughed. "That's the funny part of it. I cleared five thousand on the bonds, and twenty thousand when I fenced the bills I printed. Later, when I was in prison, I added up all that I spent and it came out that I cleared less than seven thousand dollars."

"What will you do when this is over?"

"I haven't thought about it." He gently pulled her to him and wrapped his arms around her. He kissed her and, with their lips together, picked her up and carried her into his bedroom. He put her on the bed and leaned over her.

"One good kiss deserves another," he said tenderly.

When Jonas and Seumas arrived in Chipping Camden, darkness was replacing the last orange light in a sky where clouds had gathered to usher out the day's sunlight. There was a cool briskness to the air. Jonas claimed his room at the King's Arms Hotel, dined in a rare, modest way, then went to the bar. It was a congenial room with stone walls, thick oak beams, and a fire that gave off a glow like the sun that slipped from the sky a few hours earlier. He took a chair near the fire and pulled another alongside. The waiter brought a snifter of Remy Martin VSOP.

Doan Chamberlin arrived punctually at nine. He wore a blue blazer with gold buttons over a turtleneck shirt. He smelled of aftershave. Jonas knew he had been to a party or was going to one. He wasn't dressed for a discussion of old and valuable art. Chamberlin ordered a gin and bitters.

After a brief exchange, neither spoke. Jonas seemed intent on letting the tension build. Chamberlin interrupted the awkward silence. "I've given thought to our conversation at Collyer's, and I've reached some distressing conclusions. I find it abominable that my private affairs have been poked into, and I am distressed even more by my conviction that you have done this in order to influence my decision regarding the Leonardo manuscript."

"You'll affirm the authenticity because you'll find the page is genuine. The evidence is overwhelming. But I don't want an adverse opinion because of someone's warped sense of idealism. Discovery of the Leonardos will be controversial from the moment it is announced, and if your committee is divided, the arguments will fester and ultimately impact on the value of my discovery."

"Are you asking me to deliver a unanimous vote?"

Jonas swirled the brandy against the sides of the glass, then inhaled the fumes. "I was surprised you had no recollection of David Latcham, particularly in view of the fact you lived together."

"My wife would find that quite ridiculous."

"I'm not suggesting Latcham shared your home in Mayfair. Has Mrs. Chamberlin been to your house here in Chipping Camden?"

"Damn you, Kalem. What do you know about David?"

"David Latcham is a graduate of Columbia University and completed his advanced studies at Yale. He's very ambitious and an outstanding art historian." Jonas stared through his thick lenses at Chamberlin. "David Latcham was your lover."

"He was my protégé," Chamberlin countered. "When I discovered how extremely brilliant he was, I took him on as a collaborator. It's a common practice, you know."

"It was the publisher's advance that permitted Latcham to research and write your book. I assume you edited the manuscript to add touches of your style."

Chamberlin nervously rubbed his hands. Jonas noticed how small they were and how precisely the nails were manicured and polished. "When did you learn about David?"

"He once worked for me. After Columbia and before Yale. He never liked New York, preferred London. Occasionally he wrote. In one of his letters he told me of his association with you. His last letter was post-marked from Reigate."

"He used me to advance his career."

"You've never forgiven him for walking out on you."

Chamberlin finished his gin and bitters. "It's over. Would you rake it all up?"

"David is out of your life, yet you continue to spend weekends in Chipping Camden. Is that because you discovered another young man of equal ability and promise?"

Chamberlin bit on his lips. "What do you want from me?"

"You are the senior member of the committee. You have considerable influence."

"Gilsanon deals in scientific measurements. There are no abstractions to his findings. He will consider that your technical report is prejudiced, that it can serve only as a guide. But even should Gilsanon and Knowles grant a positive decision, Robin Mackworth-Young will insist on corroboration. For the money it'll fetch, any buyer will."

"I have no damned intention of selling the drawings to the Royal Library. They are free to bid along with everyone else, and if they want additional proof, that's their prerogative."

"What of Freebury?" Chamberlin asked. "I've seen him go mawkish over a new discovery, then waver and be indecisive."

"He concerns me. Freebury will know it is genuine, but be opposed on the principle that it will have too great a value. He believes art is for the masses."

"Edgar is idealistic, but he's no fool. His professional integrity is at stake. My integrity is also on the line. If we authenticate it, your discovery will have a value I couldn't begin to estimate."

"And well deserved," Jonas added firmly. "When it becomes known you have played a role in its authentication, your fortunes will greatly improve."

"Are you suggesting I will receive financial reward for a favorable opinion?"

"I suggest the announcement will cause a vast amount of publicity and you will be a part of it. Your lecture fees will increase and more of your books will be sold." Jonas allowed his words to sink in.

"If you believe the work is genuine, why are you taking this extraordinary measure to meet me in secret and threaten to expose my personal life?"

"For two reasons. Freebury must vote his professional opinion, and I want an early declaration. I must have a decision in days. Not months."

"Why so impatient? Would a few weeks matter?"

"I've invested enough time, and the time has been costly. I want accreditation *now*." Jonas added emphasis by rapping the table with the flat of his hand.

After an uncomfortable silence, Chamberlin got to his feet. "I'll do what I can. My report will go to Pimm and you will hear directly from him. Now I must go."

Jonas watched him make his way past the bar. He signaled for the waiter and ordered three fingers of brandy. Again he inhaled the rich fumes and sipped from the large bowl. He reviewed his brief encounter with Doan Chamberlin, asking himself if he had been forceful without provoking the proud art scholar into a vengeful attitude. He had been careful to solicit Chamberlin's influence with Freebury and steer him away from a rash judgment based on misguided idealism. And he had asked for an early decision. He was pleased with his performance. He drained his glass and set off for his room.

As he passed through a square-shaped hall he was handed an envelope by the hotel manager. The paper was thick and expensive. The flap was engraved and when he drew the envelope close, he saw, represented in Korean characters, the unmistakable name of Madame Sun. The paper was scented and gave off the familiar spice and floral fragrance he recalled from their first meeting. He read the brief note:

Dear Mr. Kalem:
    There is great urgency in meeting with you. Please be so kind as to join me in Room 16.

Madame Sun's signature was rendered in a single, bold Korean character.

"Wally, I've been trying to get you all afternoon. Have you heard from Oxby?"

"I'm happy to say I haven't."

"Don't be too sure of that. He called to learn how to contact you. Told me that Kalem arrived in London on Thursday. Jack's got his own information network, and when the fat man hit Heathrow, Jack knew in thirty minutes."

"I know he's in London. What's he up to?"

"Oxby said he'd fill me in later . . . that it was important to make contact with you."

"He doesn't stand on ceremony. He knows where to find me. We've had another one of those unfortunate accidents."

"Good Christ. Who this time?"

"Giorgio Burri." Deats gave a brief accounting. "You'll have a report in a couple of days."

"You're sure he was murdered?" Heston asked.

"It's too much of a coincidence. First Sarah Evans, now Burri. Both accidents?"

"But what's so damned important, Wally? Two people are dead."

"We'll find that out after we defuse Waters."

"I think Oxby wants to be there when that happens."

"Our plans are complete. We're moving on Tuesday morning with or without Oxby."

"Do me a favor, Wally? Don't play the hero again. I'd like to catch some salmon with you this autumn."

Jonas had carefully chosen an obscure site for his meeting with Chamberlin. He was baffled, but more angered, that Madame Sun had been able to follow him. His initial reaction was to ignore the note. But he relented and climbed the stairs and found his way to Room 16. He was admitted by a smiling James Sun.

"You've come early, Mr. Kalem."

Madame Sun was dressed in a tailored suit and cream-colored silk blouse. She seemed taller than on their first meeting, but still diminutive. She greeted him graciously, saying, "It has been several weeks since we met. Much has happened."

Jonas was determined to make the meeting brief and declined the invitation to sit. "Why have you followed me? You knew how to arrange for a meeting in London."

"You must understand our determination. We made arrangements to learn when you were at Collyer's to present the Leonardo. But you drove directly to the country and James followed you. I have just come from Brussels to meet you."

"For what purpose?" Jonas demanded.

"The page from the manuscript contains a rendering of the *Mona Lisa*. It becomes the first-known study of the lady ever to be found. We want it."

Among the members of the committee the logical source for a leak was Gilsanon & Knowles. Gilsanon said he would put his crew to work immediately and a crew might be a dozen workers. "How did you learn this?"

"It matters only that we know," Madame Sun said with finality. "We have been able to put a value on your discovery."

"The value will be determined by the auction. It will be entered at Collyer's winter sale in February."

Madame Sun did not respond immediately. She turned to her son and nodded. James handed her a folder and took up a position by her side. Slowly her fingers leafed through the half-dozen pages, then, her eyes wide and staring, she spoke in a reverential manner.

"We will pay eight million dollars. The money will be deposited to your bank within twenty-four hours of the signing of this agreement."

Jonas sat. The reality that he would be paid so large a sum came with a sudden rush of exhilaration and fear. He had vainly tried to put a value on the manuscript, but couldn't trust his judgment. Selling privately would attract little attention. Offering the pages one at a time at auction would create demand, higher prices, and worldwide attention.

"I will need time to consider your offer. There are many advantages to the auction."

"I have reviewed your astrological chart and it distresses me deeply. You, or someone close to you, remains in grave danger."

"Damn your chart! You make an offer and tie it to warnings of danger. Is that really what your astrology is all about?" He had dismissed her ominous prophesy before, but in spite of his outburst he could not shrug off his new respect for the foretellings of Madame Sun's *Ming Shu.*

"There is something more which is not part of your astrological chart," Madam Sun intoned. "You have stretched your financial resources to the limit. Your bank has refused further credit."

"That's absurd," Jonas protested. He had assigned the balance of his assets, including his first editions and the Childe Hassam he had been so profoundly proud to loan the Museum of Modern Art. "Searching for lost treasures is not for the timid."

"*Il Diodario* has been an expensive luxury. You must allow me to visit there."

Jonas got to his feet. Madame Sun looked up to him, her face composed and smiling. James was behind her, a hand touching his mother's shoulder. He, too, was smiling. They seemed poised for a portrait, but to Jonas they were a threat to everything he had worked so long to achieve.

"I'll consider the offer," he said.

"We are certain that you will." Madame Sun handed him the folder. "The terms are most reasonable. You will also find a telephone number where you can reach me with your decision."

Jonas took the folder. He scanned the first page, then walked to the door and turned to look back at the tableau of mother and son, smiles frozen to faces as if they were masks covering lifeless robots.

# Chapter 31

A black sedan stopped in front of Torno's *municipio*. From it emerged Bruno Brassi and his deputy assistant, Dario Zingoni. Two uniformed men remained in the car. Brassi had not called beforehand, aware that doing so might frighten Torno's chief of police off to a quickly conceived "emergency." Brassi brushed aside an indignant sergeant and strode directly into Pavasi's office.

Seated behind a cluttered desk was a man in the full bloom of dissipation. Seeing the *comandante*, he began fussing with a black tie wrapped loosely around an unbuttoned shirt a size too small. A bulge of fat rimmed the collar. His eyes were swollen, his lips puffed. On his blue serge uniform was stuck a gold pin to one lapel, the other missing.

"This is a surprise, Bruno. You should have phoned."

"Why? So you can make believe you are busy?" He picked up an empty wine bottle. "So you can hide these in the *rifiuto*?"

"You haven't come to spit your insults at me."

"Hardly that. It would be a waste of time. Tell me what you know of *Il Diodario*. Your men are posted on that property around the clock, and I find it difficult to understand how they can serve the people of Torno and guard the villa at the same time."

"They volunteer for the extra pay, Bruno. You remember how it was to earn extra money?"

Bruno remembered and had done the same. "Who pays them?"

"The money is from Signore Kalem, the owner."

"Who puts the money in their hand?"

Pavasi went to a mirror and finished knotting his tie. "Of what concern is it? The men get paid."

"I'm authorizing Lieutenant Zingoni to review all records and interview your 'volunteers.'"

"Bruno, please listen. The American pays me and I pay the men." He waved his arms. "Isn't that all you need to know?"

"How much for Pavasi? How much is lost at the tables in Campione? And last week you play the big shot in Monte Carlo."

"I win and I lose. It's no one's business."

"You gamble with your money? How much does Kalem pay you?"

"I made a contract with Signore Kalem. How much is for the guards and how much is for me is my affair." Pavasi grew excited and the button at his neck popped loose.

"How many volunteers guard the old place?"

"I have a contract. I am honor bound to put men on the property."

"Your honor is twisted. Your first obligation is to the people of Torno. But enough of honor and money, the investigation will speak for itself." He sat across from Pavasi and signaled for Dario to close the door.

"You are aware that Signore Burri from Cernobbio was found dead on the lake Friday?"

"A terrible thing. *Un attacco cuore,*" Pavasi said somberly.

"You knew it was his heart?"

Pavasi looked surprised. "Doesn't everyone know?"

"Everyone? Did you learn this from the people at *Il Diodario*?"

"I haven't been there in a week."

"Then by telephone?"

"I talk to Signore Kalem every day, but he was away this weekend. He came back on Sunday."

"You met him at the airport," Brassi said flatly.

"You knew?"

"It is my business to know. What did you talk about?"

Pavasi looked away. "Nothing of importance."

"Perhaps not to you, Luciano, but however trivial, I want to know why he calls every day."

"Usually about the guards. Yes, he asks about the guards."

"What else?"

"He wants to know if I have heard from a certain Englishman."

"The name?"

"I have it here someplace," Pavasi said, trying to forestall the inevitable. He sifted through the litter of papers. "Here. The name is Deats."

Brassi got to his feet.

"Everyone in *Il Diodario* must be interrogated regarding our investigation of Burri's death. I want you to telephone Kalem and advise him that it's urgent you meet him tomorrow morning at ten o'clock."

"Tomorrow is not good. I have a meeting I must attend in Como," he said importantly.

Brassi glared. "There's no meeting in Como. You've been in Brissago on Lake Maggiore every Tuesday for the past two months. You spend the day with Anna Manucci." Pavasi had been spending his new riches profligately, leaving a trail that Brassi's staff could easily follow. "You must not tell Kalem we have met. Is that clear?"

Pavasi's head was bowed. Brassi barely heard him reply. "*Sì*. It is clear."

Brassi slammed the phone onto the desk with such force the bell inside rang, and Pavasi bolted halfway from his chair. "Get Kalem on the phone. Now!"

Pavasi dialed and, when he reached the last number, put the receiver down. "Bruno, in the name of the Holy Virgin, what do I say that won't make him suspicious?"

"Tell him you're having difficulties with the guards. That they want more money."

Pavasi dialed all the numbers again and soon had Jonas on the line. He said as little as necessary, but an appointment was confirmed.

Brassi returned to Como. Dario Zingoni assured his superior that Torno's police chief would not wander off and would be on duty when the *comandante* returned the next day.

Harold Pimm had arranged the Monday meeting long in advance. He had not anticipated the added pressures of the Leonardo and could only trust that his committee had made progress since their meeting with Jonas Kalem the previous Thursday. The committee had other paintings to consider in advance of the February auction. Deadlines were approaching for photographs for the catalog. The Old-Masters auction was a tradition, once an occasion for social mixing, now an important event in the art world. Old Masters were gaining in popularity and price. When word spread that a Leonardo was to be offered, the numbers of collectors, curators, and agents attending would require moving the auction to a hotel, where it would be covered by the media. A great, visual event for television. Of no little consequence, it would mean record profits for Collyer's.

Doan Chamberlin was the last to show and the first to speak directly to the principal purpose of the meeting. "I trust we can present our opinions and arrive at an early decision."

"I am in no rush," Edgar Freebury protested. "If we affirm, that piece of paper becomes more valuable than it deserves to be."

"Is that a reason to deny its authenticity?" Chamberlin challenged.

"Quite right," Pimm chimed in. "All of you agreed to evaluate the authenticity of the Leonardo, not put a price tag on it or worry that when it is priced, it will bring too much or too little." Pimm eyed each man in turn. "The opinion which will ultimately be expressed by Collyer's will be unprejudiced." He turned to Paul Gilsanon. "Have you had time to complete your technical findings?"

Gilsanon handed a folder to each man. "We worked round the clock," he said proudly. "I've given you a summary of our findings, and if you're confused by the technical jargon, I will answer questions. We've completed forty-six separate tests on the paper, inks, chalks, and intaglio impressions created by the writing instruments. The paper is of the period and indigenous to the vicinity of Florence... probably from a *cartiera* along the Pescia River. Our chemical analyses show both inks and chalk to be similar to those found in other Leonardo manuscripts. The spectrographic examinations compare favorably with similar tests released by the Musée Français and the Ambrosiana. Titration tests were also made, as well as docimasy analysis indicating a familiar crude iron had been used in formulating the inks.

"Lately we have utilized a computer procedure pioneered by the Fogg Museum in Cambridge, Massachusetts. Tricky stuff but effective. We have programs that contain all that is known of the way an artist went about creating drawings or paintings. In the case of Leonardo, the computer knows he was left-handed, his brush strokes were more often left to right, and he achieved chiaroscuro effects in his unique fashion. Everything known about his handwriting, and his manner of spelling or use of abbreviations, is also in the computer. Then we entered similar information from the document under study and made a computer match. So far, so good. We're greatly encouraged. I expect to find corroboration from Cambridge on my fax machine as early as this afternoon.

"In balance, we find the work authentic, subject to such vagaries as usually attend granting an unqualified ascription to an artist in circumstances where a work of this great age has no history and no provenance. Our studies, and I point this out most forcefully, do not immediately declare the work is fraudulent, but neither can we declare that it is unassailably authentic."

"Good Christ," Chamberlin burst out, "until your final equivocation, I thought you were going to make a definitive statement for a change. But you've gone off as you usually do, shifting the responsibility to the historian."

"Come off it, Chamberlin," Gilsanon replied testily. "You are as aware as I am that this page and others like it that may come before us will be argued over for decades. We take an adversary position; we try to disprove authenticity, not prove it. To that end, we've made a firm declaration."

"We invite dissension by weaseling our words," Chamberlin shot back.

"I have not equivocated. Read the report before pointing fingers."

"I've read other reports from Gilsanon & Knowles. Each one reads like the last. Six-syllable gobbledygook couched in a goddamned language that adds up to pure obfuscation of facts and no clear-cut conclusion."

Pimm's eyes were closed. He had anticipated Chamberlin's sniping, and when he felt the squabbling had run its course, he called on Edgar Freebury.

"I agree with Ed Gilsanon with respect to the antiquity and authenticity of the paper and inks. I am concerned with content and style, and speak now as an historian.

"I have concluded that Jonas Kalem has made an incredible discovery. The page fits neatly into Leonardo's *Treatise on Painting* and contains preliminary thoughts and sketches he made before the final draft. Our special reward, of course, is the head of the enigmatic *Mona Lisa*, rendered, I presume, very close to the time he worked on the painting.

"From my perspective the drawing can be attributed to Leonardo. I feel his hand touched the paper, that he wrote the words which I've translated to my satisfaction. Quite naturally, I have considered that a student—perhaps Melzi—toyed with some parts of the drawing, but whatever might have been touched is minor.

"As I studied the handwriting I was occasionally persuaded that it was not da Vinci's, but I must quickly admit I am not qualified to judge whether he actually penned the words. I am satisfied with the content and the vocabulary."

Freebury placed a folder on the table. "Here is my report. Brief, but complete."

"And you vote to affirm?" Pimm asked.

"In spite of my finding, I will not vote for accreditation."

"Have you lost your senses?" Chamberlin said in disbelief. "What in hell will you do?"

"Abstain. I am repulsed by the thought that what we say will make a piece of paper worth millions."

"Goddamn it, our job is to say it's real or fake, not put a price on it."

Pimm fanned the pages of Freebury's report. "Edgar abstains for personal reasons. From what he has said, and from all I see in his report, he has found the manuscript page to be authentic. Have I stated your position accurately?"

Freebury nodded.

"The equivocation continues," Chamberlin said boldly. "First the caveats, then an abstention. We sound like mice doing lion's work."

"Then dispel all the vagueness," Pimm rejoined. "Are you claiming for or against attribution?"

"For it," Chamberlin said with a firm voice. "The fact that Giorgio Burri had somehow become involved prompted my only reservation. His provenance made interesting reading, but my decision turned on the drawing itself. I have not concerned myself with paper and inks. That is for Gilsanon and all his magic machinery to study."

Chamberlin placed his report next to the others. "Leonardo, among all the great artists, produced a uniqueness never equalled by another artist. A Leonardo doesn't look like a Botticelli or Perugino, or Signorelli or any of his contemporaries. When Leonardo copied another artist, he left his indelible mark. No one then or since has produced a drawing or a single sentence to be confused with the Master's. It is quality and only quality that decides whether a drawing is an original, a copy, or an imitation. And that ultimate measurement is *in our feelings.*"

Doan Chamberlin had prepared his little speech carefully and warmed to the opportunity of presenting it to his captive audience.

The committee continued its deliberation until after six o'clock. Harold Pimm waited patiently for small arguments to run their course, taking from each new pieces of information that would help him dispel his own doubts. He was not bound by the group's decision yet was pleased there was a positive agreement, including Edgar Freebury's abstention, which was obviously hiding his approbation. A work by Leonardo would bring a gargantuan price at auction. At year's end, Pimm would enjoy a share of the profits.

A false claim and its subsequent exposure would have a contrary effect. The loss of his share of the profits would be overshadowed by a loss of prestige, or in the extreme, termination from a position he prized.

When finally the discussion and arguments had run their course, Pimm called the conference to an end. He reached out to touch the three reports, then glancing at each in turn said, "Your work is complete. Mine begins."

In truth, Harold Pimm had devoted as many hours to the project as the others combined. He had begun his study of the drawings and handwriting the previous Thursday and, with very little sleep, had probed and analyzed and come to his own conclusion. He had personally delivered the precious manuscript page to Jonas at Heathrow on Sunday afternoon, then returned to the Victoria and Albert Museum for a confidential meeting with an old colleague with whom he had collaborated on previous attributions.

He set the reports in front of him, and as he read each one he made notes to compare to his own. Gilsanon's findings were still troubling. The handwriting analysis was incomplete and neither Chamberlin nor Freebury had proven persuasively that Leonardo had written on the page. Pimm knew how scholars argued over Leonardo's squiggly lines, yet he was fascinated by the artist's own account of how he invited musicians to practice while he painted and how their laughter resulted in the relaxed smile on the face of the young wife of a Florentine merchant.

He labored over the reports for several hours, sustained by several pots of tea heavily laced with a pungent Cuban rum. At ten o'clock he wrote a brief note to the managing directors in which he confirmed his committee's agreement to grant accreditation. Then he placed a phone call to Jonas as he had promised.

Jonas listened to Pimm's news with childish delight. It was a sweet victory. But there was no delight in Harold Pimm's voice when he learned that Jonas was unwilling to guarantee that he would put the Leonardo into auction.

"I assembled the best authorities in the UK. They came through damned quickly. We're counting on featuring your Leonardo in the Old-Masters show in February. That's your part of the bargain, Mr. Kalem." Pimm's voice was hard and without its usual friendly musicality.

"I agreed to use Collyer's if I put the drawings to auction," Jonas replied.

"Are you planning a private sale?"

"Possibly. I'll have a final decision in the next few days."

Jonas agreed to phone Harold Pimm no later than Friday. He immediately called the number given him by Madame Sun. His call was answered by a woman who repeated the number Jonas had called, then asked simply, "Have you a message?" Her voice was clipped, English, efficient.

He gave the woman his name, telephone number, and a brief message: "News from Bruton Place very favorable."

He had expected to talk with Madame Sun and was disappointed that he could not share the news from Harold Pimm. He had weighed the merits of the private sale against the publicity of an auction. Pressures to replenish his depleted resources were growing and argued for an early sale. Pride gave way to the practical. "There will be other pages," he concluded, "a little fortune now, fame later."

"Pavasi's a shit. He cares only about this." Brassi rubbed thumb and forefinger together. "But his little world is about to come apart. Here, in the heart, he is frightened."

"Any chance he'll tell Kalem what's going on?"

"Dario won't let him out of sight. I trained him myself."

Brassi and Deats were seated at a table in a corner of Caramazza's dining room. The *comandante* elected to tell Deats personally of his plans for Wednesday morning. "I want to get inside that damned castle without fuss or suspicion."

"Waters has a dozen ways to get out of that building you call a castle."

Brassi shrugged. "Out of it? Yes. Off the grounds? Perhaps. Escape from the lake? Never."

Caramazza joined them. "My American guests ask so many questions. Where to buy this? How many miles to there? I never know the answers." He smiled. "Signore Deats, I almost forgot. There is a telephone call for you."

Deats took the call behind the small reception desk.

"This is Oxby. Have you heard from Elliot?"

"We talked on Saturday. Where are you?"

"I'm in Como."

"How long have you been there?"

"I came on Sunday. I was on the same flight with Jonas Kalem."

"Elliot tells me you've been on Kalem's trail since July. Why didn't I know this?"

"You never asked."

"That's a bad answer, Jack. I need to know what you're up to."

"You don't need to know. You go your way, I'll go mine."

It was classic Oxby. Secretive and obstinate. "Stop playing games, Jack. What are you up to?"

"I'm going to pay Mr. Kalem a visit, but I don't want to interfere with your plans."

"We're taking Waters tomorrow morning."

"That's good news." Oxby actually sounded enthusiastic. "What time?"

"Ten o'clock."

Oxby did not answer. The silence lengthened and infuriated Deats.

"Who have you teamed up with?" Oxby asked.

"Fuck off, Jack. If you want to cooperate, then join us tonight. I'm in Moltrasio at the Hotel Caramazza."

"I know. There's no point in getting together, but you can do me one favor. When you take Waters, don't rough up Kalem too badly. Cheerio."

Deats heard the click. The call enraged him. He returned to Brassi, where, unable to conceal his fury, he spilled out the brief conversation. "I don't know what the son of a bitch is up to, but it's typical Oxby. He didn't leave a number. He could be anywhere in Como."

"My men can check every hotel, every *pensione*."

"No good. You can put all the police in Italy on the hunt. If Jack Oxby doesn't want to be found, he won't be."

Jonas remained in the solarium following the call he made in accordance with Madame Sun's instructions. The one camera still working in Stiehl's studio was once more sending a distorted picture. Stiehl had located the cameras and all but one of the microphones. Jonas complained to Tony, arguing he had a right to know what Curtis was up to. "Watch him more closely," he had told Tony. He was also concerned that Eleanor was spending too much time with Stiehl. What had he told her? Had he shown her the drawings? "No, Curtis is too smart to do that," he said aloud. "Eleanor must not know. That would be dangerous."

He waited impatiently for the phone to ring. He opened another bottle of wine. An hour slipped by and he was certain he would not hear from Madame Sun until the morning. Then, shortly after midnight, the phone rang.

"What is your good news?" Madame Sun asked.

"Collyer's will grant an attribution to the Leonardo," Jonas replied triumphantly.

"Without condition?"

"Only because there are minor gaps in the provenance."

There was a pause, then Madame Sun continued, "Have you come to a decision?"

"Yes. I agree to sell, but the money must be transferred to my bank at the time I give you the manuscript. I must have confirmation."

There was a pause. "That can be arranged. You have the drawing?"

"Of course," Jonas answered.

"We are anxious to have it, Mr. Kalem." Madame Sun spoke with an authority that was not to be denied. "Our representative is in Milan and can meet with you tomorrow morning. Would that be convenient?"

Jonas hesitated. All that he had set in motion years before was racing to a climax. It was after midnight, he was tired. Why so soon? Then he threw all those thoughts away. Pavasi was coming. Security would be at full strength. "Yes," he answered. "Ten o'clock."

I regret that I cannot visit your *Il Diodario*. But another time," Madame Sun said. "Our representative will have the necessary papers and will telephone the banks for the transfer of money."

"What is his name?" Jonas asked.

She did not answer his question. "I am pleased with your decision, Mr. Kalem. Very pleased. Good-bye."

# Chapter 32

A taxi boat eased against the bumpers lining the stone dock. An oddly dressed man reached a short leg up to the landing, but quickly stood back when he found he was peering into the barrel of a rifle held by one of Pavasi's off-duty *polizia*. A burst of animated shouting followed, and when it was over, the guard extended a hand to the passenger and helped him scamper up beside him.

"What a strange little man," Eleanor called out to Stiehl from the studio window where she had watched the boat approach and the visitor come ashore.

"Anyone we know?" Stiehl came beside her.

"Look how he's dressed." She laughed. "A jumble of stripes as if he's been cast in some awful farce."

The man wore blue seersucker pants and a striped shirt and tie topped with a blue and orange blazer. On his feet were thick-soled boots, and a white cap ballooned above his head like a giant soufflé. A leather briefcase was clamped under his arm. Eleanor was amused by the little man's strange costume, but she admired the way he confidently strode to the portico where Tony stood waiting.

"Forgive me if I'm a bit early, Mr. Kalem, but Tuesday is market day and I wanted to avoid the traffic in Como."

Jonas looked down to the small man. He had expected Dong Shim, the one who had telephoned to arrange the first meeting with Madame Sun, and whom he expected had been in the Berkeley Hotel that first evening. They entered the solarium. Tony took position behind Jonas and never looked away from the strangely dressed man who had come to execute a rare and possibly historic transaction.

"This letter will introduce me." The little man handed Jonas an envelope.

The letter was brief. It confirmed that Julian LaConte had represented Madame Sun and her husband on numerous occasions, and that he was a lawyer acting with full power of attorney. Though he was small of statue, there was a largeness about him. His long nose dominated a face that was strong and intelligent. His eyes were unusually big and brown, and framed by thick brows. His upper teeth protruded slightly, seemingly more so because they were large and very white.

"I'm expecting others," Jonas said. "But our business is more important, and I damned well don't want to rush through it."

"This should not take long." The little man's voice was a rich baritone, another incongruity that Jonas noted. "May I see the Leonardo?"

"It's here on my desk." Jonas took the drawing from a slim metal case.

"And here is the agreement." LaConte handed the papers to Jonas. He then took a magnifying glass from his pocket and examined the page closely. He moved the glass slowly over the handwriting and seemed to be reading the words.

The bells in the church of San Giovanni in Torno pealed out the tenth hour. Jonas glanced nervously toward the dock.

"It is truly beautiful," LaConte said quietly. "But so small. I expected it to be from a larger manuscript."

"Only the Leicester Codex is larger," Jonas said knowingly. "All of Leonardo's manuscripts are less than eight-by-twelve inches."

The agreement was a scant three pages long. Jonas was asked to provide the name of his bank, the account number, and a bank officer who would confirm that the monies were deposited.

Jonas wrote in the information. "They've killed off the advantages of dealing with Swiss banks," he grumbled.

"It's still easier to move money around in Switzerland," LaConte said without looking up.

The Bank Julius Bar was serving as agent for Madame Sun. Jonas knew it as a private and prestigious institution. The deposit would be in Swiss francs, and the agreement stipulated that funds would be transferred immediately, but limited to two million dollars the first week, and subsequent withdrawals of two million weekly for three weeks. Furthermore, all withheld money would earn interest at the prevailing rates and deposited to Jonas's account.

"I never agreed to these terms." Jonas was obviously angered that strings had been tied to the arrangement.

"Merely a reasonable precaution," LaConte insisted. "Your money earns full interest. I'm certain you would do the same if you were the buyer."

"But I'm not. There will be no restrictions."

"Then there is no agreement." LaConte put the glass in his pocket and slipped the papers back into his briefcase. He made a move toward the door where Tony stood, arms folded across his chest. LaConte turned to Jonas.

"If you have a change of mind, I will be available to meet another time."

Jonas stared at the little man and past him to Tony and then to the lake and an approaching boat. "Bring me the damned papers."

LaConte obeyed. Jonas signed two sets, retaining one and handing the other to LaConte, who now had the telephone in his hand.

"One final detail, Mr. Kalem. A call to the bank in Zurich will assure that money is transferred to your account by this time tomorrow." Jonas nodded.

LaConte spoke to the operator in fluent Italian. And a moment later he issued a stream of instructions in perfect French. "It is done. I will return tomorrow, and after you have confirmed that a deposit has been made to your account, I will take the drawing."

He put on the white cap and started for the door and as he did so, the briefcase slipped from his hand and the papers scattered. "You are clumsy, LaConte," he scolded himself. He reached down to retrieve the papers.

A van pulled off the road by the unused gate high over *Il Diodario*. The doors opened and nine men leaped out, each dressed in green-and-mustard yellow combat uniforms. The leader pointed to the top of the wall and barked a brief command. One of the men held a length of thick rope, a grapnel attached to an end. He threw the hook over the wall, then pulled the rope taut. In turn, each man scrambled up the rope, then dropped onto the other side. The last over pulled up the rope and let it fall to the ground, where another coiled and concealed it in the brush.

They huddled around their leader. Three carried Pietro Beretta BM59 Alpine rifles, the others had sidearms. Below them was *Il Dio-*

*dario*; they looked down to the tiled roof, the hill so steep that in descending it, one feared falling on top of the mansion. Instructions were reviewed: five headed north, the others south toward the docks. They began a slow descent through the thick brambles.

A motor launch moved leisurely along the lake's edge. Two men dressed in white stood on the small afterdeck. One held a microphone and once each minute announced the ship's position. Above them a blue-and-white pennant fluttered in the mild breeze. They were flanked by two smaller craft that looked very much like pleasure boats. When they were directly abeam of *Il Diodario*, the man with the microphone gave instructions. One boat continued to a point a hundred yards offshore in front of the boathouses and anchored. A man appeared with a fishing pole and threw his line in the water. The launch took position off the dock, and the third boat cruised slowly in a wide-sweeping figure-eight pattern.

The hovercraft that normally rushed directly up the center of the lake came into view and sped past the villa to disappear beyond the Torno landing. It made a wide turn, slowed, then dropped into the water, where it bobbed in its own wake. The commuters and tourists had been replaced by men in white and blue uniforms.

A pontooned helicopter sat in the harbor at Cernobbio, its engine idling, the rotors moving imperceptibly. The pilot watched the second hand on his chronometer reach the top of the dial. He accelerated, then lazily the copter lifted, its nose tilted over, the blades clawing the warm air.

The distinctive sound of the helicopter grew louder. Eleanor tried picking it out of the sky. It was directly in front of the villa before she saw it coming in low over the water.

"Something's going on out there. Come look."

Stiehl joined her at the window. She pointed to the dock. "Two boats are tied up and two more just sitting out there. Another is running in circles, and now a helicopter has joined in."

"Who came in the second boat?"

"Two men. I've seen one of them before. He wears black and has gold buttons."

"They beefed up security," Stiehl said. "I counted five yesterday. One was still in his police uniform. Now you know why you can't go shopping."

"I'm no threat to anyone if I'm off buying panty hose or having my hair done."

"Jonas thinks you'd be a threat as soon as you leave *Il Diodario*."

"Why? What am I supposed to know?"

Stiehl took hold of her hands. "It's what Jonas *thinks* you know. I'm going to find a way to get you away from here. But you can't ask questions." He repeated in an almost threatening voice, "Is that clear? No questions."

"It's clear that I'm a part of whatever's going on. I spent all those months finding paper and formulating inks and, if you won't tell me what you're doing, I'm damned well going to get it out of Jonas."

She was genuinely angered, her face flushed and her eyes wide. Stiehl was sure she was also frightened. "Be careful what you ask Jonas."

"I have a right to know. You tell me!"

He shook his head. "Understand this once and for all. You're not to know." He kissed her.

"That helped. I'm frightened and it's an awful feeling." She put her arms around him, hugging tightly. She slowly pulled away. "That's better." She looked up at him. "I didn't have any breakfast and I'm starved. I'll fix lunch."

"Great idea. Give me a few minutes and I'll be down to help."

Walter Deats sat next to the pilot. Brassi gave him the choice of the *comandante*'s launch or the helicopter. "This is your show," Deats had answered. "I want the best seat and that's in the air."

Pavasi's guards came together after their patrol. "Who is with Luciano?"

"They went through the door before I could see."

"The other one? The little man with the odd hat?"

"Someone to see Signore Kalem."

"But the boats"—a finger pointed to the motor launch—"especially that one."

"*Dio!* The *comandante*'s pennant is flying from it!"

Before either said another word, arms reached under their chins and tightened against their necks. Their eyes bulged like little balloons. Then, breath spent, they sagged. "Tie them up. Carmine stays with them. The rest take your positions."

"*Scusi*, Signore Kalem. I did not know you had a guest." Pavasi reached the entrance to the solarium just as LaConte put the last of his papers in the briefcase.

"Our business is over. Mr. LaConte was just leaving."

LaConte patted his briefcase. "Thank you again." He tipped his cap and scurried past Pavasi and the man who had come with him.

"What's so damned important with the guards?" Jonas was clearly irritated. "And you didn't tell me you would bring a guest."

Brassi, who was wearing a business suit, forced a smile. "Forgive us, signore. Luciano is not responsible that I am here. I insisted on joining him."

"That is true," Pavasi said apologetically.

"Then why *are* you here?" Jonas demanded.

"I am Bruno Brassi, *comandante* of police for the province of Como."

Tony stepped back. He felt as he had in London when the police cars, their sirens wailing, flashed past him on Fleet Street. He edged toward the door.

"Luciano will talk with you about the guards. I am here regarding Giorgio Burri's death. I am told he visited here often."

"Several times," Jonas answered.

"What had you heard concerning his death?"

"A tragic accident. He drowned."

Brassi looked past Jonas to Tony, who stood by the door leading to the long hall beyond. "I am sorry, but I have not met the other gentleman."

Jonas turned. "This is Mr. Habershon, my assistant."

Brassi stepped toward Tony, his hand extended. "Welcome to Como, signore."

Tony put a hand forward. Brassi glanced down to the back of the hand gripping his. "It's a pleasure to be here," Tony replied dryly.

"The circumstances of Professor Burri's death are puzzling," Brassi continued. "He was not a young man, but strong, and from all signs, in excellent health. The autopsy revealed that he died from a heart attack, and yet he was found with his upper body out of the water and a rope twisted around one leg. We can perhaps understand the heart attack, it can happen at any age, at any time. But the rope..." His voice trailed off. "Forgive me, my mind was talking."

"I'll miss him," Jonas added. "He was good company."

"What exactly was your relationship?"

"We were friends."

"And you last saw him?"

"Monday. In his home. He was proud of his wife's cooking."

"Not since then?"

"I flew to London on Thursday. Luciano met me when I returned on Sunday."

"*Sì*, Bruno is aware of that," Pavasi said.

"Luciano tore himself away from the gambling tables so he could meet you," Brassi said scornfully.

The chatter from the helicopter grew louder, and as it passed over the villa, all conversation ceased. Jonas showed irritation at the invasion of his privacy, but Brassi knew differently. It was a signal.

"Signore Habershon, when did you last see Giorgio Burri?"

"On Monday. I was with Mr. Kalem."

"Not since?"

"No."

"Where were you on Friday morning?"

"Here, in the villa."

"You have witnesses?"

"See here, I don't like this silly questioning at all." Tony masked his own angry fear with Habershon's effete indignation.

"It is my responsibility to ask 'silly questions.' Are there witnesses?"

"Of course. Others saw me. I don't know who. I don't keep lists of the people I run into each morning "

"Signore Kalem, is there a young woman here named Eleanor Shepard?"

"Yes."

"And a Curtis Stiehl?"

"They are guests."

"And Anthony Waters?" Brassi's eyes were on Tony when he asked the question. When Jonas failed to answer, Brassi turned back to him. "Anthony Waters, signore. Is he among you?"

"I no longer employ Mr. Waters." Jonas had composed himself and stood at his desk, sorting through papers as if he were about to go about his usual business and the *comandante*'s presence was an unnecessary intrusion.

Brassi moved to the front of the desk and positioned himself so that Tony was on a line directly behind Jonas. "I am not concerned if you employ him, only if he has been here in your *Il Diodario*."

"There are four of us," Jonas replied firmly. "And you have an accurate identification of each one."

"Mr. Habershon," Brassi called out the name in a loud voice. "I must ask to see your passport."

Tony bolted from the solarium like a shell shot from a rifle. He knew every turn in the old building—every door, the hidden rooms, the corridors behind walls. He raced to the pantry beyond the dining hall.

Brassi broke for the door leading outside and ordered his men into the villa, singling out one to remain with Jonas. Suddenly the room was empty, save for Jonas and a young man standing with his right arm across his chest. He was holding a pistol.

There in the doorway through which the others had disappeared stood the strangely dressed little figure who thirty minutes earlier had scampered away with his briefcase tucked tightly under his arm. He touched the visor of his cap as if in salute to the surprised guard and proceeded past him. Jonas had retreated to his command chair, his arms resting on the fat pillows on each side of him, his eyes staring blankly through the thick lenses.

"I realize this is a very distressing time for you," LaConte said "The tranquillity of your *Il Diodario* has been rudely interrupted and you have been left in the company of this young man who holds what I am certain is a fully loaded M51 pistol." He smiled. "I failed to present you with three sheets of paper which will fully explain why I have returned."

"First you should know that my full name is John LaConte Oxby. I am by profession a member of the Arts and Antiques Squad, S01, Scotland Yard." Oxby showed his identification to Jonas, then to the young guard.

Jonas was breathing heavily, his white skin shining.

From an envelope Oxby removed three documents and placed one on Jonas's lap. "I am authorized to serve this arrest warrant for the sale of purportedly authentic works of art, and which you are accused of causing to be created by persons whom you have employed for that purpose." The paper slid to the floor.

"Filthy nonsense!" Jonas cried out. "The drawings are genuine as attested to by experts at Collyer's and a provenance researched by a Leonardo scholar."

"You refer to Giorgio Burri, whose death is being investigated this very moment. A very timely tragedy," Oxby replied.

"Police departments don't authenticate works of art."

"Mine does," Oxby replied.

"But you can't arrest me. I'm an American and we are in Italy."

"Your facts regarding nationality and geography are correct, but before dealing with them, I must serve a second warrant for your arrest. This time for complicity in the murder of Sarah Evans, who, when killed, was serving on special assignment for my section. We police people don't take kindly to having one of our own killed." Oxby placed a second sheet of paper on Jonas's lap. Jonas brushed it away and it fell beside the first on the floor.

"That's as ridiculous as your first ill-founded charge. I've never known such a person. I repeat, I am an American citizen and we are in Italy."

"My, but you are being difficult, Mr. Kalem." Oxby sighed "That is why I have a third piece of paper. This last one has been issued by the Italian government. It authorizes me to arrest you in compliance with Italian law. You will be retained by the local authorities until all the extradition procedures can be smoothed over. You may retain counsel."

Oxby allowed the third sheet to fall to the floor on top of the others.

Eleanor put the finishing touch to the lunch. She searched for a flower to place on each tray and smiled at her success. She went to the refrigerator for cold drinks. Loud voices came from other rooms, then Tony burst through the door into the pantry.

"Fix your own. These are spoken for," she said innocently. He grasped her arm and dropped to the floor, taking her with him. He ran his palms over the wood floor as if feeling for a lost coin. She twisted free, and as she tried getting to her feet he pulled her back.

"Stop it!" she shouted. "You can't—"

The palm of his hand swept across her cheek. It stung, but she was more frightened by the anger in his face.

His hands rubbed the floor, then, magically, a square section of the floor opened. He wrapped an arm around her waist. "We're going for a ride." He pushed her to the opening.

"There's a ladder inside. Climb down or I'll push you down."

She fought to free herself. "Curtis! Someone!" He covered her mouth and forced her into the opening. Her legs swung wildly, groping for the ladder. The pantry door opened. Stiehl had come to help with the lunch.

"What in Christ are you doing?" He leaped at Tony, who turned and sent a heel directly into Stiehl's stomach. Eleanor, suddenly released from Tony's grip, fell screaming into the black hole. She dropped a dozen feet onto soft dirt, too frightened to know if she was hurt.

Stiehl charged again, but Tony turned gracefully and kicked a leg high into his shoulder, spinning him backward. Like a mole escaping from a cat, Tony disappeared into the hole, and as he did so, the door slid back into place. Stiehl pawed at the smooth floor, searching for a way to open the trapdoor. Dowels held the lengths of wood together. One was larger than the others and set slightly below the surface. He pressed on it. The trap raised a half inch. He pulled it open. Then he lowered a foot to the ladder and climbed down. He thought he was in a cave; it smelled of damp and moldy earth. The trapdoor had automatically closed and heavy footsteps paraded over the floor above. The noise ceased as quickly as it had come.

He reached his hands into the darkness and touched the wet stones that lined the wall. He felt a draft and faced into it. As he stepped ahead the air moved faster. He was in a tunnel, another gift from the Italian army.

He moved faster. After fifty feet the tunnel gradually turned. There was light ahead reflecting dimly off the wet walls. Another fifty feet. Now he could see the end of the tunnel, a rectangle of brilliant light. He began to run.

Tony had half carried, half pulled Eleanor through the tunnel. They emerged at the first row of boathouses where the speedboat was moored. He forced her into the boat.

"Don't do this! Let me go!" she cried.

He slapped her hard on the cheek and she lashed out, her nails cutting into his arm. He struck her again. Then a third time with more of a fist than an open hand. She put her hand to her head. "Don't hit me," she said with a voice tight with terror. "Please, don't hit me." Her body was trembling.

Tony glanced at the fuel gauge. He always filled the tanks after a run over the lake and had enough to reach the Swiss end of the lake. He opened a locker and took out a German rifle. It was heavy but accurate and took a thirty-round clip. He put a 9mm pistol under his belt.

He flipped the key to start the engines, and heard a noise behind him. He turned to see Stiehl jump into the boat. He reached for his gun but Stiehl was on him before he could pull it free. Stiehl grabbed him around the neck and pulled him onto the deck of the boat. "Get out!" he shouted to Eleanor. For an instant she was frozen, then she extricated herself and jumped to the dock.

"Run! Get the hell out of here," Stiehl yelled.

Tony rolled over and onto his feet. As he straightened, his hand found the grip of the automatic. Stiehl faced the wrong end of the gun.

"I don't want to kill you, Stiehl, but I need one of you with me . . ."

There was a loud report, then another. Bullets tore into the spot where Eleanor had been standing seconds before. The shots came from one of Brassi's men. Stiehl lunged at Tony. Another shot was fired. Then another that was louder than the others. It came from Tony's revolver. Stiehl spun and fell. His right side was on fire. He put his hands where he had been hit, and felt the warm, sticky blood.

Tony brought the engines alive. He poked the nose of the boat away from its berth. There was more rifle fire, deadly shots kicked up water sprays and tore into the dashboard. He thrust to full power, turning south. Then in a zigzag course, he turned the wheel and aimed north. Two patrol boats were waiting and vectored on him. Tony saw the maneuver but maintained course until it seemed he would collide with one of them. At the last instant he swerved, and as he ran by he aimed his rifle at the stern of the patrol boat. At least one of the rounds he pulled off struck home. The back of the boat exploded. For a harrowing few seconds half a boat floated on the water, then sank.

The second patrol boat rushed in to pick up the crew. Now, Tony faced the hydrofoil that had come out of hiding. It was as fast as the white speedboat but not as maneuverable. Above was the helicopter, turning and twisting as if signaling.

One at a time, Tony thought, his eyes flashing from the helicopter to the hydrofoil. He ran as close to the shore as he dared; the hydrofoil followed. He cut the engines and was almost instantly becalmed. The hydrofoil flew past, but the helicopter recovered and remained above, lurking in the air like a giant buzzard.

He turned to full power and set after the hydrofoil. It was making a wide sweep, apparently circling to come up behind Tony. He cut the circle in half. As the hydrofoil seemed to be bearing down on him, he made a crisscrossing pattern directly toward it. His eyes never left the port pontoon, a slim section of metal on which the craft relied for half its ability to raise its hull above the water. He took dead aim on the strut holding the pontoon. The pilot tried to swerve off, but was too late.

The bow of the speedboat sheared the pontoon; the hydrofoil sped on a short distance then fell on its side like a wounded goose.

Tony stared up at the helicopter. "Fucker."

Deats looked down at the white boat streaking away from the disabled hydrofoil. "He's got a bellyful of confidence." He motioned to the pilot to stay behind the boat. The pilot nodded and took the craft down to fifty feet over the water.

Deats put a map in his lap and estimated their position. Within minutes they would pass Bellagio, an unpromising goal for Waters. Beyond Bellagio, it was likely that he would choose a landing well north. Deats put his finger on Colico. From that small town one could take the military roads to the Julier Pass and the safety of St. Moritz.

"Tell Brassi he's headed north. To either Colico or Gravedona on the western shore." The pilot spoke into his microphone. Deats set aside the binoculars and put a rifle across his lap. It was beautifully crafted, and so new the oil on the stock smelled with a rare freshness. Deats aimed at the white boat ahead. Through the telescopic sight he clearly saw the body lying behind the man he had pursued so long. The stiffness in his hand was still an annoyance, but the finger on the trigger moved easily.

The speedboat continued north past Bellagio. The helicopter kept a discreet distance behind. Then the boat slowed and Tony left the controls, went to Stiehl, and bent over him. The radio in the helicopter buzzed. It was Brassi, speaking in Italian. The pilot acknowledged the message. "The *comandante* is coming. They are approaching Bellagio."

Deats was concentrating on the activity in the boat below. "My God! Look what the bastard's up to."

Waters had picked up Stiehl's limp body and draped it over the railing. Tony climbed back behind the wheel and accelerated. The helicopter followed.

Once again the boat slowed. Tony stood, looked up to the helicopter, then pushed Stiehl into the water.

"He's forcing us to go down for the poor blighter!" Deats shouted.

They were directly over Stiehl. Tony had throttled to full speed and was making his desperate run for one of the northern towns.

"We can't stop for a dead body," the pilot called out.

"He's not dead." The wash from the rotors created ripples in a wide circle around the body that was feebly flailing its arms in an attempt to stay afloat.

The pilot radioed his *comandante*'s boat. *"Presto! Presto!"*

Stiehl sank out of sight, then bobbed to the surface. Deats yelled to the pilot. "Down!" The craft dropped to a few feet over the water. Deats crawled onto a pontoon and reached an arm to Stiehl. "Grab hold!" he shouted. Stiehl managed to get a hand out of the water. Deats took hold of his wrist but lost his grip. They tried again. This time he grasped tightly. There was a horn blast. The launch had caught up. Two men dove from the boat and swam to Stiehl's side. Deats climbed back into the helicopter.

"Go. And fast!" was his simple command.

The helicopter banked and rose. They flew up the center of the lake and at three hundred feet had the harbor of Menaggio to the west and the small town of Varenna to the east. The warm sun had brought out a fleet of pleasure boats and a hundred white triangles played in the breezes. It was a dismaying sight to Deats. Tony could duck in among the boats and be lost. They hovered over the armada of sailboats while Deats studied the map.

"Go into the harbor," he instructed the pilot. "If we don't see him, we'll go north." He glanced at his watch, then again after they had flown over and beyond the harbor. They had consumed a valuable three minutes going down for Stiehl, and there was no guarantee they had not overflown the white boat. Deats pointed away from Mennagio. *"Presto! Presto!"*

The pilot swung the ship into a speed attitude and headed to the center of the lake. The helicopter was an old workhorse, probably retired from the army and rehabilitated for a more sedentary assignment than chasing after a powerful speedboat. It vibrated and the engine's shriek was too loud to permit voice communication.

Deats signaled with his hands that he wanted to move closer to the easterly edges of the lake. He chanced that if Tony was still on the water, he was headed for Colico. It was a gamble. The lake was three and a half miles wide and they could not fly over both shorelines.

He scanned the water beneath and ahead with field glasses that were difficult to focus in the shaking aircraft. By Deats's calculations, they were a minute and a half from Colico. Then the pilot tapped his arm.

He pointed directly ahead to the telltale rooster's tail pluming up from the deep blue water. "Faster! *Presto!*" Deats urged.

As they were coming up over him, Tony turned his boat around and sped directly under the approaching helicopter. He had locked the wheel, and as he passed, he fired at the plane's belly. Bullets crashed through the thin skin; one tore into the cockpit, narrowly missing the pilot. Tony ejected the clip and inserted another. The pilot turned sharply and flew back in a rocking motion. Again they passed and Deats fired at the boat's controls, but his shots were wild. Tony triggered a stream of bullets, again striking the underbelly, this time sending a shard of metal into the pilot's leg. He yelled out and grabbed where it felt like he'd been stuck with a knife. Deats crawled behind him and bound a piece of cloth over the calf where the blood soaked through the pants.

"Stop weaving," Deats shouted. "I can't take aim." The pilot acknowledged and indicated with his hand that he would fly low then swoop up and over the boat.

The helicopter banked, then dropped to ten feet over the water. The rotors whipped up a fury of spray, nearly enveloping the helicopter. Tony turned at a right angle to the helicopter's line of approach. As he did so, the aircraft rose up directly over the boat and hovered.

Deats took careful aim, the crosshairs centered on the shoulder. "I don't want to kill you," he said calmly. "That might be too good for you." His good intentions vanished as Tony brought the rifle up and took aim on the superintendent.

The crosshairs moved to the chest. Deats fired. He fired twice more. He saw red circles on the white shirt. He raised the sight and saw the face contort in anger, then dissolve into bewilderment.

Tony fell back against the wheel. The white torpedo, its fierceness spent, turned in a lazy circle through the wavelets as gently as a rising autumn breeze that wafted across the quiet lake.

# Chapter 33

"Put this in front of the little man with the long nose." Caramazza handed a bottle of Cinque Terre to a young waiter. "He dares say our white wines are inferior to the French. Let him learn how wrong he is."

The waiter presented the bottle to Jack Oxby, uncorked it, and poured the wine into a stemmed glass. Oxby sniffed the slightly fruity wine, then sipped it. He smiled appreciatively and Caramazza put his thumb and forefinger together at the corner of his mouth and made a clicking noise with his tongue. It was a gesture meaning great taste and approval.

"Our host is determined to prove there are good Italian whites," Oxby announced to his dinner companions. He faced Bruno Brassi. "I had not meant to offend him, nor you."

"I am no expert," Brassi replied. "All Italian wines are *saporito*."

"You criticized his wine, Jack. For God's sake, compliment his food," Deats chimed in.

"I'll have no trouble doing that. He rates a Michelin star."

Caramazza said good night to the last of his guests and came to the table. "Did you enjoy the wine, Signore Oxby?"

"Very much. A solid flavor, much like Montlouis, or a Vouvray. *C'est bon*."

"That's enough wine talk, Jack. You'll be lucky to have water if you keep it up," Deats scolded.

"*Sì*, enough of wine. I wish to hear more about today," Caramazza interjected. "I knew something was happening when I saw the helicopters fly back and forth over *Il Diodario*. Any injuries, *comandante*?"

"One of our men took a bullet in his left shoulder." Brassi put a hand above his heart. "Lower and he would be dead. He was on the patrol boat that was blown up."

"And the American?" Caramazza asked.

"He is in the Ospedale San Anna. He was shot at close range. The bullet entered here." Brassi rubbed an area below his rib cage. "Such bleeding: I feared he would be dead before reaching Como. He had been taken from the operating room when I visited him. He is a lucky man, but still in danger."

Caramazza turned to Deats. "There was a young woman."

Brassi answered. "She is with him." He shrugged and smiled. "She is very pretty, and would not leave his side."

"But the one that drove the white speedboat. You could not capture him?"

"I wanted him alive but he was prepared to die if he couldn't get away." Deats opened and closed his right hand, rubbing it where he had seen the scar on the back of Waters's hand. He was silent for several moments, then continued, "We caught up with him near Colico. That's where we had it out."

"We don't have to worry about extradition now." Brassi smiled weakly at Deats. "He is going back to London in his own box."

"Not what we had in mind," Oxby offered.

"Not at all. We wanted him tried for Sarah's murder," Deats said. "And when he was found guilty, and I know that would have happened, I wanted to wring a confession from him that he killed Giorgio Burri."

Oxby lifted his glass. "You did something that was very difficult very well. I salute you."

Deats brightened. "We flew back to *Il Diodario* and that's when I saw you for the first time. Remind me to get the name of your tailor so I can be sure to avoid him."

"You didn't like my outfit?" Oxby laughed. "It's not easy putting together a wardrobe where absolutely nothing matches. Surprising how it works, though. All the attention on what I was wearing, and not on me."

Deats continued. "I was worried about Miss Shepard. She looked like bloody hell, her face cut and her clothes torn. But she recognized me." Deats relished telling the others how he had disabled Eleanor's car, then played the gallant Samaritan. "She was spitting mad that Stiehl had been shot. There was no quieting her until we took her to the hospital."

"You understate her anger," Oxby said. "She cried at Kalem, and called him every obscenity she'd ever heard. But he wasn't listening. His grand scheme had crumbled and he was in total shock."

"When did you put all the pieces together?" Deats asked.

Oxby ate the last of his dessert, then pushed his chair back from the table.

"It's fair to say that luck plays a role in a case like this. My first encounter with Kalem was in Paris, where he gave a talk on the lost Leonardos. There aren't many people running about predicting the imminent discovery of great art or, in particular, the recovery of an entire Leonardo manuscript. He seemed too confident and I thought it a good idea to know what he was up to. I have a network of friends located in all sorts of odd places, some in galleries or consulates. I had photographs and sent them to my contacts in the major airports. Keeping an eye peeled for someone with Jonas Kalem's proportions isn't difficult.

"In mid-September he was seen in Heathrow and I guessed he was in London. I assumed his taste would run to one of the luxury hotels and it was an easy matter to trace him to the Dukes Hotel. He had a suite with the other American."

"Curtis Stiehl," Deats interjected.

"Quite. I searched out the charwoman, an accommodating Mrs. Palmer, who looked after the rooms. I dressed as an employee and accompanied Mrs. Palmer into the suite. I discovered an elaborate accumulation of artist's supplies, photographic equipment, and a hundred sketches and photographs of two skulls. Not ordinary skulls, but from Leonardo's anatomical drawings in the Royal Collection."

"From the Windsor Library?" Deats asked.

"I didn't make a connection at the time," Oxby replied. "But eventually I saw a definite link between Anthony Waters, the library, Sarah Evans, and Leonardo's drawing of two skulls."

Caramazza placed a bottle of grappa on the table next to the Cinque Terre. Oxby frowned and declined a glass of the strong-tasting brandy.

"I am very fond of a Korean woman who came to London with her family a few years ago. She is a stunning person of great talent, and so I solicited her assistance and arranged for Kalem to meet her in the Berkeley Hotel. Jonas was convinced her name was Madame Sun, wife of an American lawyer, and the young man with her was her son James. Mostly true except for James. He's a struggling actor I help when I can. Madame Sun is an astrologer and advocate of *Ming Shu*. She prepared Kalem's astrological chart, to which I added a few embellishments. Kalem acknowledged he planned on taking a Leonardo to Collyer's for authentication, and that presented a small problem. I know all the right people at Sotheby's and Christie's but not at Collyer's.

"We were watching Heathrow much closer now. When he came in again, he was followed to Collyer's, then out to the Cotswold, where he met with Madame Sun a second time. I had rather hoped he might slip the manuscripts by Collyer's and the miracle is that he did. They will be embarrassed to learn the drawing is a fake. I've seen the manuscript page and can say it's the most masterful work of forgery I've ever come upon."

Deats interrupted. "How much of this was passed on to Elliot Heston?"

Oxby answered the question with equanimity. "Eighty percent? Or half? I'm not a compulsive reporter. My job was to catch Kalem with evidence. He had to commit himself to the forgery charge. I could have called his tune earlier, but he'd have gone on to some other trickery."

"But Tony Waters. We might have nabbed him alive."

"Yes, but more likely he would have disappeared again and found another role to play." Oxby looked at his empty glass. "You pretty much know the rest."

Oxby took the bottle of Cinque Terre and refilled all the glasses. "I would propose a toast if I thought this were a fit occasion. We've been through it before. The excitement is over and tomorrow will be another ordinary day. Perhaps that's as it should be." A smile covered his face.

"But damn it. I'll miss the chase!"

# NEW YORK ART DEALER
## *Trial Date Set*

SPECIAL TO *THE NEW YORK TIMES*

LONDON, Oct. 22. Facing charges of complicity in the murder of a Scotland Yard agent, New York art dealer Jonas R. Kalem has been extradited to London for his trial, scheduled to begin November 27.

Special interest is being focused on the case as it has not yet been established through the courts that policewoman Sarah Evans was murdered. Suspected of causing the fatal car accident in September was Anthony Waters, who was killed recently in Italy while attempting to escape from local police. Scotland Yard has announced a special investigation to establish Mr. Waters's guilt.

In addition, Mr. Kalem faces charges of fraud and conspiracy, for allegedly creating and selling manuscript pages ascribed to Leonardo da Vinci. Also implicated is Eleanor Shepard, recently of Washington, D.C., and Curtis Stiehl of New Jersey.

Ms. Shepard and Mr. Stiehl are currently in Italy, where Mr. Stiehl is recuperating from a bullet wound suffered during Mr. Waters's attempted escape. According to government authorities, the two Americans do not face extradition proceedings.

# About the Author

**THOMAS SWAN** has chosen art crime and thievery as the backdrop for his thrillers. Currently a director of the national board of the Mystery Writers of America and previously vice president of its New York Chapter, Swan is committed full-time to his writing life, having retired from his position as a vice president of marketing at American Express. *The Cézanne Chase* marked his hardcover debut; he is now finishing his third novel, involving a missing, priceless Fabergé egg for Newmarket hardcover publication in 1999. He and his wife Barbara live in Short Hills, New Jersey.

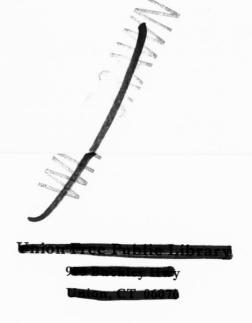

DEMCO